I0699632

SARAH ZIMM

EVERY THREAD OF LIGHT

EVERDARK PRESS

Edited by J Mercer

Book design by Okay Creations
Hardcase artwork by @lesyablackbird
Map design by Chaim Holtjer and Jennifer Bruce
Chapter illustrations © Sarah Zimm, gate illustrations by Shelby Schena at Maple Projects
Character art by @lesyablackbird, @koijix, @ladyhedi and @lictoria_art

HC ISBN 979-8-9878859-7-0
PB ISBN 979-8-9878859-6-3
Ebook ISBN 979-8-9878859-5-6

Printed in the U.S.A.

First Edition March 2025

Everdark Press

Author's Note

My Dear Readers,

I knew that as the Whispers of Dust & Darkness series unfolded, the characters and subject matter of the story would mature. Please take note that *Every Thread of Light* contains explicit adult content and dark themes that some may find triggering. For a full list of warnings, turn to the last page.

With that, welcome back. As you venture deeper into the world, I hope you enjoy your return to the Kingdom of Magus and what lies beyond.

Sarah Zimm

Guide to the World

The opening chapters of *Every Thread of Light* highlight major events that took place in *Every Dark Shadow*. The next few pages offer a recap of the world, magic system, characters, and terms for readers who want a refresher.

AGE AND SEASONS EXPLAINED

Time passes in Magus like in the human world, but those born with abilities to wield magic (Magies) age slower than those without magic (mortals). And those descended from the primordial gods (Descendants) can live millennia, though they can be killed.

Seasons (spring, summer, autumn, winter) are controlled by the moons. They don't flow linearly, but as the gods deign, shifting when a great ebb in power occurs, such as the birth, death, or ascension of a Descendant. Smaller moon events occur within each season and are believed to bestow different gifts, like knowledge, on citizens. Magies, who draw power from the moons, are highly sensitive to moon events and changes in season. For example, the recent Darkening that plunged Magus from spring into winter was thought to be spurred by the Darkwielder freeing his god magic from the Dark Shadow Dagger.

THE PRIMORDIAL GODS & THEIR MOONS

EREBUS: God of darkness, creator of the crimson moon, and father of the Witchists.
SELENE: Goddess of light, twin of Luna, creator of one of two gray moons, and mother of the Matterists.
LUNA: Goddess of light, twin of Selene, creator of one of the gray moons, and mother of the Morphists.

THE MAGIE GUILDS

WITCHISTS
Guild of Spellers, born of the god Erebus, bearing the ability to summon ("call" another Witchist mind to mind)

Shadowcasters: Witchists who can conjure and manipulate shadows at will. Arguably the most powerful Magies. In the Belly, they've often served as guards to the territory bosses.

Spellcasters: Practitioners of the grimoire, known for creating wards, shields, potions, and elixirs. Of a rarer subset are healers and seers. Healers call on magic to mend wounds, and seers read memories, experience visions, or receive prophecies. These subsets of Witchists often serve as academy sages or private tutors.

Animaters: Witchists who have the ability to store objects inside their skin, such as weapons or items of sentimental value. These objects, when stored, appear as tattoos that flow like silver on their skin. One of the rarest of the Witchists, they have been known to serve as Magie smugglers and mercenaries for hire.

MATTERISTS
Guild of Influencers, born of the goddess Selene,
bearing the ability to manipulate the mind or elements

Benders: Matterists who develop an affinity for flame, air, or water with an ability to influence their element's state, shape, and flow. Commonly found serving in the king's Special Army and often staged at front lines in battle.

Enchanters: Matterists who can sense and influence others' emotions, wills, and actions. Unguarded and mortal minds are easiest to seize. Prized by and often indentured to royalty or aristocratic families.

MORPHISTS
Guild of Transformers, born of the goddess Luna,
bearing the ability to mold the physical

Shifters: Morphists able to take the form of other entities, including mortals, Magies, and beasts, using the lightlines on their necks. Shifters have a particular lightform they can take, specific to them, and they may also use their affinity to shift others. For this, they're often at the sides of high-ranking officials.

Fabricaters: Molders who can forge metals, fabrics, and other materials into differing substances. These Morphists often work in textiles, weaponry, metalsmithing, or other such trades.

THE (FORMER) SPECIAL ARMY
Army of Magies that served King Osiris Lestat

After their ascension (a ceremony where their full powers manifest), members of this army served at a keep called the Pyre, working their way from grunts to titled positions (in order of rank): *priv, privfir, lieuten,* and *serge.* Among hard-to-stomach duties, soldiers were responsible for conscripting Magie children to the king's academy to train their powers, until "Captain Rivmere" (Jasper Salt, the Darkwielder's proxy) staged a coup at Wythe, turning half the Special Army to the Darkwielder's side. Loyalist soldiers fled Wythe with the crown. Those who followed the Darkwielder became part of his new legion.

THE CONSTELLI
The Academy of Magie Sciences

Opened decades ago by the king to educate Magie children in their powers so as to use them in service to the crown. Magies live and train at the academy under strict, if brutal, tutelage by the sages of their guild (Witchists, Matterists, or Morphists). At sixteen, students undergo *Asenti*, a ceremony to instigate the full manifestation of their affinity. They either become an apprentice at the Constelli on a path to sageship (teaching) like Rune Ethera, are sent to the military like Hart Aurum, or go into other trades or jobs that serve the crown. Until the events at Wythe, Grimm Hermes was headmaster, working in secret to aid Ophelia's mission to find the relics while she was hidden off-world.

MAJOR CHARACTERS

OPHELIA DANNAN (Oh-FEE-lyuh DAN-inn): Orphaned fugitive of the crown and last living Descendant of the Matterist goddess Selene, who has not yet mastered control of her power but whose mission it is to find the three primordial relics of the gods and destroy them to end the war for power. Currently on the run with Falcon Thames in the Underbelly.

FALCON THAMES (FAL-kn Temz): An Animater of the Witchists Guild indentured to the Underbelly's bosses with a reputation as a ruthless *smugger*, able to get Magies safe passage off world. One of three men who took oaths to guard Ophelia across time. Family origins not yet revealed.

HART AURUM (HAHRT OR-uhm): A Shifter of the Morphists Guild who can wear any likeness. A former soldier in the king's Special Army and Ophelia's oldest friend. Orphaned as a child. Other family history not yet known. His location currently unknown.

RUNE ETHERA (ROON Eh-THER-ah): An Enchanter of the Matterists Guild who was apprenticed to Grimm Hermes but forced by enchantment into killing the headmaster at Wythe. In staying behind at the battle to give Ophelia, Falcon, and Hart a chance to escape, he was taken prisoner by the king.

GRIMM HERMES (Grim Air-MAZE): Prior to his death, he was the oldest and most powerful living Spellcaster in known existence. He reset Ophelia's mind and created passages between worlds, across time, to keep her hidden from the crown.

OSIRIS LESTAT (Oh-CY-ruhs Le-STAT): The half-breed Spellcaster king of Magus with a unique ability to siphon others' magic to stay young, with whom the Darkwielder has just waged war.

TRIX FARROW (TRIK-s FARE-row): Spellcaster who aided Ophelia's crew from New York to Magus and chased Wick Sneed (who stole Ophelia's locket) through a passage. Whereabouts unknown, but Falcon has just received a summons from her in the Belly.

VALKIERAN (KIER) BALCOMB (Val-KEY-ran (KEY-er) BAHL-kowm): Publicly known as the Darkwielder, the last Descendant of the Witchist god Erebus, who stole back his relic (the Dark Shadow Dagger) and waged war on the crown. He was injured in the battle at Wythe and seemingly survived, but his whereabouts and plans are unknown.

OTHER NAMES & TERMS

ASHË (AHH-shee): A Shadowcaster we are soon to meet

DRECORA (Dray-KOR-uh): A breed of northern dragons that guard the icelands

JAGERIN (Jay-guh-RIN): Magiesian, translates to "little slayer"

KAMFE (KOMM-fee): "Fight"

KÚZLO (KOOZ-low): The northern capital made up of three valleys surrounded by the icelands

LIEUTEN (LOO-tehn): 4th rank in the former Special Army

MAGIE (MADGE-ee): Those born able to wield magic

MAGUS (MADGE-iss): The mainland kingdom ruled by Osiris Lestat, currently at war

MAETHER (MAY-thur): Translates to "breath of life"—the fabric of magic in all living things fed by, made of, or able to wield magic that Ophelia Dannan can sense

MATHIAS STOLM (Muh-THY-uhs STOW-lm): A Bender of Flame in the Matterists Guild and officer in the Darkwielder's new legion

MIGTH (MIGG-th): A combustible, powerful moon metal derived from the mines in the icelands, guarded by drecora

NAKOMMEN (NAHK-o-mehn): Translates to "young warriors" or "warriors in training"

NOMME GESEH (Nomm Guh-SEH): A northern conclave of seers

PHILO (FAI-low): A Spellcaster employed by the Darkwielder whom we are yet to meet

PRIMORDIAL RELICS (Pry-MOR-dyal REL-ics): Three instruments that bare the power to amplify or siphon magic, forged from the moons and essence of the original gods to balance power among the Magie guilds

PRIV (PREEV): 1st of the four ranks in the former Special Army

PRIVFIR (PREEV-fear): 2nd of the four ranks in the former Special Army

RAKÚA (Rah-KOO-uh): An ironspade drecora welded to Kessan Aksander

SAIRA BALCOMBE (SY-ruh BAHL-kowm): Introduced in the novella *Darkwielder*, Kier's mother

SERGE (SARE-guh): 3rd rank in the former Special Army

SESHEN (SEH-shinn): Northern warriors who fly dragons

STÄRKE VAS (Stare-kuh VAHSS): Translates to "strength unseen"

TERICHEN (Tear-EE-chin): "Teacher"

TRINŪTEN (Trin-YOO-ten): A northern prayer

VICLUMENI (Vick-loo-MEN-ee): An ancient term from the Magie rule to which we're yet to be introduced

WESHAN (WESH-ann): "War"

WESHKAMFEN (Wesh-KOMM-fen): "Competitors"

WOLVEN (WOOL-ven): Mythical wolf-like beast

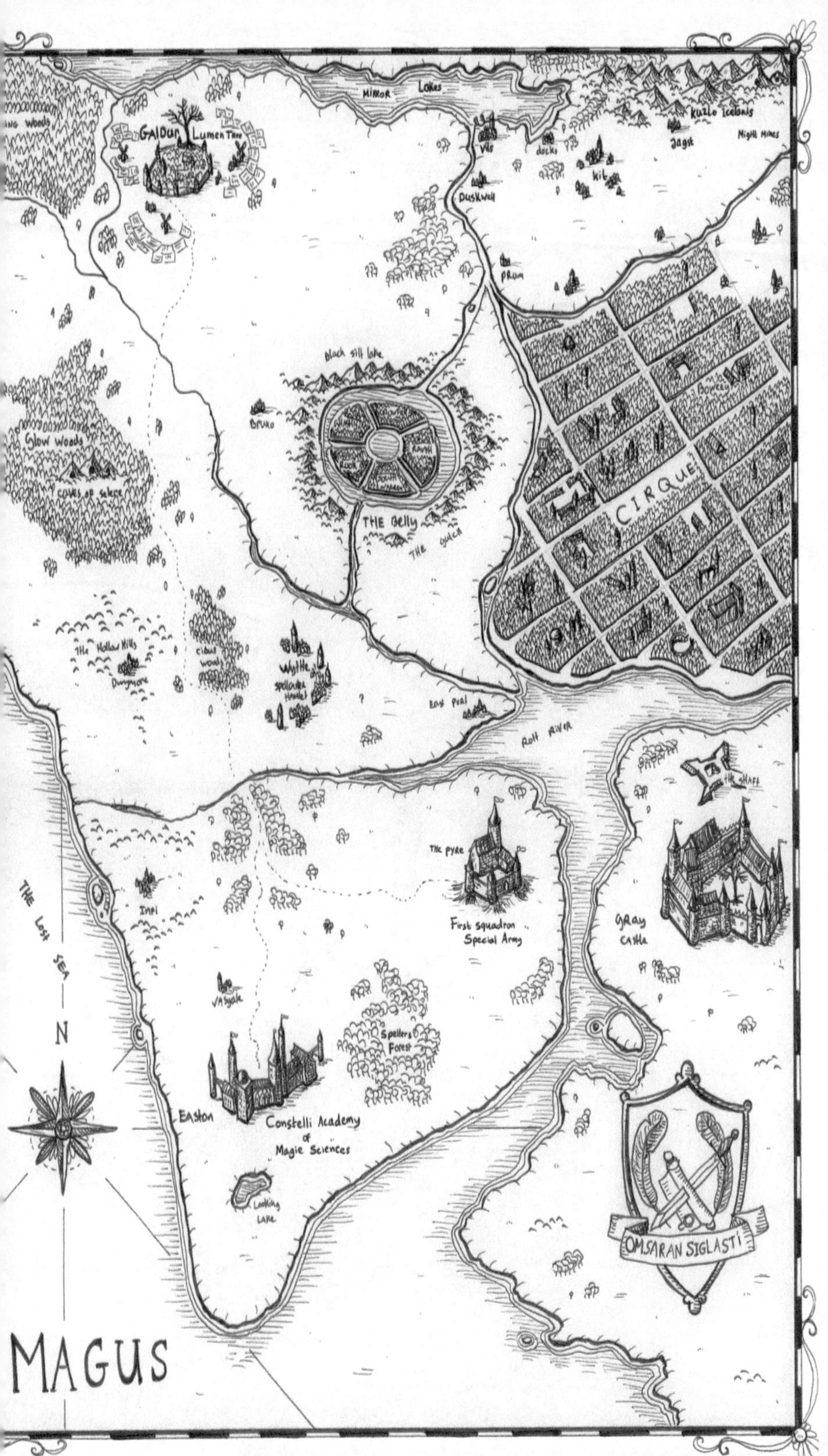

MIRROR   Lakes
ng Woods
Kuzlo Icelands
GalDun LumenTaro
Jagst
Mig'll Mines
Vilf
docks
kil
DuskWell
Prim
black silt lake
Slow Woods
Bowers
Bruxo
CIRQUE
Caves of solace
look
Ravel
THE Belly
The Hollow Hills
THE GULCH
Dungmore
Cibus
woods
Wylfle
spellcaster
Hamlet
Bay Pearl
Roth RIVER
the SHAFT
Inni
The pyre
GRAY
Castle
First squadron
Special Army
Vasgale
THE Lost SEA
N
Spellers
Forest
Easton
Constelli Academy
of
Magic Sciences
Looking
Lake
OMSARAN SIGLASTI
MAGUS

ICELANDS OF KUZLO
NESTING GROUNDS
THE SHELVES
VALLEY OF ICE
FLIGHT FIELD
THE BINDER
VALLEY OF
FLIGHT FIELD
MAIN GATE
FLIGHT FIELD
NAST STARK

THE VIRSTONE
NORTHERNMOST GATES
FLIGHT FIELD
VALLEY OF BONES
HE COLOSSEUM
SESHEN CAMP
DRAGONWOOD
IGTH MINES
MIGTH MINES
RON
HOUSE OF BONE
THE BOWL
AL SERSIE

For those with the courage to dream to the moons.
Embrace your magic, and let your dragon roar.

EVERY THREAD OF LIGHT

The primordial relics were forged to prevent a great war among the gods of Magus three. But it stands to reason that anything forged in treachery is destined to breed deceit.

—GRIMM HERMES
Headmaster, Constelli Academy of Magie Sciences
Philosophical Guide to the Gods, recovered compendium

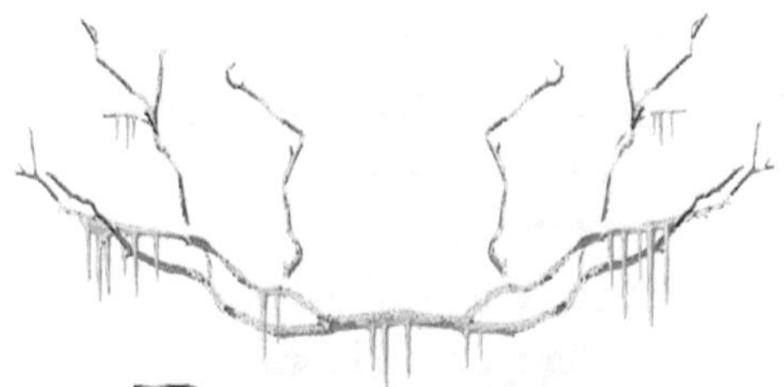

BEFORE

At the edge of the world, a northern lord commanded a coffin of ice to rise.

Braced at a steep ledge wearing his white pelts, Kessan Aksander concentrated into the mountain's shimmering abyss, determined not to fail, even though his spellstaff shook in his broad-boned hand with the effort of maneuvering the block between fists of narrow rock.

It was not the first body ever fished from the mines. It was, confoundingly, the first discovered frozen this way.

A jolting screech rang into the tunnels.

With the snap of his concentration, the ice slab lurched mid-air, scraping a cliff face, and gasps filled the cavern from the tribal council—ten warriors draped in furs and hoods who knelt against the cave walls, giving Kessan a wide berth.

When another shrieking *hreeeee!* pierced his ears, he cursed the giant beast circling the mountain outside. Behind his rib bones, he could feel the pound of Rakúa's white, leathery wings, a constant since he welded the north's fiercest drecora a few years earlier, but today she knew he needed absolute concentration.

Insolent dragon.

Reeling his attention back, he steadied the block, his hands shaking to seize every speck of control they could.

The tribal council watched.

Between steadying breaths, he reminded himself that using his spellstaff would not diminish him in the elders' eyes. They knew how temperamental magic was here in the sacred inner cavern. They would not judge him. And yet, it was embarrassing with his father, the *volorost*—the high lord of the north—among them.

A miner had woken his father with news of the body before dawn, and Kessan overheard the report. He was a light sleeper like every young lord, every son of a *volorost* over the centuries who would eventually vie to be heir and had it beaten into him to keep one eye open. He had volunteered his affinity for this task knowing this was a chance to prove himself as heir. Technically, the *volorost* had six other choices.

Sweat caught in Kessan's brows, and as the ice block crested the rim, a chanting began to stir in the cavern, low and rhythmic, pounding in the cage of his chest: "Adaren ma! Adaren ma! Adaren ma!" *Raise it! Raise it! Raise it!*

At the rim, the oblong block landed with a wobbly clank—not his smoothest spell—and he expelled a breath of relief as a hush knelled through the cavern, his father and the elders pressing in.

Kneeling to inspect the block, Kessan braced himself for the ice-scorched remains of a miner he might know. Instead, a sharp current jerked his head back as a torrent of images flooded his mind. His vision spun forward in time, causing him to forget the weight of the white pelts on his shoulders and any need to prove himself.

Horrific scenes unfurling in his mind's eye, he only saw the trouble to come—a trouble in three: *the river, the ice, the amulet.*

Stumbling out of the vision with panic pulsing through him, he braced a hand against the block before reeling back, blinking his eyes clear.

His father lumbered forward at his side. His father who would normally be the one to see a vision this grave. Catching closer sight of the contents inside the block, the *volorost*'s old eyes narrowed like sharp gems. He grabbed Kessan's arm, voice low. "Ka has nen gesehen?"

The young lord—the seer—swung a wild gaze to the tribal council members, who were trading vexed looks, before rounding back to his father's question.

What had he seen?

"Weshen," he whispered in the Magie tongue. "War like the North—like our world—has never seen."

ONE

TRICKS OF THE DARK

CHAPTER 1
ALIVE & UNWELL

Ophelia wanted to be done with hiding. No more resets. No more stories. Yet, under a dangerous midnight sky glittering with winter, magic, and the anticipation of war, it seems she's the fugitive once more.

High above the streets of the Underbelly, she studies the reckless gap between rooftops sprawling before her and, with a muttered prayer to the goddess Selene, flings herself into the frigid winter wind as if she bore wings.

She lands on a knee beside a rough-shaven *smugger*, her a ravaged ship come to shore, Falcon Thames a tower of vigilance. Something stirs in her chest—a flutter—when he perks a brow and offers her a warm hand up.

Falcon's fingers slip from hers to graze the lightblade in his baldric as they approach the roof wall. "Not far now," he notes, tucking his chin into the high collar of his coat.

"Good." Gods willing, reconnecting with an ally will put them one move closer to freedom.

Ophelia has felt the anticipation of seeing the Spellcaster for hours since leaving Rook, since Trix's summons came as jolting as winter's fall on Magus. A winter, and summons, as unexpected as the silence now sprawling through the city of pleasure six stories below.

In the middle of night with snow burying the streets, wind dragging its sharp claws across her skin, the Belly—the Darkwielder's sanctuary—should pulse like a wild, beating heart. There should be Crats, basking in drunken debauchery, especially here in Ravish.

"It's too quiet," she mutters, unease an unwanted passenger as she surveys the scene, feeling the need to triple check they left no trace to be followed.

Falcon nods, as if between the pricking snow and curtains of magic that cloak the night he can feel it, too.

"Let's go," she says. Her hands numbing at the fingers, she starts to rise just as the wind carries a scream that could cut the cold.

A man in a gray coat barrels up the street with the fear of the gods in his gait, chased by a dark streak nipping viciously at his heels. With a lurch in her chest, Ophelia realizes it's a shadow at the same moment Falcon curses.

Gripping the edge of the roof, she sees the man veer and shuffle on the ice. He collides with the façade of a derelict apartment door that's rotting at the hinges. "No," he moans. "No!"

Under the snow-dusted glow of a gas lamp, an unfamiliar figure in dark clothes steps forward. A Shadowcaster, his silhouette carved with sharp edges. "Crat," he spits like a curse. "You've been coming into our city like you own it, but that's all changing now, isn't it?"

Ophelia starts to her feet, magic humming inside, but Falcon clasps her arm. "This is the Belly, Teacup. We can't be seen."

The man lets out a wailing cry as the shadows lunge. With a crack, the Crat's cry cuts like the scratch of a song and the man folds to a heap.

Her nails bite the brick of the roof as the shadows rip back to their caster.

She has lived in danger her whole life. Run from it. Slept in its midst. More recently, faced it head on. But Falcon is right about the Belly. There's nothing safe or friendly about the city that's harbored magic like an incubator. Especially now, with news of the revolution spreading.

Waiting for the street to clear, she fills her lungs with a shock of winter air and the stench of Ravish—that reek of petrol, perfume, and wet stone. The scent of danger. Lifting her gaze to the sheens of dust that dip and dive in the night, her senses come alive—fully alert—amidst the magic that has no master.

It's a reminder of what they fight for. *Freedom.*

Four bells faintly chime in succession across the city. "Dawn's coming," Falcon notes. "We need to be off the streets." He pats a hand on the wall, looking through his lashes at her. "Ladies first?"

She snorts. "When have you ever called me 'lady'?"

With his chuckle echoing and the cold nipping, she alights down the rails along the length of the stone façade, her woolen dress and fur cloak billowing. Her satchel, hastily packed before they left Rook, jostles at her hip when she slips to the street.

She doesn't look at the dead Crat.

Keeping their heads down, they traverse in silence the rest of the way to Ravish, the Belly's eastern-most territory. As is habit, she memorizes the route, drawing a map in her mind of the mazing alleys, the trinket and smoke shops, the canals where boatmen sleep under thick wools in tied-off dinghies.

When they reach a hotel bricked black and trimmed in gold, she scours the natural shadows, nearly missing the woman on the corner with her arms crossed over a thick coat and trousers belted at the waist to hug her slight frame.

"About time," Trix calls, pushing off the lamppost where she's been waiting.

Ophelia's struck by how changed she looks—not just all the leather she wears, but the hard edge in her eyes. She wastes no time pulling the Spellcaster into a hug, but almost right away Trix stiffens in the embrace.

Pulling back, Ophelia swipes at a rogue tear that's slipped to her cheek, then takes notice how the Spellcaster frowns, folding her arms like a barricade as if uncomfortable by all the emotion. "Sorry, " Ophelia says. "I'm just relieved you're alive."

With a rueful smile, Trix shakes her head. "What did I tell you about apologizing?"

Women are always doing that.

But Ophelia's own smile weakens at the sight of the taut lines etching Trix's face. Evidence the woman's been bracing against pain, hardening herself.

Memories of Trix's twin, Cleo, barrage Ophelia like a battering of snowflakes, pushing a lump into her throat. Trix must blame her. Getting involved with Ophelia got her sister murdered.

"Wick Sneed," Ophelia starts, and just his name stirs a spark of fury. "He didn't hurt you?"

Trix casts a look down the street as though she half-expects to see him there, sneering in the murk of the budding morning. "I didn't catch up with him."

"I can't believe you went after him. That was—"

"Goddamn stupid," Falcon cuts from where he's been watching their reunion. Stepping onto the curb, he combs the Spellcaster over, a smirk coloring his lips. "Trix Farrow. Seems you've got as many lives as you had cats once."

Trix stares with mock loathing at him, as she always has. A flicker of the woman Ophelia began to call a friend. Setting off toward the hotel, she calls, "Unless you two enjoy this bloody weather, follow me."

Ophelia was expecting a place they could lie low and recalibrate, not heavily weaponed Magies guarding the front doors of a hotel.

After passing through an old-world foyer dotted with crystal chandeliers, she runs eyes over faded-gold wallpaper in a long hall strewn with tasseled rugs, dark wood paneling, and polished sconces. Décor that's a nod to a more prosperous city—maybe a city that was safe once—before the Belly became somewhere magic-born hide.

Trudging beside Trix up a curving staircase and down a narrow hall, Ophelia counts twenty more Magies who look like they've seen plenty of fights. The men and women are well-muscled. Some of their noses are bent, and many bear scars on their brows or hands. Each wears an assortment of colored leather and wool, and an array of weapons stuffed wherever they could find a sheath.

They stop sorting through food and medical supplies, their gazes lifting to follow her.

Once upon a time, her mother taught her to run, but Ophelia has since taught herself not to cower. She stares back at the Magies, surprised to feel Falcon's hand hover at the small of her back.

He leans to catch Trix's eye and lifts a brow. "This place was full of Crat guests a few weeks ago."

Noting his protective hand, Trix shrugs. "Things change. We'll be using it as a base now for a citizen's militia."

Falcon huffs. "Right. When Wyatt Kercher finds out you seized his hotel, his dogs will just give up the bone."

"He won't be a problem," she assures as they round another hall. "We've already started recruiting Magies who want to learn combat."

Ophelia cuts a glance at her in surprise. "That was fast. The war just started."

"Did it?" Trix asks. Sconce light flickers over her serious features as they approach the end of the hall where she gestures ahead to a set of double doors. "Ophelia, you can take the suite." She flicks a hand toward an adjacent door as they near it. "This one's open for you, smugger."

Ophelia tenses. She doesn't want to admit how much she wants Falcon to stay, not in front of Trix, but the idea of being alone with her memories is suffocating. To her relief, he walks straight past the offered room without a word, striding toward her suite.

With irritation simmering in her eyes, Trix follows, her mouth clamped shut.

Their mutual annoyance and sniping are oddly comforting. The two act like siblings, and it reminds her of how it was sometimes growing up with Hart.

In the suite, Falcon drops their satchels on the bed. His eyes crawl the gold- and red-papered walls, drapes, and fine furnishings before they narrow back toward the hall of Magies. "Can't say 'combat leader' doesn't suit you—I've seen you fight—but who the hell are your friends?" he asks Trix. "I don't recognize them."

The Spellcaster leans casually against the door frame. "You don't recognize them because you've been...gone." Her gaze drops to the floor, a small acknowledgment of the horrors they relayed to her via summons earlier, about what happened in Wythe and why they're here, two people short.

Don't think about it now.

"The Magies here are newly free," Trix explains. "They didn't all get a chance to prove themselves, what with the arena closed, but they're out of their indentures and hungry for vengeance. They're good fighters."

Falcon's brows knit. "The fights are shut down?" *Barbaric fights,* from how he's described them. Crats throwing their Magies into pits, waging bets, forcing them to tear one another down for a chance to earn their freedom.

"They stopped about a week ago," Trix says. "And don't worry about my friends. They're on the right side."

Side. *Magies versus the monarchy,* Ophelia considers with a quiet little simmer of wrath in her chest. *One side fighting for freedom, one to keep control. And what is each willing to become to win?*

While Falcon busies himself prowling the suite, inspecting every tapestry and closet—even the bolt on the balcony door—Ophelia settles at the wall beside Trix. From the corner of her eye, she studies the woman's sharper edges, the lack of usual color in her wardrobe, the baldric she has slung across her shoulder that's replaced her spellbag in favor of blades.

Ophelia could drown in guilt. Maybe Trix is a woman who makes her own choices, but Ophelia's at least partly to blame for the caster's circumstance and all she sacrificed when she followed them to Magus.

She steals her friend's eye. "I'm sorry about your sister. I know that's not enough, but are you"—she swallows—"are you truly okay?"

Trix's face is a mask as she chews a lip and studies the floorboards. "I will be."

Ophelia touches her arm. "What happened after you passaged here?"

Trix glances to where Ophelia's hand rests. "I found a purpose." Stepping out of reach with a smile that doesn't quite light her eyes, she backs through the door. "You two look like something my cats coughed up. Get some sleep."

Night explodes inside a dream.

The ground clefts, shaking and trembling as guns and magic spark. In the throes of battle, Wythe's great temple burns and screams ring from children trapped inside it.

Death is everywhere.

The king is escaping.

And the darkness inside Ophelia, drawn from the Gray King, is a river of ice that settles so comfortably in her bones she might believe she was born of shadows instead of light.

"Kill him, Ophelia!" The Darkwielder's plea cuts across the dais to her.

Catching sight of him hanging in a chasm, she goes still as stone. His power, a tether between them, resounds in her, calling her to act.

Beyond a doubt, she knows what he wants her to do—kill the king and catalyze the revolution. But this is a nightmare and she knows what's to come instead.

The Darkwielder will fall and lose control of the shadows that spin like a hurricane around the Spellcaster hamlet. The darkness will waterfall and beasts will spring up to claw men, women, and children to ribbons. And when it happens, Ophelia will face an impossible choice—extinguish the king's life or vanquish the shadows to save the innocents. There won't be time to do both.

As the Darkwielder loses his grip and shadows leap, her decision plays out.

The tingle of *maether* gathers in the golden ridges of her arm as she teeters on the edge of a command. Then she sees herself, standing on that broken dais, looking nothing like the girl who hid in the mortal world for four years in fear. She is a woman with hair as wild as her mother's and dark eyes threaded with golden light—a goddess incarnate.

In that moment, she wonders if there might be a way, after all, to do both: save the innocents and free herself from the king.

In the nightmare, her hands rise to press firmly against her chest as she takes a single, determined breath, imagining a different ending to the battle of Wythe, and thinks, *Destroy us.*

A thousand suns explode through the dream.

To her panic—and relief—light tunnels from her arm to the ground and missiles straight into the abyss, seeking the Darkwielder before shattering her own heart...

Ophelia bolts with a cry in bed, clawing at her chest. In a fury of shoving covers away, her foot snags on the sheets and, with her heart slamming against her ribs, she slides onto the hard floor, smacking her knees upon the wood.

Panting, she realizes where she is—*when* she is. It's just the hotel.

Vaguely, she registers the low dimness of the room hugging darkened shapes of furniture. She's slept the whole day, and the evening has set.

Pushing to her feet against a wave of adrenaline, she searches for the reassuring outline of Falcon in bed, but he's not there.

The nightmare presses in. Panic climbs the rungs of her chest, up her throat, and sends her scrambling toward the washroom.

She doesn't make it to the toilet.

Ophelia's eyes water as she retches into a porcelain tub, hands gripping the edge of the clawfoot where she kneels on the cold tiles. With a cheek resting against the edge, she fights for control of her breath and notices a glow pulsing into the narrow room from a small square window.

Outside, particles shiver against the glass, making little pings. When they have her attention, a deluge of soft whispers fills her throbbing head, warbling over top of one another, as nonsensical as ever.

Her head aches, and aches, and in her mind, she sees blood. Grimm's blood, before his body disintegrated and became *dust*. It still doesn't make sense. Why would he become particles when other magic-born die and become ash?

The whispers breathe louder—like bees.

"Leave me alone," she rasps. Maybe it's selfish, but in this dark moment, she can't bear the light.

A prattle comes again, the dust vibrating like shaken stars, pressing itself closer against the pane as if to see her better or be let inside.

"*Go away,*" she wills, clenching her stomach. Yet it whorls in protest, like she's asked it to do the impossible. Picking her head up, she begs, "*Please.*"

The shimmers of light scatter like an unkindness of daws, taking the glow and whispers, leaving her head mercifully silent.

Clinging to the tub, waiting for her tremors to ease, she tries to gate against the lingering snatches of her nightmare. But this is it—everything that's happened catching up. Rune's vacant eyes as he stabbed a pick-blade into Grimm's chest. Falcon and Hart being beaten with the butts of soldiers' guns. The feel of Hart's hand slipping out of hers before they all jumped for the passage. Only two of them making it through.

With a bare arm, she wipes a tear off her cheek and releases her grip on the tub to draw her legs into herself.

I am Ophelia Dannan, the daughter of Elora, the direct descendant of Selene, the goddess of light and protection. I am of the dust, the breath of life. I am stronger than my darkest hour, and I will not break. Whatever I must do, I will free this kingdom.

She recites the words again. And again. But alone in the dark, experiencing echoes of what they lost and left behind, she can't feel the conviction of the words. Can't forget she let the King of Magus live and failed to save Grimm Hermes. Failed to keep them all together.

Beyond the washroom, a door rattles and clicks.

Dragged from her thoughts by the sharpening awareness that someone has entered their suite, Ophelia scrabbles to her feet and snatches the blade sheathed at her thigh.

CHAPTER 2
WAR & HEAT
WEST RAVISH
2ND DAY IN THE NEW WINTER
OPHELIA IS WITH FALCON

F alcon's familiar swagger sounds in their room, followed by the grunt of clothes being removed.

Ophelia expels a breath but stands there, vexed at the foreign sensation of his *maether* washing through her, stunned to realize she can distinguish his magic as she would his signature on paper or his laugh in a crowded tavern. A progression of her power, she wagers, now her affinity has returned.

If only she could slay her guilt and make that nightmare her last.

Relaxing the weapon in hand, she listens as Falcon's boots pause outside the washroom door, holding the breath inside her lungs until his weight shifts on the floorboards, until he steps away and there's a familiar clank of his weapons belt being laid on the bed.

Silence pervades, except for a few soft murmurs that sift through vents and walls from other rooms. Moving to the sink, laying down her blade, Ophelia flinches at the sight of her own sharper edges in the garish mirror.

Two nights and her dark eyes are larger in her narrowed face. She traces the length of her neck to the collar of her nightgown and stills at the outline of something foreign beneath it. As fast as her hands will move, she unfastens the fabric, tugging it down over a shoulder.

Her breath hitches when she sees the mark.

She can nearly feel the Darkwielder's phantom touch, how it trailed like melting ice when he returned the locket she now wears. But it's the pattern on her skin beside the necklace, below her collarbone where a marking stains the skin, that elicits panic.

Darker than a bruise, it has the intricate look of a mortal tattoo, if that tattoo were inked from the inside out. Its shape conjures a serpent, the way its lines wend over her heart and up to her left shoulder.

She listens with the intensity of a creature gauging threats, terrified she might hear his voice. But it's quiet—in the hotel and in her mind.

At a soft squeak of bedsprings, she draws her nightgown closed, forcing her attention to the objects laid out by the sink: fresh water, clean cloths, and Falcon's mint paste.

After a moment, a fraction of warmth beats into her.

She's not sure how she'd feel about Falcon knowing of her nightmare and how she envisioned the battle at Wythe ending differently—with her death—or that she feels like she could drown in the lifetime of memories that've returned to her.

Falcon has his own demons.

In New York, they both suffered nightmares. Her, dreams of fire, though she didn't understand the connection to the Constelli then. And Falcon, sometimes thrashing in his sleep, moaning and calling out strange names or places.

"Echoes of the past." That was all he'd say about them.

After washing the unsavory taste from her mouth, Ophelia cracks the washroom door and pauses in the threshold. She's met with a soft, dancing light from the hearth and an unexpected sight that makes her breath catch.

Sitting on the bed with his features half-lit in the room's glow, elbows resting on the leather of his pants, Falcon polishes a wicked blade. He wears nothing above the waist save for the spelled tattoos covering his arms, chest, and neck—Animater ink that shimmers silver across his broad muscles, a sign of the weapons and other effects he holds beneath his skin.

It's not the first time she's seen him bare chested, or felt the attraction. But watching him press down on the knife in his hand until it disappears into the silver glow near his ribs, she's not prepared for the pull she suddenly feels to him. Or how envious she is of that blade, that it gets to be buried in his warmth.

Before her next breath, that envy prods her feet toward him, but a sliver of memory stills her: Rune, brandishing a crooked smile at her from the bottom of their favorite lookout spot, holding up a flask and picnic basket.

Guilt washes over her, and she feels like trash. More so when she blinks and her mind carries her back to the Constelli, to the night after the academy burned when Hart sat quietly with her beneath a tree while her tears fell in ugly rivers.

One keeper, her first love. The other, part of her soul.

With two important people missing and the world plunged to war, she shouldn't be wanting Falcon this way—*needing* him.

When he catches sight of her, his hand stills completely on the next blade he's about to sheath. In the glow of the room, she guesses the fabric of her gown doesn't obscure much beneath it. He's seen her in as much before, but his lips part as if in shock, or awe. Or both.

That feeling behind her heart prods, and as his gaze grows intense, all she wants is his arms around her, chasing away the dark and hideous things she's done and dreamt.

Absently abandoning his knives, Falcon's attention fastens wholly on her as she comes to stand in front of him.

"Hi," she breathes.

His hooded eyes comb the curve of her breasts. "Teacup," he warns, even as the corded muscles of his neck twitch. The world's gone to war, but right now she's only aware of the battle here—a dance of wills that began when she met Falcon, her equal.

Dropping her gaze to his knives, she leans to draw up a blade, the letter *A* winking at her from its unfamiliar hilt. It looks as if it were forged in stone, or something as hard.

"A new one?" she asks. In every city they've ever traveled, she's noticed with curiosity how he collects them. She's come to know most of them well, but not this one.

He's distracted at first, still staring at her. When he notices what she holds, a fist flexes as he swallows. "An old one."

"It's beautiful." Not steel, but a light gray—almost white—with wings carved into its hilt. It fits well in her hand as she knuckles it, angling the narrow shaft so its point gently hovers at the skin over Falcon's heart. She lets the tip just graze along his flesh, and when his chest glows silver, activating his magic for her, they trade a look of wonder.

That's new.

Silver pools where the tip presses, growing with each inch Ophelia feeds the blade in.

Falcon shudders under her hand as the knife is swallowed up, shaft to hilt, until its entire length is buried.

Just watching his ink skitter and settle makes an unexpected ache bloom between her thighs. She clenches them together, wondering if he's feeling a shred of the same need. If he's on the cusp of losing control as she is.

When her gaze trails to his, she finds an echo of that heat staring back.

Her words a mere breath, she asks, "Have you looked your fill? Because all your gaping seems wasted if you refuse to do anything about it."

With a growl, Falcon pulls her into the space between his legs, where the front of her thigh grazes the shape of him that's growing harder.

She gasps, on fire for him instantly.

"Ophelia." He groans as if the past four years are catching up to him, his forehead dropping against her chest beside her locket, his nose grazing the swell of her breast.

She can't keep her fingers from raking up his soft, stubbled cheeks, or from burying in his windswept hair. She squeezes to relieve some of the tension she feels, and when she tugs his head back, intensity blinks at her and, trash or not, she says, "Hold me, and let's forget what happened just for one night."

His breaths come ragged, and as long as he wars with that perplexing intensity, she's half sure he'll push her away. Finally, he shakes his head. "There's no just holding you anymore, Ophelia."

Her hands still in his long tresses as the implication flames desire. She doesn't analyze that on arrival in the Belly, he told her *no*, or why he might feel different now.

All she says is, "I know."

His eyes flash a darker blue—carnal, ravenous. Launching to stand, Falcon draws her flush against him, driving a fury of energy through her—his *maether* and hers, tangling.

She's a paper moth to his flame, and he's the antidote to the chill in her.

Falcon claims her mouth with a fire that could burn the bed. Tongue parting her lips, he hauls her up around his waist, and as she clasps her legs at the ankles to drive him closer, they spin.

He backs her recklessly against an empty wall, so fast that gravity disappears, the wall shakes when they land against it, and light flickers from a sconce.

He tastes like a fire-smoked night, like sweet mallows and autumn rain. His breath is hot against her mouth as he hovers there, growling, "Tell me you want this. That you'll have no regrets."

"Yes." *Gods, yes.*

"Tell me," he grates, squeezing the back of her thighs.

"I won't regret you."

Falcon shifts to set her down, hands roaming under her nightgown. When two of his broad fingers brush the sensitized curve where her bottom meets her thigh, desire strikes a heady blow to her core. She moans as he touches just shy of the trail where she's growing wet.

"*Falcon.*" He captures the word with his mouth, giving her heat as he kisses greedily down the soft slope of her throat, his tongue leaving delicious tingles along her pebbling skin.

Bracing her against the wall, he frees the hand exploring under her shift to wrestle the ties on her nightgown open, as if driven by manic need. He draws a torturous trail down her ribs before cupping her breast, then makes a delicate feast of her flesh, taking the swell of her into his mouth. With a flick of his tongue, her nipple peaks and a little groan escapes her lips.

She's fantasized this moment in fragments for so long, she's lost to the sensations, forgetting her nightmares, the marking over her heart, her guilt, even Rune and Hart and the war—everything but the mystifying thing that burns between her and Falcon Thames.

Tangling her fingers in his hair, she draws him closer still, so distracted by the friction of his leg against her core—needing more of it—that she's only vaguely aware her nightgown has fallen off both shoulders.

When Falcon's mouth finds her collarbone, a chill writhes through her—a slither of cold serpents beneath her skin.

Appearing in her mind is a face pale as ivory, with slate eyes narrowed and expressive lips pulled to a frown that mouths, disapprovingly, *"Ophelia."*

She reels at the voice—at her imagining of it—and heaves it away from her.

No, it's Falcon she heaves. He groans and she's suddenly on her feet, panting, all the warmth in her gone.

Falcon stands a foot away, his wild blue eyes narrowed in confusion, his forehead creased with concern.

"I didn't mean to," she starts, trying to get a grip on her breath. The shift from heat to ice, desire to terror, was so sudden.

It wasn't real.

Falcon shakes his head as if it will clear whatever consumed him, his gaze still wild as it slides to her collarbone. To where her nightgown's askew.

She hastens to straighten the fabric, but it's too late.

Falcon's a firestorm. "What the hell is that?"

"It's nothing," she says, keeping a palm over the marking.

"Ophelia," he warns, on the cusp of losing control.

She can't lie to him, not ever. "I think it's from pulling the Shadow into me when I cured the king."

His eyes go lethal, treating her to a glimpse of the *smugger* he truly is, standing before her bare chested and feral. "He marked you?"

"I don't know." It feels like a stain, like a consequence of making the wrong choice in Wythe. Like a mark of her guilt for leaving things such a mess.

His eyes blade closed a brief moment. "I'm going to take him apart, piece by goddamn piece."

"No." The objection fires without thought, as if on instinct. Quickly, she adds, "I won't have you killed fighting my battles." She waits for the veins in his arms to settle, his fists to uncoil. Quieter, she says, "I'm sorry I pushed you away just now. I don't regret—"

"It doesn't matter." He looks up, the muscles in his jaw flexing. "I shouldn't have... There are other things we need to talk about."

"What things?"

"I got a line through to Gray Castle." His expression is grave. "It's not good."

CHAPTER 3
RIVERS & QUESTS

Every cell inside Ophelia wakes. "A line to Gray Castle? Why didn't you say?"

Falcon eyes her a long moment. "You're distracting. Put some clothes on." He turns on his heel to fish a log off the hearth to feed the fire, and the thump of the wood against the grates resounds in her chest.

Taking up an iron poker, he throws an irritated frown over his shoulder as she draws beside him.

Residual heat blooms at the idea he is still bothered. "I could say the same to you." She thrusts a hand out at his bare chest, where his tattoos are as disheveled as her nightgown, all rearranged in different patterns across his skin.

Falcon wrenches the poker under a log, sending sparks up the flue. "That's..." He growls, and how long he stares into the fire, she can tell he's bothered by something else, too.

"Tell me the news."

He stops his jabbing. "The Darkwielder survived." Flames catch in the fire, and Falcon glances up at her. "He used his power to forge a river that's cleaved Magus in two and cut both sides off from the other."

A rush of blood thrums in her ears as Falcon raises the poker to gesture out the window, where the still-dark sky shows so thickly with particles that the moonslight hardly glows. Farther beyond, the Gulch's sharp silhouettes climb to wall in the city.

"Are you certain?" she asks, though she knows in her bones it's true.

Iron clangs as Falcon replaces the poker. "My source's partner serves the northeast's representative. In a council meeting, he saw them map a river a mile across that runs from east of the Constelli clear up to Duskwell." Falcon's tattoos ripple in the firelight, ink pooling over his heart to offer him a crisp, rolled parchment. Unfolding it, he hands it to her.

On a map, Falcon has traced a thick line that centers widest at the hamlet of Wythe. Or, what was Wythe. When they fled, it was in shambles. Stretching almost north to south, the line—this dark river—divides the kingdom east from west.

As if he sees the horror on her face, he says, "This wasn't your doing, Teacup. It's a hell of a lot bigger than that seam you forged when you cured the king. Those who've seen it say the shadows are thicker than water. He made a goddamn river of the Dark Shadow."

The night before, lying in the borrowed bed in Rook, Ophelia felt an odd trembling. She thought the quaking was her. "Has anyone tried to cross it?"

"Royal Army units, just yesterday. Every boat they sent was swallowed up. Flames don't touch it, wind won't move it, spellwork's a bust."

She peers at the map. "We're directly in the river's path, but it hasn't breached the Belly's walls."

"The Belly is the Darkwielder's sanctuary," Falcon points out as she traces a finger along the dark line.

"The West and South grow more than half the kingdom's food. With no trade access, and winter coming, people will starve." It's a sickening thought. She's known hunger—true hunger—in her early years when she and her mother had little but each other.

Falcon nods. "Even the Crat bastards will have to start rationing. I give it a month or two before they grow desperate and figure out the only path left to the West is—"

"Here." The implication reverberates in her.

Falcon's quiet a moment. "The passages in the Belly are down, too. As far as Trix can figure, there's a ward up to keep anyone from casting in or out."

"You already told Trix?"

"I didn't want to wake you. She's going to hole up, scour her spell books, and see if she can tell what kind of magic's at play. A ward might protect the Belly from its enemies a while, but Osiris has his own powerful Spellcasters. If they figure a way through..."

"We're trapped." Fury rises like her own personal beast, pushing Ophelia to pace the suite. "The Darkwielder must know what his river's done and that the king's likely to retaliate. They'll bring the fight here."

Falcon turns toward the window, the tattoos on his back roaming his skin in agitation. "I haven't been able to get summons west to figure out what the Darkwielder's doing, or who with. And a daw's useless if I don't know where to send it."

Her magic nudges, offering an answer. Ophelia drops her hand from her mouth. "I'll do it."

Falcon spins, fists steeled. "No."

She bristles, caught off guard by his adamance. "If I connect to the dust outside the Belly, we can see past the Gulch. It's the only way."

His gaze dips to her collarbone, to the Shadow's mark. "After you learn to shield your mind." The flicker in his eye is a reminder Falcon was once a twin, that for privacy he would've learned to shield his mind from his sister.

"I won't stay here and hide when I can do something," she argues.

"There's goddamn *darkness* inside you! You want to risk calling our enemies straight to you?"

His words cut through that stain on her chest, down to her bones, but she stacks her spine. "I thought you wanted me to fight." His eyes glint a wilder blue and she can see she's driving him to snapping, but she won't back down.

He shakes his head. "You're strong. I'm not arguing that. But every time you travel, someone senses you. Given we're stuck between two men who'd give their nuts for you to win this war, our one advantage is that neither know you're here."

She glares at him—this man who gets under her skin so well—and thinks how she'd like to snap him in two. It's a precarious thought—one that seems to come from elsewhere, but catches quick as a spark.

Too fast, her magic is moving, bleeding to the surface of her arm in a stream of light, then into her fingers. She can feel it searching for Falcon, to do just that. Throwing a desperate gaze toward the fire, she steels her will and channels her frustration there.

The energy releases like an axe, cracking the firewood and grate beneath it in two.

As Falcon whips his neck at the sound, she shakes with spent energy and fear. That was too close, and a terrifying reminder that she lacks control of her power.

With a soft curse, Falcon faces her, looking only half as agitated now. "I'm not trying to stop you from fighting. I'm asking for a few days. If we're caught, it'll be a whole lot harder to find our way to..." He pauses as his mouth starts to shape the next word. She braces for him to say it—*Hart and Rune*. "To the relics," he finishes.

The relics.

At the mention of the god-forged instruments, she's back on a muddied country road in Galdur, four years old and saying goodbye to her mother while Aunt and Uncle stand on the porch watching.

She can still feel the warmth of Elora's whisper—a whisper she only recently remembered: *"I have a relic from long ago, dove. Dangerous people want its power. I need to make it disappear."*

It was years before she understood the danger of the relics. That in the hands of the right wielder, any of the three—the dagger, the amulet, or the lightstone—were capable of amplifying or stealing worlds of magic. It was years more before she remembered the green pouch where Elora used to stow the relic of their guild. A pouch she never opened.

Her mother left her to find a way to make the amulet disappear, and Ophelia's throat thickens, thinking of how Elora must have failed in her quest. Because the tomes say the Gray King has the relics, apart from the dagger now, and Elora's magic passed to Ophelia.

Falcon's quiet, watching her, letting her have her thoughts.

"I have to finish what my mother started," she says, "or the past four years of hiding—dragging all of you into this—will have been for nothing."

"Not for nothing," Falcon says softly, dipping his chin to her, and she feels the spark fan again. He clears his throat. "Master shielding. Then you scout the West and find the relics. And when we end the war, maybe we all find some goddamn peace."

"Peace?" She searches his face—the slightly crooked slope of his nose, the blading edge of his jaw—then scans down the wide planes of his chest to the broad hands that've taken men apart...and caressed her skin. She can't see him sitting around whittling wood after the war. "What would Falcon Thames do without something to fight for?"

His ice-chip gaze darkens on her. "I can think of a few things."

The fire crackles.

"Dangerous things or pleasant things?"

"*Pleasant* is for picnics in the country, Teacup. Is pleasant what you felt with my hands on you?"

A rush of a heat steals through her core. She bites a smile, giving him a long sigh. "All right, shielding first. Not because I don't plan to travel or because you're good with your *hands*, but because Grimm never got to shielding."

On the map she still holds, she rubs a thumb over the spot that marks the Belly, frowning. "We need allies, and to warn people the war's bound to come here."

Falcon glances out the window to where the pleasure district sprawls and lights cluster a few streets away. "Before hell broke loose in Wythe, Jasper Salt implied the Belly bosses had no clue about the Darkwielder's plans."

Jasper Salt. "Captain Rivmere." The snake so willing to sacrifice her mentor for the Darkwielder's cause.

She blames herself for what happened that night, but one day when she's mastered control of her magic, she hopes to meet Salt again, if only to give him his dues. "You need to tell the bosses about the Shadow river and what's coming."

"Trix suggested the same thing, but I'm on Vesh Derringer's shit list."

"All the more reason to go to him and get back in his good graces. There are thousands of innocents here and the king's well-versed in war. We need allies," she stresses. "And the bosses might know a way around the wards."

Falcon rubs the scruff of his chin. "It'll take a couple days to track them all down." He hesitates, and she can see a glimmer of worry pass over his face. "I don't want to take you out in the streets. Not with that." He motions to her nightgown—to the marking beneath it. "But something tells me not to leave you alone here, either."

"I don't need a keeper." The words sail hotter than she means off her lips. Frowning at wherever that came from, she amends, "I'll be all right. When you go, I'll have Trix."

CHAPTER 4
COFFERS & CORPSES

The club reeks of lust and sweat.

Vesh Derringer flicks his lighter. *One-two-three. One-two-three.* A soothing pattern. Green sparks catch the contents of his pipe, illuminating his shaking hands. Drafting a long pull from its stem, he lets the mawkish smoke seep from his mouth to his lungs, lungs to his blood. Holding it too long, he sputters.

The fit earns him a snigger from across the circle, where Wyatt Kercher and Arkimen Proffit have coordinated their little reunion in a curtained-off area in the back of The Roux.

Vesh never comes here. His cousin's brothels are profane, notorious for "anything goes." If Crats can pay, Kercher's entertainment delivers. It makes Vesh's skin crawl enough to take another long drag.

He's no magic hopper, not like those who come to his territory in Crowfell, strung out and looking to steal from his card tables. But tonight his nerves aren't something whiskey will fix. Neither will the woman approaching his chair wearing only a web-silk skirt slit to the thigh and a string of beads draped between bare breasts.

He flinches as her long, thin fingers slide to his leg and she starts to seat herself on his lap.

Vesh appreciates no one's touch apart from his own. He recoils so abruptly that the woman slips off his lap. Scrambling up, she retreats, and the hazy smoke of his pipe curls in her wake.

Anxious, Vesh works another sweet breath into his lungs while running a sweaty hand over his trousers. Laughter filters between the tacky red tapestries that hang around them. Beyond the curtains, he can see the half-empty alcoves where more illicit smoke fogs the air, glasses clink softly, and moans escape from compartments.

Worry spreads through him. Only a dozen patrons in The Roux tonight when there should be a hundred. It's not a good sign.

Puffing, he flicks a look between his cousins. Arkimen's stoic, succumbed to drink. And Kercher's lost in a feast of flesh.

Vesh shouldn't have come here. They rarely convene all together, even in the best of times. He's learned never to leave his clubs unsupervised. When the cats are away, the rats descend. He's been telling Jasper Salt the dens and hoppers have to be dealt with, and that business has been slowing with the kingdom's unrest. But Salt's communication has been sparse the past year.

With a roll of his knotted shoulders, Vesh feels the tension leak from his muscles as they start to tingle.

"Hey," Kercher calls lazily. "My entertainment not to your liking? Why do you look so uptight?"

Unlike Arkimen, who stares into his third dram of whiskey, Kercher's splayed like a peacock in his wingback chair, groping the breasts of a madame in his lap. Behind him, a pair of male hands knead his neck.

Vesh looks at his cousin incredulously. "I don't know, Kerch. Maybe because Desi hasn't spoken to us for months and now she's calling us to meet. At your filthy club, of all places."

"Maybe she misses me," Kercher drawls, head tipped to welcome the male's mouth at his throat as the madame kneels between his legs.

As she takes Kercher's length in her mouth, Vesh looks away. "You've never been Desi's favorite." On a long exhale, he worries aloud, "Her fabric shops don't need the Crat business the way we do, but maybe things are spilling over to Rook. The slow-down, you hear me? Or she's heard something we haven't heard. Fuck. It's been too quiet."

Vesh sent a daw to Ghastly requesting a meeting with Jasper Salt three days ago, after rumors of Magies trying to take the West filtered into the Belly. His request went unanswered until this morning, when a letter showed up on his desk with the Darkwielder's sigil.

Wait, it said. *Word is coming.* Kercher and Arkimen received the same message.

"Desi must have gotten a letter," Vesh realizes. "Fuck."

"You swear a lot when you're stressed," Kercher grates out.

"You know the Darkwielder has history with the king. What if he decides to get involved in this war? What would that mean for us?"

"Would you relax?" His cousin lets out a long groan as the female between his legs picks up her pace. Because this is Kercher's house, Vesh averts his gaze again and says nothing. "We've been running his Belly fifteen years, haven't we? Even if he got involved... *Shit*." Kercher moans, bucking his hips, fisting a hand in the female's dark hair. "It doesn't mean he'd turn on his friends."

A shiver climbs Vesh's spine. "The Darkwielder has no friends." He looks to Arkimen to back him up, but his quiet cousin's attention is fixed out the dark, frosted windows at the back of the room.

Returning to Kercher, Vesh scoots forward in his seat. "A war will draw harder lines between the Magies and mortals. No more Crats to fill your brothels. Not even our coffers are full enough to lose the kind of money a war will cost, Kerch. Why the hell aren't you more concerned?"

A glass slams on a table behind them. The sound rings hard enough to make them peer through the tapestries.

A woman in a blue-ruffled blouse and dark trousers parts the curtains and looks directly at Kercher. "He's right. Maybe you ought to stop running your bawdies like your own personal harems."

A slow grin spreads over Kercher's face. He tracks Desi as she seats herself across from him in the only open chair. With a hat tipped over her forehead, her face is shrouded from the lamplight that dances above and at her back.

Vesh squints through the wispy smoke of his pipe to see her better. She looks different somehow. Each of the bosses are nearing fifty-five years, but no one could tell they're over thirty. They frequent *gisen* to keep themselves looking young. A strategy to keep appearing capable.

Maybe it's her hair. Desi's always preferred short, blonde bobs but tonight her locks are long and brown, side-swept under her favorite hat.

Resting a hand on the head of the female still pleasuring him, Kercher whistles. "That really you, cousin? You look good."

Desi huffs sharply through her nose. "Dismiss your pets, will you? I have news about the war. And a delivery for you."

Vesh's focus narrows on her as he snuffs out his pipe, hastily pocketing the instrument in his pants. "What is it?"

From his wingback, Kercher grips the armrests, panting, then lets out a long groan as his body shudders. The sound devolves to a slow chuckle as he straightens in his seat and finally flicks a hand to dismiss the female between his legs.

Wiping her mouth, she leaves with his male plaything. Meanwhile, Kercher fastens his pants and eyes his three cousins. "Why does this feel like a funeral?"

A slow smile curves Desi's mouth. The expression takes Vesh off guard. Unfortunately, he knows his cousin's mouth, thanks to a drunken night a few years ago, the last time they were all together when Vesh almost more than kissed her.

It's her teeth, he decides. They're straighter. He tries to remember if he's ever met a *gisen* who can alter teeth so well.

A rumble cuts Vesh's wondering short.

He peers through the tapestries to investigate, and that's when The Roux's front doors fly off their hinges. One lands a heavy blow to a wall. The other takes out a row of tables.

Lashes of darkness tear in, faster than Vesh can get a look at their source. Gasps, screams, and the sound of snapping bones break across the brothel as the shadows rip through the room. Vesh vaults to his feet, Arkimen and Kercher following suit, looking equally horrified and calling for their guards as bawdy workers flee, their bare skin spattered crimson.

Vesh turns in a circle, panic both sharpening and clouding his mental state. His own men were just at the wall, but they must have fled.

Waving a hand to peer through the pipe smoke, he takes full notice of the quiet. An utter hush has fallen across The Roux. Trading fearful looks with his cousins, he creeps to the part in the tapestries.

His guards are there, standing among several other Magies in the center of the room where the floor is littered with dead Crats.

Vesh's mouth falls open like a shocked wooden puppet as each of the casters calls their shadows back into their wrists.

His guards were in on this?

"What the fu—" Kercher's words trail off over Vesh's shoulder.

At the same time Kercher grabs for a pocket blade, Vesh digs in his waist for his revolver.

"I wouldn't do that," Desi calls.

Hand stilling, Vesh whips his gaze around to see Arkimen, shaking on his feet, and Desi, rising from her chair with a smirk.

The tapestries around them fall to the floor, and Vesh whirls again, stepping back as a bevy of Shadowcasters hulk into their private area to make a circle around them.

"What is this?" Vesh panics.

Desi crosses her arms. "It's a message. Please, take a seat."

Shadows lash in vicious strikes, swiping the ankles of the three male cousins. Vesh crashes down, seated in his chair.

Desi smiles, and Vesh's eyes latch on her, his pulse pounding. "Years ago, you brought your money into the Darkwielder's sanctuary on the guise of protecting Magies. What did you get in return?"

Vesh's mind spins as the horrible feeling he had earlier wedges itself in his gut. Sobered, Kercher rights himself in his chair, all traces of pleasure replaced with nervous twitches. Arkimen is simply pale.

Desi tilts her head to one side. "As Jasper Salt tells it, the Darkwielder gave you power. Let you get richer. But it wasn't enough for you."

"Of course it was!" Kercher says.

Extracting an envelope tucked at her back, she flicks it onto Vesh's lap. "Someone's been talking with the Gray King's representatives, sharing information about the Belly, proposing trade agreements…"

Vesh shakes, swallowing. "Never."

Desi slings a cruel laugh that sounds nothing like her. "You thought the Darkwielder wasn't paying attention, but he sees everything that happens in his house."

At her silent command, shadows leap from the circle around them, fisting Vesh's neck and hauling him off his feet.

Kercher and Arkimen suffer the same fate, until all three dangle, kicking, in mid-air.

"His *shadows* see everything," she amends quietly.

"What did you do?" Kercher chokes at Vesh.

"It was business!" Vesh claws at his throat, feeling his eyes bulge from the pressure around his neck. "Things were"—he grunts—"slowing down," he sputters. "Needed...an influx... Money! The Darkwielder expects..."

"He expects your *loyalty*." Desi steps into his eyeline. "As Salt tells it, that's what you swore to him."

Drips of a conversation from fifteen years ago, at the start of the last spring, filter into Vesh's head.

The Darkwielder was still "Kier Lestat" then, when he called the four of them to a valley city in central Magus. Newly surrounded by an unfathomable wall of rock, it was the place that would become the Belly. A place he talked about making a haven for Magies, until the time was right to change history.

It'd all started so nobly.

Desi stalks between the three of them. Eyeing Kercher, she points. "Frivolous." Turning to Arkimen, "Complicit." And rounding last on Vesh, her features harden. "And his biggest disappointment—a greedy club rat who tortures Magies."

"What?" His question chokes in the shadow's hold.

"I hear you keep trophies in your bedchamber, Derringer."

Shame colors Vesh's face a deep burgundy as he thinks of the little vials of ash he rolls between his fingers to calm his nerves—remnants of criminals his blade-for-hire, Falcon Thames, has procured.

"You had a sister who liked to bully Magies, too."

Vesh's eyes flash. He's back in a ballroom at Gray Castle, having his first conversation with Kier, just after his stepsister, Nisha, plotted an assault against him on a boarhound hunt.

The truth hits him. The Darkwielder has harbored resentment all these years. He *is* going to war against the monarchy. Against Crats, like Vesh.

But... "You...?" Vesh coughs. What had he and his cousins done that Desi would turn on them?

A slow smile lights her face. "Things have changed. That's what I've come to tell you."

Vesh struggles harder against the shadowhold, needing to look Desi in her midnight eyes, to implore her. They're family! "You know...how magic...gets out...of control! It needs...consequences!" he sputters, and the shadows grip him tighter.

She gazes pitifully at him. "You sound like the Gray King. And the Darkwielder has no more need for you. You're just a reminder of things that won't be welcome at his court."

Court? Vesh gurgles, but no words come out.

Desi raises, then drops her arm. And the shadows rip.

Panic.

After one horrific moment, Vesh realizes he isn't dead, right before two other heads roll off their perches. Carved like stone in pained silence, Arkimen's face stares straight up. Kercher's, landed on its side, is stuck in a grimace. As their bodies tumble in heaps, bile climbs the walls of Vesh's stomach. "No!" he wails, wrenching his eyes shut.

Desi scoffs. "You order smugglers to take Magies apart, but you can't stomach seeing it done?"

When he opens his eyes, she's looking at him with an odd tilt to her head.

Then the shadows on Vesh's neck wrench him up, and he's tossed against the far wall. A lancing pain splits his back, and he cries out, falling forward on his knees in a fit of coughs.

Vaguely, he hears the clack of his smoke pipe hitting the floor.

Bending to retrieve the instrument, Desi stares at its contents, nostrils flaring a long moment before stuffing it in her pocket. "Think I'll keep this. *My* first trophy."

"Desi," Vesh pleas. But when she steps into the brighter lamplight, his eyes round.

She shakes her head at him slowly, reaching up to remove her hat and toss it aside. She looks at him, and he wonders how he didn't see it.

"Not Desi," she says. A rush of sudden words—an incantation—hurries off her lips, and her hands fly out to stir a burst of energy so vicious it's as if a hole has ripped in the wall behind Vesh.

A wicked passage—the only kind in all of the Belly open at present—snatches Vesh up in its mouth. The moment he's spinning inside it, the walls start snapping, and he's sure he's headed straight to hell.

CHAPTER 5
SPIDERS & SERPENTS

M osaics of silk banner in the nipping headwind as Falcon weaves through a thickening crowd on Market Alley. His head ought to ring with calls of merchants, market-goer chatter, and pops of cart wheels, but in the thin, gray light of morning, it seems the crowd isn't feeling friendly.

Bodies shove in from adjacent alleys, joining a flood of citizens who elbow into line at food and fabric carts.

The air's frigid, but squeezed into the throng, his chin low, Falcon's chest is warm as a goddamn furnace. His Animater skin helps. The cold's tolerable if he keeps his ink moving, so the metals, ores, any other material he's got sheathed, stay good and malleable. It's easy to do with his agitation mounting as it has since he left the hotel.

Ophelia can take care of herself.

Even still, his ink pulls, discontent at the distance. It's hard to ignore the urge to turn around as he ventures farther away toward the Crossing, but he's got to cut over to Crowfell soon, into Vesh Derringer's territory.

Slipping into the crowd, he focuses on the task at hand—get to Crowfell unseen, find and warn Derringer, get the ball rolling on allyships, and see if the boss knows anything about the wards. Then he can get back.

A dusting of snow hugs the path he shuffles down. This alley's all brick on both sides and slick with moisture. Around him, he notes the scowls. Magies clutch coats they've fashioned out of cut-up rugs and blankets—whatever they can afford—because most can't foot the steep price Fabricaters charge to tailor wardrobes.

The disgruntled edge of the crowd keeps him watchful. From the corner of his eye, he notices two market-goers at a fruit cart jostling for a peck of apples. Farther on, a woman slips a pack of meat off a cart and into her bag.

Tucking his chin into his coat to avoid eye contact, his collar rises to meet the soft stubble of his jaw and he catches a distinct smell of the past—northern oil.

A long time ago, this coat was hewn special for him. Stitched with fabric folks can't get just anywhere. Fabric imbued with a spell that protects its wearer. Along with the cold, that scent of oil takes Falcon back to boyhood—to frosted breaths, smoky fires, screeching beasts, and thick pelts. Things long gone from his life.

Slurs ring out in the old tongue as he reaches a line of fabric carts. Spectators are drawn around two women who glare, spitting mad, at one another.

"Misen!" *It's mine!* one shouts, yanking a fur-lined cloak to her chest.

"Nast! Nast, misen!" The second woman shoves, and the first lands on her haunches. Before she even rises to her feet, flame catches in her palms.

Damn the gods!

Fire sails.

Falcon tears forward, breaking cover, and whips his jacket off to throw it atop the second woman, whose threadbare coat has caught flames. The crowd collectively gasps and steps back as he pats, snuffing the burn. When he pulls the coat off the woman, her hair's singed and she's crying. "You all right?"

As she nods, a hiss whistles through the crowd. Falcon launches to his feet and backs into the fold a breath before the shadows reach the scene.

The ropes race around the woman who's still lying in the street and catch the wrists of the Bender who threw the flames.

Two guards stalk up the alley, shouting for everyone to move along. Falcon knows them instantly. They're low-rate guards who like to gamble. In fact, he's taken them for more than a few shinies at the Crowfell tables. One's a hefty brute in South Warren suede. The other, thin as a beam in the sleeker garb Kercher's men wear in Ravish.

Falcon flows with the foot traffic in the opposite direction from where he needs to go, slipping his jacket on. It carries the acrid sting of smoke now, which masks the scent of the past.

It's getting worse in the Belly—the bickering and fighting. In a city where magic hangs in clouds, no one ought to go without. But magic requires disciplined wielders, empathy and morals, and raw materials to work from. War and winter are already making everything scarcer.

Falcon curses the Darkwielder for starting a revolution without preparing people. As far as he can see, he's left them to their own devices. *Everyone for themselves*—that's what it's come to. Rune would have something idealistic to say about it, if it were him here with Ophelia. Rune could talk some sense into people.

Falcon's teeth stab his chapped bottom lip. The past few days, working with Ophelia on shielding, he hasn't found the right time to tell her everything. He still doesn't have words for what shook loose in him when he looked at her three days ago. Or what he learned about Rune Ethera.

He feels an empty pang at his side where his skin sheath is lighter of the two items—the letter and the book—that he was stowing since Dwymore.

Halfway up Market Alley, there's more trouble.

Falcon perks his ear to where a small crowd's gathered, where gossip is being passed around like a virus. Past the ringing that's tinkled in one of his ears since he was seven and a reckless choice cost half his hearing, he strains now to the catch the half-truths whispered in Magiesian:

"They burned every last Constelli sage alive and wiped out the Special Army!"

"Beasts are running loose around the kingdom!"

"Crats are hanging their magic-born!"

"The cold's gonna kill trade across the whole kingdom—we'll starve!"

A curse under his breath sends an exclamation of white into the air. The bosses will have a shitstorm on their hands if thousands of Magies get themselves more riled up. At the thought, he hustles.

An old merchant steps into Falcon's path, thrusting an apple at him. "Obst? Obst frishon?"

Falcon eyes the fruit with irritation. "Nast." Darting by the merchant, he makes for a shortcut to the Crossing, where the Belly's five territories meet. There, he spots a familiar fabric cart, its shelves laden with colored metal trinkets and stacks of fabric.

A shop owner's eyes widen on him. The septum ring they wear winks as they shake their head, beckoning Falcon over.

Glancing around, he sidles behind a curtain of patterned colors.

The owner glances at him from beneath the hood of a notched blue cloak, keeping attention on the fabric they're folding.

"Mayra?" Falcon registers their silver-sheened fingertips, nails worn to nubs. "You're doing the market these days?"

Mayra's hands pause before resuming folding. "Desi Graves was murdered last night in Rook. I was hoping I might hear something."

"The fuck?" he asks, stunned. *Desi Graves is dead?*

Head down, Mayra says, "You haven't heard, then. I wondered, given your circles."

He doesn't bother telling them he's not quite in those circles these days. His head spins. A goddamn boss is dead?

A fresh slew of shouts rings up the alley, and a barrage of fabrics take flight in a magic-spurred wind as a man makes off with stolen goods.

"Spiders," Mayra mutters, craning to watch.

Spiders in a jar. They've shared the sentiment before about too many Magies in one place.

"Tangled webs," he agrees.

Mayra looks troubled. "War and winter at once. Why do the gods punish us so?"

He won't opine on the deities, though he's sure they have little to do with the state of Magus; Erebus, Selene, and Luna haven't been corporeal to walk among their creation in centuries. He doubts they pay it mind.

Tipping his head, he says, low, "Who've you told about Desi Graves?"

Mayra sets a folded cloak on a neat pile. "I didn't think it wise to feed the unrest. I only saw guards bring her body out at all because a late customer was knocking incessantly on my shop door. A friend of yours, I believe."

"A friend?" He splays a hand on the wood of the cart, keeping an eye on two shoppers who've stopped to inspect Mayra's wares. "Who?"

"The redhead with the temper."

He cocks a look at Mayra. What would Trix need in Rook after business hours? "What'd she want?"

Mayra shrugs. "A new look from my *gisen*. She was insistent."

The shoppers glance at them, and Falcon lowers his voice, feeling the ink shift across his heart. "I'm heading for Derringer's. I'll find out what's going on. For now, keep things quiet."

Ophelia's always felt better running.

As a child, if she was sprinting through forests in knee-deep snow clasped tightly to Elora's hand, she was focused on what came next and not the danger in their wake.

Sounds of their heavy breathing, sticks breaking under boot, and the swish of their cloaks kept her senses sharp when she fled village to village with her mother. Kept her from panicking at the memory of that last time, when two soldiers had ripped them from bed and declared that they'd found Elora Dannan at last. Then the soldiers vanished. Ophelia hadn't known how then, only that she'd feel safe again once they were running.

Fleeing was her plan when she and Hart arrived at the Constelli, but he never believed two penniless, *unascended* Magie children would get far on their wits. And in those early days, Ophelia still hoped her mother would return and they'd run together again—with Hart. But that hope withered with each passing year. It died entirely as her affinity manifested far greater than any other Matterist, and she pieced together that her mother had been a Descendant. That her magic passing to Ophelia meant one thing: Elora was dead.

At a mirror in the Ravish hotel suite, she straightens the dress she's put on—the one Trix left for her, which feels a bit formal for the hotel. Thick, silk velour of the faintest gold. A vee in the neck and long sleeves to her wrists. She checks her locket, then grabs a matching cloak off a hook. Still fighting a chill, she drapes the fabric around her shoulders before readying a satchel.

She feels compelled to stay packed with Falcon away to warn the bosses of impending war. If her childhood of running taught her anything, it's that nowhere is safe and she must always be ready.

Pausing, she feels along the edges of the mental shield she's been working on the past few days.

Falcon suggested she picture herself amid mountains, making new walls rise around her. "Forge them of ice and iron. Make them impenetrable."

"Why ice and iron?" It wasn't a combination talked of in classes at the Constelli.

Then again, Falcon never went to the king's academy. "Magic can't penetrate them as easily when they're forged together," he said.

She tries to imagine those iron walls, rocks cut of ice rising to hug them. What she brushes up against, though, feels more like a sand castle, fragile and easily trampled.

She'll keep practicing.

With Falcon away, she plans to help Trix find the spell that will breach the wards keeping anyone from casting a way out of the Belly. There has to be something.

Reaching for a scarf to finish packing, she stops short at the sight of two objects stacked on the dresser. A thick piece of cream paper, folded neatly and sealed with blue wax bearing the Special Army sigil, rests atop a white book—Rune's white book.

Memories spate her mind and make it hard to breathe.

Focusing on the paper, she can see the suggestion of faint blue ink. It stirs an echo of Hart's deep voice. "What do you want, Lia? To visit the sea? I'll paint it for you." And he did, because they couldn't go.

At the Constelli, Ophelia kept a folded map as a bookmark in whatever she was reading. So worn was it from running her fingers across it to plot paths from Easton to Inri to the ports of the Lost Sea—adventures she longed for to search out her mother.

"It's only a hundred miles," she'd tell Hart in hushed whispers as they sat on the floor of her room eating sweet bread she'd sneaked from the kitchens. "We could make it and be gone."

"No, Lia. There's nowhere the two of us could run in Magus that they wouldn't find us. We'll end up dead."

"You don't know that," she would insist.

"I do."

The childhood conversation, their whispers, and their sticky hands on the map fade as Ophelia's gaze slides to the white book that holds memories of other lives.

She remembers snatching glimpses of the book across time and place. Tucked into Rune's high-waist trousers at the breakfast table, where they sat every morning in a flagstone farm kitchen in 1854. Or slid quickly into a drawer in his room at the orchard in 1852, when Ophelia entered without knocking.

Only once did Rune draw the book out openly. It was 1835. She was wearing a blue and pink-flowered day dress. Rune, a white tunic and brown pants. They'd just declared their feelings, and he asked her to journal how she felt...

A tinkling against glass interrupts her reverie.

Tearing her attention to the window, she sees a vast cloud of particles drag themselves like fingernails down the pane. In that same moment, a chill ripples beneath her skin.

Her stomach tightens at how furiously the dust begins to vibrate, how quickly its whispers flood her head. They sound like a warning.

Stuffing the book and paper into her satchel, she hoists the bag around her back.

When she arrives at the window, the dust peels itself away. Its whispers beat like beetle wings through her mind as she gets a clear view of the street below and goes rigid.

A formidable black phaeton is drawing next to the hotel.

At the sight of the serpent sigil on its polished door, power stirs in her. Magic that raises the hair on her arms and screams at her to *run*.

She races from the room and down the stairs, the layers of her dress a flurry, until she reaches the main floor of the hotel.

Panic rising in her throat, Ophelia pounds on Trix's door.

At no reply, she hammers her fist again against the wood. "Trix!" she hisses.

Movement down the hall refocuses her fear. Under the domed ceiling of the foyer, several militia members—friends of Trix—congregate.

Ophelia opens her mouth to warn them of what she's seen, but there's something about their attire that makes her shut it again. They no longer wear that mottled clothing, but polished uniforms instead.

She raps faster on the door. This time, there's a loud thump, followed by the crashing of glass.

Ophelia jiggles the knob with fervor, and a muffled groan replies.

"Trix!" But the door stays stuck. Gaze catching on the sconces where light dances in the hall, she thinks, *Yes! But carefully.*

Concentrating, she senses for the *maether* in the flames fed by a lumen tree not far from the hotel. Magic of the gods. She connects to it and makes it hers. Then, as if plucking golden threads from the fire itself, she pulls the energy into herself, letting it well in the ridges down her arm where lumen healed her a week ago.

She can do this. It isn't the Constelli or Wythe, where high emotions drove her to destruction. It isn't a year ago when she awakened and panicked at the memory of what she'd done. It's a doorknob for gods' sake.

Her mind screams to hurry, but she makes herself grasp the knob with care. Light filters down her hand like water, causing the knob to glow brighter and brighter. *"Open."* She twists, and mercifully it clicks.

In triumph, and as the light in her hand dims, she shoves through the door. It looks as though Trix has just fallen into a table and shattered a vase.

"Gods," Ophelia mutters, bolting the lock hastily and dashing to her friend's side.

The window's open, letting cold air funnel into the room.

"Did you just come through there?" she asks as Trix hauls herself to her feet, swatting away Ophelia's outstretched hand.

"I'm fine." The Spellcaster plucks a shard from her palm, and blood wells.

Ophelia's stomach writhes. There was so much blood at Asenti after she lost control protecting Hart from the *prüstrot*.

Shoving the nausea down, she says, "We have to go. There's a carriage outside just like the Darkwielder's; I think he's come back."

As Trix frowns, holding her palm, Ophelia scours the table for a bandage, absently registering the unopened grimoire, empty bowls, and the fine layer of soot over everything.

Finding a cloth, she grabs Trix's hand and dabs. "Falcon's gone to Crowfell to talk to Vesh Derringer. We need to find him and get out of Ravish."

Hurriedly, she pockets the stained cloth to fetch a fresh one, bandaging Trix's wound. Just as she ties it, voices sound from the hall, muffled by the door.

A familiar prickle climbs her spine.

God calls to god.

"He's here," she breathes, throwing the hood up on her cloak, lunging for the window that's ajar.

Trix steps in her way. "We run, and then what?" Nose to nose, she notes the odd chestnut color of the caster's hair, the red stains on her blouse. "How has hiding worked out for you, Ophelia?"

Trix's tone takes her off guard. "What?"

"You're down two boyfriends and an ancient Spellcaster, last time I checked. Hart. Rune. Grimm Hermes. And no closer to the relics you and your warden keep talking about."

The words are barbs. "We're wasting time. The Darkwielder's going to find us." As she steps around Trix to work the window up higher, a breath-stealing stab of cold greets her.

Out on the rails—footholds that stack like a ladder on the side of the hotel—she prepares to climb, when Trix ducks her head out. "What if we stay and fight?"

Ophelia grips a frigid bar. "Fight the Darkwielder? Until I'm as practiced with my power, he'd eviscerate us."

Trix shakes her head. "No. What if we stay and fight with him against Osiris? Isn't fighting what a Descendant of the gods would do?"

Ophelia squeezes the rail tighter. "I will fight. I'll find every relic and end this war, but I won't ally with a monster just because we have the same enemy. I won't lose another person I care about for the sake of revenge." She starts down the façade, but a chilling gust of wind catches her hood, forcing her flat against the building.

With a curse, she glances sharply below, where at the mouth of the narrow alley half of the phaeton's high, black wheels are visible and she can see passersby gawking at the carriage. Men and women in dark uniforms guard it.

"So not that way," she mutters.

A grunt draws her attention upward to find Trix climbing out the open window, gripping a rail as she calls, pointing up, "This way!"

At the roof, Trix reaches for Ophelia's hand as if to pull her up, but instead, she holds her there. "We could align with the Darkwielder's cause."

"Are you out of your mind?" Pulling against the caster's grip, Ophelia swings herself onto the roof, scouting for an efficient route off the hotel. "You didn't see him kill a hundred men like it was nothing. We were chased through a passage by *his* Shadowcaster, Trix. We lost—" Emotion chokes her words. She's kept her sorrow locked away the past few days, as best as she could behind that washroom door, but she can feel it clawing to get free.

When she comes around, Trix's eyes are sharp as fresh-cut gemstones. "We've both lost people. If we aligned, we'd have enough power to end half a century of oppression like *that*. We'd have safety. Isn't that what you've wanted?"

It's like every wound reopens.

Ophelia has always looked over a shoulder with dread, knowing that someday, someone or something would come for her as they must've come for her mother. The only moments she hasn't—exploring the countryside with Rune, counting stars on city roofs with Falcon, or lost to her writing while Hart painted—were based on fabricated stories.

"I want freedom," she answers, bitterness leaching to her voice. "Where no one is hunted for power, where *I* am not hunted. But I won't be a cannon in their war."

"Stop being so noble. This isn't just *their* war." Trix takes her arm, lowering her voice. "If you run now, you might never get another shot."

Before Ophelia can ask what she means, Trix steps away, straightening as if at attention.

A breath of ice shivers across Ophelia's skin, but not from the winter air.

She presses a hand against the marking over her chest, where coldness rises through her cloak to greet her palm, just before she hears the low, rasping voice that's been haunting her.

"Hello, goddess."

CHAPTER 6
TETHERS & FOES

RAVISH
5TH DAY IN THE NEW WINTER
FALCON AND OPHELIA ARE ON THEIR OWN

Something's coming. Or it's already here.

The air feels prickly, charged, as Falcon weaves down Market Alley. He's ready to cut over to the Crossing to hit the shortcut into Crowfell and Vesh Derringer's territory, when foot traffic parts at the mouth of another alley and a flash of black fabric makes him bolt mid-stride.

Instinctively, he draws a blade from his hip and lowers it to his side, searching the throng of shoppers and merchants intently.

Between bodies, it flashes again—a black cloak out of place in a sea of mismatched, colored garbs. It disappears into the crowd heading toward North Ravish, not the direction he needs to go.

He idles, debating whether to stick to his plan or make sure this isn't a threat. If it is a threat and he lets it go, if something happens to Ophelia because of it...

Memories sift of soft thighs in his hands, mouths smashed together, Ophelia's hands in his hair, and that crazed, manic feeling to claim her.

With a curse, he charges down the side alley after the cloak.

The Darkwielder arrives on a wind of shadows, as powerful as Ophelia remembers.

One second, there's nothing. The next, mist is climbing the walls and darkness unspooling, pressing into corners, blanketing every inch of the roof until she can barely see what's beyond the short walls.

The chill she feels is paralyzing, but heat—*light*—also pulses in the sky, a million urgent fireflies. The budding storm of dust separates itself from the vaster veil that's thick above the Belly and descends, sweeping with agitation amongst the shadows that have carried her enemy here.

Out of that thick mist, the Darkwielder takes shape. Her heart slams her ribs like a hammer as his striking pale face catches a fraction of light and his starlight eyes seize hers, beholding her where she's rooted, where she's blocking Trix.

A smile ghosts his lips. *"Did you miss me, Ophelia?"*

It takes a moment as she fights the feel of his power to comprehend his mouth hasn't moved. More horrifying is the way something inside her preens at the purr of his voice in her mind.

He's real. He survived.

Wick Sneed proclaimed the Darkwielder wasn't done with her and now he's before her, feline in the way he surveys her, the object of his fixation.

Ophelia laid witness to his shadows swallowing royal soldiers, how he rendered them nothing but ash with so little effort.

She reaches for *maether*, searching for just a fetter to grasp—but there's so much of *him* here. She settles for swiping a throwing blade she's sheathed in her boots. Keeping keen eyes on him, she notes the silver of his rings, the faint pink scar above a dark brow on his forehead, and the blackness that folds at his back. Not wings, but the illusion of them.

She grips her weapon. A blade won't stop the Darkwielder, but perhaps it will distract him enough that she can disappear with Trix down the building, slip into the growing crowd, and find Falcon.

I am no one's pawn. I will not let him take me.

Before the Darkwielder has drawn two steps, she expels a breath and hurls the knife. It careens through shadow to stab straight through where his raven cloak billows at his side, making him stagger as it pins the fabric against a few narrow inches of wood along the roof wall.

She whirls for Trix.

The sight of the Spellcaster on one knee, head bowed, bolts her in place. "What are you doing? Get up!" When Trix doesn't answer, or move, a horrible notion pulses behind her ribs. "Trix!"

There's too much silence before the caster answers, "This is the only way."

A stabbing rhythm to the tune of betrayal pounds in her veins as Ophelia vaguely hears the tearing of fabric behind her. She turns—straight into the Darkwielder. And his smirk.

"That was my favorite cloak." It flaps, shredded on one side like a bird whose wing's been maimed, but the feathered shoulders are still imposing as he holds her gaze. "Don't be afraid, Ophelia."

Like his darkness, the soft command curls seductively around her. For a moment, she wavers, fighting against a part of her that wants to lean toward that voice, that power.

Monster. He is the monster who turned half the Special Army, cursed the kingdom, and commanded the beasts that nearly killed Hart. A villain whose own proxy marched Grimm Hermes to his death.

"I'll forgive you the cool reception," he allows. "Benefit of the doubt, for keeping my creatures in line for me when I was indisposed at Wythe." The Darkwielder drags a long finger over the scar on his forehead—it must be from falling into that chasm, before his shadows got loose. He inches ever closer.

He's trying to intimidate her. With that power of his shuddering around her—*in* her—it nearly works.

Let him get close enough, Falcon would tell her. *Then strike.*

The Darkwielder lifts a brow in her direction as he raises his knuckles—the ones with tattoos that cross and snake like bands of shadow. He brushes them against her cheek. "I've felt your despair these past few days, goddess. I've come to help ease it."

She can't bear his touch. Wrenching her face away, she swipes another blade from her boot, leaving her with only one still sheathed. "Don't call me that," she seethes, her nose a breath from his as she lays the knife's edge to his throat.

"It's what you are."

"I—" She hesitates, registering something he said. "What do you mean, you *felt* my despair?"

When he shrugs, her eyes forge daggers of their own. "Get out of my mind."

Shadows veil his shoulders, angling around the two of them. "I didn't put myself in your mind, not this time, if that's what you fantasize."

She lays a palm over her heart where that stain of a marking resides, punctuating, "You marked me."

His deep, resonant laugh is so unexpected, she drops the hand in a fit of fury. "What?"

"You called the Dark Shadow, Ophelia." His slate eyes glint like cold metal at her as his fingers tease a shadow nudging his side. "It was an unexpected but pleasant surprise to find that you forged a bond between us. That I could sense you again and feel what you feel."

Her breaths scrape in her ears. "Forged a...?" Snapping her mouth shut, she considers the last few days. The washroom. Her nightmares. The intimate moments with Falcon against the wall in their suite. He sensed all that? Felt what she felt? She knuckles the knife in her hand so hard, it presses to his flesh.

"I'm sorry you didn't get to finish," he says coolly. "That was uncomfortable for everyone."

"You're vile."

The briefest flicker in his eyes. "You have a lovely spirit. Here I've come to offer aid, and you can't stop pulling knives. Which are beneath you, goddess."

"*Aid*? You ravaged an ancient hamlet full of innocent people! If that's your aid—"

"Are we so different?"

Her fury beats against the bones in her chest. *Grimm told him.*

Before securing the Darkwielder's allyship to go after the relics, Grimm must have told him that she burned the Constelli. She had no idea then who the headmaster chose for allies, or why; they'd thought it safer that way, that there would be time to debrief once she was woken from the spell. But none of that went to plan.

"If you know what I've done"—she sneers—"then you know I could make you disappear. I could think you to nothing." If she could control her power. "I haven't because I am nothing like you."

Amusement glitters in his eyes. "You haven't because you fear yourself, and because you feel me." She keeps a tense eye on the Darkwielder's hand, where he rubs his fingers together. "We are tethered—lives linked by my shadow you called. A shadow you accepted as part of yourself," he muses. "It's fused so fully with your light, I can feel your warmth. While that power is inside you, you'll want me breathing. If I die, you die."

"Lies." But at his unwavering brow and the knowing look in his eyes, she lowers the knife to her side.

The Darkwielder's attention drifts to where Trix still bends a silent knee. "Ms. Farrow. You've been most helpful, but there's more to be done. Ready your soldiers for what's next."

As Trix obediently rises, that vicious betrayal thrushes heat through Ophelia's veins. The dust around her swarms to every angry heartbeat, pulsing faster, hotter, when she sees no shred of remorse on Trix's face. The caster turns for the wall, making quick work of disappearing down the side of the building.

Ophelia stalks after to peer over the ledge, catching Trix's glance once more before her supposed friend greets the soldiers lined along the street. Soldiers who've been residing at the hotel this entire time.

Ophelia's fists mallet to the point of pain as the truth fully dozes her over. The table of unused spell materials, the grimoire unopened... Trix was supposed to be finding a way out of the Belly, but she never even tried. From the time she summoned them to the hotel, she must have known the Darkwielder was coming, and when Ophelia and Falcon told her of their plan to win over the bosses, Trix encouraged it. She knew Falcon would be away today.

"She's chosen the wiser path."

Ophelia spins, centering her fury on the Darkwielder.

I am the daughter of Elora, the Descendent of the goddess Selene. I am no one's weapon but my own.

A sliver of light sparks beneath her sleeve. "Is your own power not enough that you must have me, too?" she demands.

"Who wouldn't have you? You're so amiable." He manages to make the words sound like a caress and, tether or no tether, she wants to wipe the smirk off his face.

At the slip of a cool tendril across her neck, rage bests any lingering fear of him. "You have infinite power and, from what I've seen, no conscience to stop you from killing anyone in your way—nothing that might've prevented you from forging a river of shadows that traps us here and kills anyone who crosses it," she grates. "So why," she punctuates, "do you need my power?"

Menacingly soft, he replies, "For now, we might differ in the lengths we're willing to go, but you'll find sacrifices get easier the longer you live. We have the same dream, Ophelia, and fight for the same thing—our people."

Every breath strains with her anger. "People you've trapped behind the walls of the Belly."

Like a gasp, the darkness recedes—every last tendril—and the roof floods with the gray gloom of morning.

Only once her eyes have adjusted does she see the Darkwielder fully, dressed in his foreboding dark leather uniform. There are no shadows at his back, none on his fingertips, but somehow that feels more dangerous. He looks a man. A striking, deadly man whose amusement is gone, replaced by a furrowed brow.

"No one is trapped here," he says. "I've taken pains to fortify the city for its safety and named your friend an officer to amass soldiers we'll need to overthrow the king." He prowls around her with intensity, graceful as a panther. "People are tired of cowering, suffering, being punished for who they were born to be. They crave a chance to seize true freedom."

"What is freedom under the rule of monsters?" Does he think he can fool her? "People will fight for you or they'll die? Is that right?"

"They'll fight for their gods."

Her spine straightens. "You've come to force me to swear an oath to you. To help you crush the Gray King, so you can rule? Well, you have come for nothing because I will not go with you." She has to find Falcon, but how?

The chill inside her presses down, almost painfully heavy. She flattens a hand against it, failing to fill her lungs.

"You don't look well, Ophelia." The Darkwielder turns a palm over to call a single tendril of shadow from his wrist. "Trouble sleeping?" In his hand, a small creature grows from the vapor, thickening until it sprouts wings and flaps to one of his shoulders, where it grows again. It's a replica of the creature that split itself in two on that dais in Wythe, and it stares directly at her with empty eyes.

She's surprised to sense the shadow's curiosity, rather than the deadly thirst it had for the soldiers.

The Darkwielder pets the creature, and when a tender ache stirs against her shadow mark, it feels as though he's running his long fingers across her chest.

He smiles. With a flick of a wrist, the beast is vapor again and folds into his skin. "You belong at my court," he tells her. "With someone who understands your power. I would force you to go with me and it wouldn't be pleasant, but I don't have to, do I?"

Pounding—in her neck and head and heart. Can he sense it? His gaze suggests so as it makes a hostage of her.

"You want to come with me," he decides. She doesn't. "You imagine what it would be like." She can't. He steps closer and those cold, granite eyes are a pestle, aiming to crush and grind her resolve. "In my court, no one will touch you. Your affinity will fully manifest, and we'll show the kingdom that its gods have not abandoned them. Together, we'll make the world our sanctuary."

She can almost imagine it—a better future for those she loves, and for herself. No more hiding, no more running. But she is no fool.

She doesn't have Rune's inclination to see the good in everyone. Her wariness and skepticism have been sharpened like a stone over years of abuse in the king's system.

She doesn't trust the Darkwielder. She could never.

And having already lost Hart and Rune, there is no possible way she will separate herself from Falcon, not after all they've been through.

"You will," the Darkwielder says quietly.

He's listening to her thoughts, right now.

Ophelia's cold smile falters. The certainty in those two little words—*you will*—makes her search the street below, suddenly terrified what might happen if Falcon returned to this hotel.

CHAPTER 7
BAWDIES & BARGAINS
RAVISH
5TH DAY IN THE NEW WINTER
FALCON AND OPHELIA ARE ON THEIR OWN

Falcon shoves against the current of market-goers, chasing that bad feeling.

Where the hell did the owner of that black cloak go? It's taken twenty minutes to double-back toward Ravish where he saw them slip away.

Finally, the path slopes and he breaks from the throng onto Bawdy Row. He pauses there, on the edge of Wyatt Kercher's district, scanning the street. He's just a jaunt from the piers and Black Silt River, where magic hangs heavier and casts a darker hue, like a morning that can't quite dawn. Lamplights burn there all day.

Gods, he's chased the damn cloak in a circle. He's not far from the hotel.

An instinct tugs. With no sign of the black cloak, maybe he ought to go back and check in.

Relaxing the hand on his blade, Falcon wonders if he's being paranoid, overprotective, whatever he's become since he almost lost Ophelia.

Then a scream. A cluster of passersby race down the cobblestones. Women rush with skirts in their hands, men hold their hats.

"What the hell?" he mutters. As a man passes, Falcon grabs his arm to stop him. "Ka passen?"

Eyes widen on him. "Miharan. Miharan en The Roux!"

Murder. At Kercher's club?

Falcon drops the stranger's arm and hustles toward the peaked awning of the brothel. The door's busted open and glass trails out. Knuckling his blade, he creeps forward, his chest already aglow, ready to gift him something substantial.

He isn't prepared for the massacre inside.

It's like a bomb's gone off. Mortal limbs are strewn in bloody piles around the club, lamplights flicker, and all the furniture looks demolished. In the back of the room, a single tapestry hangs, half-torn, from the ceiling. The rest are pooled on the ground.

Only a blue wingback chair sits upright.

How many times has Falcon made a run for Kercher and seen the Ravish boss holding court in that chair like a king himself?

He's not now, though.

Falcon's pretty damn sure that's his body without a head, crumpled on the floor. And gods of Magus—he strides farther in—Arkimen Proffit?

Shouts in the street turn Falcon's good ear. "He's returned! The Darkwielder!"

With a flashing bolt of fear, Falcon thinks of Ophelia. Just as he starts back toward the door, a shadow moves in his periphery. He whirls, blade ready, to see a snake-like smile and an eye patch meet the light.

Wick Sneed steps out from behind the tapestry in a black cloak—*the* black cloak that Falcon had been following—with what looks like a fresh shadow mark on his neck, and an angry pink scar over a lower eyelid. It matches the one on Sneed's ear.

"Falcon Thames." Sneed grins in goddamn glee. "You never could walk away. My good luck you followed me here."

In a blur of motion, Falcon extracts a second knife from the ink at his neck—a lightblade this time. He fists a weapon in each hand.

Sneed's laugh is shrill. "So eager to settle scores." His gaze flicks at something across the room and back. "I hear you found that pretty little redhead. And *Ophelia*"—he draws her name out slow. "How's our goddess?"

Falcon lunges. Blinded by rage, he doesn't hear the shriek until it's too late. Shadows cut across the club to intercept him, sending Falcon off his feet and sailing toward a wall. His head smacks the sharp edge of an alcove as he lands. Groaning, he rolls to his side.

The ringing in his ear tings louder as his head spins. Shoving to his knees to shake it off, he realizes that he's dropped his lightblade and is only holding one knife.

By then, half a dozen Shadowcasters he vaguely recognizes surround him. Three men and three women who must know his reputation—what Falcon can do if given a chance. Their shadows lunge for his arms, holding him in place as Wick Sneed casually bends to retrieve Falcon's lightblade.

After flipping it in his palm, Sneed traces a finger over his scarred eye. "One day I'll return the favor, *smugger*. As it is, we've got a job for you, and it'll require your sight."

At Sneed's nod, the shadows squeeze and Falcon's vision darkens.

Ophelia doesn't like that a crowd is gathering below the hotel. It's too dense to tell if Falcon is among it.

He can't take on the Darkwielder. He'd never win. And a world without Falcon is...inconceivable.

She assesses her adversary, the fact that he stands so close and can call his shadows at will, while Ophelia hasn't had the time or enough training to fully control her power. Still, she has to do something.

Drawing *maether* from whatever nearby source she can sense, she lets the energy hum beneath her sleeve.

"Come," he says. And as he extends a hand to her, she glimpses an unmistakable onyx blade—the one thing that *could* make her go with her enemy willingly—and her magic wavers.

The Dark Shadow Dagger seems to pulse from his belt. Or perhaps that's the blood in Ophelia's veins.

Her primary goal is to bring all three relics together in order to nullify or destroy them. One of them is right here.

She remembers Trix's coaxing: *If you run, you might never get another shot.*

As a plan forms, a million whispers of warning fill her ears, but she focuses on the Darkwielder. "Swear you won't harm Falcon. Any of my friends."

Her enemy looks disappointed. "They're of no importance to me personally, and I want you well, Ophelia. It wouldn't serve to harm them."

They're of no importance? *Arrogant prick.*

Swallowing her desire to murder the Darkwielder, she forces a nod, then slowly takes his offered hand. She tenses at the shock of his essence—a heady storm of rage and heart and hollowness that mingles with the coolness of his skin.

When he sweeps an arm around her, she's enveloped by the scent of smoking leaves and cloves. Faster than a breath, darkness rises and launches them off the roof, delivering them safely to the Belly streets below.

As a phaeton door opens to her, she makes a quick circle on her forehead and prays to the primordial goddess of her line: *When word reaches Falcon that I went with the Darkwielder, let him trust I have a plan.*

TWO
WOLVES TO SHEEP

CHAPTER 8
PLAYERS & PARTS
SOMEWHERE OUTSIDE MAGUS
5TH DAY IN THE NEW WINTER
FALCON IS ON HIS OWN

Falcon's ink simmers like a cauldron.

He's been trapped in a shadowhold with a sack over his head for hours, plotting the painful ways he's going to torture Wick Sneed the second he gets free. But when the carriage he's stuck in slows and the sack's yanked off, it's not that prick he sees.

Trix sits among four Shadowcasters from The Roux, hair tied back, with an expression that's only half as full of temper as the day she slung an arrow at his chest.

It takes a second to process, to register the black uniform she wears, patched with the Darkwielder's serpent-dagger sigil.

The version of Falcon Thames that wouldn't hesitate to lop a limb off—the *smugger* with no soul—boils so hot that a weapon rises on its own from his tattoos, the base of its hilt protruding from his chest.

Trix leans forward. With a palm, she calmly shoves it back into Falcon's ink. "You can't kill me, smugger. Not if you want to know where they took Ophelia."

He blazes. "What the fuck did you do?"

Wrenching against the shadowhold, he manages an arm loose. When it frees, he doesn't hesitate. Extracting a smaller lightblade from the ink at the side of his neck, he slices through his hold.

The shadows hiss as they split and draw back.

He's a madman then, leaping across the seat, straight for Trix's neck.

The Shadowcasters grab for him, but Trix's hand flies up. "Stand down," she snaps.

Mayra's words play back at him as he glares at her: *The redhead with the temper.* He angles the tip of his blade near her windpipe. "You killed Desi Graves. The others, too?"

Trix's throat bobs against the blade as she swallows. "I gave the orders." Eyeing her entourage, she says, "Give us five minutes alone."

Falcon glares at every single one of them as they shove out the carriage door.

As they go, snow blows in, bitterly cold. He doesn't get a good look at where they are. All he sees is white.

"Talk," he barks when they shut the door.

Under the blade, Trix draws a long breath. "For every Crat who ever laid a hand on me and every Magie who fought in the arena, watching the bosses die was a perk. I liked it. But I didn't warn you what was coming because if you knew, you wouldn't have left Ophelia alone. And she wouldn't have gone with the Darkwielder."

His hand tremors—with fury or fear, it doesn't matter. He's a second from ending her.

Brave or stupid, Trix doesn't look afraid. "She had to go with him, Falcon. My sister saw her fate."

He stiffens. Trix's sister who used to see the future. "Cleo had a vision?"

"Yes." The light filtering into the cabin makes knives of Trix's eyes. "She was never wrong, whether it was army raids or deaths or card games. When Cleo was dying in my arms, she told me I had to help Ophelia. Said it was the only way we'd win the coming war. I trusted her. It's why I went after Sneed. I needed him to lead me to Jasper Salt."

He can't fucking breathe. "You're working for Salt," he seethes. "What did Cleo see? *Exactly.*"

Trix looks at him with regret. "If we all play our roles—including Ophelia, including us—Magies win." She lets the prophecy sink in, a grave look on her face.

"We win at what cost?" When Trix lowers her gaze, it's all it takes for him to know they don't all survive.

Chewing her lip, Trix shakes her head slowly. "I'll tell you everything, if you want. But you should know that Ophelia chose to go with the Darkwielder. She took his hand and got into his phaeton of her own accord."

"Does she know, then? About the vision?"

Trix's amber eyes narrow. "I didn't think it wise to tell her just yet. She's marked."

Marked. The goddamn Dark Shadow.

"Fuck!" He rips the lightblade from Trix's throat, his lip curled in a snarl. "She went with him because he has the dagger and she thinks she can swindle her way to it." Falcon knows it's true, because he knows her. He taught her. And it's what he would've done.

A smoldering sort of pride roots in his chest at her courage, but when his imagination thrusts upon him an image of Ophelia taking the Darkwielder's hand, that pride is quickly brambled by a strange flare of possessiveness.

Trix sits forward. "You trust her, don't you?" He scowls. "Let her play her part, smugger, and you play yours. For her and for the war you've been waiting to wage." Trix reaches to crack the carriage door and steps out into the white air.

With an inward curse, Falcon follows. Disbelief widens his eyes on the landscape that greets him. A hill overlooks a valley city he could never forget. One he hasn't laid eyes on since he was young, since he left his homeland behind.

They're well outside the Belly, then. Outside Magus. The city of Jagst—the gateway to the Kúzlo icelands—sprawls below, a cluster of clay stone buildings veiled in snow.

He whips a look at Trix, seething under his breath, "What the hell are we doing here?"

"Playing our roles," she answers as a pair of soldiers from a second phaeton join the four Shadowcasters who were holding Falcon back.

With a pit in his stomach, he takes note of their fur-lined cloaks, the heavy pelts over their uniforms, the boots made for trekking through deep snow. The pit deepens when he realizes they put the same boots on his feet, though he's still got his leather jacket. He feels the collar rise up to meet his chin now, the material thickening around his chest as its magic weaves more layers against the cold.

He wonders if it senses he's returned to where it was spelled.

As the wind tangles its cold fingers in his hair, Falcon paces, until the sight of a blight flowing a half-mile south catches his eye and halts his step. A dark river. *Gods of Magus, it's true.* He may have a bad ear, but even he can hear the quiet hiss and groans, the snapping.

Bracing against the relentless wind, he faces north to Kúzlo's perilous blue mountains of ice, nearly impenetrable without an invitation. Which is more dangerous, he wonders—the Shadow river or the icelands? The darkness or the home just beyond Magus's borders that he was forced to leave?

As memories dredge of caverns, winged beasts with breath as cold as ice, and a boy staring hatred up at Falcon from a trap in the frozen ground, his bones ache.

Soldiers hand Trix a thick pelt, and she drapes the knee-length coat around herself. Then they hand him one, too.

He cuts a hard look at her as he shrugs it on. Whatever this plan is, it's suicide, which should tell him all he needs to know... But he has to know.

Under his breath, he demands, "The cost of winning, Trix. Tell me everything."

CHAPTER 9
MARKS & CAGES

J oon nearly pisses himself.

A half-mile north of the Gulch, he waits in formation at the edge of camp with forty-nine other rebel soldiers. In their stiff, black uniforms bearing the Darkwielder's sigil and leather shoulder guards cut like sharp feathers, they make five formidable rows.

Joon stands straight as an arrow, wishing he could wipe the bead of sweat off his brow, but it's enough just to hide the tremble of his chin.

A hundred yards away, the Shadow river roars like a nightmare. In his ears, in his chest, in his veins. Daw birds from the East have been dropping like stones as they attempt to breach the West. Sent by the crown, Joon assumes.

He shudders.

Even if the river's snapping claws and teeth didn't gut a person, the mournful hisses and aching shrieks might be enough to drive a man mad.

"Soldiers!" With *Lieuten* Price's voice at the front of formation, a puff of frigid air coughs white. "Each of you survived the battle at Wythe to get here! If you survive the morning, you'll be given a permanent place in the Darkwielder's legion." He stalks the rows of soldiers, but most eyes are trained forward on the river. "By General Salt's authority, whatever your rank in the king's Special Army—*lieuten*, *privfir*, *priv*, or grunt—those titles mean nothing. In the legion, we're all servants. We fight for one thing—to free our kind from the tyrant king!"

Soldiers throw fists in the air, shouting assent.

Joon feels hope swell in him, despite his anxiety about the river. Hope for his freedom and that of his younger brother and sister, who are somewhere on the other side of this new border. Hope that he'll do more than the work of the yard grunt he was a week ago.

"Once a grunt always a grunt." Terk's whisper to Ezren floats to Joon. He feels their eyes as the two *priv* snicker.

"We're servants!" Price cuts a look at the men as he paces by. "For our gods and our true king, after this day we'll bleed the same color!"

Black, Joon thinks, lifting his gaze to the river.

"Not all of you were privy to the plans in Wythe," Price acknowledges. "Some of you are yet unmarked by the Darkwielder's power. But you chose your side in battle, and now the Dark Shadow will have a chance to choose you."

As he angles his body to half-face the river, Price shouts, "And who will the Dark Shadow choose?" He pauses, letting the silence speak. "The loyal! When I call your name, step to the edge of the river to receive your marking."

Joon watches with his stomach in his throat as Price calls forward a soldier named Pedyr, another first-year, an unmarked Bender of Water. Joon's shared yard duties a few times with him, a boy who likes to hum while he hauls around food.

The lad looks nervous as he walks stiffly past Joon's row. His fingers round into fists, and Joon hears a low, prayerful tune on the soldier's lips as he marches. At Price's nod, he stops a few feet from where the ground splits and darkness flows.

Nothing happens at first. Then the shadows that writhe over themselves in the river take notice of Pedyr, and thick bands begin to rise. The shadows surge, coalescing to form an eyeless face with long teeth that leans forward to sniff the soldier.

The humming seems to grow louder, not quieter, as Pedyr faces the Dark Shadow.

Joon barely breathes, every muscle locked as he waits for it to accept the soldier and mark him.

With barely a warning, the beast rears. As if it's smelled something rank.

An ear-splitting shriek cuts Pedyr's humming, then the Shadow opens its jaws and swallows the soldier whole.

*H*e wasn't worthy.

Under the triple moons that night, Joon tries not to see Pedyr in his mind. He presses a palm to the chilling mark on his neck and lets his gaze drift past the dinner fire.

All the adrenaline of the day leaks out. First the river, then the raid on a convoy of commoners.

His hand shakes. He can't make out the river this late, but he can feel it—still hungry, despite the six men it devoured. Men deemed unworthy, not loyal enough for the battle to come. All Joon thought when he stepped to the edge and stared into the empty vastness of that power was *give me a chance to prove myself*, and the Shadow dragged a single claw across the side of his neck.

Along the camp's perimeter, torches breathe to life by the hand of two Benders of Flame.

Joon's attention draws to the yard where each lit torch illuminates an iron enclosure, one after another, until there are five rows holding hunched shapes—the prisoners from the wagon, brought to camp a few hours ago.

Beside him, Terk leans forward to catch Ezren's eye, talking over Joon. "What do you think the Captain wants with them?"

"Hell if I know," Ezren replies under his breath. "Don't see how low-born mortals are worth all that iron."

Joon frowns as he warms his hands and stares at a girl in one of the enclosures.

Terk elbows him. "What's with *you*, eh?"

"He's never been on a raid, is what," Ezren laughs.

"That's not it," Joon protests, trying not to think how his gun shook in his hands when they intercepted that caravan and marched all those people like animals into cages.

He's saved from saying more by the war song that starts up low, bawdy but poetic, around the fire. Joon steals a closer look at the young commoner woman.

In the torchlight, her tangled hair looks a golden sunset. Her figure's slender, huddled under a woolen blanket and resting against the iron bars. She's striking, but he shouldn't be looking at her or thinking her worthy of sympathy—he's a soldier in the Darkwielder's legion now, and she's mortal.

Ezren's elbow catches him. "Sing, grunt."

Joon rubs his chest. "You heard Price," he mutters unhappily. "There're no grunts here."

Terk throws his head back to laugh. "Once a grunt, always a grunt."

"'Lest he prove otherwise," Ezren allows.

"I got my mark, didn't I?" Joon motions to his neck.

"'Cause you smell pretty," Terk howls. "Pretty as that fine-spun blond silk you call hair on your head and that precious beard you're trying to grow." He whoops harder.

Joon glowers at them both. But he sings. He's no good—*a cat stuck up a tree*, his older sister used to say—but he sings because, like everyone here, he's superstitious. After drills, before patrols, they sing to Erebus for fortitude, to Selene for protection, to Luna for victory.

Though it's quiet tonight, the war is coming. Joon swears he can feel it in the air, ever since the river this morning.

Price said their job's to keep watch, hold the river north of the Gulch, and watch for enemies. There are plenty stuck on this side of the divide, given the academy, the trade routes, and the representatives that keep homes in the West.

As his mouth moves, Joon's gaze tracks again to the cages. To the girl. He understands war, but he can't quite understand the threat a bunch of commoners pose. Still, he sings a prayer. One for the courage to prove he's no grunt.

As the song swells and food comes round, Joon tears bread off a loaf but hesitates to put it in his mouth as his gaze catches on the cages again. He can hear the pleas of the prisoners.

Lowering his ration, he considers it. Then tucks it into his uniform.

An hour later, the songs have dwindled and the fire smolders.

"All right." Price stretches to stand in the midst of them. "To bed or to posts."

All but a handful disperse to the tents.

Someone clasps Joon's shoulder.

He turns to see Price, the tall, fair-haired young officer with a bent brow. He towers over Joon. "First post tonight," he notes. As if he can read Joon's empathy, he says, "No talking to the prisoners, Orteven."

"No, sir." Joon shakes his head, then buggers off in the direction of his post, pulling on his gloves.

For the next hour, he swivels his gaze evenly among the rows of cages, his hands twitching at his side with every moan. It's so cold, the hair in his nose has frozen. And Joon has fur lining his cloak, a hat to match, and gloves.

When the moons perch high overhead and the camp finally hushes, Joon risks a glance to his left.

The girl watches him.

Debating, he edges away from his post until he's close enough to see her cheeks are cherry red, her forehead filmed with dirt.

A gust howls, loud enough to mask any voices at a distance.

No talking to the prisoners.

But they're commoners. Tired, cold, in no shape to be a danger to soldiers with magic and weapons as potent as theirs.

Joon steps to her cage and extracts the bread. "Hello," he says. "Are you hungry?"

The girl inches forward, but her chains clang to halt her. "I am, thank you," she rasps. "But I'm afraid I can't..." She lifts the heavy cuffs, which are bound to a stake in the ground.

He glances over his shoulder. He has direct orders—this is idiocy.

"What's your name?" the girl asks.

Joon finds her watching him keenly, huddling into her thin blanket. Why didn't they give her something thicker?

"Orteven," he replies. "Joon Orteven..." He mulls over how to address a prisoner of war; his mother taught him manners, and this girl is pretty. So pretty. "My lady," he decides.

"You're a gentleman, Joon Orteven." She says it as though she regrets it. "And...a Fabricater?" She squints. "It's hard to tell from here."

Joon catches movement in the next cage—someone tossing in their sleep.

He edges closer to the girl, strapping his gun over a shoulder. "I am a Fabricater—a good one." Not that anyone's noticed.

"I thought so. I knew a Fabricater once. You have the look of him. Strong and broad-shouldered, capable hands. I bet there's no material you can't mold."

Joon stands taller in his boots.

The camp is quiet. The fires only smoke now. Sneaking a glance behind him, he puts the other patrols in sight. They're silhouettes at opposite ends of the grounds.

He stretches out his fingers. "A minute won't hurt."

She works herself to her knees as he hovers a hand to open the lock on her enclosure. He'll weld it back together quick enough.

He's about to offer to feed her the bread when he gets a closer look at her wrists—an angry red from the shackles.

One minute.

The girl watches Joon as he waves a hand over her manacles. "You're sweet, like my brother was," she says. "He always did the right thing, too."

Joon's pride swells as her clasps fall away. *More than a grunt.* Setting them aside, he offers her the bread and watches her mouth as she takes a grateful bite.

He shouldn't ask. "What's your name?"

Her eyes flick at something in the distance, then back to him. Chewing slowly, she replies, "I'm Willow, like the tree."

"Willow," he repeats. A name for a girl who looks strong, beautiful, and kind. "I'd be burned alive for letting you free. Better hurry."

Willow doesn't seem able to chew the bread faster, though. It must be the cold, or her mouth is dry.

Joon is reaching for his canteen when a sharp scream jolts him, causing his head to smack against the cage.

A second wail, like someone's *dying*, makes him jump to his feet in panic. But the girl. He searches the ground in the dim light for her restraints. Where are they?

A third horrid scream—from the next cage over, he thinks. Throwing his gaze into the night, he sees a bulky shape in an enclosure rolling around in distress.

He spins to the girl. "I'll be right back. Don't move!" Dashing in the direction of the noise while freeing his gun, Joon skids to a stop in front of the prisoner in the next cage who's wrestling around under a blanket.

"Halt!" he shouts, aiming his rifle.

"Help..."

Joon combs the torchlights for signs of the others on patrol. They're still walking the perimeter.

"Please," the man cries in anguish. "It's killing me!"

Joon can't get a look at what's harming the prisoner. But he can hear Price in his ear, this morning after they returned to camp and filled these cages. "Jasper Salt wants them alive," he said.

Focusing on the padlock, he hovers a hand. At the snap of iron, he charges in.

The prisoner goes still as death.

Joon's heart is in his throat as he creeps forward in the hush, poking the barrel of his gun at the thick shape.

It doesn't move.

Swallowing, Joon hunches over and slowly coaxes the wool back with the nozzle of his gun.

A man with short-cropped hair and dark skin lies still, eyes shuttered.

The raid was so chaotic, Joon doesn't remember all the prisoner's faces. He angles his head at the scarf tied around the man's neck. On closer inspection, there's something familiar about him. Leaning in, Joon's interest catches on something gold. A tattoo under the scarf.

The prisoner's eyes flash open, and fast hands grab for Joon's gun.

He barely registers the murderous look in the man's eyes before something hard lands a blow to his forehead.

Stars. A silvery taste. Something wet dripping into his eyes.

His bell rung, Joon falls sideways in a dizzying swoop. Vision blurring as he tries to put the male prisoner in sight, he only hears grunts, like an animal, amid loud snapping sounds.

The man hunches as the sounds continue, and though Joon is spinning, he swears the prisoner's skin grows lighter, that his whole body changes shape.

It sparks something. In the part of his brain still working, Joon envisions himself sitting at a dinner table at the Pyre, weeks ago when a soldier towered over him and scared him out of his seat. The next time he saw that soldier was Wythe, on a raised platform in the hold of a shadow.

This prisoner's not mortal. He's Morphist. A Shifter, at that. A fugitive.

The snapping sounds stop, and the face that looms darkly over Joon isn't the Shifter's anymore. It's that of *Lieuten* Price.

A female's voice calls out, "Hart!"

Joon blinks, but he can't move or speak as the Shifter stalks freely out of the cage.

Managing a roll to his other side, Joon gasps as pain wails in his head and he sees the would-be *lieuten* embrace the girl. Willow, who Joon left unshackled.

He can hear Terk in his head, laughing. *Once a grunt, always a grunt.*

Joon's vision winks as the prisoners disappear through the torchlights.

CHAPTER 10
PRISON & BREAKS
REBEL ARMY CAMP, WEST MAGUS
5TH DAY IN THE NEW WINTER
HART IS WITH WILLOW

The air smells foul, laced with dirt and urine and hunger.

Hart Aurum slips silently out of an officer's tent and wipes a smear of blood on his stolen trousers.

Weeks ago, he would've loathed injuring anyone. Now, shifted to take the likeness of *Lieuten* Price, he scans the rebel camp where Willow's people have been caged and hopes the gash he gave the officer leaves a scar. At the least, Price will need a healer when he wakes.

Hart sheaths a revolver in his coat to hide the glint of the barrel. With the fur blanket he snatched beneath an arm, he weaves around the tents trying to tamp the anger that's been notching since soldiers raided the Dwymoran's convoy.

The camp is dark except for torchlight. Just before the cages, he pauses near a tent and gives a soft whistle—their call—and two brave eyes shine in the night at him.

Willow's too exposed in a dress and light blanket, her hair a tangled mess thanks to a soldier's shadow ripping her from a wagon.

Anger throbs inside his fists, but Willow doesn't complain. She nods at him.

Hart casts a single glance up the road that cuts through camp, at the end of which sits the Dwymorans' unattended wagons.

It's time.

He stalks toward Willow with the confident gait of a *lieuten*, settling the warmer fur blanket on her shoulders. She lets him turn her around and pin one of her arms, then he hauls her against him. Nudging her forward, he leans to her ear. "Two patrols, at the north and south end."

She turns her face so abruptly to look that her mouth swipes his.

With a jerk in surprise, Hart's step falters.

Two brows raise at him. "Was it that terrible?"

Frowning, he urges Willow toward the cages.

They wait. It's a minute before he glimpses the sheen of a gun heading toward them. He wipes his brow, not liking how unsteady his shift feels. It's not his first of the day, unfortunately. Before they were captured by his former comrades, Hart had just enough time to swap his likeness for someone the soldiers wouldn't recognize. So they wouldn't realize they had a defector in their midst.

Shifting again in the span of hours, while hungry and tired, was a risk.

"Price?" a voice calls as that gun bobs nearer. "Something wrong, sir?" A fourth-year Hart vaguely recognizes hastens forward.

"Wait," Hart whispers in Willow's ear, feeling her tense in his grip. Then, as *Lieuten* Price, he scowls at the approaching soldier. "This one got out of her cage, right under your nose."

"I'm sorry." As the soldier snaps a bow, Hart notes the dark, clawing mark that brands the young man's neck.

Hart heard the soldiers talking earlier about the river, about the mark of the Dark Shadow that connects them to their master.

"You're sorry?" he scoffs, making a show of tightening his grip on Willow. "What were your orders?" *Do tell.*

The soldier pales. "Keep eyes on the prisoners."

"Do you not understand why that's important?"

"Yes, Sir. Captain Salt's coming for them tomorrow. He needs them all. I'm sorry, I'll take her back right away."

Hart vexes at the reply—Salt is coming to take these prisoners. Outwardly, though, his expression remains even as he releases Willow's pinned arm. For her ears, he mutters, "*Now.*"

Hart throws her at the soldier.

Before the soldier can recover his surprise, Willow's hands are cupped to his head. In seconds, he's on the ground, writhing at whatever she put in his mind.

Hart's known a few talented seers like her, who've honed secondary gifts within their guild. He has to admit, it's convenient at present.

"How long will he be like that?" Hart asks.

"I saw his greatest fear—he thinks he's in a pit of spiders," Willow replies. "It should buy us an hour."

As Hart divests the soldier of his rifle, Willow shocks him with a grin. In the short time he's known her, he's come to recognize it as her favored coping mechanism in times of stress.

"There's never an uneventful day with you, is there?" she asks. "Though I didn't see our first kiss in a war camp, with you as an officer."

"*Kiss?*" he balks. "That wasn't—"

Willow spins for the cages.

Stalking after, he digests the implication that she's imagined them kissing. Ophelia would've ribbed him endlessly about that awkward encounter, when they were young.

Among the enclosures, they find the old woman first.

Hands resting in her lap, nearly frozen in the manacles, Mammy's mouth clamps in a hard line when she sights Hart.

Willow creeps ahead of him, shucking off the heavier blanket he gave her. "It's okay, Mammy. Hart's just shifted."

The woman's severeness dissolves as Willow wraps her in the blanket.

Fishing heavy iron keys from the pocket of Price's uniform, Hart frees Mammy. He doesn't savor their reunion, though. There are thirty more cages.

A weight settles on his chest as he surveys row after row of enclosures. They're spaced to give each prisoner a clear view of the river in the distance. Which he can't worry about now, either.

Thirty more cages.

Thirty more mortals somehow his responsibility.

You nearly destroyed their village, and still they took you in.

He approaches a cage where a man with salted hair matted to one side stoops. Pete something. The old coot who works metals and talks incessantly while he does it.

Four days ago, he melted migth *from a gun to solder your shattered knee. It's why you're walking without a limp.*

The old man recoils at the sight of Hart in his shift.

"Pete," Willow whispers. "It's magic. Remember what Hart can do?"

The man slowly relaxes.

Like all Willow's people, Pete discovered Hart was no mortal after the battle in Wythe. After the passage refused to take Hart with Ophelia and Falcon, and he fell a hundred feet or more from the ancient Syca tree.

By the time Hart realized he wasn't spinning in a passage, the ground was meeting his legs. Splayed out on his back, he watched the snow descend, the sun come up, the moons rise, and each once again before he woke to Pete and two other Dwymorans dragging him through the snow.

They didn't perform the rescue for his sake. He remembers Willow's voice, ordering them on. With Hart's next blink, he was lying in a bed in Dwymore, pain seizing his legs. He wasn't cuffed as he was the last time she helped him, after the beasts in the Glow Woods, but his heart leapt the same at her familiar halo of ashen hair, the scent of cotton and flowers in his nose.

In the camp torchlights, another cage appears.

"Cora!" Willow breathes in relief.

"Willow?" the girl cries. She's caged with two small children. Extra mouths, slow feet, nonstop chatter as they convoyed from Dwymore.

Children may hold the only joy left, his subconscious points out.

After several more cages, there's a budding trail of commoners at Hart's back.

"Stay to the shadows," he orders them.

He tried to dissuade these people from following him north. He planned to set out alone to search for Ophelia and Falcon. Now, fearful white eyes moon at him.

Freeing three more prisoners, he moves to the last enclosure in the row, stewing about what the soldier said earlier.

What could Salt want with commoners?

Taking prisoners is an effective war tactic when your enemy cares to barter. But the Gray King will never be swayed into surrender to spare a few low-born lives.

At a clang of iron, Hart whips to see a Dwymoran stumbling against a cage door, then registers the sheen of a gun barrel near the northern perimeter.

"Who's there?" a female voice calls.

Panic powers Hart's steps. In less than a minute, the soldier will realize half the cages are empty and alert the camp. If the soldiers they took care of earlier aren't already rousing.

Counting faces behind him—*twenty-nine*—he takes Willow's arm. "Who's missing?"

She rakes them over, this motley group that's cold, exhausted, worse for wear, and clinging to one another. "Shep," Willow confirms. "Shepherd."

The man-child Willow treats as an errant brother.

The one who fetched you food and drink for two days when you were healing from your fall.

He inspects the enclosures, searching for silhouettes. There. Halfway down the next row over.

Hart hooks Willow's gaze. "Take your people to the wagons." He motions to the road. "It's far enough from the tents to escape unheard, so long as the camp sleeps. Get the horses tied and everyone inside. If you hear gunfire, go."

Willow grabs his arm, but he can't look at her. The last time he met a woman's eyes before rushing into danger, he lost her.

And here he'd thought he had no one left to lose. "Go," he grits out. "We'll be right behind you."

Putting the patrolman in sight, Hart draws a long breath that stabs of winter, then turns on his heel.

He feels like he's swimming, which isn't good. It's a warning. When he reaches Shepherd's cage, a bone snaps, and Hart buckles against the iron door with a grunt.

A bear of a man sits up, his face tight with fear.

Concentrating, Hart rights himself. "I'm here to free—" The crack of his leg makes him fold.

Shepherd's chains rattle.

In Hart's starry vision, he can see the man's afraid. Hart tries to explain who he is, but his words choke the second his shoulders separate and widen—the worst part of his shift back to true form.

The pain sends him to a knee.

Breathing deeply, he forces his arm up to fit the key in the lock. It takes fumbling. When it clicks, he reefs the iron open.

In the distance, a gun bobs closer. Another soldier.

Snap.

Hart's hand braces his weight on the ground.

Returning to form cuts the more he fights it. But once he surrenders, he'll be useless for minutes, unable to fully defend himself or anyone. If he'd eaten today, if he hadn't shifted once already, it would be different.

His back cracks, and that's it.

Collapsing, he clenches the keys in a fist and tries to put the frightened Shepherd in view.

"I'm going"—he grunts—"to free you. Then you run to the wagons. To your people. Do you understand?"

His spine strives to lengthen, and Hart clamps his jaw, struggling to crawl to free the chains.

He should have left this man. It was because of him that Ophelia and Rune were taken by the Royal Army in Dwymore.

Willow's face flits into his mind.

With an elbow, he heaves himself forward to raise the key. Shepherd holds out his hands. And it's in. One more breath, a twist, and the chains fall away.

Hart falls with them, and the shift takes full hold.

Bones and muscles lengthen and fill. A deep shade of ebony floods his skin. It's a minute before the snapping ceases and Hart can manage to lift his head.

The Dwymoran is rooted in place, having watched the transformation.

"What are you waiting for?" Hart snaps. "Go!"

The idiot stays.

He feels a thick pair of arms wrap his chest, trying to hoist him.

In response, his stomach revolts. He's wiping his mouth on a sleeve when he hears the tread of boots in the snow.

Shepherd's arms disappear, dropping him to his knees. Knees he shattered days ago but, reforged from *migth*, don't register the pain.

A soldier with a bolt of blond hair and a rigid posture gapes at the sight of Hart. He doesn't recall her name but remembers her excelling among the Matterists in the Special Army training yards. Unfortunately for him, she's a talented Bender.

She's confused at first, taking in the scene—Hart, the empty shackles, Shepherd who still stands there. Her eyes narrow. "Hart Aurum."

Damn his face. Damn that he was once a fixture at "Captain Rivmere's" side and seen by everyone.

The Bender's gun snaps bullet-quick to her shoulder, training on Hart. "We have orders to bring you to Salt on sight. What are you doing here?"

"Isn't it obvious?" He sways. "I'm stealing your prisoners."

CHAPTER 11
MERCY & RUIN

S loppily, Hart lunges.

The Bender soldier sidesteps him easily, and he surges to the sod. From where he lands, he sees her raise her gun.

She fires a deafening shot—not to kill, probably to alert the camp—then presses a hand to her neck over the Dark Shadow mark. It's disconcerting how fast shouts echo from the rebel tents.

Hart scrambles to his feet as she raises her hand, brows narrowed in concentration. There's no time to reach for his revolver. His mouth begins to water. In short order, a current floods his lungs, his throat. On his knees, he gasps against the small river filling his airway. Clutching at his neck as light pricks the edge of his vision, he falls face forward, water bubbling from his mouth.

A voice calls to him, but the sound is garbled by blood rushing into his ears. He vaguely registers the sound of a hard smack. A deep scream.

As quickly as the current surged in his throat, it's sucked away.

Sputtering a barking cough, Hart feels cold hands lift his head. Voices murmur, and arms scoop beneath his shoulders to lift him upright.

Burning. There's burning as breath ekes into his lungs and everything rushes in. The night. The shouts. Willow's wild eyes on him.

Willow.

He scowls disapprovingly at her, or tries to. She didn't go.

She shakes him. "The camp's awake, Hart! Hart! Look at me, we have to run!"

A shot of adrenaline sharpens his senses. Bones are still settling, but he manages to move his legs enough to let Shepherd and Willow steer him, to let each brace him under an arm as they flee before they're seen.

The wagons loom into view, but the horses aren't strapped yet—what was Willow thinking?

A gun pops.

The air shifts as a bullet sails by.

Willow urges them faster, but Shepherd, bigger and slower, labors in his gait.

"We need to separate," Hart pants.

"No." Willow guides them down another line of enclosures. It looks like two more rows to the wagons. Two more—

Pop.

The support gives at Hart's left shoulder, and he stumbles sideways.

Willow tumbles atop him, and when she lifts her head, her eyes reflect the moons. It takes a panicked moment to realize it isn't her that's been hit.

"Shep!" she screams, clawing over Hart to reach her friend. "Shep!"

Hart drags himself up in search of the shooter, spotting him not a hundred yards away with a rifle frozen mid-air, blood smearing half his face. Separated from his unit, it's the grunt they duped into freeing them.

Hart stares menacingly at the boy. Instinct makes him reach for his lightblade, but he ditched it when the rebels raided their convoy so they wouldn't realize he was Magie.

He clasps the revolver instead.

The young soldier, face awash in horror, has already lowered his rifle and sunk to his knees. He stares at the weapon in his hands as if he can't believe what he's done.

Shepherd rattles a cough from where he's rolled flat onto his back. "Willow? Willow, are you here?"

"I'm here, Shep." She runs a hand over his forehead but looks to Hart, pleading, "Help me get him up!"

Keeping one eye on the grunt, Hart lowers to kneel beside her. A red stream oozes from Shepherd's chest, and they have no healer.

"Is it morning?" The man's eyes cloud. "It's—Willow, it's so cold."

"I know, I know. *Hart*," she begs him.

Shepherd moans as shouts cut across the camp, the soldiers gathering fast.

"He won't survive the hour," Hart says. "And the army's trained to torture first—they'll use him to find out who we are. Tell me quickly what you want to do."

Realization darkens Willow's expression as her gaze flits to the gun in his hand. She knows what he's offering: a quick death for her friend.

"No." She shakes her head emphatically. "We can make it. We can—"

Fire plumes in the sky. A collective of Bender flames illuminates half the camp yard. They'll have a minute, maybe two.

Grabbing Willow's arm, he barks, "Tell me."

Shepherd moans. "Willow, I can't see anything. I'm—I'm scared."

Pain shines in her eyes as she squeezes the man's hand. "It's okay. It's going to be okay."

"It hurts. Make it stop. Please..."

"It's going to be okay," Willow whispers again, straining to control her breathing. Her face is nearly white as she nods just once at Hart and turns Shepherd's face toward her with shaking hands. "Do you remember the song you sang me when I was little after my father died?" she asks Shepherd. "About the man in the moons? We sat on the well and threw wishing stones down and you played your guitar afterward."

Shepherd stops moaning, a serene look falling on his face.

"Let's sing it," Willow urges as Hart raises the gun to hover near Shepherd's temple.

Bile is rancid in Hart's throat, though this is not the first man he's put out of his misery.

As Willow runs delicate fingers over Shepherd's eyes to close them, the two sing softly together. She allows a tear to fall from her eye before nodding again at Hart, and when she shutters her eyes, he pulls the trigger.

The pop is deafening.

Feeling the ring of it through his body, he drops the gun, a bullet of grief piercing him as Willow's soft voice chokes on her song. But there are soldiers a few hundred yards away who must have heard the gun go off.

Hart takes Willow's arm. "We have to run."

She clings to Shepherd's coat.

Wrapping his arms around her waist to pull her away with him through the natural shadows, they find their way back to the military carriages and wagons.

He sinks with her behind a carriage wheel where he can feel her trembling.

"Hart." His name makes frost in the air between them.

He brushes her hair aside. "I know."

Loud as a New York train, something whistles through camp. At the familiar shriek, he stiffens, then presses an eye to a wheel slat. Shadows, and not the eking kind but vicious tendrils that remind him of the Darkwielder's beasts. Beasts he knows too well.

Through their markings, the soldiers must be tapping the power of the Dark Shadow—the river.

The army descends on the road. "In the wagons!" The voice belongs to *Lieuten* Price. He's awake, and a bevy of soldiers in black surrounds the Dwymorans on all sides.

Shadows and soldiers encircle the wagons.

You told them to wait here.

Willow moves as if to go to her people, but Hart yanks her quickly back, nearly to his lap. "Shepherd was an accident," he whispers. "The rebels have orders to keep them alive."

She stops struggling, but they're both tense as he holds her, while men and women Hart once shared halls and meals and assignments with wrench open the wagon gates.

"Cora, Mammy..." Her eyes widen. "We can't get them out."

A stone pit forms in his gut. "No." He releases his hold on her. "We can't."

This isn't supposed to be Hart's problem. It can't be. He's gutted for what he had to do for Shepherd, but there are things—important things—he needs to do. He has to find Ophelia. He has to tell her things. He can't... He...

Willow's hand finds his, squeezing it in the dark.

A curse leaves Hart's lips. Searching the area, he says, "This way."

While the army's pulling people off the wagons, he dashes with Willow into the dark toward the intake tent where four horses are tied.

Hart's hands work deftly to pad, saddle, and free the largest of the steeds. For a moment, he weighs the gruesome idea of cutting the other horses down to thwart being followed. But the officer carriages can operate without steeds.

Once mounted, he reaches down for Willow's hand.

She stares at it. "I can't just leave them."

When she steps back, utter panic makes him snap, "The soldiers won't kill them. Take my hand, Willow. Take it now!"

But she steels her jaw. "Maybe not *kill*, but there are worse things, Hart. You know that."

He can't see all the scars from Willow's childhood, but losing her brother, as Hart lost his own family, binds them.

Leaping from the saddle, he takes hold of her arms, a promise rushing out before he's thought it through. "If we get free, we can track where they're taken from a distance. Plan a way to them when we've got more strength."

Willow looks at him. "We?"

The relief he hears in that single word might be his ruin.

CHAPTER 12
SKIN & SECRETS

WEST MAGUS
5TH DAY IN THE NEW WINTER
WILLOW AND HART ARE TOGETHER

As they ride, Willow is haunted by the sounds of death: the crack of guns, the abrupt ceasing of a song, Shepherd's silent chest, the cries of her villagers.

Braced between Hart's broad arms on the siegehorse, they race under the cover of night toward the Howling Woods, a forest of spindling beeches where the trail forks—one path straight and even toward Duskwell, the other steep and sloping up a bluff.

As they climb the slope to find shelter, her body starts to numb. Snow is falling in earnest, whipping at her cheeks. It'll guise their tracks but may freeze their limbs.

After what feels like hours up a snaking path, Willow's grateful when Hart slows the horse under a cover of red leaves still clinging to their branches.

Seems winter was as much a surprise to the forests as it was to her village. To the whole kingdom.

Sadness settles at the base of her throat, but she lets it be, as Mammy would advise, and they breach a snowy clearing where silence betrays the chaos of what they've run from.

"There." Hart jerks his chin at a low stretch of rocks and leads the steed to an opening in a short cave wall half-hidden with boughs. She used to go hunting with her father, a long time ago, and recognizes it as an old animal den.

Stiff as ice, Willow dismounts and hands Hart the steed's heavy blanket. She surveys the empty wood as he ties the horse out of the wind, working quickly as if he's traveled under duress a thousand times. She's both sorry for it and comforted by his competency.

In the den, the ground's softer under her boots. The moonslight shining off the snow outside lights the curve of a squat tunnel. They hunch, following it around until the den widens and they can stand.

It's the size of a room at the Weeping Bell, and littered with a large nest of leaves and a few animal skeletons. Her nose is too cold to smell if there are traces of blood or urine, but there's nothing she can see to suggest the den's been used recently.

"It's empty," Hart confirms.

The cold fully clutches Willow as she stands there, her shivers deepening to the point her teeth start to chatter. The culprit isn't just the cold, but the shock of it all. The raid on their wagons. The screams of her people being shut in cages. Knowing what they still face in that camp.

Shepherd is mortal. He deserves to be buried, but he's still lying there alone.

Hart observes her, a frown on his face. "They'll have figured out two escaped by now. We can't risk a fire."

"I know." It's almost painful to let the blanket fall from her shoulders, but she hands it to him. "We'll have to share."

"This scrap?"

Willow shakes her head. "Skin."

As she lets the fabric of her dress—Cora's dress—fall to her waist, Hart's eyes widen. "Willow—"

"I know you don't want this."

"What?"

"To help me. You want to go find Ophelia. If we'd gotten everyone out tonight, you'd have left first chance."

Hart's focus snaps to her eyes, but he doesn't correct her.

"It's fine." She rubs her bare arms. "But if you help me get Mammy, Cora, and the others somewhere safe, I can help you find your friend. I can see inside minds, remember? Memories of soldiers, officers...captains."

The notion washes over Hart's face—how useful her affinity could be if they found the right mind to search. She lets her dress fall to the ground. "But who can we help if we freeze to death?"

Hart stands there, gaping, awkward. If she weren't half in shock and terrified for her people, freezing where she stands, she'd laugh at how uncomfortable he looks. Then she does anyway and can't seem to stop once she starts. The laughter that echoes in the den sounds maniacal.

A deep crease splits Hart's brows. "I'm failing to see what's funny."

"Nothing." Willow hiccups, sobering. "There is not a single funny thing, but it's ironic, isn't it? Our first conversation, you were on your death bed. Our first kiss, in the midst of a prison break—"

"That wasn't a kiss—"

"Our first undressing, so we don't freeze to death. If I didn't know better, I'd say the primordial gods are toying with us."

Willow can picture the triple crosses on her cottage in Dwymore, the ones that burned with the second wave of royal soldiers. Her Da hung them long ago. They used to be a comfort.

Hart glowers. "The primordial gods have been toying with my life since it started. Why stop now?"

She tilts her head. "You don't believe they offer protection?"

"They're the reason we're at war. The reason all my life I've had to—" His jaw clamps shut, and muscles ripple down his neck. "You should've turned the four of us away when we came to your inn. At the least, taken your people the opposite way of me two days ago instead of trusting me to get you to safety."

Amid her violent shivers, she observes, "Fear makes you bristly. For how bristly, you must fear a lot."

He steps back as if she knew this because she'd touched him, and the expression on his face explains how he might feel about her actually reading his memories. Such would be very unwelcome.

She tries not to take offense.

Taking the blanket carefully from his hands, she gives him her back to spread the fabric out over the nest of leaves, then lowers her chemise.

"Well?" She glances over a shoulder. "Do you plan for us to freeze, or do you want to live to find your friend?"

With a curse, Hart shucks off the thick cape he wears. The coat next. His broad fingers hover on the tunic. "You see into minds by touch?"

"If I know it's coming, I can shield."

Still scowling, he pulls the tunic over his head and tosses it aside.

Her heart skips at the sight of his smooth, dark skin. At his nipples that peak with the cold, as her own do beneath her shift. At the scar that looks like sunbursts from his fingertips to forearm, a remnant of a curse cured. At the thick, knotty muscles twitching across his chest and abdomen.

Willow takes him in openly. "I see fear makes you strong, too."

"You have a lot of theories," Hart grumbles. He draws a circle in the air with two fingers, motioning her to turn around.

A smile ghosts her lips at his modesty. "It's only skin, Hart."

"And do you share your skin often?"

She leans to pick up the cape he dropped. "I've never been freezing to death, or in love."

"There are other reasons to bed someone." He clears his throat, as if he's said too much.

"True," she allows, wrapping the fur cloak around herself before shimmying out of her shift and going to lie down.

Hart's hands ball at his sides, but he walks to the edge of the blanket.

"The pants, too."

He stops. "There's nothing beneath them." A shiver threads his irritated tone.

"It's only skin," she repeats softly. "But if it makes you feel better, I won't peek." Shifting to her back, she fixes her gaze on the rocky ceiling. At the slip and tug of fabric, she wills herself not to look...for all of two seconds.

Hart's backside and legs are pure muscle. Thick, but lithe as a stallion, carved for quick bursts of strength. He turns, and his length—she swallows—is considerable.

Directing her gaze up again, her pulse skips as leaves rustle and Hart slides in next to her. He adjusts the cape and blanket, wrapping the two of them in a cocoon.

Willow walls her affinity, bracing for his touch as he inches toward her. His foot grazes hers first, then a leg. But he hesitates there.

"Hart, we won't keep all our toes like this." Beneath the cape, she finds his hand and splays it across her belly, just below her breasts. Rolling to her side, she tugs him closer, fitting herself snug against his chest. But cool air still snakes through the small gaps he's careful to leave between their lower halves.

Willow inches her bottom toward him, hoping for the warmth of his thighs, but the curve of her bare backside finds something else—something that twitches instantly in response.

Hart curses under his breath, and as he hurries to tuck himself away, she has to stifle another laugh.

"Are you okay back there?" She twines her legs with his, pressing the top of her feet against his calves.

He jolts. "You're ice!"

"Thus our sleeping arrangements," she says over her shoulder.

He lets out a long growl and slides his right arm under her neck to cradle it, leaving his other hand where she still holds it to her stomach.

"Better?" he asks.

"It'll do."

After a few minutes, the drum of their hearts spreads warmth between them. It takes longer to radiate to Willow's limbs, but Hart's tense arms finally relax around her.

She could almost nod off when he speaks. "I'm sorry I was bristly."

She smiles. "I'm growing used to it. But thank you."

"For what?"

"You're a trained soldier and know the army. I've—I haven't lived with magic-born in a long time. Thank you for staying."

Hart tenses. "I didn't agree out of the goodness of my heart."

Willow twists her head and meets serious, dark eyes. Too serious. They could both use some lightness.

"Tell me something to distract from the cold." Looking forward again, she tries not to enjoy the feel of his muscled legs against the back of her thighs. "Have you ever been in love?"

"I've been with women, but it rarely meant anything," he murmurs. "I was trying to ignore..."

Willow cranes her neck again to look at him. "Ophelia?"

His nostrils flare. "Do you ask every question that enters your mind?"

She shrugs in his arms. But she recognizes the look of longing that mars Hart's face. Tuck cared for Willow like that, and she hated the feeling of that one-sidedness. The imbalance. "You love her."

The muscles in his chest flex against her back. "She's important. We grew up together. It was only the two of us after the raid on our village." He shakes his head. "Never mind."

"Tell me," she insists. "We're not going anywhere tonight." As she angles her body to better see him, his arm grazes her breast, and she clears her throat to hide the hitch in her breath.

It's only skin, she thinks. This time, reminding herself.

Hart sighs an exhale, the lines of his face softening. "Sometimes we'd help my mother make pies." He rolls his eyes, as if it's a ridiculous confession. "Ophelia loved them. She talked my mother into telling her the secret to their sweetness—picking the fruit before sunrise, after the berries had a full night to bask in the moons. From then on, once a week, I'd catch her slipping into the woods before the farmers woke to harvest them. It wasn't safe for Magie children to be alone out there, so I'd follow her. Keep a distance. Just in case she needed me..."

Hart blinks, threading his bottom lip between his teeth like something painful has dawned on him. "Ophelia never needed me, though."

"But she cares for you," Willow says thickly, recalling the memory she saw of Ophelia destroying a shadow beast in the Glow Woods. "Not that it matters. You'd love her regardless, right?"

After a moment, he replies, "There are different kinds of love. She and I—" He narrows accusing eyes at Willow. "Why do I get the urge to confess things to you I'd never tell anyone?"

She smiles. "All the near-death, maybe. You really should stop getting so close to it."

"Close to *you*," he growls. "And we're not dying tonight." There's no malice in his vehemence, and this makes Willow's pulse thrum faster.

"You said before you aren't here out of the goodness of your heart. But you are good, Hart. Your loyalty to Ophelia, what you did to spare Shepherd from being tortured, staying with me…"

A pang hits her as she looks at him. A pang that scares her—the feeling she's known him far longer than she has and wants to know him better. Better than she has any right to if he loves someone else.

She's never loved anyone, not with the desperate, aching need Mammy has always reminisced about feeling for her Da. But Hart is a man who'd be easy to fall for, if she isn't careful.

"*That*," Hart suddenly snaps, startling her. His eyes shutter a moment. "That look you give me, like *you* need me. No one's ever…" A flash of his dark eyes. "That look is why I stayed, and if you don't stop, it will be my undoing."

Her heart's a herd of horses off to race, and Willow's all too aware of every bit of skin that touches between them. Her chin lifts of its own volition and for a long second they stare at one another. Then Willow turns away from him again.

Hart isn't hers to need like that.

She forces lightness. "I do need you, Hart Aurum. I need you to keep my feet warm."

The rest of the night slips away in silence. Once warm in the clutches of sleep, Willow finds she isn't haunted by the sounds of death anymore, but vivid dreams of a boy playing in a frosty wood. A ball slips from his hands and rolls to a stop against a thick tree. Retrieving it, he pauses to peer inside a dark hollow that clefts the trunk open, calling, "Who's there?"

His question echoes and the boy laughs in delight. Something stirs violently to life in the hollow and knocks him to his haunches. From there, he gapes at the fist reaching out from the hole.

"Shhh," its owner's deep, male voice warns as the hand opens to show the boy a gleaming object.

Hart's dragged awake by a forceful pull in his chest. One he's only begun to feel again recently.

Ophelia.

But at the sight of Willow, cheeks pinked like roses, silken hair spilled over his shoulder, he lets a long breath go. He must've been dreaming.

They're still entwined, and heat radiates between them. With a snort, Hart realizes he can still feel all his toes.

And then, another jolt.

He stiffens.

The tug is a wire yanking him to his feet, out of their warm, sleepy nest. Heart pounding, Hart dresses quickly, then draws the wool around Willow before hastening toward the pull's call. Hurrying down and out of the tunnel, he's greeted with a dawn that bathes the clearing and snow falling in heaps off trees.

It's warmer than last night. Hart shields against the brightness.

When the sensation pokes again, he barrels into a thicket, spooking the horse as he passes. Making his way through the trees, his foot slides and sends a bevy of rocks clattering down a steep, craggy outcrop that meets the vast horizon.

His hope falters.

It's not Ophelia, but the rebel army camp, spread out below. Hart can make out the cages he so recently escaped, the monstrosity that's the river of shadows, and the wind-worn groves of the Gulch.

Chest surging with raw energy on the cusp of release, Hart stares in the direction of the Gulch as if he might see through it to the Belly on the other side.

Could Ophelia be there with Falcon?

The thought's interrupted by a small hurricane that seems to erupt in the face of the magic-made Gulch, splitting open a passage that's large enough to let three slick phaetons speed from its mouth.

The Darkwielder's carriages.

"Hart?"

He spins at the voice, a hand on the revolver belted at his waist. But it's only Willow, fully dressed and wrapped in the blanket.

She peers at him with concern and sidles up next to him. "I thought you left…"

In the rebel camp, her people are being escorted from their cages toward the arriving phaetons.

"They're moving them." Willow's voice pitches. "We have to follow." Turning on a heel, she dashes through the thicket before Hart forms a response.

His gaze lingers on the Gulch, shoving aside the prickle of the passage, focusing on that other, stronger call. It's not unlike what he felt when shadows stormed Wythe in the battle at the knoll. Or what he felt at *Asenti* when Ophelia ascended to her power.

It's the call of a strong affinity he can feel like the beat of his own heart. And it doesn't come alone. Guilt is its companion, whispering in his ear as it has since he was a child, reminding him, *You're keeping secrets from Ophelia.*

He doesn't have a choice. He never did.

"Hold your hand out, Hart," his mother told him that night long ago in their kitchen. "It won't hurt much."

Barely five, he hadn't met Ophelia Dannan yet. The blade was sharp and swift. His palm split cleanly. A rolling tear tracked down his cheek as his mother pressed her own cut hand to his. Then his father did the same.

"By the sharing of our blood," his mother said, "we are bound to this oath. For the safety of our family, as long as we live, never will this secret pass our lips unless the gods release it."

Staring at the Gulch, Hart remembers the sealed paper he gave Falcon Thames to store in his ink.

Has he given it to you, Lia? Have you made sense of it?

A gallop of hooves stomps behind him. "Hart, we have to go!" Willow cries out from the steed.

Backing toward her, he watches the passage snap shut and the peaks of the Gulch dip out of sight while calming his racing thoughts with assurances: Hart didn't make it through the passage with Ophelia, but that means Falcon did. And Falcon Thames swore to him that he'd take Ophelia somewhere safe. Away from vicious kings. They're together, and once Hart aids Willow, he will find them both.

Then...

Blood oaths be damned, he will find a way to tell Ophelia the gods-honest truth.

CHAPTER 13
GATES & STROLLS

D read follows Ophelia through iron gates.

From the phaeton she shares with two escorts, she watches the crowded Belly streets vanish, the Gulch disappear from view, and Ghastly—a city rumored to spur nightmares—rise instead like a dream.

She drinks in a glittering world where night is presently reigning, carved of snow and obsidian rock and dark waters in the distance.

The phaeton jostles down a narrow road between endless trees shaped like towering black spears that reach toward a dust-filled sky. She can see only one light in the forest and knows instantly by the faint hum that it's a lumen tree.

Face pressed to the glass, she's shocked to make out in the far distance the spires of a dark palace, nestled into vertical walls of mountain.

Her first thought is, *This can't be the Belly.* Her second, *Where in Magus is he taking me?* She doesn't recognize the landscape at all.

Stealing a glance behind her through the rear window to be sure the gloomy city where she left Falcon Thames is truly gone, her stomach plummets. There's only the iron gates and one other phaeton, where the Darkwielder rides separately attending to some important business. Nowhere are the hordes of citizens who trailed their slow convoy across the territories all day, vying for a view of the myth himself.

Eyeing one of her escorts, a soldier who sits across from her, she asks, "Did we just passage?" She's only ever gone through one on foot; she's not sure what it would feel like, driving by carriage.

The soldier named Stolm, an officer in what the Darkwielder called his legion, rolls a guarded gaze from the window to her. "It is not for you to know."

He has a rasping accent, sculpted and shaped by a cold place, a clear indication the modern tongue isn't his first. Its harsh melody makes him sound older than the mid-twenties he looks, and reminds Ophelia of Falcon's abrasive lilt, just enough that an ache stretches in her chest and for a moment she questions what she's done coming here freely.

No regrets, Teacup. Regrets get you killed, she can hear Falcon counsel in another life.

In the dim light, Stolm sits forward to remove the glass from a lantern hung on the carriage door. Rubbing two dexterous fingers together, he sparks a modest flame on his flesh and sets it to the lamp so the phaeton fills with an orange glow. A Bender of Flame with the sort of control Ophelia envies.

Stolm's hair, curled behind the ears, catches stark-white in the light, along with his straight nose and clean-shaven chin. She studies his serious expression, demeanor, and attire as though he were an opponent in a card game, trying to make out his character and his weakness.

The rebel uniform he wears is a formidable yet flexible material fabricated like overlapping feathers. It looks custom sewn for his broad shape. The cloak is finespun as well, resting beneath a warm pelt of fur that pins at the collar. Though fabric hugs Stolm's thick neck, there's no hiding the whorl of shadow that brands his skin below his jawline.

It seems everyone beholden to the Darkwielder has been marked in some way.

"I think we did passage," Ophelia wages, watching Stolm's reaction.

He doesn't blink, but the brown in his eyes does twitch, and it's telling enough. They passaged. She didn't feel it because the passage wasn't recently cast—it's permanent—but she's right. The Darkwielder's residence, the real Ghastly, isn't in the Belly.

There's no room for panic now. She'll find a way back to Magus once she has the dagger.

Cold fingers brush against her mind, and she tenses.

Watch your thoughts, Falcon warned her only yesterday after they finished sparring and moved on to shieldwork. *From now on, act as if he's listening.*

Eyeing the Shadow marking on Stolm's neck, she asks, "Why is the Darkwielder hiding this place?"

The gloved hand on Stolm's knee balls as he glances to Ophelia's other escort, a sage who appears older, whose pale hair falls in waves past the shoulders to his thick robe and sash. He's spoken not a single word to her all day. His eyes have been white as fog the entire trip, connected to someone or something elsewhere.

Returning to Stolm, the more likely source of information, she says, "The Darkwielder must have told you who I am." She scoots forward in her seat. "If you tell me about Ghastly, I could help protect it."

Considering her, Stolm mutters under his breath to the sage, which sends the man's eyelids rapidly fluttering.

"What's he doing?"

"Searching the future. Aman is the true king's seer."

She considers his white eyes. "The Darkwielder keeps him in that state?" The idea is horrifying, and she thinks of Rune enchanted by those twisted twins, which was different but no less terrifying.

Stolm balks. "Aman is glad to do it. He has served the true king a long time. Erebus's line, even longer."

"As in, when Magies ruled." She's been hunting for knowledge about her ancestry since she was young. "Does he foretell events? Or locate people?" *Did he see me coming?*

"Aman is not that sort of seer," Stolm says in that wind-grooved tone. "He maps intentions. Right now, he is deciding if we should trust you."

Under the scrutiny, her fingers itch to rub her locket, but she keeps them folded in her lap.

When Aman's eyes settle white, he nods once. Stolm excretes a long sigh and says, "The heart of the city that the Underbelly citizens know as Ghastly is..." He struggles for the word. "Fatamorga."

She can't hide her surprise. "A mirage?"

At the accurate translation, Stolm tilts a look at her, his rigid shoulders relaxing a fraction. "The dens and markets are meant to distract, but if anyone approaches the gates they see only a dark estate and feel a sense of fear that keeps them away. Few know what is beyond the mirage or where the true Ghastly lies."

"And you live here with the Darkwielder?" She can't fathom it, that he has loyal followers after all he's done.

"We live under his protection."

She almost laughs, unable to reconcile that the master of those horrifying shadow beasts could be nurturing.

Aman's eyes twitch with that odd, rapid flutter. She catches flashes of color before they cease their movement, then the sage raises a long, pale finger toward the window.

Stolm readies a hand on the carriage door. "You will walk from here."

"Walk?" At the abrupt slowing of the phaeton, she grips her seat.

While Aman stays in the carriage, Stolm exits, and Ophelia hesitates only long enough to take a steadying breath. Then, clutching the strap on her satchel, she greets a stark new world.

He's there.

Looking etched from the scene itself so that it's difficult to tell his ivory skin apart from the snow or his coiffure of dark hair from the dense trees, the Darkwielder stands with an arm at his back, the other outstretching a palm to her.

Because she needs the Darkwielder to trust her, she makes a choice that would stir a storm in Falcon and lets her walls of iron and ice fall, dropping her mental shield.

A question breathes in her mind almost instantly. *Shall we?* His palm flexes.

"I can manage."

He looks amused, retracting his hand. "I'm glad to hear it."

Air whistles through the loose tendrils of her hair, but with all the trees snow-laden, the world feels shrouded. Cold, but comfortable.

When the phaetons disappear with the Darkwielder's entourage, Ophelia's met with the full, hypnotic view—those mountains of midnight painted with snow and the palace sculpted from rock, the dark and perilous water that looks vast as a sea. No people, though. No busy court, carriages, horses, or army. But everything else—the landscape, the palace, the glittering blanket of magic—is breathtaking.

"Do you like it?" The question, like his soft voice close beside her, catches her off guard.

"I didn't expect this," she admits.

"What did you imagine, Ophelia?" His curiosity ebbs almost as viscerally as his shadows.

"Perhaps more of your monsters."

He smiles, but it's cold. "I'll endeavor not to disappoint you."

He walks then, and in this strange dream of a place, she has few options but to follow. Keeping step in the carriage tracks beginning to disappear in the soft, swirling wind, she observes with suspicion that the distance to the palace looks immense. "Why are we walking?"

He slips a hand into a pocket, the gesture shockingly casual. "It's a beautiful night."

CHAPTER 14
COURTS & SPIES

Once upon a time, Ophelia wanted to be everything.

A student of life, a writer of novels, a reveler of art, and a sailor of the One Sea. Exploring the nooks of every known and unknown world, she would traverse mountains by day to feel her own insignificance in the call of the wind and lie all night in the grassy hills beside a man who saw her faults and kissed them like treasures. They'd gaze at infinite stars, bathe in the moonslight, and make love, feeling the edges of the world narrow even as the universe grew and her magic—part of something bigger—grew with it.

But dreaming was a privilege reserved for the lucky in Magus. All her life, the crown viewed her as property, as something to chain.

And here she is, still a captive, even if a willing one. Yet, as the Darkwielder leads them off the road toward Ghastly, snow blanketing the black canopy of the woods, she's surprised to feel a lightness in her chest. Freedom, where she once felt shackles.

Lanterns flicking along a cleared trail suggest the Darkwielder comes here often.

Ophelia slows mid-stride at a sea of purple buds perking through the white surface. Stubborn little flowers she's always loved for the way they grow in impossible conditions.

Sitting amongst similar blooms in Notting Wood, her younger self first coaxed a flower to dip its petals into her hand and nuzzle her palm. It was then being Magie first felt real, when she realized what she would need to become to survive in this violent world.

Like a tome that weathered time, like a sword with unbending steel, she would need to be strong.

Though not in bouquet, the flowers feel like a gift. She resists the urge to gape too long or run a hand through them. She'd bet a song the Darkwielder wants her smitten.

Instead, she sweeps a discrete gaze through the woods, committing to memory the slopes of the land, the distance to the road, the curving path, and even the orientation of the mountain peaks and position of the moons.

"Did Stolm tell you about Ghastly?" the Darkwielder asks, his stride and posture at ease here.

"He called it a mirage. Seems like a lot of trouble to go to."

"There are things to protect here above all else."

"With spells and an army marked to serve you? Is that the price of safety—trading one's will to the Dark Shadow?"

"The Shadow gives them my protection. It doesn't enslave them." He sounds so affronted, she glances in his direction, vexed that he almost looks hurt.

Feeling something dangerously close to sorry, she forces her gaze to the sky. She's not seen anything like the way it eddies purple to green to blue, a kaleidoscope undiluted by village lights.

She's never had a true home for long znd can't get a read on where Ghastly is, but it feels far enough for homesickness to plague her. Far from nights that winked over Notting Wood where she wrote girlish stories by the glow of lanterns she and Hart stuck in tree branches, far from laying on her back beneath the mortal sky with Rune, and even farther from the rooftop in New York, where in Falcon's arms she'd felt both safe and free.

Ophelia can feel *him* watching and it makes her tuck her weakness away. "What?" she bites out.

"You have immense power, but the smugger was right to be worried about your mind. There are seers in every region who read memories, thoughts, or intentions. Without strong shields, everything you know would be theirs, and we can't have that, not here. Have you never learned to protect your mind?"

She spears him with a glare so he might not see how this unnerves her, how deep down she hates herself for running all those years—years she could have been training. She replies through gritted teeth, "I'm working on it."

"What have you mastered?"

"Don't you know?" *He* is in her head, after all.

The Darkwielder delivers a look that's more weary than wicked, thumbing the black crown ring on his finger. "I suppose the crown keeps a tight leash on information that doesn't serve it. I won't be surprised if the library at Ghastly paints a fuller picture than the one at the Constelli. Or you can ask me whatever you wish."

Stunned by the seemingly earnest offer, she nearly missteps at a bend in the path where tree limbs tangle above. She assesses his serious expression, the smooth lines of his jaw, his clear-gray eyes. "I'm still trying to discern why you brought me here, specifically. If you've rifled enough through my mind, you know I have no intention of being a queen."

"*The* queen." His eyes penetrate hers and he peaks his brow, smug as a cat. "And give yourself time to consider what you truly want. Because you do want."

Before she can catch herself, her gaze drops to where the Dark Shadow Dagger is shrouded on his belt. She averts her eyes as quickly, but it's too late. A dark chill curls against her shields, and that arrogant curve of his mouth tells her he knows. He knows exactly what she wants—what she came here for.

"The relics," he muses grimly. "It was a feat to procure one. But together we might finally bring them all home and eliminate further threats to our people."

"And I should believe you want that? Grimm—" At his name, the phantom knife speared through her dislodges and she bleeds anew. Her throat clenches. His death feels too fresh; her heart is still impaled. She takes a steadying breath. "Grimm Hermes made you an ally and the only relic you sought was your own."

The Darkwielder doesn't break stride. "Trying for all three wasn't possible. The other two aren't inside Gray Castle."

He has her full attention. In fact, every shred of her focus narrows to him. And his insufferable smirk.

She hates to further expose her disadvantage by asking, but along with the dagger on his hip, information is why she's here. "Where are the others?"

"Well hidden, I imagine." He spares her a pondering glance. "Retrieving one was enough to spark a revolution, and your return. Now, here we are." As he sweeps a look around the wood, it's as if the black-needled trees curl toward the trail.

"I would've wagered you stole the dagger to satisfy a more personal vendetta."

"War is always personal. Who sacrifices everything good in themselves without being provoked?" The words are filled with his wrath, and a bitter sort of regret.

Everything good.

The dust glitters above the canopy, casting a natural shadow on his chiseled expression as he says, "You're here at Ghastly because I want you here—as queen, but also an equal. And as my agent."

She stops walking and, without even thinking, reaches for his arm to stop him. "Your agent?"

The Darkwielder glances at where she touches him, his brows folding and his black hair falling slightly from its coif.

She drops her hold on him instantly, swallowing against the power he exudes—against how, here in the wood away from his legion, he looks so different. Almost approachable. Barely twenty-five, though she knows he's lived much longer.

For a moment, his lips turn up at the corners, as if liking her fascination.

Hate fills her.

Hate at him for convincing her to come here willingly. Hate at herself that she can't look away from him as he tucks the smile away and says, "While my officers grow our legion to face royal forces, there are politics to play. Both the Constelli and its sages are within our territory now, as are several of the regions run by Osiris's representatives. We need to turn their loyalties as we stake claim to the throne."

"'Stake claim' how exactly?"

"Once we've convinced those with withering ties to the crown to throw their resources behind our rule, we'll have an event. A coronation."

Her surprise is genuine. "Why would you bother with the time it takes to turn representatives when you have the power of Erebus? A relic, a river…?"

He fixes so intently on her that the tether connecting them thrums. "There are wards my shadows can't breach, and the Royal Army is ten times the size of our legion at present, with weapons that rival magic. Allyships win wars."

"And what part do I play in securing them?"

"Shadows may be warded, but the *dust* does not bend to weapons or spells. It bends to no one but the Descendant of Selene. You can travel, Ophelia. Spy here and afar. Help me protect Ghastly. Eventually, with the mastery of your affinity and the other relics, nothing will stand in our way."

She furrows a brow at him, processing what he said—that there are places his shadows cannot go—and trying not to shiver at the dark look in his eyes. What must have been done to him to put that look there? It's the same expression he wielded before allowing Jasper Salt to murder Commander Jory Dagon.

Almost under her breath, she says, "You mean there's nothing you won't do to put the king's head on a pike."

The Darkwielder offers a wicked grin that should not make him look so handsome. "There's that," he admits.

So this is why he's keen to play politics rather than strike at the king swiftly and head on. The Darkwielder isn't impulsive. He's the cat who toys with the dying mouse and likes to watch it bleed.

"You want the Gray King to suffer before you behead him, and you want me to help you do it."

"And will you?"

She studies her hands. Osiris deserves to pay, but spy for the Darkwielder? He did live at Gray Castle once, probably knows how the king thinks, and knows places yet to search for the relics. He knows more about everything, she suspects, and training to be his agent could work in her favor—if she's careful. Because it would never be a true alliance; she could never trust him.

She can almost hear Trix—the Trix she first met: *You don't have to trust a man. Just be smarter than him.*

The Darkwielder watches her eagerly as she resumes their pace. "So you'd run court and the military," she says. "I'd spy on allies while searching for the other relics. And once we establish power, we take the rest of Magus."

Darkness glimmers in his eyes. "Simple enough."

"Nothing is simple." As their boots softly crunch, she thinks more about the relics. "What if our vision isn't the same?" *Our alliance would end, and one of us would try to kill the other, tether or not.*

His granite eyes reflect the snow shimmering off the trees. "Maybe you'll change your mind, Ophelia."

But the relics were used to steal a throne; there is no world in which she'll change her mind about fulfilling her mother's mission, or about being queen.

As they trek deeper through the woods, he urges, "Take some time to think it over." Before she can reply, he hastens his gait. By the time she catches up, her thoughts are on the pressing urge in her belly.

Peering ahead, she sees a stone bridge, more trail, and snow. No sign they're closer to the palace. "How much farther?"

"Eager?"

She clenches her pelvic muscles. "It was a long ride. I need a washroom." Why does it feel like she's admitting a weakness? Even Descendants of the gods have to piss. Though, it's hard to picture the Darkwielder coloring the snow yellow.

"You need to relieve yourself." He looks amused. "There are plenty of shrouded spots here. If you need me to hold your dress, I'll gladly assist."

Seething a look at him, she stalks in the opposite direction, into a thick grove of trees. *Bastard.* She traipses several minutes farther than necessary, until she's sure he's out of view. It's quiet and peaceful in the dense cover, snow spattering from trees that grow close together. She can see the glittering sky through the canopy, and whorls of dust that weave freely.

The beauty is all part of his game, surely. He wants her to see and fall in love with Ghastly. How much easier to convince her to his side.

Ducking under a black bough, she finds a tree slim enough to wrap an arm around and sighs with relief. After, she's straightening her cloak when a howl cuts the silence. It's chased by a rush of darkness that makes the dust-lit woods flicker.

She feels a burning in her instantly. Hot *and* cold as the ridges on her arm spark with golden light and the dark marking on her chest chills to ice.

Through the trees, in her ears, fervent whispers arrive as if to warn that something's near.

Ophelia traces her footprints to follow them back the way she came, but foliage rustles straight ahead. A rapid trill of *maether*, quick and sharp, vibrates between her and whatever creature creeps in the trees a jog away.

She's reaching for her blade when a shape breaks through the cover of midnight trees.

Her focus narrows to a four-legged beast that stands as tall as she, with a fleece of white fur and glinting, gold eyes. Its lips are stained red and peeled back over razored teeth.

She knows the animal at once. An ancient beast with a thirst for blood.

Wolven.

CHAPTER 15
MYTHS & BEASTS

GHASTLY
6TH DAY IN THE NEW WINTER
OPHELIA IS WITH THE DARKWIELDER

Erebus made wolven to guard his palace. An aggressive northern beast, they've not been seen in Magus since the primordial gods walked among us. But should even the most skilled Magie fall upon a pack, gods help you. If you value your life, do not let a wolven close enough to leap.

Monsters and Myths of the North,
scribed by Headmaster Grimm Hermes

I t's too late to run.

Hackles raised, the creature stalks forward with its head lowered until it's just short of pouncing distance, eyeing Ophelia as a continuous, low growl rumbles in its chest.

She holds utterly still while, in the woods, a chorus of bays echoes. Several other white shapes hulk into view, surrounding her. The dust doesn't like that. Swooping like starlight, it dives from the canopy to make a shield around her.

Ophelia clutches her arm where light begins to glow from her lumen mark, and she holds the gaze of the largest of the wolven.

Its pack paces, unsettled, watching the trees.

This may be reckless—really reckless—but following her instinct, she abandons the idea of using her blade or commanding the dust against these creatures. Instead, she outstretches a hand and feels for the wolven's essence, remembering Grimm's words: *The very breath of magic. Anything made of it, with it, fed by it... You feel its essence as if it's part of you.*

As they gaze at one another, the largest wolven steps forward, its paws light on the snow despite its massive size. It stalks so close she can feel a huff of its hot breath. When a wet nose meets her palm, his wild and anxious *maether* gales through her.

She can feel him like she felt the woe of the tree at Gray Castle and the Sycas falling in the Glow Woods. She can feel his courage, his fear, his honor, his...protectiveness.

Shapes move in her periphery—a second wolven stepping closer. A third, and fourth.

A rush of darkness slams against her mind. *"Ophelia!"* An unmistakable hiss of shadows cuts through the woods, causing three sharp yelps.

Her chest plunges with a chill.

The wolven before her reels back as she throws a hand to her chest, struck with the animal's pain and a sorrowful feeling of death, as though it were her own neck the Darkwielder's shadows just snapped. A menacing growl rips from the wolven's throat as it whips its neck around.

The Darkwielder steps into the clearing. Everything about his face, his posture, and his energy is lethal, and Ophelia's stomach pits when she sees his shadows return to him from the woods, mist clinging to his skin.

He doesn't take his eyes off the wolven between them. The wolven who's just lost his pack, whose *maether* tremors with what feels to her like bloodlust.

"Kill it!" the Darkwielder shouts.

Kill it. Kill the leader.

Kill the king.

Memories mingle. But this isn't the king. The Darkwielder sees a deadly beast in the wolven, because that's who he is. He doesn't feel the creature's pain the way she does.

"Ophelia!" He sounds panicked, and before the wolven can lunge, darkness claps, throwing a wall of unseeable night around her.

At a clash of teeth, a yowl, she screams, "No!"

A surge of light erupts, melting the snow beneath her as it gobbles through the darkness, spreading like wildfire until every last shred of the night the Darkwielder sent to crush the wolven scatters.

The creature lies on its side, whimpering, panting heavily.

From a tree he's been thrown back against, the Darkwielder groans, straightening to his feet with a loathing look.

Ignoring him, she rushes for the wolven to lay a gentle hand on its leg where shadows have snapped bone. Light flows quickly down her arm, into her hand, and beneath the white fur. As its leg begins to mend, she feels intense relief.

She didn't destroy it. She healed it.

Moments after, the wolven's molten eyes soften on her as it lugs itself to its feet, shaking out its fur as if nothing happened. Its leg faintly glows, like a starburst.

"Go," she whispers, her head dizzy from the effort of wielding the dust.

The wolven listens.

When it disappears from view, she begins to stand but it's a struggle to get off her knees. How light her head feels, how heavy her limbs.

She hears his footsteps before taut arms scoop her up against leather armor. "You're farther along than I thought," he breathes in her ear. "Hold on."

At a gasping speed, the woods and gravity disappear beneath her in a billow of shadows. The mist carries them, and Ophelia's cocooned by the Darkwielder's infinite power, which is amplified by his relic. She clutches his neck to keep from falling to her death, and a sickening thought comes.

Did those wolven happen upon her, or did he send them?

"They were already near, Ophelia. But now I know where to start with your instruction."

Her blood chills. "You killed that pack to test me? To see what I could do!" she shouts above the rushing wind. Mid-air or not, she shoves against him—hard.

But the Darkwielder holds her tightly. *"Lesson one, goddess."* His voice, a hiss in her head. *"Even evil can show its heart. Let empathy slow your sword with the wrong beast, it's you who will end up on the pike."*

They summit the wall into Ghastly the way birds would, soaring on a cut of wind.

Ophelia fumes, refusing to look at him, but as they land and his shadows clear to reveal walls of mountain around a Gothic courtyard, she's forced to tuck away laments of wolven and his test.

An outdoor garden unfolds like a secret. Towering brightly in its center is one of the grandest lumen trees she's ever beheld, pulsing with energy so intense that at first she can't speak. Its light flows in beads from roots to limbs, its branches spindling and twining with a neighboring tree—one whose bark and leaves are dark as coal. The effect of their meshing is a tangle of lightness and darkness that feels all too prophetic.

In awe, her gaze sweeps over marble benches, mazes of hedges, and vibrant bushes that bear fruit and buds despite the falling snow. Throughout the courtyard sprawl walkways that shimmer as her gaze shifts, as if someone bottled the sky and architected every surface with it. There are towers to the north and east and a very large domed structure to the west.

In any direction, the gardens trail inside the hugging mountain.

Who could've built this palace but a god?

Across the garden, she sees a few men and women harvesting fruit or flowers. Servants who look comfortable in either dresses with long aprons or vested shirts and pants. All that lacks here is a bustling court.

"Welcome to my home," the Darkwielder breathes in her ear.

At the realization he still holds her, she quickly extricates herself from his arms, and a familiar voice calls out across the courtyard, "Am Kosost!"

Officer Stolm is all posture and urgency as he approaches, flanked by soldiers in those intimidating black uniforms.

Vanishing are all traces of the Darkwielder's smirk, his casual tone—any vulnerability at all. Shadows sift to his pale skin, and the power that seeps from him shudders behind every rung of her ribs.

Outside these walls, he was infuriating. A man-child. Here, he's every bit the dark king, whose mere presence seems to cause Stolm to keep a few paces between them.

"Ka nes?" the Darkwielder asks. *What news?*

"Gefeshi, Kosost, nah Easton," Stolm replies.

While the men confer, Ophelia translates enough to surmise there's been an ambush on legion soldiers who were en route to secure the Constelli for the Darkwielder, that a Royal Army unit outside Vasgale surprised them.

"Twenty lost, but we have taken the academy," Stolm says. And there's more—an incident in a legion camp north of the Gulch, where prisoners tried to escape.

She assumes Stolm's referring to captured royal forces, but their lowered voices and quick speech make the conversation difficult to follow. As she tries to grasp details, movement near a hedgerow pulls her attention.

A woman in layers of dark skirts and scarves lingers with a hand on a long-stemmed flower, as if she is listening. Intrigued, Ophelia traces her shroud of long, dark hair with its distinct swaths of gray, just making out the shape of a delicate tattoo on the woman's cheek. With her gaze fixed on the flower she holds, the woman curls her hand around its bud, then rips the petals from the stem to let them fall and scatter at her feet. She's placing the thorned stem into her basket when, as if sensing eyes, she looks over.

"Goddess."

Ophelia whips back to the Darkwielder and Stolm.

The Darkwielder's gaze lifts to where her attention was fixed, his face darkening with displeasure. He angles his tall frame to obscure her view, noting, "You must be tired."

"No, I have questions."

"And it seems I have pressing business." He sighs. "Stolm will see you inside. We'll start your instruction in the morning."

"Instruction?" Her volume catches looks, but how dare he presume after what he pulled in the woods that she'll be preening for his mentoring.

Switching to thoughts, she sends them—loudly—across the tether: *"I haven't agreed to your alliance yet, let alone lessons from you."*

The Darkwielder spares her a withering look before stalking away. *"We begin at breakfast. Come hungry, goddess."*

The mountain isn't the oppressive fortress Ophelia imagined outside.

Darkness does color the marbled floors and winding staircases, the walls and tapestries, as well as the windows framed in the rock. But the golden finishes, the lavish carpets and candelabras, and the well-placed lanterns and hearth fires that blaze every dozen paces, make this vast palace carved inside a mile of rock...inviting.

Trailing Stolm through a great hall and up to a balcony, she rakes a gaze over the impressive ceiling. A mural spans its length. The scene depicts a steep hill with a silvery lake at its base. Beside the water lies a beautiful woman with long, golden hair, sprawled in a fountain of sunshine.

She's painted so tenderly, and with such exquisite detail, that Ophelia could write her story.

"Where is everyone?" she asks at the next floor. It's so quiet she only hears their own footfalls. "If this is court, shouldn't there be people?"

"This is the Darkwielder's private wing," Stolm replies.

Private wing.

The knowledge sharpens her curiosity as they walk.

Dust and moonslight ripple through a bay of windows, lighting on fine artwork mounted in gold frames. These have an intimate tone, with hands holding delicate blooms, a palm cupping a woman's cheek, lips meeting a ruby apple. Things softer than war or shadows that snap wolven's necks.

"This is the east wing and tower." Stolm halts before a set of thick doors that crest to an impressive arch. "Your chambers," he says.

The room is a dream.

Ophelia can hear Falcon telling her to check every possible exit, every window. Once she has, she takes in the beauty. A carved writing desk with ample ink pots, quills, and paper. An armoire she imagines is filled with fine clothes. Shelving that spans the length of a wall, crowded with books. A four-poster bed beside an impressively large hearth. And a separate room with a toilet and tub from which she can hear soft voices.

Two women rush into view. They wear matching dresses that sway at their ankles and soft leather aprons tied neatly in front.

As they bow, Ophelia's gaze meets the eldest woman's. She has gray-threaded hair and umber eyes with a familiar, kindly look. There's hope in them.

Stolm nods at the two. "Your attendants will clean and feed you. Help you with any...woman things."

Ophelia nearly rolls her eyes at him. Is she a dog? Instead, she glances toward the door they came through. "The Darkwielder mentioned a library. I'd love to see the tomes."

"It is late. If you require something before morning, your attendants can summon it for you."

"He said I'm not a prisoner," she replies through clenched teeth.

"Not a prisoner. A guest he wishes to keep safe."

"Am I not safe in a mountain?"

"Of course," Stolm replies. "But there are spells that ensure it. You would not wish to walk into one unintentionally in our unfamiliar halls."

Spells in the halls. "What sort of threat is he worried about?" Ophelia can't imagine how enemies would even find Ghastly, let alone infiltrate the mountain.

"Nothing to concern yourself with," Stolm assures her. "Only precautions any sovereign takes."

As he bids her goodnight, Ophelia's too tired to press the matter.

The elder of her attendants approaches, her eyes twinkling in a way that reminds Ophelia of Trix—only with affection instead of cunning.

"I'm Hannah, Am Kososten." The woman's warm tone is a comfort, but *Kososten*?

She doesn't wish to offend the woman, but the title makes her blanch. "Please, call me Ophelia."

The woman shares a look with the second attendant. "How about *lady*?" Hannah compromises.

"All right," Ophelia agrees as the other attendant takes her cloak.

"I'm Isolde, my lady," whispers the young woman, both her deep-brown skin and eyes the color of the sea radiating softness and warmth. With hair wound into braids at the nape of her neck, she looks about twenty and...awestruck as she beholds Ophelia.

She doesn't wish to be worshipped, but she would welcome friendship, considering there are spells in the halls apparently preventing her from exploring at night.

When Hannah ushers Ophelia into the washroom—yet another dream—she sets aside her plotting.

Stretching across the domed ceiling is a beautiful mural of golden trees, their roots reaching down dark-green walls that flicker with mage lights. Yet another fire laps in the hearth, near where a velvet chair faces a deep porcelain tub.

"I hope it feels like home," Isolde says, her accent lighter than Stolm's, but still there. "You're the first guest we've had in the east wing." She reaches for Ophelia's satchel.

Ophelia clings to the bag. "I'll keep it with me, if you don't mind."

Isolde bows, still smiling ear to ear as she disappears to retrieve bedclothes.

Hannah fills the bath. With the jewels in her leather cuffs shining red, she waves a hand over the water until steam begins to rise.

Ophelia marvels at the woman's gentle magic, little vibrations soft as butterfly wings against her skin.

Every few moments as the water heats, Ophelia senses curious eyes, but she's focused on the milky water and the scent of jasmine. More than uncover Ghastly's secrets all in her first hours here, she aches to melt into the bath. When Hannah leaves her to soak, she savors the warmth that eases a bit of the tension in her muscles and allows her exhaustion to take full hold.

She won't think about how she's left Falcon behind, or what the Darkwielder did to the wolven. She won't think of anything but this bath.

Drifting, head heavy, her chin lowers to brush the water. Her eyes are drooping, closing—when a beast made of shadows leaps at her, gnashing its teeth.

She jolts with a gasp, forcing water over the rim of the tub as sharp fear drives her to her feet, and wildly searches the washroom.

There's no beast.

No beast.

Only her reflection in the chamber mirrors, showing her long, wet hair cascading water down her breasts, her belly, and her thighs. Her chest rises rapidly where the dark marking taunts her, anxiety keeping a grip on her throat.

It was only a nightmare. But it lingers as she dresses for bed, as she sips at the delicate soup Hannah serves her. She doesn't object when her attendants dim the lights. Climbing under pillowy sheets, she listens to the two women's hushed voices while they gather dishes, then quietly leave her to sleep.

Covers to her chin, the solitude pressing around her, Ophelia's eyes fall on the contents of her satchel where it rests on the writing desk. She can just see the charred corner of Rune's white book peeking out at her. At the sight of it, the day—the entire week—seeps inside her like its own shadow. Truly alone in the Darkwielder's mountain palace, she feels every tender bruise and ache she's been holding together by will. The sharpest ache is that of leaving Falcon with no explanation in Ravish, but there are others.

She wants to see them—all the men who've become her family. To feel Falcon's arms around her waist, his cheek against her belly. To watch the hard lines of Hart's face smooth as he spreads paint on canvas. To see the light and mischief working in Rune's eyes at one of her bold ideas.

She slips from bed, needing to hold something they've touched. Taking the white book, she hugs it to her chest as she lies back down. The feel of the leather and scent of its spine make her thoughts narrow to Rune, stirring an idea.

I could search for him.

She swore to Falcon she'd wait a few days to try traveling again, until she could visualize a shield protecting her mind. It's been a few days, and things have also changed—she's walked willingly into the Darkwielder's palace.

Closing her eyes, she searches beyond the bed, beyond the room and the window, until there are no barriers between herself and the dust that veils Ghastly. She pictures Rune. The last she saw or spoke to him was after she shoved an amplifier stone in his hand and begged him to fight the Enchanters who had just made him murder Grimm.

He stayed behind for me. I need to see him. I need to know he's okay.

At first, she doubts herself, doubts whether the dust—or any part of her magic—can hear her in this mountain, but swift enough she feels the rush of some reply.

The white book slides from her hands as every part of her grows much, much lighter.

CHAPTER 16
DREAMS & NIGHTMARES

GHASTLY
6TH NIGHT IN THE NEW WINTER
OPHELIA IS ON HER OWN

Her bed is gone. *Ghastly* is gone.

Tingling like she's tapped a lumen tree, Ophelia startles when her vision clears on a claustrophobic cell that's walled entirely by stone, where a man hunches over himself in chains on the floor.

She could swear her heart stops.

It can't be.

Wrists shackled in his lap and a bowl of something putrid rotting between his bare feet, he sags like a beaten, broken vessel. His dark curls are a wreck, his head bobs as if his neck strains to hold its weight, and his eyes... They're a travesty. A dark, lifeless green—the green of molded earth—they stare at nothing.

Rune.

Ophelia traces every feature of his gaunt face. And, gods, his neck, his chest—so much of his exposed skin—is marred with deep, slashing lines. Open wounds left to their own healing. And the color of his skin... He's as ashen as the alabaster moons.

She can't quite breathe, and she struggles to tell if this is real or simply a manifestation of her guilt.

Looking at Rune, a horrible notion takes hold of her. If the king's army did capture him, this is what they'd do to him—imprison him in the Shaft at Gray Castle.

Because of her.

"Rune," she whispers, feeling the word leave her chest. Her hand roves to her locket, then to the silken nightgown in which Hannah dressed her, sliding up into her long, loose hair, and finally to the skin of her cheek.

Ripping her touch away, she stares at her fingers. They're translucent and...glowing, as if she's becoming corporeal.

Startled backward, she meets bars of iron that lock this cell. Still, she searches for winking particles, or a sure sign she hasn't traveled and this is actually a nightmare.

Turning in a circle, she sees a stone tunnel beyond the cell that's lit by lanterns. She has no idea what's happening—she is not made of the dust, yet this doesn't feel like a dream.

Clank.

She spins at the sound to find Rune's head tilted in her direction; he's softly scraping together the shackles that bind his wrists.

An impulse rises in her to get him out of here, whether this is real or not real, whether an escape is even possible.

Think.

She sweeps a gaze over the contents of the impossibly sparse cell. There's no lamp, no books. Only a mattress, the rotten food, a basin, and the smallest window.

His shackles scrape, scrape, scrape, drawing her back to him.

"Rune." His name breathes between them as Ophelia steps forward.

His lifeless eyes flicker and his muscles twitch as she kneels, positioning herself shy of his legs to avoid the bowl of whatever's gone sour. He seems to see her but struggles, as though fighting to remember.

"Rune, it's me. Fellie."

He flinches, a spectrum of ugly emotions shading his features.

This close, her breath catches at how sharp his cheekbones angle. Her hand has a mind of its own, reaching to cup his wrists above the leaden shackles.

When their skin touches, it's a shock to her system. In most living things, she's come to sense some breath of life, but Rune feels nearly empty.

She yanks her hand away, and as she withdraws her touch, Rune jerks. "She's here." His voice is barely a rasp. Scrape. Scrape. Scrape. "She's here." His body quivers in agitation as he clanks those shackles together.

Anger clenches her teeth. He's chained like an animal, drained to nearly nothing.

"I'm going to get you out." There's not a speck of particles to be seen, but there are flames in the lanterns.

Shuttering her eyes, she feels for the heat. *Just like the lock at the hotel.*

The pinpricks come first, devolving to a rippling of tingles from her chest to her fingertips. Grasping the flame's edge, she calls it into herself and wastes no time funneling the *maether* down to her hands, placing them again on Rune's shackles.

"*Open,*" she begs.

With a heavy click, the iron clasps thud to the stone.

Rune frowns at his wrists, rubbing two fingers where they've bitten his skin raw.

Slowly, because he gives her the impression of a wounded creature, Ophelia rests a hand on his sleeve, sliding it up to his shoulder, then to his cold cheek. As his eyes focus on her, she says, "I'm so sorry, Rune." Sorry for Grimm. Sorry for not remembering him. Sorry for her split heart.

She's reaching to pull him up with her when Rune's hands lash out angrily for her neck. They squeeze—violently.

"Ru—" She chokes in surprise at his sudden strength, a fervor that sends her reeling onto her back where she kicks her legs.

The bowl of rancid food shucks across the cell as Rune straddles her and steals the air from her, repeating, "She's here!"

His vehemence sets off a chain reaction in the tunnels, in other cells that've been quiet but now ring with the clanking of iron and the shouts of prisoners.

Her eyes widen on Rune—the absence of him and his kindness, his lightness, his love. This is not the man who cares for her. It's a man who wants her dead.

She feels a jolt of *maether* in him, from wherever it's been buried, as he lurches up and heaves her off her feet, charging forward to slam her back against the bars of the cell. "You shouldn't have come." The words are a hiss—Rune's words, yet not.

As his eyes bore through her, a groan of metal grates outside the cell, long and heavy as if a door's being dragged to open. A stampede of boots in the tunnel follows.

Thrashing wild, she claws at Rune's punishing, crushing, bruising hands.

"Surrender." The command washes through her—Rune's will, his enchantment—and because her shields are down, because she didn't even try to keep Rune out, the desire to stop fighting consumes her, telling her she should let go. Maybe this is what she deserves for the lives she's cost, for allowing the king to escape and for breaking Rune's heart.

"Rune," she gasps.

A flicker. Something fighting to the surface in his eyes. For a moment, Ophelia feels the pressure under his hands ease. But it's only a second before his eyes dull and harden again and the pressure resumes.

"Surrender."

"No—" she chokes. *Let me go!* she screams inside.

Light.

So swiftly does light rise in her, bursting like a breaking star and throwing Ophelia backward through the iron bars. There's a rip as her thrashing hands catch in fabric, then Rune Ethera and his grip are gone.

F ire laps.

When she blinks, choking for air, Ophelia's relieved to be sprawled on the rug beside her bed at the Darkwielder's palace. A dozen candles blur from either side of the marble hearth, flicking from candelabra stands.

It's two more long breaths before the door to her room flies open, and she braces for the Darkwielder's shadows, or the Darkwielder himself. Mercifully, it's Hannah and Isolde, wearing nightgowns and worried looks.

Hannah forgoes formality and drops with Isolde to Ophelia's side. The women startle when they see her up close. "We heard you scream."

Pressing a careful hand to where the skin on her neck throbs, raw, Ophelia can't find the words to ask what they see as they pull her to her feet and settle her onto the bed.

Hannah glances around. "Was anyone in your room after we left, my lady?"

"No," Ophelia replies, meeting the woman's eyes.

With a frown, Hannah brings the covers up to Ophelia's chin and brushes a hand over her forehead. The gesture makes her ache; it's so like how her mother used to tuck her in.

"A bad dream?" Hannah asks as Isolde fetches water.

"Something like that," Ophelia answers quietly.

As Isolde sets a cup beside the bed, she and Hannah exchange wary looks. Then Hannah leans forward to gently lay a hand to Ophelia's neck.

Warmth comes. Tingles. Relief.

The ache in Ophelia's throat is fading when Hannah warns, "Don't speak of where you were." And, rising to her feet, she adds in a lighter tone, "Just a dream, my lady. We'll be close by, should you need us."

Ophelia's heart pounds long after the women go.

Hannah's words and Rune's madness both linger in her mind as she lies on her side facing the fire. A tear streaks her cheek and her blurry vision drifts to her hand.

She opens the clenched fist, and the torn piece of Rune's tunic lies there, clutched in her sweaty palm.

CHAPTER 17
IRON & BLOOD

When the tentacles on his mind release, Rune drops to his knees on the stone floor of the cell, chest heaving.

Voices hiss in the tunnel.

"Almost had her."

"He was close."

"Not bloody close enough."

"You think another session?"

"Too soon. It'll kill him."

Metal clicks, and the drone of iron groans as the cell door opens. The tunnel light shadows as an iron chair wheels forward, and with unfocused eyes Rune traces the monarch of Magus's movements.

Osiris Lestat is regaled in his lavish, jeweled coat that buttons to hide half his misshapen throat. Vaguely, Rune registers the stiff silhouettes that hover in the tunnels.

"Apprentice." The Gray King's low voice fills the silent cell.

Rune's gaze lifts, by his own volition or an invisible rope—it's hard to tell anymore—and he meets a reflective silver mask that covers one of the king's eyes and part of his forehead.

"She found you faster than we thought, didn't she?" The king casts a look around as if searching the cell for evidence. "No particles. Fascinating. You're certain she was here?"

Rune doesn't know who *she* is, but his head bobs.

"And how did she get away?"

He feels the inclination to answer, albeit through his teeth. "I don't know, Your Majesty."

"Give him truth," something wills.

"She was—" Rune searches his memory from the past half hour, trying to recall her name, her face, and why she feels like something to him, but it's like peering into murky water. "She was marked. But...it was light...that took her."

The king assesses the crease in Rune's forehead and his supplicant posture, then throws a question to his retinue in the tunnel. "Is he fighting it?"

"Barely at all now, Your Grace." Lux Locke, half the pair always at the king's side, sounds proud.

A thin smile crooks the king's mouth. "Ahead of schedule on all fronts." At a motion of his head comes the sound of armor.

Rune is hoisted off his knees to face the king. Slowly, the monarch rises from his chair and accepts the cane brought to him, settling his weight onto it as he steps forward to circle him.

No one pulls the rope in Rune's head. For two riotous seconds, he's himself—and he screams inside, wishing for death as he thinks of *her*. Ophelia. Fellie. It was Fellie. She came for Rune, and he almost killed her.

He'd wanted to kill her.

A pale eye steps into Rune's line of vision to inspect him closely, and the riot inside him quiets.

The monarch's nose sniffs within an inch of Rune's neck where his wounds haven't yet healed. Straightening, he leans on his cane. "You think I'm torturing you."

Rune doesn't feel compelled to answer this time. He braces for the king's blade, another session. But it doesn't come.

The king's eye twitches. "What I've been doing is building your strength and capacity for what's to come, Apprentice. Like a father would. You could think of me as such. You have no father of your own."

Rune strains to remember. Father. His father was… He had a name that started with *J*.

The king looks with pity at Rune. "Such histories our ancestors wove with their choices. Choices children and their children paid for dearly." Reaching into his jeweled coat, the king extracts a small paper. A picture, maybe. "You're nearly ready, so I'll tell you a story that begins with my father—a rigid man of conviction with a hard hand and harder morals. Not an ounce of give with his opinions or his belt. I was his pride, though. Until I was…no longer his."

The king looks to the tiny window, where the smallest hint of moonslight spills into the cell.

"Some say a Magie forced himself on my mother. The truth? She was bewitched into bed by a Spellcaster who served our home. My father found them together, in fact, when I was eight." Osiris glowers. "The man—my sire—was hanged in the tree in our front garden, beside my whore mother."

The king's eye glazes, as if seeing it now. "I lost my position as firstborn, my inheritance, and my only brother. Even before my cursed affinity showed itself, I was sent to Easton to an orphanage for Magie boys." The monarch's gaze snaps to Rune. "I was tortured, too. And I'm grateful for it. Do you know why?"

The king taps the picture in his hand that Rune can't see. "I became a man with a purpose, if not one with family."

Family. The word conjures thick fields, campfires, a white mustache, a wealthy carriage.

"I knew *your* family," the king says. "I knew him well."

The cell sways.

"Your grandfather. Your mother, too. A beautiful woman, Cenna. I wasn't informed she had a son. Not until after my Enchanters found you with Ophelia Dannan in that wretched village and I had records pulled."

The king's cane clicks against stone.

"I had to know what was so special about you—a half-breed boy with no instances of disobedience, a star apprentice—that the headmaster chose *you* to be an accomplice to the rebel cause. When I uncovered your ancestry, it made complete sense why Grimm Hermes felt compelled to keep you close." He snarls the words.

The past and present blur in Rune's mind. Warm kisses in the sunlight. Tomes. A lake. A dim library and pair of shrewd Enchanter eyes. His own bloody hands. The king's stone face. A swarm of soldiers. This cell.

"Rune Ethera." The king turns his name over. "You took your Magie father's name. I can't blame you, rejected as you were by your grandfather."

The slow gears of Rune's mind churn to an old conversation with his grandfather outside the Constelli: *Get your sageship, boy. Then perhaps you can see your family.*

It was all he'd wanted for so long.

The king slides a finger along the edge of the picture he holds. He jerks it away just as fast, as if the paper bit him, raising it to inspect a bead of blood at the tip. "Not to worry," he says. "It pained me, but I dealt with your grandfather for failing to declare you, as was his duty to this crown." The king sucks the blood from his finger, then his eye falls to Rune. "Hiding you away was unforgivable—a breach of trust—given your grandfather and I had recently reconnected."

Murmurs sound in the tunnel.

"I might have been the bastard in our family, but your grandfather was always the weaker of us brothers."

Rune stares uncomprehendingly—his head is tar. Rune's grandfather and the king? Brothers?

"You," Rune rasps.

"Me." The king leans in. "Your great uncle, by blood." He finally holds the picture out to Rune. In it, two boys pose in a study wearing academic uniforms from another time.

In a haze, Rune recognizes his grandfather—the man's wide face, straight nose, stern brows—so like the boy pictured beside him. The only difference is their eyes. His grandfather's were green. The other boy's, the same shrewd blue that watch Rune now.

His legs give.

The soldiers that grasp Rune's arms bear his weight as the king takes a final look at the picture. "I was mistaken once," he muses. "Twice, in fact, thinking I could make an heir. But you and I—not only do we share blood, but each of us have a foot in two worlds as half-mortal, half-Magie. Who better to occupy the throne than men who understand, who have lived firsthand the corruption that magic wreaks?"

Corruption.

Like Rune's mind?

The king's hand curls, white-knuckled, on his cane. "I am forced to quench a siphoner's hunger if I want to stay alive and keep that corruption in check, because I had no heirs to pass my kingdom to. No one I could trust with my secrets or the future of Magus. And you..." The king steps closer. "You were bewitched by magic to the point of abetting fugitives. You were tortured, made a murderer, so many atrocities..."

Rune's head falls. There's one more second where a small voice in him riots—screams of love and equality and peace.

But what did that get you? he asks it. *Everything the king said and more.*

The epiphany curls like smoke, choking at the riot, the last of those screams. Why has Rune never seen before what magic has stolen from him and those he loved?

Rune, as the king's nephew, rubs his fingers together, imagining ash coating them. The death of magic. Of corruption. The notion spills like oil through him: Ash isn't something to fear, but justice. If they'd captured Ophelia Dannan tonight, perhaps the kingdom, and Rune Ethera's heart, would finally be at peace.

Studying him, the king says, "The hardest lessons are learned first-hand, but they're effective. Sometimes we must be broken before we can be great."

Of course. The king had only wanted Rune to understand how magic corrupts, so he showed Rune that corruption, let him experience it firsthand. All the children captured, the students brought to heel, the siphoning, and the fear he evokes... Lessons.

Rune has been his pupil.

The king stows the picture in his coat and retrieves a second. "Your father and grandfather are gone, but your mother is not." He holds the picture out.

Rune's mother has the same raven hair he used to curl his small fingers in. The same gleaming green eyes that smiled as she ducked her head around a tree when they played hiders-seekers. The small, curving smirk she reserved for Rune's father.

He thinks of these memories as if they belong to someone else.

In the picture, Cenna sits in a parlor with a book in her lap, the sun drenching her features. Two small girls sit beside her.

Rune realizes his eyes are wet and his fists clenched as the word *family* beats with each of his breaths.

Tucking the picture away in his coat, the king says, "Cenna lives in Bowery with your mortal sisters. Prove your loyalty and take your place in this house, and you'll have your way to them."

Rune's head drops in a sweeping bow. An answer.

Footsteps sound in the cell, and a slender young man in a red-stitched coat folds in, trailed by a servant carrying clothes—not a tunic and trousers, but things bejeweled and finely stitched.

"Mend him," the king orders. "Then take my nephew to chambers more befitting the prince of Magus. We have a great task ahead of us."

CHAPTER 18
LESSONS & PASTRIES

O phelia's awake with the sun.

It spills a buttery glow into her room that belies her dark mood and washes the books, the rugs, the fine drapes, the bed, and the desk where she's been writing half the night in a shower of light.

Setting down the quill, she blows on the fresh, wet ink in Rune's white book as she stares out the arched windows that overlook the eastern side of Ghastly, where ice-coated stonework and narrow stairs hug the façade.

She managed to doze a few hours, but spent the better part of last night at this window, nurturing her hatred for the Gray King of Magus and feeling the ghost of Rune's hands on her neck. How Osiris Lestat must be torturing Rune, for him to become *that*.

Shutting her eyes, she fights the image and forces her grip on the book to relax. She knows what Falcon, Hart, and *her* Rune would say. They all agreed. They swore. If any of them were ever captured, they should do nothing to compromise the mission.

Her instincts tell her the Gray King won't kill Rune. But torture... She swallows.

It was part of the deal, Teacup, she can hear Falcon say. But after what she saw in that cell, she doesn't care. They can't abandon Rune, though she can't go back to him now, either. Not without an idea of how to break the hold they have on him. Not without knowing, exactly, how she traveled physically.

All night, she's been replaying how she could've folded her body across space, across the kingdom. She didn't travel on the dust. It felt like the once-dormant part of Selene's magic she used a year ago with Hart, when all it took was fear and will to make objects disappear.

Maybe those objects hadn't vanished. Maybe, like her—and like the Darkwielder's shadows that she scattered—they'd simply gone elsewhere.

She's hoping the library holds answers. Answers that might allow her to travel that way again, with more control. Because with this ability, she's not just equipped to spy for the Darkwielder. She could go anywhere.

"I was holding you and thinking of Rune," she mutters to the white book. "But how did I get back with his shirt—"

Don't speak of where you were. An echo of Hannah's earlier warning causes her to slam her mouth shut.

It was an odd thing to say, unless Hannah knew of Ophelia's tether to the Darkwielder.

She checks that her shields feel firm, taking a last look at her coded words in the white book. In the pages, she captured what happened at Gray Castle, what Ophelia couldn't say to the maddened Rune, what's been on her heart since her memories returned.

It felt good, at least, to be writing again.

Slipping the book into her satchel with the scrap of Rune's tunic, she hauls herself to her feet, avoiding the full-length mirror.

Her head swims with sudden lightness. Her stomach rumbles, empty. Apart from soup, it's been more than a day since she's eaten.

With steadying hands against her bodice, she takes a long breath. The dress she found in the wardrobe is silken to the touch, pale as the Darkwielder's complexion, with sheer sleeves and a threaded pattern of tree roots. Fitted at her waist, it spools to her ankles, impractical on multiple levels. Namely, it's winter. But the fabric is heaven against her skin, and she can move freely in it. To spar. To run.

She feels for the blade secured just above her new boots. No one bothered to check her for weapons, and the weight of it brings comfort, a realization she has something of everyone she loves here, with the exception of Grimm: her mother's locket, Rune's book, a letter from Hart waiting to be read, and this knife Falcon gifted her yesterday—the new-to-her blade with etched wings she'd been admiring.

Has Trix told Falcon the truth of her betrayal? Has she told him where Ophelia's gone? Is he trying to find her?

Perhaps with this new ability, she can go to Falcon and tell him herself.

But first, information. She can't waste this opportunity here. To know where to look for the relics, she has to discover everything she can about her ancestry, her power...and her opponents.

She stows her satchel deep in a drawer, letting the thought of Rune being tortured fuel her resolve.

A rap sounds at the door.

Stolm enters briskly in a uniform without cloak or pelts. "Enost," he greets with a tight nod. "I have come to escort you to breakfast."

"Enost," she replies, noting how he works hard to keep his gaze averted from the dipping collar of her dress. Reason number two it's impractical. "Don't you have more important things to do than see to my stomach?"

"I am to be your guard while you are here, my—"

"Please don't say 'queen,'" Ophelia interrupts. Following Stolm into the hall, she flinches at a prickle that comes with crossing the threshold of her chambers. "Was my room warded?"

"He ordered it spelled this morning," Stolm says.

"The Darkwielder?" He said he can sense her—does he know she traveled? Did he see to where?

Stolm seems to note her worry, elaborating, "When he returned from business this morning, your attendants said you had a difficult time sleeping. They suggested a ward might give you peace of mind." Tension releases in her chest as Stolm nods at the doorframe, where the air faintly glimmers. "It allows you, your attendants, and I—as your guard—to enter the chambers. And whomever you invite."

"Not your king?"

"He wishes for you to feel safe at Ghastly."

Ophelia puzzles at that. "So he keeps saying."

On the stone staircases they came up the evening before, Stolm's brows are deeply knit. In a low tone, he asks, "Why do you not wish to be queen?"

She'd sooner gouge her eyes out, sooner no one had this unfettered power she and the Darkwielder possess. The kingdom might do better if its people had a true say, but she'd rather make Stolm a friend than an enemy, so she keeps that to herself.

"Magus doesn't have the best history with sovereigns. I want to free the magic-born, but not from a throne where I'm feared."

When the officer angles a surprised look at her, she fears she's offended him anyway, but he remains quiet, his expression turning pensive as they reach the landing above the great hall. The murals look even more brilliant by daylight, and the fires still burn. The sun also douses the hall, filling it with so much extra warmth that the sheerness of her dress makes some sense.

As Stolm begins his descent, Ophelia gently grabs his arm. "The library. Do we have time to see it?"

Stolm looks at her hand, then glances around them before asking, "Sen sagen Magiesian?"

She drops her hold. Is he asking if she speaks Magiesian because the tomes in the library are writ in it? By his peaked brow, she senses it's more. Some sort of personal test of trust.

"Jes," she replies. "Am arast melusan de reshen. Rigti komfan." *Yes. I love the melody of the language. It feels comforting.* Her words aren't as fluid as Stolm's, but she's pleased how they come back to her, how familiar they feel off her tongue.

He looks impressed, motioning his head as he leads them past the stairs. "Jes, rigti komfan." He pauses. "It makes me think of home."

"You're not from Magus," she wages. His accent lacks the drawl of Belly citizens, and there's only one other place she knows that still speaks in the Magie tongue.

He says, "I am from the Northern Territories. The valleys of Kúzlo."

It rings familiar. Icelands, she thinks, sure she's heard Falcon mention it. "I thought the North isn't bound to the monarchy's laws. Why did you leave?"

The corners of Stolm's eyes pull taut. "It was not an easy choice. There were always difficulties. Harsh weather, little food. The valleys survive by trading with other northern cities, using spellwork to grow what we could in greenhouses within the mountains. But over the years, the *volorost*, our high lord, began entertaining trade talks with the Gray King. His soldiers were rough. The risk, high. The council voted to decline an agreement for a long time, until the loss of several elders three years ago. The *volorost* promised King Osiris *migth* from our sacred mines to power industry."

"And power his army," Ophelia realizes with a sinking feeling.

Stolm shakes his head as if the idea is sacrilege. "In exchange, we had access to passages that let us bring raw materials from Magus into Kúzlo. It angered many tribesmen and those of us who disagreed left."

"Three years ago," Ophelia echoes. While she was hidden away in the mortal world. "It must've been hard to leave people you loved."

"My cousin," he admits, looking pained. "But I should not complain. After my father died, the Kosost found me in Duran, working for little money at a baker's cart. I am in his debt." Stolm clears emotion from his throat as they enter a wider hall with arched ogives. "This is the north tower."

It's deep in the mountain, where the walls grow jagged and the windows are scarcer, dimming the light and feel of the particles. Halfway down the hall, Stolm finally motions to twin doors that arch in a sweep of thick, dark wood a full two stories high.

"The library," he says. "But I am afraid you will have to explore later. We will be late."

They walk clockwise toward the eastern end of the palace, the lightness returning in Ophelia as the daylight and dust filter more generously back in through windows. She's noticed the particles rarely roam indoors here. Like her, they seem to prefer the open air, the lack of walls and doors, and a means of escape.

"Which part of the north do you come from?" Stolm asks her.

It seems easiest to say, "Western Magus, actually. Galdur." She was too young to remember where she was born or even the names of places she and Elora stayed. It'd been winter then, too.

Stolm looks doubtful at her. "That is no western accent you have."

Breakfast turns out to be through the next archway at the top of a solarium. It's warm as summer, despite several opened windows that stand among tall, marble pillars wrapped in lush, sprawling ivy.

They climb iron stairs that wind behind a red bounty tree dripping with fruit, and Ophelia's just grateful it isn't a Cibus; to face the Darkwielder, she needs all her wits.

Before she sees him, shadows curl against her mental shield, where she hasn't felt his presence since the courtyard yesterday. Among daylight that kisses plants, more glass, and pillars, he sits at the head of a filigreed table spread with every kind of decadent meat, elaborate platters of fruit, and delicately iced pastries.

Her mouth waters at the food. She's so hungry, she could eat it all.

The Darkwielder looks up from the correspondence before him. "Did you get lost?" A steaming mug meets his mouth. His sip is so casual, Ophelia might forget he's the same man who broke the necks of those wolven.

Stolm bows. "My fault, Kosost. I let her sleep late."

Ophelia puzzles that Stolm doesn't divulge their conversation or their stroll to the library while the Darkwielder studies him as if he's tallying something.

"Any report on our little project in the West yet?"

Stolm hesitates, then nods. "The first will arrive soon."

As the officer takes his leave, Ophelia asks, "Project?"

The Darkwielder shifts his emotionless gaze to her. "Measures to make mortals in the West safer during the war." He flicks a wrist, and there's no mistaking him for anything but who he is then, as a shadow snakes to the floor to yank a chair out for her.

Ophelia takes another seat a modest distance from him and ignores his budding irritation. Her stomach betrays her again with a loud growl, but as she reaches, ravenous, for a plate of pink moonberries, darkness sings forward and shoves the dish away.

"Your shields are weak." He punctuates each cold word in her mind, and she realizes, with dismay, that in her hunger she let her walls down. "With the tether between us, it's harder to shield me out, but you really must fortify yourself."

Turning a slow look at him, she asks, "Can you spy through the shadow inside me, or only rifle through my thoughts?"

"Secrets, Ophelia?"

"Of course not."

He ponders her, sipping at his mug. "The only shadows I'm able to see through are those I wield."

Taking that to mean he didn't see where she went last night, she relaxes.

Setting down his mug, he angles his head, those slate eyes skimming over her. "That dress is lovely. But you still look unwell."

"Dreams of monsters," she mutters, wishing it had been a dream. "And I haven't eaten." She raises a brow as she reaches for the pastries to her right.

Shadows rush across the table, and with growing ire, she watches the pastries mold and blacken from the inside out. A blight. A stain. A damn curse and waste of food.

Angrily, she reaches for a plate of muffins to her left.

His darkness burrows, rendering anything within her grasp to the same spoiled fate. "Second lesson, Ophelia," he says with chilling calm. "Enemies don't wait for you to strengthen your armor. They'll use any weakness to crush you."

Hotly, mockingly, she replies, "Good thing we're gods."

Calling a shadow to coil his finger, he toys with it, letting it slip under and over each tip. "Even gods can be weak." He says it as if she doesn't know this already—as if she doesn't blame her own weaknesses for the destruction she's wrought, for the men she's lost.

With a vicious look at the Darkwielder, she imagines herself a spear. A spear that might teach *him* a lesson.

From out the solarium window, she sees a sheen of dancing dust suddenly freeze, then rush through the open pane like the wind itself, cracking a marble pillar on its way toward the Darkwielder.

In a fluid motion, he's a moving phantom. Shadows clap, enveloping the particles and snuffing their heat with a blanket of darkness Ophelia can feel like a plunge of cold water. When the light disperses, he's standing across the table wearing a reprehensible smirk.

She's distracted for the briefest second by his casual dress—black pants with a fitted shirt left open at the neck, a tattoo peeking through.

When he continues to smile, her anger gets the better of her, spurring her to reach for her ankle to free Falcon's wing-hilted blade. Vaulting to her feet, she stabs the knife straight through the plate of decayed pastries to prove no other point than she won't sit there and take what he dishes at her.

The pastries *hiss*, and the Darkwielder's eyes narrow on the blade, recognition alighting in his gaze. Flicking his attention back to her, he says, "Your reflexes are impressive. If our enemy were as capable as pastry, you might be ready for war."

Simmering, she rips the knife from the plate, returning it to its sheath while she keeps her eyes on him. "I know exactly what my enemy is capable of."

The Darkwielder splays two hands on the table and leans forward, as if the words are a personal challenge. "Do you?"

Nails. Cold, sharp talons drag down her mental walls, ripping them open—ripping her open.

She lowers to sit as pictures move in her head, catapulting her into the mind of someone surrounded by soldiers in a dim, sprawling bedchamber.

Terror swarms Ophelia's senses as, across the room, the Gray King comes into view. He towers over a small shape and draws long, siphoner's breaths. Feeding on magic, feeding on...a little boy.

Oh, gods.

On her knees, straining against the hold of soldiers, a young woman with a golden braid down her back screams. Face wet with tears, she reaches for the boy.

Pain—ugly, hateful pain—implodes through the body and mind she's inhabiting. It grips their lungs so tightly, they can't breathe. They fall to their knees. Soon, ash swirls across the chamber floor, and death pervades the room.

The images fade like falling stars, and Ophelia's gripping the filigreed table, feeling as though she's the one who can't breathe. "What...What was that?" It was horrid. It was...

"A memory," he says darkly.

She cuts a look to the Darkwielder, shocked to find his gray eyes shining with moisture. "Yours?"

"Yes."

As she processes that he showed her a memory of himself at Gray Castle—that with this tether, he can do that—he turns away, stalking down the length of the table to retrieve a dish.

"I can't have you destroying Ghastly," he says, glancing at the cracked pillar as he sets the plate before her.

A spread of mouthwatering cheeses, moonberries, and meat, untouched by his shadows.

"Eat," he instructs, eyes still haunted. "Then I'll show you what we're protecting here."

CHAPTER 19
GUILDS & GAMES

GHASTLY
7TH DAY IN THE NEW WINTER
OPHELIA IS WITH THE DARKWIELDER

The Darkwielder moves like a ghost.

Through a hidden door that masquerades as a grand fireplace, he disappears so quickly that Ophelia starts to call out after him. Only, she isn't sure how to address him after the personal memory he showed her.

She slips after him into natural shadows where a single lantern suffuses rough walls and a wooden staircase with light, carving the Darkwielder's pale features with a deadly sort of beauty.

From a hook near the door, he hands her an unremarkable cloak. "Wear this, unless you're ready to announce yourself."

Taking it, she says, "People call you 'king' or 'Darkwielder.' What's your true name?"

He pauses in the midst of shrugging on a longcoat, caught in surprise that threads his raven brows. "You...want my given name?"

She swallows. Why does he make it sound so intimate? "If we're to be equals."

"I was born Valkieran Balcombe." His brows hold their frown. "Anyone I was...close with...called me Kier." His name creaks out slowly, painfully, like a door that hasn't been opened in a long while.

"Kier," she echoes.

The way his eyes soften, she fears it was a mistake to ask for it. It's too easy to sympathize with someone when knowing their name feels like a gift.

Blinking the softness away, Kier pulls his coat taut. "Come."

Cautiously, Ophelia ties the cloak around herself and follows him up the stairs.

"The histories of the Great Siege are replete with lies," he intones as they climb.

The stairs are narrow enough his arm brushes hers, and she hates that it sparks the smallest tingle. "What does Osiris taking Gray Castle have to do with Ghastly?"

He glances at her as they crest to a door. "You'll see." Pulling his hood up, he pushes out and Ophelia's struck by the sound of muted chatter as they enter a dim alcove curtained with velvet fabric.

Shadowing her view, he steps so near that Ophelia can scent his heady mixture of smoke and cloves. She finds herself holding her breath as he lifts a hand toward her cheek. Reaching past it with a smirk, he draws up the hood of her cloak to shroud her, then steps away, motioning her out of the alcove.

With an exhale, Ophelia leads him into the light. "What is—" *Maether* washes over her, taking her question captive.

They've come out on the top floor of a grand foyer and stand on a balcony that wraps the opulent hall below in a full square. With every inch swept in marble and intricate gold filigree, it's not the dark comfort of the east wing. It's royal. The ceiling is domed and bedecked with a hundred ethereal murals, and the space is filled with pillars, candelabras, ogives, and statues that Fabricaters crafted in celebration—not condemnation—of Magiesian history.

No doubt Osiris Lestat would shudder to see it.

No doubt he'd burn it to the ground.

She's filled with awe, and something she can't quite name, at the way this part of Ghastly sings an ode to the Magie rule. A rule the Darkwielder seems determined to resurrect.

They follow the balcony, him leading her around the square hall past a statue of the primordial goddess Selene.

Ophelia has to look twice at the deity up close. The goddess's high cheekbones, the spill of hair shaped down her back, her pointed chin—they bear a likeness to her mother. She's grateful her own hair is spun half-up and she wears a hood. It wouldn't be a stretch if someone saw her with the Darkwielder, next to this statue, and wondered who she is. She's not ready for that yet.

"What do you feel?" he asks, as though he's genuinely curious.

She feels...energy. Quick and light, but also deep and slow. Strong as steel and slippery as silk. A mingling of textures and life and...

"Everything," she breathes.

When his lip curves in understanding, his smile is nearly boyish. "See the staircases?" He flicks a tattooed finger.

At equidistant points, three separate stairs forged of marble and flecked with gold descend to meet another square hall like the one in which they stand, with sweeping doorways and a bustle of activity.

Passing one of the staircases, Ophelia notes a long flag bannering down a wall. Its red threading forms the image of a throne and, if she's not mistaken, the likeness of the Dark Shadow Dagger.

She finds two more flags across the hall—one with blue thread that forges a stone on its throne, and the other with green stitching that draws a third throne and a necklace. An amulet.

She slows in her stride. Her mother, the majestic Elora Dannan, once possessed that relic. Where is it now?

"Are those the original guild flags?" she inquires.

"They were made at Ghastly and tailored by Spellcasters. The first were burned." The word—*burned*—leaves his lips like a blade.

Once she's taken in their surroundings, the people walking the halls pull Ophelia's attention. So, this is court.

"They're all Magies," she mutters.

Men and women, young and old, are filing out of doors, trudging up the stairs, laughing and speaking the old tongue like this were any ordinary life. They look healthy, wearing fine cloaks and coats, their dresses and pants fabricated to perfection. They look as though they've never wanted for anything.

Among the faces, she seeks anyone familiar. It's futile—Elora is dead—but looking for her is an old habit, a bruise of a hope.

"They shouldn't exist," Kier says, his face drawn as he watches his people.

"Why shouldn't they exist?" she asks.

Kier looks at her. "The stories say Osiris slaughtered the guilds. That there were no survivors."

"They're survivors of the Great Siege?" With widened eyes, she looks anew at the faces passing by.

The differences between Magie orders are as pronounced here as in Magus, but there's an air of pride in the way people walk. She can pick out the Matterists by their fluid silken frocks, and the Morphists by their stiff gaits and jackets that gleam with buckles, buttons, or snaps. The Witchists may be most obvious, though, for how they favor lovely jewels and specks of vibrant color. No one wears black, she notes. Perhaps here the color is reserved for the Darkwielder and his legion.

Where the square hall turns, Kier steers them beneath the Witchists' banner. In a subtle little alcove where a statue of Erebus stands, he presses against the seams. A half-wall opens up and inside, down a hall, there's yet another hidden door that leads down a back staircase.

One could get eternally lost in this palace.

"Do you use passageways often?"

As they climb down, Kier says, "The former Witchist king liked his hidden passageways once, too."

"The former king," she echoes.

"My father. He filled what became Gray Castle with tunnels, from the bedchambers to the wings, the library and kitchens. They were excellent for spying and disappearing quickly." At his raised brow, she gleans he knows them firsthand. Passing through the glow of a lantern, Kier says, "While Osiris ravaged the main wings of the castle, survivors of his attack fled with children through the walls."

Her heart thumps. "Tell me more of the survivors?" Her mother would've been an infant among them. Who might she have escaped with?

"Servants, distant kin of the Magie rule, some others. They scattered across remote northern villages," he says. "Children grew and had children of their own. It took time to discover them and create a place they could reunite."

"A safe place," she says, the words an echo of Falcon's only weeks ago. The thought of him stirs an ache in her chest.

When Kier holds the door ajar for her, she looks up, not expecting the view.

They've bypassed all the common areas and stand at the base of a tall, grand dais. Black-carpeted stairs ascend to where three thrones sit. At the back of the chairs looks a shrine forged from golden statues. It spires to the ceiling in the shape of a tree and connects to a grand chandelier.

"Do you want to go up?" he asks.

She certainly doesn't.

If he's brought her here to convince her she ought to stake her claim and take her throne, he's achieved the opposite. It's...too much.

"I'm tired," she says.

Wending back the way they came, Kier's expression is sullen, the slope of his jaw taut. Something he said earlier strikes her, but she waits to ask him about it until they resettle near a balcony overlooking the guilds.

"If your father was the Witchist king, how does that make you Osiris's nephew?"

"It doesn't," Kier says flatly, pressing a thumb against the crown ringed round his finger. "That's only what he told me. My mother and I survived his siege, but we didn't escape Osiris." A shadow ebbs to the surface of Kier's hand where it rests on the railing. His eyes darken on the tendril, so menacingly she can feel a shiver in the marking on her chest.

"Does your mother...still live?"

He nods, but doesn't elaborate.

"What did Osiris do to you?"

Kier looks at her. "It's a long, tragic story. One I don't feel like telling."

Though she hasn't tried to breach Kier's mind like he has hers, she can sense his walls rise.

Forcing her attention back to the people, she mutters, "So you found survivors and brought them here."

In passing conversations, she catches enough to glean that Magies have lives at Ghastly, even jobs. There's talk of classes, sages who teach, healers, studies in science, cooking. And in the hall far below, she notices several people gathered in front of ornate, golden doors. They appear to be measuring, making notes in a book. Perhaps preparations for the coronation Kier is planning.

"How often do you visit this side of the mountain?" she asks. "Do you ever show your face here, or just lurk at balconies and in the walls?" Does he have friends?

He frowns, and she's not sure whether she shouted that last question across their tether, or it's in response to the notion that he lurks about. "Once a week, there's a council," he replies. "When you decide to trust me, you can meet the appointed members from each guild."

Trusting him is not in her plan. And yet, her empathy festers the longer she observes him, the more she suspects Osiris kept him and his mother prisoner. Hurt them.

Maybe it's the tether, but behind the wicked smirks and terrifying shadows, she can sense a blanket of woe that makes her feel something other than loathing for Valkieran Balcombe. She senses he knows what it is to take abuse for being Magie, what it is to be hunted and made to hide. He knows, like her, that the Gray King will never stop pursuing them, not until every god's line is under his heel.

That's why Ghastly exists. That's why Kier made it.

She can feel his cool touch brush against her mental shield, a gentle finger tracing a cheek. "What are you thinking?" he asks.

I'm thinking you can't know what it means to me to see this place, to have ancestors and answers so close after wondering so long.

Except...he can.

Come with me, he said to her in Wythe. *You'll be safe. And we will rebuild this world together.*

They're two of the same. Seemingly the last two in existence to wield god magic, their histories are as interwoven as their fates.

"I'm thinking I can't forgive the things you've done as the Dark-wielder," she admits, "any more than I can forgive myself. But I understand some of it." Among his crimes, he let many in the Belly and elsewhere suffer, hoping to keep the Gray King's focus from Ghastly and the last of their ancestry.

She flattens a palm over her locket, conscious of how her mind is clouding more with each moment she's here. He hasn't paraded her around or announced she's the goddess returned. Nevertheless, as an earnest smile shapes Kier's mouth at her confession, it feels like a weight being draped over her shoulders, as though he's settled a queen's robe around her.

The thought makes her take a full step back. Maybe he's more cunning than she thought.

As residents pass by, Ophelia tucks her chin and drops her mental walls to speak in his mind: *This is why you said to wait to give you an answer, isn't it? No matter what you've done, you knew I'd agree to ally once I saw this. All you had to do was bait me to Ghastly.*

In the glow of candelabras, he is every bit the Darkwielder again, eyes unreadable.

When he doesn't deny her claim, she thinks of the curse she extracted from the Gray King—the curse the Darkwielder unleashed inadvertently on Magus. Inadvertently... Because of his hatred. She'd felt that hatred. His curse was cast out of vengeance, to make Osiris suffer. Except...

Her stomach drops.

No. No, it couldn't have been orchestrated for something as childish as getting her attention, as devious as forcing her return to Magus so he could get her to Ghastly.

Kier steals the distance between them in a single step. Quietly, coldly, he says, "I would have done far worse to get your attention, goddess. To get you to see what's at stake and work with me to find the other relics and restore our rule."

She blanches. No. She cannot be standing here feeling a morsel of empathy for a man who is monster enough to risk the very kingdom he claims he wants to save.

He bends a cheek near hers, so they might look like lovers whispering, and says, "If I have to be the monster a thousand times for you, I will." She stiffens at the threat. "Or," he counters, "you can agree to trust me and we can work together. For our people."

Agree. He keeps saying that like trust is a choice. For the first time, it dawns on her that maybe it is.

She needs to learn control, but if the Dark Shadow Dagger weren't on his hip, or she had the Matterists' amulet, Ophelia would be as powerful as he. Maybe more, because she commands the breath of magic.

She could bring Ghastly to the ground, or help save it.

This is why Kier wants her on his side. This is why he wants her alliance.

If trust is a choice, it's simply the choice to work with him, instead of against, which brings her back to her mission. "You said the other relics are well hidden. Do you have ideas about where to look?"

He angles his head back, gaze dark and intense, his power so immense that her cells seem to shudder. But she will not so much as lean, let alone flinch.

A devilish smirk. "Will telling you about the relics buy me some trust?" At her leveling scowl, he chuckles. Running a thumb and a forefinger down the sides of his chin, he says, "Osiris kept the lightstone in the vault at one point, but it wasn't there when I finally robbed him of the dagger."

"How did you free your relic?"

His expression clouds. "Like a ghost."

She rolls her eyes in irritation. He's playing with her now. Fine. "And the amulet?" She hopes she doesn't sound as eager as she feels.

Kier rests his elbows on the balcony. "For as paranoid as the Gray King was, he rarely checked the walls at Gray Castle. Eavesdropping was too easy." He fiddles with the crown on his ring. "Osiris was in a rage once about 'the source.' He lamented to his commander that it wouldn't matter if it—you—were undiscoverable, if he could just find the amulet. I realized many years later what he meant."

Ophelia releases a breath. "Osiris doesn't have it." Though he let the kingdom think so.

Apart from counting on Ophelia to cure his curse, it was this absence of the amulet that drove him to hunt her. The amulet is the only relic Osiris never possessed. The last threat to his reign, until Kier stole back the dagger for the Witchists.

Which means whoever fled from the palace with Ophelia's infant mother all those years ago must have had the amulet, and must have given it to Elora when she was old enough to keep it safe.

Ophelia thrums with hope. If her mother was the last to have the Matterists' relic, then the key to finding it is figuring out where Elora went after she left Ophelia in Galdur.

She's ponderous until she feels Kier shift beside her. "Well, goddess?" he asks. "Do you trust me yet?"

The allyship.

Watch your queen, she can hear Grimm tell her, back when they used to play chess in his office at the academy.

She chooses her reply wisely, as one should when making deals with a god, so if things go awry or some hidden magic were at play, rendering it an oath, one wouldn't be bound to those words to the point of peril.

"All right. I agree to your instruction and to spy. Whatever it takes to obtain the relics."

At the ghost of an arrogant smile returned, it takes every effort not to throw him off the balcony.

THREE

MOVES &
COUNTERMOVES

CHAPTER 20
SERPENTS & WINGS

GHASTLY
8TH DAY IN THE NEW WINTER
OPHELIA IS WITH THE DARKWIELDER

Even indestructible, unending darkness flees in the presence of light. Therefore, let us not waste energy fearing the dark. Rather, the failing of the light.

Primordial Gods: A Forging of Power, Section IV—A Study in Balance by Virginia Knowle, sage in the Matterists Guild

From beneath the tangled limbs of the lumen and shadow trees, Ophelia surveys the courtyard and wonders if, apart from her attendants, the staff at Ghastly were told to keep their distance from her, or if it's knowing the dark king could arrive any moment that keeps them so focused on their task, plucking fruit in the frosty morning.

As she awaits Kier—her instructor—something brushes against the back of her cloak.

A flower lies on the ground, so blood-red it might be black, its bud tapered to a point. Careful in retrieving it to avoid the thorns nestled along its stalk, she looks up to find the woman in black. The one who was lingering in the gardens on Ophelia's arrival.

Posed near a hedge, the woman holds a basket of stems, watching her.

Ophelia hesitates, straddling the line between curiosity and suspicion, as she always does. At the Constelli, her suspicion of those in power kept her alive, but also fueled her bold mouth, which sometimes earned her bruises.

Curiosity wins at present and she moves in the direction of the woman.

Power.

Cold, taut, and emanating, it stills Ophelia mid-stride.

"Throwing you to vultures first thing after breakfast isn't the instruction I had in mind." From just behind her, Kier comes round to pluck the thorned stem from her grasp with two long fingers. "Fortunately, the woods will be less...crowded."

Frowning in the direction of the woman, he tosses the stem aside, shifting to obscure Ophelia's view and command her full attention. The space vanishes between them as he wraps an arm around her waist, like she is a ship and he a bloody marauder.

As if he can feel her irritation rise like sails on an angry wind, he whispers, "Do try to stow your ire until we've landed this time."

Her eyes flash, recalling how last time they flew she shoved him mid-air. "You deserved that and worse."

As a buoyant mist envelops them, he only laughs.

High above Ghastly, the network of stone stairs sweeps into view around the steep mountains that shield the palace. Beyond is the empty road they traveled in on. Farther, miles of forest.

Kier alights them onto a slope of land that offers a distant view of Ghastly and the unfamiliar dark waters that lap at it, gesturing to the woods. "This should work."

Her boots crunch snow as they walk to a spot where the ground is even.

The wind is harsher in the open, not that Kier seems to notice. She's grateful for the layered shirts and fur-lined leggings Hannah showed up with this morning, after Ophelia told her she wanted to train outside Ghastly's walls. Lest she lose control.

Kier holds up a wrist, allowing shadows to seep. They uncoil themselves to form a wide circle around them in the snow.

The sky winks, and she isn't surprised to see the particles that veil this part of the wood gather. They're either curious or suspicious about whatever's going to happen. Or perhaps it's she who is suspicious, after his lesson with the wolven.

Kier hardly looks like he's concentrating, and his power pulses swiftly across the tether to her, so viscerally it feels as though she could touch it.

At his behest, the shadows that forge a circle rise into a wall around them.

Panic licks up her spine.

The wall's not spinning like it did in Wythe—it's not even a hundredth of that size. All the same, her chest tightens and her breaths grow ragged at the memory of flashing teeth and talons, at the echo of children screaming, at remembering the sacrifice she couldn't make—*kill the king or vanquish the shadows.*

"Take the wall down," Kier says.

She throws a hand toward the relic on his hip. "You'll just raise another one. What about sparring or shielding?" She's better at those—and they don't stir her nightmares.

His expression holds no compassion. "You agreed to instruction. I suggest we start by addressing your weaknesses. Take down the wall, Ophelia."

"I can't," she grits out. Not permanently, not without her own relic.

"You can."

The wall starts to spin.

She shakes her head at him even as a serpent flashes out from the darkness, slithering with a hiss across the snow—but not toward her.

Fangs bared, the serpent fixes on its master.

"What are you doing?" she shouts at him.

In her mind, she sees shadow beasts leap, vicious teeth tear a soldier's neck, the hamlet burning, bodies falling, the king escaping.

She fights the images of her nightmares back in order to focus on the serpent that lashes toward Kier. "Call it off!" she screams.

Kier only stares harder at her. *"Take down the wall."*

This is ludicrous. Perhaps it's a bluff. Perhaps the serpent can't hurt its master.

But it lunges, sinking fangs into Kier's calf. He growls with the pain of it, but doesn't so much as swat at the creature.

Of course his shadows can hurt him. The same way fire can singe a Bender of Flame who isn't careful. Like a spell can turn on a caster inept at their craft. Like Ophelia's own scorching light could swallow her up if a single intention were misinterpreted.

Magic can be ruthless at destroying one's enemies, and just as capable of destroying oneself.

She calls the dust, willing it to eviscerate the snake. It does. But it doesn't matter. Two more serpents skitter from the wall, and when the light of the particles scatters them, too, four more emerge, then eight.

She growls with the frustration of this damn lesson, trying to target each one, to be careful the light doesn't touch Kier, all while he stands there—looking at her—enduring bite after bite from his own shadows.

"Try harder."

She could draw *maether* from the elements into herself, like how she picked the lock to Trix's hotel room. But that approach is a crutch, easier than what she keeps tamped down. Easier than the thing that rendered part of the Constelli to ruins. Easier than the magic she accessed deep within herself in Wythe that vanquished a hundred of Kier's beasts.

Her raw magic—the wild light in her bones.

Tapping it left her unconscious last time, unable to ensure Rune stayed with them. The idea of reaching for it... It feels too close to her nightmares.

But there are maybe fifty serpents lashing at Kier's legs now, and sweat crests his brow.

"Ophelia!" He quakes on his feet, emanating power but refusing to use it. Waiting to see what she'll do to the shadows he has unleashed—to *his* raw magic.

She cannot destroy the darkness, but maybe she can take its power by giving it what it craves.

From the ridges of her lumen mark, light spills out of her like treewater from a Syca spile—so much light—seeping until it begins to form a shape the way Kier's shadows do. What glows before her, inconceivably, is a massive golden dragon with wings as wide as the circle Kier's shadows forge.

Kier's eyes reflect its light, and his shock.

Maybe she should tremble at the sight of it. She's never seen anything like this. Yet, there's something familiar and inevitable about the existence of her lightform, as though it's been there all along, waiting for her to be strong enough—ready enough—to wield it.

The darkness slowly turns its many heads. One by one, the serpents writhe over each another, reaching eagerly toward her lightdragon.

She doesn't have to tell it to devour the darkness. It's wise and knowing. It's her, or an extension of her, lowering its mighty wings as if in an embrace. Then those golden wings swallow the serpents whole.

It draws a gasping sigh from Kier's direction. "So warm," he mutters, sounding relieved.

The shadow wall vanishes, and the golden dragon fades, its light crackling as it seeps into the snow, into the earth, back into her.

Ophelia feels as if she is everywhere. In the trees, in the sod under the ice and powder, in the roots and sky, in the dust that circles overhead. She is everything and nothing at once. Uniquely made but insignificant in the whole of the world. A wielder of life, yet merely a conduit for something far bigger. Something that doesn't know of limits or lament its weakness. Something that just...exists.

The woods are silent.

Kier lays his hand with the silver rings flat to his chest, as if he can feel it, too.

There's less dizziness this time, with her light returned to her. A surging sense of irritation rises, though, at Kier and his methods.

She storms at the infuriating bastard. "You couldn't warn me of your lesson plans?" she hisses, shoving at him. She doesn't care his legs are covered in snake bites. "You die, I die, right?" The tether. "I could've killed us."

"Would you have been sorry?" he grates.

She ignores the stupid question, how close it hits to her nightmares. "That wasn't training." It felt like another test. It felt like... "What was that?" she demands.

Before she can shove him again, Kier catches her wrist in his hand. His grin is wicked, his breaths rough as he spins her around, her back against his chest, his cheek against hers, facing her toward the scorched ring her light left in the snow. "That was you slaying your fears, goddess. Now, we can begin."

His touch disappears. When she turns, he's loosing a less threatening shadow to mask the punctures on his legs.

It takes a moment, while he works, to realize his lesson has driven away the guilt she's been wracked with, and her nightmare of Wythe.

That she no longer trembles with fear, but with power.

CHAPTER 21
WEAKNESS & WEAPONS
GHASTLY
10TH DAY IN THE NEW WINTER
OPHELIA IS WITH THE DARKWIELDER

She can't decipher Kier's weakness.

For two days, Ophelia searches for cracks in his armor. At breakfast, he's the irritating dark king, his shadows always near, the dagger on his hip. He doesn't drop his walls, even as he reads correspondence from the camps stationed along the Shadow river or fields reports from Stolm about "incidents."

He doesn't seem bothered by the berth his soldiers give him, either.

As far as she can tell, he has no visits from family, from friends, from any special females or males...unless they service him after Ophelia bids him goodnight. Even with Stolm, his most likely confidante, there's little banter outside war talk or planning the coronation Kier intends to hold.

On the third day, she tucks the wonder about weaknesses away to focus on her progress. Her control. She will not find herself in another situation where she's forced to fight impulsively and make sacrifices that haunt her.

Kier laughs at the idea that they warm up with steel. Rather, his shadows dart at her like knives and her light becomes shield or sheath.

Oscillating between brandishing the dust and calling bursts of raw magic forth from inside her, Ophelia revels in getting faster, surer. If or when she faces enemy magic and weapons in war, she might actually be able to unarm soldiers without obliterating them.

She misses the weight of a sword, though. Not that she could bring herself to wield one against Kier. It would only make her think about how his eyes aren't the challenging, sharp-blue of Falcon's that light at the thrill of her every thrust. And Falcon wouldn't want her distracted. He'd want her to be smart, to use every opportunity to grow stronger and find her opponent's weakness.

In which case, she shouldn't play the sound of Falcon's voice in her mind, or remember the rumble of it against her belly, the ripple of his muscles, his strong hands on her thighs, his tongue on her skin, the skittering of his tattoos.

Stay focused.

That's what she tells herself she's doing when she starts to enjoy the feel of magic flowing between her and Kier, the chill of his shadows chasing the flame of her light as they clash and dance in the trees.

It isn't until the afternoon, when her light crackles and eats up his darkness, that she starts to circle something that hints at weakness. As Kier is left empty-handed, an odd expression smooths his face—the same look of relief as when her lightdragon gobbled up his serpents.

"Mmm," he mutters, like he's savoring it, before tugging on his coat and stretching his shoulders out, readying to fly back.

She studies him, her skin still tingling, suspecting why the victory felt too easy. "Why did you let me win?" she asks.

As shadows unfurl around them, Kier settles a hand at her back and meets her eyes. "It's been a long time, Ophelia, since I felt anything but cold."

CHAPTER 22
STAGS & GHOSTS

In a gorge north of Jagst, Falcon thrusts himself like a sword, silent as a mountain cat, from his perch off a low branch.

The stag has no time to keen in surprise.

Landing at its side, he drives a stake through the artery in its neck.

The *vis stagisi*, a rare stag, falls in an avalanche of ice-blue fur.

Panting, Falcon watches its blood turn the snow red and trail toward the half-frozen stream. He's not devout, but he closes his eyes and lays a hand to its side, the way northerners do to guide an animal's spirit home.

"Gosten frist nen," he whispers to the wind. *Gods free you.* The ritual placates some guilt. He doesn't kill an animal that some call sacred lightly, but there's no getting to Kúzlo without a gift. And ever since Trix told him...everything...Cleo's vision has ticked in his head like a clock.

Trix couldn't say *when* it ends. Her sister saw flashes of a celebration, the moons looking strange, and bloodshed. She saw the North in the fight and Falcon among them.

He doesn't let himself dwell on the rest.

First things first.

His best guess is that it will take a month or so for the Gray King to set his sights on the Belly, or find some other way to attack the heart of the Darkwielder's forces. And Trix will be expected to check in with the legion soon. They have to get to Kúzlo.

It's taken six days to track the stag. All the while, Falcon's been a live wire, replaying how he looked Ophelia in the eye and told her he'd be back, thinking of her with the Darkwielder.

He scrubs his bloody hands clean with snow and, once again, fights the urge to find her that's tearing him up inside.

Getting to his feet, he whistles into the trees.

"About time," a Shadowcaster gripes as she trails Trix out of where Falcon convinced the rest of their party to stay upwind. "If we'd done it our way, we could've finished this days ago, instead of freezing our bits off—"

"You're not in Magus, Anesh," Trix says evenly. "Falcon knows the beasts of the North. Our job is to make sure he gets to the icelands, nothing else."

Falcon folds his arms at the brunette with a black-skull stud through her nose. "And as I've said," he grates, all adrenaline after that kill, "your shadows can trigger traps around here. Now keep it down, or we'll have wolven on us."

Anesh's coal eyes smolder at Falcon, but she clamps her yap shut, her gaze drifting to the trees as the other soldiers trek out. First comes a wraith called Ashë with plaited, white braids and a light footstep—a girl who lost her tongue in the fight arena and, as Falcon learned last night, plays a wicked hand of crooks and scales. She's someone Trix assured him they can trust, unlike the four Shadowcasters from the phaeton who come next. Two copper-haired, ruffian cousins who look more suited to smuggling than playing soldiers, and two others as dangerous as they might be dumb for how trigger-happy they were with their shadows the night before, scaring off dinner.

Rubbing his jaw, Falcon assesses the stag as Trix steps beside him, handing him back the thick fur coat he took off earlier.

"It didn't smell you coming," she says, pride in her voice.

"Good spell," he allows, shrugging the pelt on. If the spell hadn't worked and the stag got a whiff of him, *he'd* be bleeding in the snow, impaled on three feet of antlers, and the next stage of this suicidal plan to win the North over would stand no chance.

Above the icy gorge, Falcon checks the sky. With the moons rising, it's tipping pink. "The Gatekeeper doesn't barter passage after sundown. Let's get the stag to Jagst."

Falcon still knows the streets by heart.

On a dead-end road in the city of stone and clay, lanterns have just lit and the ritual, not to mention just being here again, makes him anxious.

Looking through a trading post window, he tenses at the sight of Dorothy Joncaire. From a distance, the elder of short stature with spider-silk hair almost looks benign hunched at the counter.

Beside him, Trix draws her face back from the pane. "The Gatekeeper's an old potion-maker? You couldn't have just sweet-talked her?"

He side-eyes the Spellcaster with a withering look. "Dorothy's not what she seems. And if anyone ought to know appearances mean shit, it's you. Right, *Desi*?"

"Fair enough." Trix's brow forms a wicked point. "So? You've been mum about the Gatekeeper. What's the deal?"

"She's three hundred years old and has more power in her ruby glasses than we wield on our best day." He looks back through the window. "Anything that goes from Jagst to the icelands goes through Dorothy, and if she thinks we pose a threat, we won't be leaving with all our faculties."

Trix rolls her shoulders. "Well, this will be fun."

Falcon's breath fogs the trading post window. "Just don't say anything about the vision. Kúzlo's only purpose is protecting the icelands." The sacred mountains. "She won't invite talks of war."

The tribe has various layers of defense, but Gatekeepers like Dorothy stationed in villages that surround Kúzlo are the first line against threats. And war constitutes a threat.

Trix absently runs a finger over the jewel in her leather cuff, her eyes darting with thoughts.

"No magic," Falcon warns. "That won't go well." He glances over a shoulder at the six Shadowcasters spreading out down the street, narrowing in on the two with twitchy shadows who guard the stag. They look like fish out of water in a city where mortals and magic-born survive by skilled trades, not blades.

"Leave your dogs outside," he tells Trix, then before she can answer, he pushes quietly into the post.

A thick waft of moss and woodsmoke washes over him, chased by a stirring scent of anise. He'd forgotten. Apart from spells that could crush a man's bones, the Gatekeeper always made damn good cookies.

The post's empty of traders this close to closing. Candles jump in holders around the store, and Falcon's surprised to see the room's still arranged with the hand-carved shelves and tables he remembers, all of them piled with pelts, oils, wax, grain sacks, Cibus tobacco, and hand-spun goods. Though, tables look a bit sparser now.

He pauses in the doorway, his gaze stuck at the back of the room, where he can almost feel the ghost of his twin. See her seven-year-old pout in the mirrors, hear an echo of Kaitriona's ire in his head as she wore out the floors. *Why can't we go back and tell them what really happened, Falcon? The tribal council would believe you, and we wouldn't be leaving with our tails between our legs. You know Reya and I were going to train for patrol someday! Now what will I be?*

When Trix steps through the door, Falcon shuts the memory down.

From the glass counter encasing potions, creams, capsules, elixirs, tonics, and oddities, where Dorothy tinkers over an open flame, the Gatekeeper speaks without looking up, "Nast plasi wist hasen, jagerin?" Her voice is thin as parchment.

"What'd she say?" Trix whispers, a hand sliding to the doubled-edged blade at her waist. Falcon can't blame her. Dorothy's got a way of speaking that comes out like she's cursing you.

"She said, 'There's no place like home,'" he translates under his breath, leaving out the last word. *Jagerin*. Little slayer.

CHAPTER 23
LORDS & GATES

The Gatekeeper remembers him, then.

Behind the counter, her black-bead eyes come up, hard as bullets on Falcon, as she slips into broken English. "I warned you about returning to the North. But you young lords. You're all fools."

As Dorothy reaches to grab a bottle beneath her counter, Trix catches Falcon's eye, shaking her head as if she still can't believe the truth Falcon told her last night. "'Lord,'" she mutters under her breath.

"A foolish one," he amends.

The Gatekeeper pours a dash of powder into her palm, taking a pinch between twiggy fingers to add to the bowl that's heating. It causes a burst of sulfuric smoke to cloud the air, and when it clears, Dorothy plucks a small object from the bowl, nestling it into a cobalt box.

Snapping it shut, she ambles down from her stool and disappears behind the counter, reappearing in a chair that wheels itself and her small frame in front of them.

As a sign of peace, Falcon lowers his chin, keeping his hands clasped where she can see them.

Her legs and wrists curl inward, more than last they met, as she gestures a hand. "You look much like your siblings. And I see you kept the coat I spelled for you." Dorothy observes it, half-obscured by the thicker fur he wears. She scrutinizes the rest of him. "You've grown strong, handsome, and...who is this?" Dorothy nudges her spectacles up her short nose, peering at Trix. "Not your sister, but as hot-headed, I sense."

"Just a friend," he replies. "We have important information to deliver to the *volorost*. In person."

Dorothy laughs, the sound like paper set to fire. "The *volorost* has initiated The Sanctioning, jagerin. He is not conducting business with outsiders at present."

The Sanctioning.

Falcon shifts his weight uneasily. "It's a little soon for the tournament of heirs."

Volorost aren't often in a rush to name their successor. Their life can march hundreds of years or more, thanks to the power bestowed on the position back when Descendants first named a *volorost* guardian of the icelands.

Dorothy runs a finger over the box in her lap. "As you are no longer tribe, *jagerin*, I cannot tell you of tribal decisions. Unless"—she drags the word out like a scratch—"you intend to declare your return as a challenger in the tournament. As the heir you are."

Falcon blanches at the word.

"Heir?" Trix asks. He can feel her attention on him. He's not sure why he didn't mention that detail.

The Gatekeeper wheels closer. "Your friend does not know who you are?"

"It didn't come up," Falcon replies. He'd rather forget who his father is, but he supposes that's not an option now.

Dorothy cracks the lid on the box she holds, turning it around so Falcon can see inside.

Reality hits at the sight of seven lustrous rings. White-silver and carved with elaborate wings, each holds a flat blue stone in its eye, blue as the mountains the gems were hewn from.

"Tournament rings," he says tightly, for Trix's benefit. "They're imbued." He wonders at the assortment of temporary affinities Dorothy's chosen.

Seven rings for seven vying heirs.

When Falcon left fifteen years ago, his father—Kúzlo's *volorost*—had nine heirs on the path for successorship. "Is..." Falcon clears his throat. "Is Kessan vying?" *Is he still alive?*

Dorothy snaps the box shut. "Are you declaring yourself?"

Falcon slides a look to Trix. By the set of her jaw, he can see she's tracking what's happening here. This is a sure way into Kúzlo. He doesn't mention, though, that if he declares himself and fights in the tournament, live or die, it's unlikely he'll leave the North again. But Falcon's been molded by hard choices. What's another to win a war he's craved half his life? A war that has to play out like Cleo saw it—with the North in the fight.

He'll do whatever it takes to get an audience with his father as fast as possible. The rest, he'll figure out.

"I'll declare myself," he negotiates, "if you imbue me an official tournament ring and let me bring the crew of my choosing from Jagst into Kúzlo. You passage us safely through the gates tonight."

A little smile forms on her crooked mouth, and Falcon suspects he forgot to ask for something. Words mean everything when you negotiate here. Quickly, the Gatekeeper asks, "What have you to give me in return?"

The price.

Falcon motions to the wall behind Dorothy's counter that's filled with the heads of every storied creature that ran through his nightmares as a boy, save for a couple no one's ever felled.

"I've got something for your collection no one else has." He signals to Trix. "I'll even clean it for you."

When the Shadowcasters drag in the carcass, a greedy light seems to glow in the Gatekeeper's eyes. Lore says *vis stagisi* bear regenerative magic. Whomever wears the hide or rack of one can restore things lost. Homes. Limbs. Maybe life itself, depending on the wielder.

Dorothy eyes its rack. "The horn." Frowning, she juts a finger to where a tip of the rack's been broken off.

Falcon can feel the new tattoo below his hip skitter. Outwardly, he only shrugs a shoulder. "If you don't want the stag—"

"It is done," the Gatekeeper says, and he feels an invisible force of energy slam through him. "You will have your tournament ring, *jagerin*, passage for eight, and nothing more."

Passage is instant. The pressure's so strong, Falcon heaves his stomach with the rest of the Darkwielder's emissaries on the other side of the *migth*-fueled gate.

Jagst is gone.

Falcon recognizes the field where they stand. It's a veritable ice bowl, a vast field of frozen shelves that bulge and jut from the ground, surrounded by steep passes and walls of blue rock. One of many flight fields for Kúzlo's patrol.

It's twilight. Particles and moonslight tango with the amber-green *migth* and snow that whorls off the shelves, making it hard to tell where the ground ends and the night begins. They might as well be standing on the northern sky. A sky that's giving him all the fucking feels being under it again.

"Is this it?" Anesh frowns from where she takes a stance near the two copper-haired cousins of the crew. They look stiff and on edge under the layers of their pelts.

"It's the way in," Falcon answers.

As planned, Trix starts to weave a shield to ward any spelled traps. The others look antsy to start hiking. Ashë, the wraith, shifts, her head tilted to the side to listen, her hand touching down over each blade in her coat like she's taking inventory. And despite Falcon's numerous warnings, the twitchy pair of Shadowcasters let darkness stir on their hands, probably unsettled by what they can't see, but can feel, in the air.

Falcon doesn't move. He can feel it, too—the buzzing.

His senses perk the same time his tattoos start to rearrange, putting his deadliest weapons closest to draw. Under his furs, he works the neck of his tunic loose, exposing the ink as that hum grows stronger, until it's a rumble like thunder from the sky traveling down the mountain walls across the ice under their feet.

It strikes him like a bolt of lightning what he forgot to ask of the Gatekeeper in negotiations. Discretion.

When the ice groans, Trix's shield wavers. "What the hell is that, smugger?"

"Dorothy," Falcon curses. "She warned the patrol we were coming."

He can't fault her. He knows what it is to be bound to an oath. He also knows there are plenty in Kúzlo who will have...emotions...about his return.

The wind kicks up, and the ground quakes with the patrol's approach.

Narrowing a look to the mountain face, Falcon eyes the rim of the ice bowl where the ridge is crumbled in places. He waits, jaw working, knowing it'll do no good to try to run, wondering how many drecora they're sending to vet them.

The first *hreeeee*! hits his ear a second later, as a massive shadow falls over the field. Another comes fast on its heels.

"Dragons?" Trix shouts. "You said the stag would buy us a clear path in!"

It was Falcon's fucking mistake. He was distracted, not expecting news of the tournament.

In the worst possible timing, he hears Trix curse, her eyes going white with a summons. But when six colossal, taloned beasts sail over the flight field, his attention diverts to the patrol.

The moons cast on leather wings that spread wide as caravels, on wicked scales painted an array of hues. Drecora. A species that evolved from the original dragons of the North to be faster, fiercer, and larger. They split off from formation toward those crumbling perches, settling at equidistant points around the rim. He can feel every breath they take as they fasten their unnerving attention on Falcon and his crew.

It's been a long time, but he remembers how patrols fly—rarely in even numbers. This isn't all of them. Where's the lead?

A seventh winged silhouette darkens the moons like an answer. As it bypasses the rim, the air shudders, kicking up snow dust, and the ground tremors with its descent, just a hundred feet away.

"Whatever you do," Falcon says quietly, "stow your shadows." But when he glances left, he sees the warning's too late. The twitchy pair of casters are rooting their stances, raising their hands.

"No!"

Darkness cannons across the ice toward the drecora, simultaneously plunging Falcon's view to blackness.

"Get down!" He lunges blindly for those near him, hoping at least to cover Trix. He can't hear if the others dive—he only registers the hair-raising suction of a beast drawing breath.

A flash of blue fire shocks the air into light. In it, Falcon sees the icepick shards, missiling on a deadly wind from the mouth of the pissed drecora. In that second, he knows not everyone's walking off this field.

CHAPTER 24
WINGS & DECEIT

For the first time since the revolution began, she doesn't dream of Wythe, but rather a dark tunnel where a thousand serpents writhe over bodies of the dead. A golden dragon, with a glinting object round its neck breaks through an iron gate and unhinges its jaw to call out a warning. But all that fills the tunnel is a river of shrieks and a wave of whispers.

The dream lingers as Ophelia opens her door at first light.

Kier stands at the precipice, a shoulder resting casually against the frame. Once more, she has to remind herself he's the closest living thing to Erebus. The dark king. Not her friend. Not to be trusted.

He wears a tunic and light, collared coat with a leather satchel at his back, and a suspicious gleam in his granite eyes. "For our fourth date, I thought I'd take you somewhere warmer."

She gives him a frosty glower, fastening her cloak. "Training sessions are not dates."

With a smile that harkens the heady scent of Cibus, he strides down the hall without reply.

They alight deeper into the woods this time where no wind breaches the canopy, where ice coats branches and layers stones and crevices, and barely a bird chitters.

Treelights are woven into the branches. They cast heat and illuminate a path to a little clearing surrounded by a lattice of snow-laden trees. At the edge, she's surprised to see a quaint, thatched cottage that looks forged by mortal hands, stone by wind-smoothed stone. Beyond is a small bluff of rocks where a waterfall has frozen on its descent into a pond, despite the fact that here in the cradle of the woods the temperature feels on the cusp of spring.

"Where is Ghastly?" she asks. "I haven't seen it on any maps."

"It doesn't exist to the known world."

She waits for him to elaborate, annoyed when he doesn't.

"I will when your shields impress me."

Yanking up her walls with the frustration of a chess player who's lost a knight, she gestures to the cottage. "Who lived there?"

Kier hesitates to look at it. When he finally does, his gaze lingers as though he might be seeing ghosts haunt the grounds. "My mother used it for a time, but she prefers the Witchist tower these days."

His mother. So she is here at Ghastly. "Are we going inside?"

"Another time." His gaze cuts back to her. In the center of the clearing, Kier lays out the blanket he brought along. "Magic needs room to breathe, and it's warm enough here. Also out of the way of most beasts."

"Not your beasts."

With a snort, he unbuttons his coat just enough that the formidable relic glitters darkly at Ophelia from its sheath. She swears it *thrums*.

Kier follows her gaze, tightness creeping into his eyes. "Have you heard the story of how they were forged?"

Her eyes snap to his, but there's no hiding she was staring at the relic. She finds it difficult not to, the way it sings. "I imagine you're going to tell me."

To her surprise, Kier slowly slips the relic from its sheath. A force presses against the air, taking her breath with a weight she can't see but can feel. The dagger's power ripples into the marking on her chest as if it recognizes its own.

The woods quiet to listen.

Kier looks upon the dagger a moment, as if seeing what's inside, and as his eyes glaze, she has to wonder if he ever lets it out of his sight. Does he sleep with it at night when he's alone, or not, in his bed?

At the picture of him in bed, her cheeks heat and she forces her gaze away, annoyed with herself. His quiet laugh vibrates through her, same as the dagger.

Damn it. Heaving her walls up again, she adds an extra layer of ice and iron for good measure.

"The primordial gods spent a millennia mating." Kier draws out the word. "When sex with mortals grew tiresome, Luna focused on setting up court and laws, while Erebus dabbled in other hobbies."

Ophelia keeps one eye on the dagger. "And Selene?"

Kier turns the relic in his hands. Treelight catches on the ancient runes etched in its hilt. "Selene was a dichotomy. She empathized with Erebus's desire to live freely, to sow his oats and have his adventures. But also with the responsibility Luna felt to their creation. It was Selene"—he glances up—"who suggested the relics as a means to ensure balance. So Erebus's mischief would not go unchecked, nor Luna's judgment cast too harsh a stone."

She's not sure she breathes. Ophelia had no idea that Selene masterminded the relics. And here she is, a Descendant of her line, intending to destroy them.

"How were they forged?" she asks.

He runs a finger along the soft edge of the dark blade, and a shiver passes through her—not altogether unpleasant. "The goddesses tricked their god of darkness."

Oh.

"Luna forged them, since she bore the affinities of Shifters and Fabricaters," Kier says. "First, she fused her essence with a piece of her alabaster moon. Once carved, the lightstone shone a silver-blue like the surface of a looking lake. A reflection of her power. She forged the amulet next, filling it with Selene's light."

Kier drops the dagger to his side, keeping a firm hold. "When it was Erebus's turn, he refused. So, one night, Selene lured him into bed." Ophelia's breath hitches. "While Erebus was buried inside her, lost to rapture, Selene bound him with her light so Luna could pierce his skin with a dagger forged of the crimson moon."

Ophelia can feel the trees shudder as Kier flexes his grip on the Dark Shadow Dagger. "They betrayed him," she says.

Kier nods. "After they took his essence, he went on a rampage. Tore up the land with his shadows, forged mountains anew, carved canyons that became the Rott River and a hundred others. He was angry because the relics bound him to the triple throne, and the goddesses. Together, they were more powerful, but they had to trust one another." He looks at her meaningfully.

She's careful to keep her thoughts, her heart, and her hands steady. "It's quite the story." It makes her appreciate the ancient dagger in a new light, knowing it was once held by the original gods. But... "I suppose that was a lesson in betrayal for me?"

Kier drags his attention from the relic to her. "Treachery has a place in war, Ophelia. But let's you and I not waste time with it. Instead, how about a game of trust?"

Cursing her niggling curiosity, she reluctantly asks, "What do you have in mind?"

"You're missing your friends. The apprentice who killed the headmaster—"

"Don't."

Kier holds up a hand. "The scholar was taken prisoner, according to my legion." So she was right; visiting Rune was no nightmare. "But the other," Kier says. "The soldier. He deserted his army but wasn't with you in Ravish."

Ophelia blinks hard at him. Why does Kier care? "And do you know anything about that?"

"I wish I did. My legion has been unable to find him." She detects a little irritation, perhaps that a lowly soldier could evade his Shadow-marked army. "Anyway," Kier says, "traveling is a skill you need to master and it would let you see if he's safe. So master it."

She nearly snorts. "You mean leave my body here alone with you."

"As you kindly pointed out, we're tethered. Your death holds no interest for me."

No interest? Like death's a game or a sport? "There are worse things," she bites out.

"Fine." To her utter shock, Kier thrusts the dagger out to her.

She stares at the thing she came here for, convinced that it would be the gateway to the other relics.

"Take it. Bury it somewhere in the woods if you like, as assurance."

Her hands ache to touch it—too much. "Would that work?" Wouldn't his shadows just sense it?

"If you are to spy for me, Ophelia, to get information about our enemies and the other relics, you need to hone this skill."

She almost tells him right then about the prison and Rune, that she's done even more than travel with her mind. It's Hannah's warning that makes her pull the truth back. Glancing at the dagger, she says, "You mean I need to trust you."

"There is that."

A rustle in the woods turns their heads. A low growl emanates from shaking boughs—a sound Ophelia recognizes even before the white muzzle appears from the shroud. Then, golden eyes. The tips of ears. Paws the size of a grown man's feet.

The wolven she healed.

Instinctively, she steps into Kier's fixed gaze, delivering him a sharp look of warning when she feels his power simmer. "Don't even think about it."

There's a tenuous truce between Kier and the beast as the animal lopes forward, offering Kier a glimpse of its knife-like teeth.

Ophelia can't explain how—he hasn't spoken—but when the wolven's eyes meet hers, there's connection. He sensed her, the way she can sense the *maether* in living things, and has come to check on her.

She glances at Kier—the wolven's source of agitation. "Stow the dagger," she tells him. "And no shadows. If you want my trust, want me to travel and spy for you, then swear it."

Reluctantly, he tucks the dagger in its sheath, and she feels its power dim. The whole forest seems to take a breath as he agrees, "No shadows."

Ophelia kneels on the blanket Kier set out. To her amazement, the wolven lies beside her. Regal, and so tall he half-obscures her view of Kier. She lays a hand on the animal's side, feeling its protective energy.

Hitching herself to the dust should be as easy as breathing by now, after all she has mastered this week. But she can still feel the dark king, the power that waves off him. He's watching her.

"Maybe you should wait in your little cottage or wherever," she calls to him. "Your energy is...distracting."

He folds his arms and takes two steps back, which must be all the distance he's willing to give. Clenching her teeth, she shuts her eyes in concentration.

The wolven brushes against her fingers, his fur warm and soft as silk. Raking through his coat, she concentrates, remembering the Glow Woods, when Hart held up her palm beneath his and she called the dust. Thinking of his hand in hers as they raced up the ancient steps around Grimm's tree home.

She reaches out beyond Ghastly—wherever it is—to look for Wythe, for the last place she saw Hart. Casting her mind out from there across clouds of dust that soar near, she searches for particles that might *know*.

It takes longer than it ever has to wade through fogs of whispers. So long that Ophelia wonders if maybe she's too far from Hart. Or if Hart is...

An answer comes faintly through the warble of whispers. A feeling, not words.

"You've seen him?" she asks frantically across a connection that stretches like a golden thread. *"Hart Aurum. I need to see where he is."*

She pictures his midnight eyes, the way he flexes his jaw when he's bottling emotions, the rare—too rare—smile he gave her before the passage ripped them apart.

In a blink, she's elsewhere, feeling light as the wind and...floating above a campfire. It takes a moment to realize what she's seeing by way of the particles—two bodies tangled under fur blankets, sleeping snuggly in the morning light.

The man's lips skim a kiss against the woman's cheek.

Hart, entwined with Willow Winter.

CHAPTER 25
MINDS & SCARS

GHASTLY
11TH DAY IN THE NEW WINTER
OPHELIA IS WITH THE DARKWIELDER

When Ophelia awakens in her body, there's no wolven, no blanket, no snow-draped woods. Coming out of that strange stasis, there's only the overwhelming scent of cloves, the firm feel of a male's mouth on hers, and breath being pushed into her lungs.

She heaves against his chest. "Get off of me!" Light flares on her arm as she shoves at his weight until his lips disappear.

Above her is a thatched ceiling...and the dark king, panting for his own breath.

Kier's eyes are blown out wide in desperation. With a frown cutting a line between his raven brows, he eases off her with some difficulty, moving to the end of the bed.

Dragging her legs up, Ophelia realizes they're inside a cottage. It must be the one she asked about earlier, but she takes no time to study it, or even reflect on the fact she just found Hart—Hart and Willow—because a pool of wet, red liquid stains her top.

Blood.

Patting her shirt, she searches for wounds she cannot feel, but there are none to be found. Other than a woozy head that comes when her consciousness travels, she's fine.

Perhaps it's the wolven that's not.

Panic mounting, she draws herself upright, her gaze tunneling on the man of shadows. At the end of the bed, he's hunched forward, cradling an arm, breathing through whatever came over him before. Shadows hum along his back.

"What did you do?" she demands. "Did you kill the creature?"

Kier swings a loathing gaze at her. "You stopped...breathing," he grits out.

"What?"

"You collapsed and the tether waned. For an hour, I couldn't feel you, and I thought..." His eyes shutter a moment with a wince of pain.

She exhales. "That...happens," she says, not wishing to examine his concern for her too closely.

"It would have been nice to know."

She looks past him. "But the wolven. You didn't—"

Kier holds a finger to his ear, then flicks it to the door. From outside, she catches a sad whimper, then the wolven's *maether* coming in a steady flow, making her shoulders relax. Until she looks more closely at Kier.

"You're bleeding." Vastly so.

He's already removed his coat, but the sleeve on his left arm is shredded, along with his skin. "Your new pet didn't appreciate my assistance."

She's stunned into silence, not only that the wolven tried to protect her but that Kier thought she was dying and took the beast on to come to her aid. It's something Falcon would do, unquestioningly, but not a god of darkness who has the worlds' most deadly shadows at his beck and call.

"I swore no shadows," Kier says, motioning across the bed. "Hand me a pillowcase."

At the moment, she doesn't care her shields are down. She doesn't know what to make of him keeping his word.

After she loosens the fabric from a pillow, while Kier wraps the wound, she steals a glance around the modest wood-and-stone room. Two windows, caked in a finger's worth of soot. Firewood stacked near a darkened hearth. Old, rolled maps, abandoned on shelves. And piles of boys' clothes, alongside an army captain's longcoat, folded neatly on a dresser.

She fiddles with her locket. "Did you live here?"

"For a few months, after I failed in my first heist for the dagger."

"You and your mother?"

"And Jasper."

"Jasper Salt?" She can't suppress the edge or surprise in her voice.

"He was the son of a friend at Gray Castle." Kier sways where he sits, red blooming on the pillowcase around his forearm. Lifting the material—a poor excuse for a bandage, the way he's tried to wrap it—he checks the wound, then quickly averts his eyes.

At the glimpse of bone, Ophelia works through a tickle of nausea. But she's surprised that he avoids looking at the wound directly, as if he loathes blood, too, when no doubt he's spilled plenty in his life.

She motions to the cut. "Why don't you use your shadows?"

"I promised..." He sways again, looking closer to passing out than drawing from his power.

Damn it. She can't have him bleeding out while their lives are tethered.

Shifting to the edge of the mattress, she angles toward him. "Give me your arm." Ignoring the nausea, she doesn't let herself fear she can't do it. She removes the pillowcase entirely.

I am the dust.

I am the light.

I am the legacy of my mother, and her mother before.

He tilts his head at her, leering appreciatively. "Look at you, Ophelia. Confident enough now to practice on the Darkwielder."

"Until the tether is gone, I have a vested interest in you living, apparently."

She draws Kier's arm to her lap, and its coldness leeches to her thighs.

As she inspects the wound, she hears echoes of a conversation with Falcon during their last sparring session in Ravish, after his sword nicked her hand and she snarled at him. She'd been stressed, tired, and anxious. Impaling her with his wild eyes, he leveled truth right back at her, saying the nick was nothing—*nothing*—compared to the wound he saw her suffer in Galdur, when he wondered if she would live, when her blood and bones shimmered at him.

The bone in Kier's forearm is polished and pale. His blood, a vibrant red.

It's not that she expected he was made of shadow... She's not sure what she expected anymore.

Calling light from within, she lets it fill her lumen mark, willing it to seep out slowly.

Kier's gaze reflects the liquid gold. As her forearm hovers over his, he closes his eyes. "Did you find your friend?" he asks, an edge to his tone that's swallowed by a sharp inhale when the light settles in his wound, and his mangled muscles begin to fuse beneath her touch.

"I found him," she replies. Hart *and* Willow.

When his pale skin smooths over, a raised pink line like magical stitches is left behind, a scar far neater than her own. Kier is looking at her, as though he's trying to decipher her feelings. "Where?" he asks.

"I'm not sure. The landscape was all snow and trees, but winter's everywhere."

"Show me what you saw."

"What?" But by the lift of his brow and the nudge that comes across the tether, she knows what he means. Show him her mind.

"A game of trust," he echoes to her. "I could send for him for you."

"You would do that?" The tether feels taut as a bowstring as she considers Kier, *senses* him at the other end of it, his mind opening to her.

He did show her a memory. A tragic one. He also trusted her light-dragon and suffered a wolven's bite for her.

"Fine," she relents.

With her walls down, she relives the memory, allowing the cold and surprise and other conflicting feelings to unspool across the bridge between her and Kier. At first, shock and jealousy at the inevitable way Hart and Willow fit, curled together like they belong with one another.

Except for a few interludes Ophelia heard rumors about, she's never seen Hart look so intimate with a woman. She has been the female in his life. This feels...like the end of that. It feels like loss. But when she examines that jealousy with a closer eye, she doesn't find herself wishing she were in Hart's arms.

Instead, it's a *smugger* with a crass mouth and wild thrust of steel who comes to mind.

When Hart and Willow wake abruptly and hop up to dress, as if they're about to be late, her storm of emotions ceases.

Ophelia tries to hover close to Hart, willing the particles she embodies to vibrate in a way he'll notice. But he's distracted, his attention narrowed toward the edge of the thicket, which he watches a long moment. He and Willow confer quietly, then rush to mount a siegehorse.

It's then Ophelia notices the convoy of dark carriages in the distance and gets a pitting feeling as Hart and Willow seem keen to chase after it. She shadows the two of them, not wanting to let go.

It's horrible to be this close to a man she worried was lost and not be able to make him see she's there.

But there's a voice calling Ophelia back to Ghastly.

Kier's panicked voice.

The memory fizzles.

She starts to surface back to the cottage, but something bright at the end of the tether holds her there. Like a tantalizing secret, Kier's mind opens to her, drawing her in.

Daylight streams through a bay of windows in a regal castle chamber where a young woman with a long, golden braid carries a stack of towels across the room. She steals a glance at Ophelia—no, at Kier. Passing by, her soft fingers brush his, causing a tingle where they touch. His heart swells in a familiar yearning.

Mouth stretching to form a boyish grin, Kier follows the young woman into a washroom and shuts the door behind them.

When Ophelia is thrust back to the cottage, Kier is running a finger along his new scar, lost to consternation. She's not certain if it's the memory she showed him or the one she just witnessed that's responsible.

Maybe she should worry more that he's just been deep in her mind, but she's absorbed by the memory of the girl with Kier. She bore a likeness to the subject of his paintings at Ghastly. A young woman captured tenderly and pined after.

"What happened to her?" Ophelia asks quietly.

Kier doesn't look at her. Eyes empty of emotion, he stands to put on his coat. "I killed her."

CHAPTER 26
GUARDS & GALLOWS

E yes seem to linger on Hart's back.

For an hour as he and Willow trail the legion convoy holding her people hostage, he peers suspiciously at the sky. Particles hover, further stirring that watchful sensation.

Where she's nestled in front of him on the siegehorse, Willow tracks his gaze to the dust. "Friends of yours?"

He vexes. "It doesn't usually follow me this way."

They've been trailing the legion at a distance for days. First south to the village of Inri where the rebel soldiers carted up more mortals. Then north to the outskirts of affluent western Bruxo. At least they have a siegehorse. Anything less wouldn't have weathered so long with them both on its back.

The prickle of eyes soon fades, and Hart's attention forges ahead where the legion is pulling off the main road and angling onto a private drive. Recognizing the stone pillars, he realizes where they've come.

At the slackening of his arms on the reins around her, Willow says. "Do you know this place?"

Hart scans for any cages, the suggestion of prison cells, or worse, but there are none to be seen, at least at the front of the estate. "This is the manor of Dorian Hobb, a regional representative of the crown."

At the edge of the property, Hart nudges their siegehorse through a copse of Syca trees. Sliding off, ass numb, he offers Willow a hand as she dismounts. She lands with a flourish against his chest, and her eyes linger on his a moment, stirring a godsforsaken flutter in his chest.

Get yourself together.

Pressed against a frozen tree, Hart tries to ignore the warmth of her arm against his and the bare skin of Willow's neck exposed under the cloak they confiscated a few days ago.

He focuses on the soldiers, the house guards, and servants who fall into lines near the front of the grand house. The staff are holding cloaks and blankets in arm, intent on the phaetons that sing up the driveway. There are at least twenty, and Hart finds it odd this is the legion's destination. But there's also cautious relief.

"It's not the gallows, at least," he murmurs.

"What is it, then?" Willow's eyes narrow in the direction of the phaetons.

"Maybe a political move." He chews on the thought while Hobb greets *Lieuten* Price at the front door.

A crown representative—a *Crat*—welcoming an officer of the Darkwielder's legion to his home? Hobb makes a flamboyant show of bowing in his tailored coat, which is a spectacle shade of purple, and Hart watches the two men confer cordially, not like enemies but acquaintances.

"Hobb isn't yet thirty, but he's influential in the Gray King's circles," Hart muses to Willow. "If the Darkwielder wants to sway that influence to his side, turning prisoners of war over could be a show of good faith."

That strategy feels like a long game, though.

Willow peers harder in the direction of the manor where prisoners are being wrapped in blankets before being ushered into the house. "So how do we free them with soldiers everywhere?"

Feeling her tense beside him, Hart follows her keen gaze to the last phaeton emptying of prisoners, where Cora and Mammy have just appeared.

Willow makes to rush for them, but Hart grabs her arm, pulling her back flush against him to feel how she trembles with intensity. Tightening his hands at her waist, he breathes, "Be patient, Willow."

When her arms relax, he releases her, ready to reason how her people are safer here than roaming the West in the dead of winter, during a war, with little food or money. But as the last prisoners fade into the house, Hart's distracted by the phaetons leaving behind most of the rebel soldiers.

Price is calling his legion into a line. Wariness needles when he orders his soldiers paired with Hobb's house guards before dispatching them to posts around the gardens.

Hart swears. "A rescue won't be simple. There's more going on here."

They spy from the woods until nightfall. Very little stirs, and Hart's legs grow restless, his stomach too empty. He can handle all that—it's par for the course for soldiers in the field—but he hates that he can't stop stealing looks at Willow, that he can't stop worrying for her or wondering if she's dying at the thought of her family inside.

He grinds his jaw, reminding himself this is a mission. He cares only about completing it so he might shift his focus—and Willow's talents—to finding Ophelia. And Willow will be in far better shape to help him if her people are safe.

When the moons perch high and they can keep hidden in the natural shadows made by the lanterns in Hobb's gardens, they creep into the yard for a closer survey.

Hart counts twenty-two guards, plus soldiers, posted at entry points around the manor. The air holds a faint smell of wet earth and cooking food and, despite the situation, his stomach complains. They ate through the rations from Inri. He'll need to hunt for them soon.

Bells chime faintly from inside the house. Hart counts to nine before the doors of the estate open, letting out a small, darkly cloaked party. He tenses at the sight of Hobb and Price, leading at the front. Two soldiers hold the rear and, between, an old man in a fur hat keeps something tucked inside his elbow. Just behind him is a commoner prisoner Hart recalls the rebels taking in Inri.

Quietly, the six walk a cleared path, lanterns swaying in hands as they wend toward the river behind the estate.

Willow is alert. "What are they doing?"

"I don't know," he admits, a pit growing in his stomach. He pulls her along with him, keeping to the tree line.

Near the river, the party's lanterns cast on a dark tent erected at the water's edge that Hart didn't make out before.

From where they stand behind the cover of a tree, Willow glances at him. "You think they're questioning prisoners?"

"I don't know," he says again, hating that it's all he has to offer her. "Taking commoners wasn't a tactic in the Special Army. I can't see what they'd know to offer an advantage in war."

From inside the tent comes a muffled sound, like grinding teeth. As minutes tick by, moans begin. This continues an agitating hour, with two soldiers at guard outside.

The pit lodges deep in Hart's gut, worry expanding that he was wrong about the strategy the Darkwielder's legion is employing here. While he debates how best to subdue the soldiers so Willow might glean information from their memories, the soldiers are called into the tent.

Clenching and unclenching his fists to bring warmth to his hands, Hart strains to catch bits of conversation, but they're too far away. Before he finishes considering whether he ought to shift himself and pose as a guard, the entire party departs, leaving the tent dark.

By lantern light, Hart notices Hobb and the legion soldiers look paler than when they went in. The man in the fur hat stares at his hands, which are coated in something dark, and Price wipes the side of his face with a kerchief, his expression marred with disappointment, disgust, or both.

Taking hold of Hart's arm, Willow breathes, "Where's the prisoner?"

A disturbing suspicion grips Hart as Hobb's party trails back up to the estate. "I think I was wrong about the gallows."

CHAPTER 27
LOCKS & LOYALTIES

K ier stays silent, refusing to elaborate on his confession: *I killed her.*

He killed the woman he loved? There must be more to the story. She can *feel* there's more to the story. But she's forced to let it go when on return to Ghastly they're met by Stolm and several legion soldiers wearing tight expressions in the courtyard.

It's broaching evening and snow whips in the air.

"Tell me inside," the dark king snaps, not bothering to slow his gait.

Wary of the urgency sharpening Stolm's light features, Ophelia follows with dread tightening her stomach as he reports in hurried Magiesian of yet another skirmish in western Magus. Worse this time. A battle ongoing with more legion soldiers lost.

Guilt gnaws at her edges that she's here behind the safety of Ghastly's walls when people are dying in Magus. But this is war—battles and bloodshed—and unless she finds her own relic, it won't stop until one side is crushed.

"Rumors are spreading by summons here and in Magus," Stolm tells Kier. "The council wants assurances of the least loss to Magie life. They wish to convene on your strategy, Kosost."

As they reach the east wing's foyer, warmth floods from the fires and Kier's nostrils flare in irritation. Darkly, he says, "By all means, let's convene."

He nods at a soldier who stands at attention behind Stolm, a female with a blunt midnight bob whose sharp features look positively lethal, and familiar. The female slashes an unsmiling glance at Ophelia, who stands at Kier's side, and it's then Ophelia recognizes her—the soldier "Captain Rivmere" ordered to cart her by shadow to Grimm's tent. Apparently she's been reassigned.

"Stasia," Kier commands. "See to it all members are present."

Stasia snaps a nod to her king before turning heel, presumably to follow orders.

To Stolm, Kier orders, "Brief me about the rest on our way."

"And her, Kosost?"

Speculative slate eyes snap to Ophelia. They look calculating, controlled. All of Kier's vulnerability—that desperation from the cottage—is entirely gone as he says, "Only rulers and appointed members attend the Council of Guilds. Have you changed your mind yet?"

He means about being queen. Tilting her chin up, she realizes the council must be a resurrection of the one before the Great Siege, in which every guild and mortal interest was represented as well as the Magies'.

She's been consumed with training and not much else the past week. If she attends the council, it would be insight into war strategy and what's happening in Magus. And it would give her a sense of the dynamics between the guilds and their Witchist king. On the other hand, she'd have to reveal herself, which would limit her ability to move unnoticed around Ghastly to search for information.

"If the war is escalating, aren't my efforts better spent on locating the relics?" she asks. "I could visit the library while the council convenes."

Studying her, Kier waves a hand to dismiss all his soldiers, except for Stolm. Swallowing her whole with that intent gaze, the dark king asks, "Following a hunch, Ophelia?"

She debates a moment whether to tell him about Elora, then lowers her voice. "I think my mother was the last to possess the amulet. If I can find out where she died..."

After a moment, he steps into her, causing his chest to graze hers and forcing her gaze up. Knuckles raise to brush her cheek and she tries not to shiver. "One more game of trust first. I want you to pay a visit to the Morphists Guild." He leans close, his breath tickling her ear. "Bring me something useful."

Morphists Guild?

As he pulls back, she looks at him questioningly. The relics are largely the reason they allied; if he's going to send her into the guilds, shouldn't it be to the Matterists' to scour for information on her line?

That smirk he reserves for her returns, as if he quite enjoys her confusion, as if he wants her to beg for answers.

She will not.

"Fine," she bites out. If he wants to send her on some mystery hunt, she'll make the trip useful. Bring him what, though? And how to sneak in discretely? Because without revealing herself, she doubts citizens would welcome her snooping.

She doesn't ask these questions, either. She's certain that deciphering what and how is half Kier's game.

When they were young, Hart taught Ophelia what it was like to become someone else.

To wear their skin.

They were thirteen when she found him at her door after lights out, breathing hard, back hunched, shirt ripped at the shoulder seams. His eyes were wet and his hand trembled holding out a small strawberry cake to her. "For you."

Darting a look down the academy hall, she yanked him inside, propped a chair under the knob, and stared at the cake he held, its tempting sweetness hanging in the air. Cake was a delicacy only sages and apprentices enjoyed.

"How did you get that?" she asked. Hart would never raid the kitchens. Not without her coaxing. Not at the risk of his hand.

As he gave her the cake, his face was a torment between pride and self-loathing. "Happy birthday, Lia."

Her heart warmed. On a day like this, they had no one but each other to make them feel seen or special. No mothers or fathers to wake them with a song, to hang streamers from the rafters or shower them with love. Wedging themselves between her bed and the wall, she and Hart laid their heads back to gaze at the triple moons while they shared his gift.

"So how did you get it?" she asked, kissing frosting off a knuckle. The little spy in her had to know.

"I shifted."

She lowered her hand in surprise. "On purpose?" He'd wanted as little to do with magic as possible since she'd known him, but there was so much potential for escaping the Constelli if he mastered it.

"Don't give me that look," he grumbled. "It was one time."

Angling toward him, she watched him chew the rest of his share. "Who'd you become?"

Hart's serious expression cracked in the moonslight as he pulled a face. "Sage Vola." His brow twitched. "I knew it would hurt, like breaking an arm. But it was more like breaking myself apart."

"What do you mean?"

He grasped for the words to explain. "I could feel myself stretching open to make room for someone else. Not their thoughts, but how they'd walk and speak. It was frightening," he admitted. "For a minute, I thought I lost myself."

She rested her head on his shoulder, taking his hand to squeeze it. So that was why Morphists carried themselves so rigidly—to hold themselves together.

Wisps of that long-ago memory fade.

Cleaned up from the cottage in the shadow woods, still tired from traveling on the dust, Ophelia chooses a long, silken dress for her jaunt into the guilds in the hopes of blending in. Peering discretely out of the same alcove through which Kier brought her into the guilds before, she spies the Matterists flag where it banners, the amulet stitched there taunting her.

It's tempting to abandon her mission, to instead search for every clue that might exist as to where Elora could have taken her relic all those years ago. But she needs Kier's trust, and to win his game.

Gaze cutting to the Morphists Guild hall, she considers that conversation with Hart. She can't become someone else like he can, but she could've traveled on the dust from the safety of her room. Only, she wants her feet in these halls, to feel rooted and part of her own history. The idea of physical travel niggles, but there's much to understand about it yet, and instinct tells her it requires knowing someone or something about where she's going, which she does not.

The simplest option is to walk in.

A trio of Morphists sit at a table focused on their work, and Ophelia eyes the cloak with a thick, gold buckle draped over a chair. With a quick search, she finds a smattering of particles lingering near the grand chandelier in the main foyer. A dusting that might fit in the palm of her hand. She reaches out to it, and it's almost instant now, how fast she latches onto its energy.

Generally, she burns to release it, to fling the force of it back out with a desperate, rushed command, but this time she holds it inside her. At first, it's like trapping steam in a locked pot and she braces to blow. But soon, the heat and pressure level, the wildness in her settling to a manageable simmer.

Testing the cord between her and the dust, she pictures the movement she wants it to mimic, then wills, *"Dip."*

The dust dives in a clumsy circle around the chandelier, skimming the side of it. She groans inwardly as the movement knocks a candle loose from its perch to land with a ceremonious crash in the lower foyer.

A surprised cry rings up.

"Stop," she wills the dust.

The particles halt, tiny shimmers suspended mid-air.

Surveying the halls, guild to guild, she's grateful most citizens have made their way elsewhere.

"All right. Let's go."

The particles sail gracefully this time, following her desire to keep close to the walls. It's heady, the feeling of life—of power—at her fingertips.

When the dust reaches the balcony between her and the Morphists' table, she wills, *"Distract them."*

The shimmer steals toward the boys like wind through an open window, setting their papers to flight.

"Pashen nis!" one shouts, and the trio vaults from their chairs to follow their roving pages down a side hall.

A thrill shivers down Ophelia's spine as she swipes the Morphist cloak.

No one perceives that a goddess walks among them. Beneath a row of exquisite chandeliers, Ophelia holds the poised, rigid manner of a Morphist as she crosses the checkered marble floor.

Hart would laugh. Falcon would commend her sleuthing. And Rune would... An ache pulses in her chest. Rune would do nothing but kill her right now.

Remembering what's at stake—Rune, as well as the fate of Magus, in the Gray King's grasp—motivates each of her steps. She flits casual glances over the filigreed details in the hall, each piece of marble or metal looking forged by the masterful hands of Fabricaters. If this were another life, another time, she would curl on a bench and admire every facet.

Voices drift from behind closed doors labeled as lecture rooms or workshops, but the hall itself is empty. Tugging on the cord that connects her to the dust, Ophelia considers where the guild might keep something Kier would find useful.

Something secret.

Thinking like a Morphist—someone with rigid walls—she eyes the dust keeping pace near the ceiling. *"Where are the thickest walls in the Morphists guild?"*

It winks in reply, dashing ahead like a speeding colt to an intersecting corridor. Following its trail down a maze of halls, she slows at what appears to be a dead end. But a woman in a legion uniform is stalking briskly toward the end of the hall, then seems to disappear into the wall.

Intrigued, Ophelia creeps after to discover entryways on either side. To the right, she ducks inside a nook that offers a view into an elaborate study, where the top half of a svelte blond man in a gold-stitched blue doublet is angled over his mahogany desk.

Brushing a rogue curl from his eye, he barely glances up at the woman who's barged in, but Ophelia recognizes the raven bob.

Stasia keeps her back to Ophelia and a hand on the belt of her legion uniform. "Lokin, the guilds convened half an hour ago. Your tardiness will only draw attention." She sounds exasperated.

The man looks just older than Stolm, perhaps early thirties, but age is difficult to tell with Magies. His angular features carve a striking face, and his posture alone implies he's someone important.

"I'm coming." Making a sharp mark with a quill on the paper he holds, he assesses it with a frown before gathering it, and several other pages, to stuff in a drawer, then waves a hand over the knob. Spinning to grab a fine cloak off a rack, Lokin laments, "He thinks because he has a relic now, every guild ought to jump at his bequest."

"Bite your tongue," Stasia hisses. "You know the walls have eyes."

Lokin glances over a shoulder before stalking from the study. "Not every wall."

"Be patient," Stasia urges, hurrying after him.

Waiting while their footsteps retreat, Ophelia marvels at the exchange—Lokin's irritation, his comment about the guilds kneeling, Stasia's reply. Neither strike Ophelia as loyal subjects, and though she's never met Lokin, Stasia appears to be in Kier's inner circle.

Something useful. Yes, this is something Kier would wish to know. Her job is complete. She could go now, venture into the Matterists Guild while she's on this side of the palace and Kier and the council are busy. But Lokin's curious behavior draws her into his study.

The room is meticulous.

Careful not to disturb anything, she strides past the plush seating arranged near a grand hearth, straight to the Morphist councilman's desk. "Whatever he was reading seemed important," she mutters to the dust that's followed her in.

The desk drawers are made of metal and open easily. All but one.

Ophelia's adept at picking locks, but this drawer has no keyhole. No mechanism. Lokin must refabricate the metal itself to seal and unseal it.

When a tangle of whispers fills her head, her instinct is to shield them out; they're hard to take for long. But she pauses this time, considering what might happen if she leaned into the din. If she truly listened.

It's slow to come, as if her ears require reshaping first. Then there are different tones. Baritone, contralto, soprano—a symphony of notes not dissimilar to the emotive melodies that used to sift from the music hall at the Constelli when Rune played piano.

She focuses on isolating one tone—a soft but strong pitch. At first, it's only a moan. Then, perhaps a vowel. A word. "*Matter?*" she asks.

The dust makes a rush to the stuck drawer, seeping through it until the surface faintly glows. Her breath catches. *Matter.* So long as something is forged with, fed by, or made of magic, she can manipulate it.

Focusing every sense, she edges her fingers along the smooth, cool metal, navigating the seams until she finds the ridge where Lokin must have sealed the drawer shut. With barely a thought, she dissolves the welding. The dust inside shoves to get free, opening the drawer and revealing Lokin's paper.

Two columns of names, with some stricken through. The document looks old, and the writing is penned in various shades of ink, as though people have been added and crossed out over many years.

The brightest mark, the most newly penned, is a circle around the name *Isaac Valoran*. She's turning the familiar surname over in her mind, when a rustle sounds in the hall.

The dust races across the room to inspect and, through their connection, Ophelia glimpses Stasia, speaking to someone via summons at the end of the hall.

Quickly, Ophelia rifles through the remaining pages, finding old addresses and coordinates, most of which are also crossed out. Could Lokin have been searching for someone and gone through all these names to find the right person? Was this Isaac Valoran who he'd been looking for? Did he find him? The final page is an old correspondence, stamped with a triple-circle sigil that must represent the three guilds.

The dust bleats in her mind, and she sees Stasia, eyes cleared and heading in the direction of Lokin's study.

As the particles whirl in an urgent flurry, Ophelia snatches up the papers and puts them back where she found them. Just as she finishes sealing the drawer, she hears Stasia grumble in the hall of a forgotten ledger and being anyone's errand woman. Ophelia presses back against a wall of bookshelves, searching for somewhere to hide, when behind her something gives.

A book she's elbowed slides askew, and the shelf swings open.

She throws herself into the hidden nook feeling lucky beyond measure—until she pulls the bookcase shut and the floor disappears beneath her.

CHAPTER 28
PAINTINGS & THORNS

THE GUILDS AT GHASTLY
11TH DAY IN THE NEW WINTER
OPHELIA IS ON HER OWN

She's not in the Morphists Guild anymore. The dust is still with her, and it's clear what she's fallen through isn't a trap door or hidden passageway. It's a ground passage—a shortcut across the guilds.

When Ophelia comes through it into a slim tower, she's perched on stone steps that curl upward like a screw. The air is damp and musty, and there are no windows. A few lanterns bolted up the walls cast wide patches of light.

The tight space presses in, too much like the places she was made to hide as a young child while her mother dealt with threats. But she can't go back to Lokin's study, so she follows the dust and stairs upward, hoping she comes out somewhere she recognizes, or near the Matterists Guild.

Where the stairs end, a door spills her into a hallway less opulent than the Morphists Guild. It's thick with the smell of potions and herbs, reminding her of Trix's store in New York. The one Ophelia, Trix, and Rune blew to the heavens to escape a small onslaught of Shadowcasters.

By the scents alone, Ophelia presumes this is the Witchists Guild—an obscure section of it, anyway. Halls filled with golden frames absent of their paintings. Instead, flowers grow from within them off the stone walls. They stretch their tentacles up toward the ceiling where a pale-pink glow mimics moonslight.

The dust whirls, beckoning her onward. Following, she feels like she's walked in a full circle when a force of energy jolts through her. She turns to face a wall woven entirely of plants. On first glance, it looks impassable, then she notes the particles slipping through the foliage.

Running a light hand over the vines, the leaves part under her touch. Ophelia draws her hand back to see through the gap to a secret path. *What would be so carefully hidden in the Witchists Guild?*

Wedging her way through the vines, she meets a hall that splits to the right, but her gaze tracks straight ahead to where sconces flicker aside a floor-length painting. It's not the subject itself that draws her in, but the *maether* she felt earlier, humming from it.

The dust races ahead.

At the canvas, Ophelia reaches a finger to trace the thick paint but a shocking prickle makes her jerk away. A barrier ward? She considers turning back to seek another way out, but her feet refuse to move and her mind's already at work on the puzzle before her. Maybe it's a trait from spending so much time with Rune.

Her hand goes to her throat, where she swallows the lump that forms at the thought of him—so changed, so angry, so...not Rune.

Shaking it away, she focuses on what's in front of her.

Wards are magic. Complex wards, like the one Kier had cast to fortify the Belly, take a great deal of power and practice to dismantle, even for a Descendant. This ward feels intricate, but smaller. Raising a hand, she lets it hover over the painting until she can sense the weave of *maether* with which the ward was cast.

A slow burning begins in her palm and travels up her arm.

There's a loosening—the feel of threads unraveling at her fingertips. When the heat dissipates, the texture of the painting ripples, thin as water, before turning to vapor, allowing her hand and whole body to pass through it.

Struck immediately by a sickly scent, Ophelia sputters a cough.

In a dark room, a man lies in a grand bed draped with sheer curtains. He has a dusting of gray in his short, black hair, cheekbones that look sallow and waxy, and brown skin that faintly glows—*glows*—from where he rests deathly still, arms at his side beneath a satin blanket.

The hum from earlier deepens in its intensity, and she has the paradoxical urge to draw closer *and* flee the room. Similar to how she feels in Kier's presence.

The light that emanates from the man flickers and wanes, and that strange smell becomes so noxious, it's difficult to breathe.

Ophelia's own voice warns it might be poison, just before her vision blurs and her balance tips.

S ometime later, a stir of voices rouses her.

"...I will take her back to the east wing."

"Because he doesn't wish her to meet me?" A grating, feminine voice. "Then perhaps he should come retrieve her himself."

"He is shouldering the war, Saira." *Is that Officer Stolm?*

There's a clank of glass as the woman scoffs. "The war, or whatever else he leaves me out of these days."

Head thick as cotton, Ophelia's eyes clear on a chandelier draped in ivy. Candles crown the centerpiece, sending it afire with little flames that reflect in a large oval mirror on a far wall—a wall with wood stained the color of bleeding roses.

There are shelves and shelves of things in the room—glass jars and bowls, herbs, and all manner of creatures suspended or wriggling in liquid.

It's a Spellcaster's workshop.

"He would wish I escort her," the male voice urges. *It is Stolm.*

"I found her in my halls unwell, Mathias. You'll do no such thing until I see to her."

A tendril of woodsmoke curls across the table where the officer grips its edge, his expression uneasy and watchful on the pale woman. She wears the same black layers of lace and silk, and clips thorns from a long stem, letting them fall into a mortar. It's her—the woman from the courtyard. *Saira*, Stolm called her. And she called him Mathias.

"But the king—"

"Who made your king?" Saira lifts an elegant hand, a finger with a long nail pointed as if to touch Stolm.

He retreats a full stride, his face an expression of pure fear.

When Saira drops her hand, there's no smile on her cupid-bow mouth. There's little emotion at all. "Tell the king his goddess is well and she will return after she finds what she seeks. That ought to please him, no? If he's sent her round here to spy."

There's a moment of charged silence before Stolm departs the spell-room.

On a daybed where she lies, Ophelia shoves herself to sit, to call after him. But the walls switch places, or maybe it's her head. What was in that room?

When her vision settles, she finds gray eyes steeled on her from behind a table, where the woman fingers a stem in one hand. Delicate tattoos fall beneath her eyes like teardrops. Ophelia stares. Elora used to have markings like that on her face.

"How much did you hear?" the woman asks. *Clip, clip, clip,* with her little shears.

"Who are you?"

Saira pauses to toss the remains of a bald stem into the hearth fire. Flames crackle, causing a bird to squawk in the corner of the room and Ophelia to clasp her chest.

"It depends who you ask," Saira says.

The woman's a Spellcaster, that much is clear. And there are other familiarities. The way she seems at home among dark things that float or creep in jars. Her black garb. Her eyes. They make Ophelia think of cursed pastries and haunting memories and how the dark king looked with loathing resentment at this woman in the courtyard. "You're Kier's mother."

Saira snorts. "I haven't heard that name in fifteen years." She lets an audible exhale go. "And you are the goddess he's been keeping to himself. The one who calls the dust and cured Magus of my son's curse. Messandra's granddaughter."

"You know about me."

They stare at one another—the mother of the god of darkness and Ophelia, a goddess of light.

"I know more than you can imagine, Kososten."

That title again. "I'm not here to be queen," she assures her.

Saira snaps a stem in two. "How disappointing." Discarding the plant matter, she plucks a new stem up and waves it in Ophelia's direction. "The dust led you to my tower. Is my son's parentage really your burning concern?"

Ophelia pushes to her feet and smooths her dress, noting the Morphist cloak she was wearing is now draped over the daybed. As she gathers her thoughts, she studies Saira and those tattoos and wonders if she knew Elora.

It's but one of a thousand questions that come, not the least of which are: Why would Kier not want Ophelia to meet his mother? Why did Stolm look at Saira as though she were made of death? And who was the glowing man in that room?

What comes out is, "Why did the dust lead me here?"

Saira's mouth curves as if Ophelia's scored well on some test. Making space, she motions Ophelia to join her at the table, where bottles have been arranged in haphazard order.

Pulling on spellgloves, Saira plucks a dried pink bud from a jar and places it into the mortar. "Foxglove to strengthen heart contractions," she tells Ophelia, adding a scant measure of a sweet black tincture. "Belladonna for digestive function." With a pestle, Saira grinds the thorns before adding a pinch of them to her bowl. "Thornbane for blood pressure." The woman places her hand over the bowl, bending air to make the mixture turn. "And a breath for breath."

Ophelia can't help staring at the woman. Keir's mother is far more than a Spellcaster; she has a second affinity from the Matterists' line—a Bender's ability to control air.

When Saira raises the scarf at her neck to cover her nose, beginning an incantation, the mixture starts to boil, then vaporize. As the air scents of that sickly stench that surrounded the glowing man, Ophelia throws a sleeve up to shield her own mouth and nose as Saira coaxes the vapor into an onyx ring on her right hand.

The scent in the spellroom dissipates as the jewel fills, brightening.

Ophelia hasn't witnessed a Spellcaster imbue an object since her time at the Constelli, but those never made her skin prickle this way.

When the jewel dulls, Saira lowers her scarf. "The dust led you here because it knows you seek the truth."

Ophelia frowns. She wanted the truth of her own line, not Kier's. What could the dust want her to know here?

Saira moves around the table. "We must hurry. It's time for another dose."

CHAPTER 29
POISON & TREASON

WITCHIST GUILD AT GHASTLY
11TH DAY IN THE NEW WINTER
OPHELIA IS ON HER OWN

Through another maze of halls that grows increasingly narrow, Saira's fat gray bird leads the way from the spellroom in the Witchist tower back to that hidden room.

It was sheer luck—nay, magic—that Ophelia found that painting at all.

As they step in, the bird perches at the bedside of the mysterious man. The smell is gone from the room, but Ophelia senses that same odd call, as if someone or something is tugging on her bones.

Saira hovers at the end of the bed, rubbing a finger over the spellring she imbued and coaxing it to life. But Ophelia will not be a party to keeping this man half-dead. She goes to reach for the woman's arm, stopping herself when she recalls how Stolm recoiled as if Saira's touch might be deadly.

Instead, Ophelia positions herself between Saira and the man, light sparking defensively on her arm. "Why are you doing this?"

Saira lowers her ring. With a sigh, she clasps her wrist and walks slowly around Ophelia to hover at one side of the bed. The floor there seems molded to her shape, as if she's stood in that spot a thousand times.

Hoping it's not a mistake, Ophelia stills the call of her magic.

The woman's attention is fixed on the figure who lies motionless between them. "He was an impressive man once," Saira says. "Honest and pragmatic. Capable of raising a city with his bare hands or rending its backbone to a mangled heap. Yet when palace children needed cheer, he gladly delighted them, remolding his own throne once into a golden toy horse that all the Descendant children could sit upon."

"Throne," Ophelia echoes. "You don't mean..."

"I've known Kane Valoran since I was a girl living with cousins at the Magie palace." She smooths a hand over blankets that don't need smoothing and shakes her head. "He would've hated all this lying around."

Ophelia looks at the man, trying to grasp the truth.

Kier is the Witchists' king, Ophelia the last of the Matterist Descendants, and, according to every tome she's read, the Morphist line died fifty years ago when Osiris trapped Kane Valoran's magic inside the lightstone relic.

The histories of the Great Siege are replete with lies.

She catches Saira's eye. "This man is Kane Valoran? You're keeping the actual Morphist King of Magus in this state and locked away?" She boils at the idea that Kier didn't tell her.

"I'm keeping Kane alive. As alive as I can," Saira says, her voice a grave of buried secrets.

"What does that mean?"

"His brain was carved from his skull the night Osiris laid siege."

With horror, Ophelia searches Kane and notes the long, distinct scar on the crown of his head.

"Fortunately," Saira says, "some of his attendants were powerful Spellcasters. They found him before his magic was siphoned and had the foresight to keep him breathing as they stole his body north." Saira caresses her spellring. "We found him many years later, lying in a nothing room in a nothing village, only his heart beating." She picks at the blanket some more. "Kane had children, but we've yet to find his kin. It's possible they're all dead. But if his heart stops beating before we find out, we risk an entire line dying, which would upset the balance of the guilds."

Ophelia thinks of the names in Lokin's desk. The circle around *Isaac Valoran*. "You need Kane's relic or someone his power can pass to, so Kier has you spelling his body while the guilds search?"

Saira looks darkly at her. "My son has no idea Kane is here. For the sake of the guilds, it must stay that way."

Her mind is a war of thoughts as she trails Saira back to the spellroom.

"You're hiding something that affects the entire rule," Ophelia says as Kier's mother steps round the work table, removing her scarf.

Kane, as an empty vessel, isn't just something Kier would find useful. He would consider it treason his own mother is keeping the existence of a Magie king secret, right here at court.

Saira holds out an arm as her bird returns to the room. It flaps to a sleeve, trembling, even as it leans in to let Saira stroke its chest. With a grim look, the woman says, "My son plotted for thirty-five years to retrieve the Dark Shadow Dagger. The things he sacrificed before your time, I won't even tell you."

Everything good, Ophelia thinks.

Saira stares into her bird's beady eyes. "Kier is not the boy who found his mother under lock at Gray Castle, nor is he the man who freed me later. I see his father in him now. The ruin he craves for all who threaten his power. The dark lengths to which he will go."

If I have to be the monster a thousand times for you, I will.

"I should've known from the start," Saira laments, walking with the bird to gaze into a glass jar on her shelf where a tentacle-like limb twitches. "In all our history, there's never been a darkwielder eager to share. Not Kier's father or his grandfather. Not Erebus himself."

Ophelia thinks of the story Kier told her about the god of darkness tricked into sharing the throne. And here, Saira is implying her son doesn't want the relics to balance power, but to keep it. Would that be out of character? She saw Kier's ruin at Wythe. Yet, she grapples with what else she's seen. The damn smirks. His memories. The concern he has for his people.

Folding her arms, Ophelia explains, "Kier and I have allied to find the relics and restore the guilds. You think if he knew Kane was here that he would kill him? Why would he end an entire line?"

Saira makes a soft snort. "Messandra would be spinning in the sky." As Ophelia frowns at her odd phrasing, the bird under Saira's hand grows more agitated. "My son has had decades of practice playing the broken boy," she says. "Don't convince yourself he can be fixed because he told you his name and—what?—that you two will save the world together?"

Her coldness makes Ophelia bristle, even as she worries the woman's right. "You don't believe in him."

"Oh, I do. I think, without question, he sees you two left in the end and he'll risk a great deal to be sure of it." Saira's gaze trails Ophelia's neck, stopping where Ophelia's hand has unconsciously gone to rest over the Shadow marking.

The woman stills. "He's tethered you."

Ophelia drops her hand, anxious at Saira's alarmed expression and how she grips the bird so tightly it squawks, trying to wriggle free.

"Have you heard of *viclumeni*?" she asks Ophelia.

The word sounds old and powerful, as if there is kindling in its syllables, but it's unfamiliar. "No. What is it?"

The bird struggles free, but Saira snatches its foot, laying a finger to the top of its head. To Ophelia's horror, it collapses to the table and the air in the room seems to gasp.

Saira walks away, twisting the spellring off her finger to gaze at it regretfully, as though she's thinking of Kane in that bed. "I've already told you too much," she riddles. "But it's something I'd look into, if I were you."

CHAPTER 30
MIRRORS & OBJECTS

EAST WING AT GHASTLY
11TH DAY IN THE NEW WINTER
OPHELIA IS ON HER OWN

On the eve of your coronation, I should warn you: The primordial relics were forged to keep the guilds in perfect balance, but their power is difficult to resist. If any offspring of the gods were allowed to nurture darker ambitions with the instruments, they could well be used to reshape the guilds.

Note found in *Primordial Gods: A Forging of Power,* from Queen Messandra Dannan to King Kane Valoran

G laring at every pretty painting she passes, Ophelia storms through the east wing, relishing the slap of her boots against the marble. She hates Saira's accusations as much as her own defense of Kier. But what she hates most of all are the secrets she now holds inside her.

She will confront him. If not to give Saira away, then at least to make him lay his cards on the table—to make him look her in the eye and tell her his true plans for the rule.

It's dusk. The harsh pink of the moons slants sharply through the windows in the east hall as she crosses it.

If everything Saira said about Kier is true, how stupid that, for even one moment, Ophelia dared hope he wasn't the monster he swore to be. She reconsiders every interaction. Every word. Every look. Every promise. She never fully trusted him, but somehow—*somehow*—she began to believe he was redeemable.

He did tell her, though, didn't he? *Let empathy slow your sword with the wrong beast, it's you who will end up on the pike.*

Standing at the threshold of his study, the peaked doors cracked to offer a narrow view into the room, she sees shelves on a stark wall, the tidy spines of old books, and a lone chair angled toward a fire within reach of a snifter holding amber liquid. She means to throw the door open, but the sight of his silhouette interrupting the fire glow stills her hand.

Kier wears none of his armor, only leather pants and a tunic, and his hair is markedly disheveled, as though he's fought with it all evening. She loathes that it deflates her anger, throwing her thoughts to what might've happened at the Council of Guilds.

"You're not supposed to be here." His voice startles her, but his troubled brows aim elsewhere in the room, toward someone else who strides into sight.

"I know," the man replies.

Ophelia's eyes flash. *Jasper Salt.* She'd recognize his voice anywhere, if not his cocksure stance. The skinny blades that clang at his belt, too—one of which pierced Commander Jory Dagon's eye through to his skull.

Salt's hair is no longer brown, but a tousled blond combed into an arrogant peak. His face appears less round—his true face, she realizes, not the one he wore as "Captain Rivmere." He's gallingly handsome in profile and looks flushed, as if he arrived just moments before her.

Kier is frowning. "I need you in the West, Jas." *Jas.* An ease, a trust, a friendship between them.

"I'm heading to Hobb's estate from here, but Gentry just heard from Trix Farrow. I thought I'd bring his report myself."

Kier gives his back to the fire. "And why do you look so grave?"

Salt bows his head. "Farrow's unit met an attack of drecora, just outside Kúzlo."

The storm of anger in Ophelia shifts. Kier sent Trix to the icelands?

The dark king's expression is chilling. "Tell me they lived," he commands, his words so quiet Ophelia strains an ear to the door.

It creaks.

Her eyes shutter a moment as dread ricochets off every rib bone in her chest. She bites her lip and doesn't move, checking that her shield is up.

Salt cocks his head, but when she makes no more noise, his shoulders relax and he continues, "We don't know. Dragonfire cut the conversation short, and Gentry's return summons still goes unanswered."

Kier's silhouette looms taller up a wall. His shadows. "Find out. I need Falcon Thames alive until he delivers the North to our side, understand?"

Ophelia recoils from the door like it's spit blades at her and stumbles into something hard. Whirling, she catches a vase as it teeters on a table by the wall.

Falcon.

Kier sent Falcon north with Trix.

Kier has Falcon.

Replacing the vase with trembling hands, she startles at the sight of herself in an oval mirror. Eyes dark and mooned. Brows narrowed to the point of looking venomous.

Kier has Falcon.

Heat consumes her. A heat that feels separate from her raw magic, from her connection to the dust. It feels ancient and primal.

Kier swore he wouldn't touch Falcon. That was their deal in Ravish.

I would have done far worse...

Her fury takes shape in the mirror. Saira's accusations about Kier were horrible enough. Somehow, this is worse. This is personal. *This is Falcon.*

Is this what Saira was alluding to? What Kier will do in the name of keeping his power? To destroy Osiris, to get his revenge, he would lie to her, manipulate her, hurt those she loves?

The throne room has three empty seats, she reminds herself.

But what if Ophelia doesn't claim her crown? What if she leaves him to rule alone?

She never wanted to be queen, but the weight of that invisible robe she felt laid upon her shoulders earlier presses down. In the mirror, golden threads of magic rise in her irises and the ghost of a crown appears upon her head—a crown of blood and lies. Her golden dragon looms just over her shoulder, its eyes like molten fire, urging her to claim it—willing her to announce herself, take the throne, and checkmate the dark king.

Ophelia backs slowly away from her reflection and the manifestation of her power, shaking her head.

She cannot be queen.

All she can think, as that strange heat flames inside of her, is *Falcon*. If he is dead... If Kier sent him to his death... Her fists clench and she loses every shred of control she's allowed Kier to help her shape.

The mirror splits—it *shatters*—with a violent crack, and glass glitters across the floor of the hall.

Kier calls out from the study. And she runs.

Flames jump on candlewicks when Ophelia bursts through her chamber doors.

From where her attendants are setting out dinner, Hannah startles in surprise. "My lady."

Ophelia shuts the door hastily behind her. She's had very little time alone with her attendants while Kier has kept her busy. Forgoing any formality now, she says, "I need your help."

Isolde casts a worried look at Hannah, but the elder woman doesn't seem surprised. "Anything, my lady."

"Did you know why I was out of my bed on the floor that night you and Isolde found me?" The night she traveled to Rune.

"You screamed, my lady," Isolde replies.

Hannah merely nods.

Ophelia exhales. "You told me not to speak about it to anyone. Why?"

In the orange candlelight of the room, Hannah's eyes glitter. "Because it's your advantage, my lady, just as it was your mother's."

Her mother. Ophelia rushes to the women. "You knew her?"

Hannah nods fervently, her eyes wetting. "She was like my own child. We heard rumors that her daughter was alive and I thanked Selene for it. I only hoped I would get to see you again, to help you."

Survivors.

"You," Ophelia realizes. "It was you who got my mother out of the Magie palace all those years ago. You kept her amulet safe."

Hannah nods. "It was chaos. King Lucius and Queen Messandra had been...slain in the throne room." With a steadying breath, the woman holds her head high. "I raised Elora as best as I could in Kúzlo. She grew. She fell in love. Then you were born—"

"Kúzlo?" Ophelia cuts in. What was it Stolm said? *That is no western accent you have.* "I was born in Kúzlo?"

"Amid sacred ice and tribal fires," Hannah says. "I kept Elora's lineage a secret, but there were seers in the tribe who always suspected. When you were born, they baptized you with dragon's blood."

Ophelia fights a wave of emotion. It makes more sense now, why her raw magic would manifest as a lightdragon; she was born in the North where her mother grew up.

"My mother had the amulet when she left me. She said she needed to make it disappear. Do you think she could've returned to Kúzlo with it?"

"It's possible, my lady," Hannah replies.

"Then—"

Shadows slip against Ophelia's mental walls, like smoke climbing iron, just as a rap comes at the door. "Ophelia?" Kier calls.

She touches Hannah's arm with urgency. "Was my mother like me?" She hopes the woman understands the question—could Elora travel physically?

The door seems to shake under Kier's knock. "Ophelia."

Hannah glances over, but neither she nor Isolde move to answer it. "Yes," Hannah says in a hush. "It's how she moved you around the valleys of Kúzlo when royal soldiers first came around."

Trade talks, Stolm mentioned. And eventually they must have discovered what her mother was—the last source of god magic that Osiris didn't have control of.

"Ophelia, why is the door locked?" Kier calls.

"A moment!" Grabbing the robe set out on the bed, she slings it around her dress. To her attendants, she whispers, "Go draw a bath."

When the water starts to run, Ophelia smooths her face. Shoving her anger down—all the secrets Saira imposed on her and her burning fury over Falcon—she cracks the door to find Kier taking up its frame.

"Are you all right?" He looks her over, dripping with worry. "Were you just outside my study?"

She doesn't blink, only gestures to her robe.

His demeanor relaxes. "Stolm said you fell into a ground passage in the guilds. You required a healer." Kier starts to raise a hand, but seems to remember the ward at her door. "I should have warned you." His eyes are flint, unbelievably earnest.

My son has had decades of practice playing the broken boy.

Kier might be well versed in deception, but Ophelia has had practice honing her poker face while swindling mortals with Falcon. She forces a weak smile. "I'm all right, Kier."

His mouth twitches to a faint smile, pleased, she thinks, to hear his name.

She motions behind her. "I was about to take a bath. Can we speak tomorr..." The word trails off as she notices the armored leather he wears, and on his shoulder a strap that usually holds the guard where his shadow creatures perch in battle. "Are you going somewhere?"

He nods, the motion sending his raven coiffure over a brow. For the casual way he smooths it back, knowing—*knowing*—he is lying to her about Falcon, Ophelia loathes him. Loathes she felt any tenderness toward him at all.

"I'll be gone a few days," he says with regret. "I promised the council I'd tamp the skirmishes in the West. It'll go faster if I see to the task myself."

She knows what *faster* means. His mist is a devourer of men. She feels suddenly cold.

Kier studies her, his thumb brushing the doorframe. "It's war, Ophelia." When she makes herself nod, he decrees, "I imagined it wouldn't interest you to go. Stolm can stay behind, show you where the passages are so you're safe within these walls."

Safe. She wants to spit that word back at him. At Ghastly, safe connotates secrets. Safe means traps set at night around the east wing because Kier doesn't trust the people in his court—which of course is why he sent her into the Morphists Guild to begin with.

She searches his face for signs of the lies, but he is that good. It doesn't matter. Nothing matters but that his legion has Falcon. That he's keeping secrets. That his own mother believes he will be the ruin of the guilds.

"I don't need Stolm to watch me," she assures him, keeping her voice light even as she adds layer after layer of ice and iron around her walls. "You've taught me well, Kier."

There's pride in his face at that. Bastard.

"Fine," he acquiesces. "But after this trip, I hope to visit with some representatives. I'll call on you, Ophelia, as my agent."

It's what she promised to do—spy for him. Her teeth clench. They were supposed to find the relics together, too. And they've done none of that.

Behind her shield, all she can think is, *a few days. I might have a few days.* Feigning a sleepy smile, she nods. "Travel safely."

As she begins to shut the door, Kier catches it. "Your walls feel stronger."

She hardly blinks. "I've been practicing."

He nods, thoughtful. Then his eyes grasp hers. "Did you learn anything useful tonight?" There's something there, beneath the surface of that question, teasing another test.

She has to give him something. If not her secrets, something he wants. On their walk to Ghastly, he told her: *You're here at Ghastly because I want you here—as queen, but also an equal.* Visualizing a chess board in her mind, Ophelia moves her queen to the center as she says, "More than useful. Seeing the guilds, I've discovered you were right."

"Right?" he echoes, sounding intrigued.

"To think I might change my mind about being queen."

Kier's eyes flash in surprise, and his hand tightens on the door frame. When he opens his mouth to reply, a voice beckons from the hall. His legion.

"A minute," he calls over his shoulder, his breath a long, frustrated growl as he turns back. "I have to go."

"We'll talk when you return." Let him think her eagerness is for him.

She tries not to shiver as Kier's gaze travels her robe, as he backs slowly away from her door. Only when his silhouette disappears from the hall does she exhale and turn away, feeling as though fate guides her next move. Falcon was sent to the same place her mother grew up, where Elora felt safe and fell in love and Ophelia was born. That feels like more than a coincidence.

Facing Hannah and Isolde, she says, "I need to get to Kúzlo now. Tell me. How did my mother travel, physically?"

Hannah rubs the ruby in her sleeve, as though the idea makes her nervous. "With an object of a place or person. But, my lady, it's dangerous. This sort of travel—your mother called it *fading*—it isn't permanent. The object remains here as an anchor for the magic. Depending on its strength, you could be called back at any moment."

She doesn't care about the consequences. She doesn't care about *safe*. All that matters is Falcon and Hart and Rune, the relics, and the end game—true freedom.

She needs an object, then, like Rune's white book. Every beat of her heart pulses to the rhythm of *Falcon, Falcon, Falcon* as she bends for the winged blade he gifted her, always tucked in the sheath on her boot.

Hannah's eyes widen and with a soft gasp, she asks, "Where did you get that?"

It takes Ophelia aback. "From an important friend." But there's no time for stories right now. Jasper Salt said Falcon might be dead. "Can you help me?"

Hannah slides a quick look to Isolde, picking up on Ophelia's urgency. "That's a special blade, my lady. You should keep it close to you. Is there another object you can use that can stay hidden here?"

Ophelia scours her mind. She has nothing else of Falcon's with her, but if he's alive, he's probably with Trix.

In the wardrobe, Ophelia searches the pocket of the cloak she wore out of Ravish, finding the thick spellcloth she used to dab Trix's hand wound. She'd hastily stuffed it there before they climbed to the roof, before Kier came with his shadows.

She holds it up. "All right, tell me how."

CHAPTER 31
SCALES & SCARS

The first time a dragon tried to kill him, Falcon was seven.

Crouched behind a boulder with his brother, a blade, and a reckless plan, he tried not to think what the elders would do if they caught *nakommen* at the base of the Virstone.

Tribal children, especially heirs, didn't belong anywhere near the volcanic mount, let alone the sleeping grounds of a hundred-sixty-eight drecora. Even the *seshen*, Kúzloan warriors welded to the beasts, knew better than to breach it.

But enough was enough. Falcon frowned at the purple knot on Kessan's cheek, the second bruise in a week courtesy of two other heirs.

Falcon nodded toward the nests. "How about that one—with the white plumes and blue ironspade?"

Kessan fidgeted. "Too fierce."

"Fierce is the point, Kess. You want to stop getting pummeled by Sunder and Xakai, you have to go big."

There were nine heirs who called the *volorost* father. *Nakommen* of nearly the same age, from different mothers, all with a jealous streak. Falcon used his fists to deal with any taunting. But Kessan was scrawnier, and Sunder and Xakai, relentless.

The bruises would make Kessan a warrior, the *volorost* had said. So long as you didn't kill an heir, tribal beliefs would stand: In the North, the strong will rise. But Kessan wasn't strong—not yet—and Falcon could see his confidence waning with every run-in.

The soft spot he felt for his half-brother pulsed as Kessan turned a blade over in his hands. "You're sure if I bring the scale back, they'll honor me?"

"They'll be bowing at your feet."

When *seshen* cut and wore a drecora's scale, it marked the beast theirs. Normally, that didn't happen for at least a few years.

Unlike Falcon, who questioned everything, Kessan believed in the northern ways to a fault. Someday, he'd be a good leader of the North, if he could survive the other heirs. He had to. Because Falcon didn't want their father's job, sitting in a mountain all his life. It would be more exciting to hunt and go on patrols, to be out in the world protecting it.

Falcon cupped a hand behind his brother's head and brought Kessan's forehead to his own. "Sei braven, nast ruchsi."

"'Daring, not dumb,'" Kessan agreed. It was what the *seshen* they idolized said before every patrol.

"Watch the traps," Falcon reminded as they set off.

In the claw of the moonslight, they weaved a careful route, quiet as ground mice around the sleeping beasts as big as homes. As they crept near, Falcon could feel the ground tremor a little under his feet from their heavy breaths. He'd never been this close to them without a *seshen*.

When they were within arm's length of the ironspade, Kessan stopped and gaped. Falcon's heart climbed to his throat. Sharp, white-blue fronds framed the drecora's massive face. Its horns were over half Falcon's body height, and overlapping blue scales shimmered where they basked under the moons, fed by the magic of the night.

Falcon felt every breath the drecora took in his own chest. Maybe this was *ruchsi*. But dumb or not, he crept toward the ironspade's tail, motioning with encouragement at Kessan, who began to reach for a scale.

The drecora twitched, its tail spasming in sleep. A low, terrifying purr grumbled through its chest.

His brother froze, but his dragonblade shook.

"Kess," Falcon hissed. They couldn't hesitate.

With a hard swallow, Kessan reached again. Again, his hand tremored. "I—"

"Do it now!"

Kessan looked panicked at the thick, deadly tail, but his hand wouldn't budge.

Prone to cursing already, Falcon let an expletive fly as he reached into his furs, drawing his own blade out. "Then I'll do it for you." He wouldn't let his brother fail.

But Kessan's eyes narrowed on the blade with suspicion, as if it was dawning on him that Falcon might want the scale for himself.

"I don't need it," Falcon insisted. "I'll give it to you."

His brother's eyes stormed with desperation and fear, and his hands twitched like they wished they were braver. Reluctantly, he stepped away from the nest.

A born warrior, Falcon didn't hesitate. He'd knifed a boarhound his first hunt last month. Said the rites. Helped clean the meat. Even now, when his heart beat against his ribs, he didn't doubt himself.

He would be Kessan's blade.

It was easier than he imagined to carve a scale loose. He sliced cleanly, just above the skin. But he wasn't expecting how it would feel to hold it in his palm. Rough as leather, but light and warm, it felt like it belonged there, with him.

"Falcon," his brother urged, stepping forward with a hand out. "Quick. The scale."

A crack belted under Kessan's boot. Stunned, the pair of brothers didn't move. Didn't breathe.

The drecora's slitting eye blinked open, and Falcon felt a hand tug at his coat. Kessan, pale as snow.

They ran.

Falcon heard the beast groan from its nest, felt the ground shake under its weight. Then, more rumbling. The hisses and shrieks of other drecora waking up.

He'd never moved his legs so fast in his life.

"Faster!" he shoved at Kessan.

Icy breath reached the back of his neck as he sprinted with his blade and the blue scale in one hand, Kessan lagging just behind him. Reaching back, he fisted Kessan's coat to pull him along, then heard the crunch of talons.

Fear shone in Kessan's eyes. His shorter legs stumbled, and all Falcon could think as his mind spun was how they couldn't both die. Not one of the other heirs were fit to run the North.

A sheen of ice, razor thin, glinted ahead like salvation. One of the animal traps the *seshen* set to catch the valley's meat.

Already regretting it, Falcon slowed, allowing Kessan to pull ahead of him, waiting until they were just close enough. Then he shoved his brother, hard.

Kessan screamed as he crashed through the thin veil of ice, falling down into a pit too narrow for a drecora to fit inside—a pit big enough for only one of them. His chin smacked the ice, and his small hands clawed at the walls on his way down.

Spinning, Falcon found the ironspade within breathing distance, the spikes on its back flexing like blades.

Then it roared. A sound to shatter ice a whole lot thicker.

He'd never heard a drecora shriek so close. It rattled his brain and would likely wake the warriors who slept a mile away.

The ironspade's fronds glinted like spears as it hulked forward, hurtling another splitting screech. This time, sound *popped*.

Excruciating pain stabbed his ears, and the world muffled as he folded to his knees near the trap. Falcon caught a dizzying sight of the drecora, saw it drawing its neck back and opening its mouth. Throwing himself flat on the ground, he narrowly missed the shards that shot from its angry jaws. With half his face pressed to the snow, he felt ice tear like talons at his furs—and the sting of a shard slicing the flesh on his cheek.

Drawing the hand that held the scale to touch his face, Falcon winced at something wet. Blood. He was delirious, maybe. But when he pulled his hand away, it seemed to shine. Or, rather, the scale did.

It took a second to realize the dragonfire had stopped. Falcon risked a glance to find the tension in the drecora's posture soften as it studied him.

He scrutinized the scale in his hand, covered in his own blood. Then the ground was trembling beneath him again, and while the pain in his ears was dulling to a deep ache, sound was still muffled.

He couldn't hear right.

He couldn't—

Falcon shook his head, trying to bring full sound back. At an indecipherable noise, he saw the ironspade whip its head in the opposite direction. Then its membranous wings unfolded in front of him, like a canopy over the ice. With a powerful push, it was off, a rush of wind cascading over his back as the beast took to the sky.

Distant silhouettes—more drecora leaving the Valley of Ice, and others arriving.

It wasn't until he saw Yuli tearing across the Shelves toward him, until the russet-haired warrior with a constellation inked on his cheeks helped Falcon to his feet, that he realized some of the welded had come. *Seshen.*

Eight stood around him moving their lips, pointing at the scale Falcon held. They didn't seem to care a *nakommen* had breached the sleeping grounds. He wasn't flogged. They hoisted him onto their shoulders to what he thought was a chant. The words came in fragments, about slaying what no *nakommen* had so young—their fear of the dragon.

"*Jagerin,*" they chanted on. "*Jagerin, jagerin, jagerin!*" While Kessan sat in an animal trap. Kessan, who Falcon had sworn to make strong.

"Kess," he tried to tell the *seshen.* His brother was there. The scale was meant for Kessan. But the chanting and ringing stifled his voice.

*F*uck, *fuck, fuck.*

When the old memory fades, Falcon sees the flight field has cleared of dragonfire. The first thing he spots are dead bodies.

Of the Darkwielder's emissaries, Anesh and a copper-haired Shadowcaster are splayed motionless, limbs tangled, their skin gone gray. Falcon curses as it starts to flake and crumble and the northern wind carries their faces, their necks, and the rest of them with it as ash.

Beside them are two more dead—already piles in their pelts.

A groan. "Gods of Magus, they breathe ice?"

Trix lifts her head from where she lies prone just next to him. Beside her, Ashë appears unscathed, drawing a blade up by her face.

"Don't move," Falcon implores them.

Running, fighting, wielding magic—each would be a deadly mistake given a patrol of seven drecora have them surrounded.

Not the homecoming he'd hoped for.

A bubbling gasp. He finds the last of the Darkwielder's emissaries lying on his back, choking on the blade of ice that impales his throat. A few more breaths, and he goes slack, too.

It's just the three of them left. Him, Trix, and Ashë.

On a ragged breath, Falcon hauls himself to his feet, raising his hands to half-mast in a gesture of peace.

One by one around the ridge, drecora lift their wings and soar from their perches, alighting with a torrent of air onto the field. They hiss and keen, talking to each other. But Falcon's focus narrows to the wide, lethal beast that just obliterated half his group. Its severe claws, like picks in the ice. Its formidable plume of white horns and the blading fronds that frame its face. Its spikes, snaking down its elegant spine to a blue ironspade tail.

Wind breezes in and out of the drecora's nostrils as if it were Falcon's own breath.

He saunters toward it.

"Falcon!" Trix whispers harshly as he leaves them there.

The drecora bares her crocodile teeth, its gigantic chest rumbling and swelling, and a tunnel of frigid air slows Falcon's step.

Its reptilian pupils dilate at him from several paces away.

Falcon's stilled by his own reflection in the silver-blue of an eye. He looks a wild man with his thick pelt, long hair, chiseled jaw full of stubble, and the white scar he got that night fifteen years ago seeming to shine down the length of his face.

"Rakúa," he says, calling the drecora by name.

Her nostrils flex like she's tasting his scent, while her eyes look straight through his soul. The low snarl she emits then is more purr than growl, vibrating in her chest.

"Talvi!" a male voice commands from above. *Get back!*

When Rakúa lowers her head and shoulders, her flyer splays a hand over her scales, using them to guide their descent down her massive leg.

With the eyes of six other beasts penetrating, with Trix and Ashë bellied on the ice, Falcon fastens a look at the flyer—a slender warrior in a flight mask, matching patrol coat, and white northern furs.

When he removes his mask and Falcon sees a blue scale set on a chain around his neck, it's like looking in a damn mirror of what he might've been. It's not the same scale Falcon took from Rakúa, and fifteen years have passed, but he knows the man instantly.

Harsh, light eyes skewer Falcon as the flyer stalks forward. "Nast sagen am drecora." *Do not speak to my drecora.*

Falcon flexes the hand that wears a tournament ring. "Technically, she was mine before she was yours, Kess."

FOUR
UNINVITED GUESTS

CHAPTER32
HEROES & HEIRS

Green flames burn in warning at Kúzlo's gate. While Falcon's every bit the outsider after fifteen years, the scent of *migth* and smoke cuts like a blade of nostalgia on his tongue.

Glancing at the drecora circling overhead, he draws out the last of his blades from his skin sheath, laying it alongside all of their other weapons—his, Trix's, and the wraith's.

Being stripped makes his skin itch. Except to clean his knives, Falcon hasn't been empty of weapons in a good, long while.

The young *seshen* inspecting the pile grunts at him. "You lose your dragonblade, heir?"

Falcon pushes away the image of Ophelia in her nightgown, when she ran a finger along the edges, how he seemed to feel it in his chest. "Wasn't exactly mine."

"No, it wasn't." Kessan draws up, addressing the young *seshen*, but staring at Falcon. "We confiscate northern weapons when people leave us in disgrace."

He doesn't tell his brother that weapon was his very first smuggle, how since he left Kúzlo he's gotten even better at hiding things in his ink.

The gate opens with the groan of the ancient stone door, tall as a drecora and bearing a winged blade crest. Kessan flanks Falcon on the right, leaving Trix and Ashë to trail behind as they enter the Valley of Iron.

Surrounded by *seshen* he hardly recognizes, their little party takes a path that still feels familiar, one that mazes through narrow rock walls where Falcon can feel the weight of stares from women in fur headscarves and men in pinned pelts. They're all standing or crouched on slabs and boulders to watch the return of the *disgraced* heir.

He doesn't miss the curses muttered in the crowd. "So you've still got them believing the story you wove," he says to Kessan, who keeps his chin high.

"The truth of your betrayal, you mean."

The words chafe as much as Kessan's still-belief in them. A man's name means something. "If I'd wanted you dead, I would've carved your throat out instead of cutting a scale for you."

"*For me*," Kessan laughs, the sound forced, nothing like the unfettered joy of when they were young and not yet rivals. "Your version of events must have made your mother and sister proud. Is that why you have come to risk your life in the tournament? To right misperceived wrongs?"

A roll of anger mallets Falcon's hands.

Not now, he tells himself. *Not with the tribe watching.*

He's here for one reason—to get the North in the war. Forget the past. Forget Kessan. He needs an audience with the *volorost*.

Falcon feels some relief when the walls widen around the procession and night unspools, cloaked in particles that undulate in a slow rhythm. Heavy clouds veil the moons over the Valley of Iron, and the city he once knew as well as his own hands breathes like a secret below the twelve mounts that form its circumference. Mounts home to the *migth* mines most will never get this close to.

This felt like home once. Tonight, ghosts of the past poke at Falcon's back.

Fires burn bright in every corner of the valley, and more flicker up on the great iron wall, where a narrow walkway connects the mines. Around the edge, small stone homes fortified with moon metal stand in an orderly fashion among old, homespun taverns and places for spellmaking, school, and trade. As they trek to the center, the wind kicks up through rows of white canvas tents.

Falcon feels his throat thicken, seeing the *yurten* where Yuli taught him to clean meat off fish and how to remove a hook from his palm. Another where he, Kessan, Kaitriona, and their friend Reya gaped at Fabricaters forging blades for *seshen* from the skeletons of dead dragons. At a familiar weaving tent, he can see himself as a kid, waiting at the basket stacks for his mother to walk back home with him to the House of Bone.

His mother who'd liked the cold because she said it was honest, given by the gods to remind them what they were made of. It was just one of the things Falcon had thought made her strong.

Their party tromps on, boots scuffing over the path where white pebbles have been laid. Falcon glances up to where the House of Bone stands like a sentry, its imposing white façade carved into the tallest mount in the Valley of Iron.

The crowds thicken as they approach, and Falcon hears a shout—"*Jagerin!*" His eye catches on a woman's fist in the air. Beside her, another rises. It's a chain reaction, and soon a quarter of the crowd wields the gesture that signifies honor and respect.

He feels the weight of what he must ask these people to risk—their peace. But they'll lose it, anyway, if they do nothing.

Amid the fists, there are also jeers. Though his blades were confiscated, taking most of his tattoos with them, Falcon can feel the phantom skitter of his ink. Winged silhouettes soar overhead, the presence of drecora making a brawl in the Bowl unlikely. Still, Falcon glances over a shoulder at Trix and the wraith. The two are tense, surveying the crowds with wariness. He told them days ago what to expect here. But it's a whole other thing to see the North.

"*Jes.*" Kessan's clipped tone draws Falcon's attention. His brother's eyes color from white to blue as he comes out of a brief summons and fix Falcon with an unhappy look. "The patrol will not spill your blood," he reports. "And given your mother took your punishment as her own long ago, you are not bound to banishment. Though some of us would be glad to welcome you back properly in the *stadhelm*."

Falcon gives Kessan a look of surprise. His brother's got a wiry build, but strong shoulders. A well-trained posture and ready stance. Maybe in retrieving that scale Falcon did make Kessan strong. "You fight there?" Falcon asks. "I might pay to see that, *bruden*."

"I am not your brother anymore."

The insult hits its mark harder than Falcon would care to admit. "Kess. Look, I'm not here to stir up personal shit. I just need to talk to Ryke. There are things coming he has to hear about."

"The war?" Kessan replies.

"You've seen it?"

Though Kessan clamps his mouth shut, Falcon imagines his affinity has grown with time; Kessan was always headed for a seat on the *Nomme Geseh*, the conclave of seers.

"If you've seen what's coming," Falcon presses, "you know Kúzlo needs a powerful ally."

"The elders are allowing you to compete in the tournament," Kessan cuts. "With special considerations. The rest of the heirs will be allowed to abdicate their matches. Their lives will not be wasted. But yours..." He trails, letting Falcon paint the picture himself.

Letting a long breath go, he surveys the crowd. "If that's the price for a family reunion, fine."

Closing in on the steep stairs to the House of Bone, where firelight dances on curious spectators, Kessan halts the procession. "The *volorost* does not need your war counsel, if that is what you think you bring here," he says, voice low. "I do not know, or care, what you have been doing all these years, but you have been gone a long time. Things are different. There are alliances in progress to ensure the icelands' protection."

Falcon's hackles raise.

"And," Kessan says, "you will not see our father, unless by the gods you make it to the final match."

"Kess—"

"I am the favored." He jabs a finger at his own chest. "I fly the most powerful drecora in existence. I will win The Sanctioning, and you, *bruden*, will be ash in the wind of the Valley of Bones."

Falcon's anger could melt the frozen ground on which they stand.

Fifteen years gone, nine goddamn years in the Belly, and he's never needed restraint. He's given his anger its outlet. He itches to unleash it, to shake the fucking daylight out of Kessan and impress on him what's at stake. But strength talks here, and a face floats from the back of Falcon's mind, where things like shame and grief and joy and love have shaped memories he'll never shake. Where *she* is always waiting with a brow raised. Ophelia.

He reminds himself on a long breath that he's not here to slay old ghosts.

Falcon relaxes the fists he's clenched to hammers, knowing he can't lay Kessan out, not if he has the *volorost*'s ear. "All right," he replies, feeling the weight of all the stares aimed their way. "I don't want blood or the title, but we'll do it your way."

With a seething look, Kessan turns, assessing Trix and the wraith. To his patrol, he commands, "Take them inside. My betrothed will get them acclimated to our ways while their *champion* prepares to train."

Kessan holds his attention on Trix. "You will be guests in the House of Bone until the tournament concludes. You will carry no weapons, start no trouble, and wield no magic if you do not wish to be fed to the drecora in the Valley of Ice. Clear?"

Trix looks coiled as a snake, despite the fact they need to be diplomatic here. She slides a gaze to Falcon, who nods.

"Crystal," she replies through her teeth.

Kessan motions his patrol to escort the women up the stairs, then follows. *Seshen* nudge Falcon with their carved, wooden clubs, and he climbs, the cold of the wind scraping his lungs.

A group of warriors stands to one side on the stairs, wearing sheaths like ribs and scowls of judgment that Falcon pointedly ignores. Among them, he's met with the sharp stare and sneering smile of a warrior with deep, bronze skin.

Even after all these years, he recognizes the heir. Braids stark-white, Sunder wears a red diamond scale around his neck and the chipped tooth he deserved courtesy of Falcon when they were kids.

As Kessan passes, Sunder steps into his path. Falcon bristles at the open hatred in the heir's scrutiny. *Goddamn ghosts.*

Before *seshen* can surround them, Sunder spews a cacophony of slander in Magiesian, but not so hastily that Falcon doesn't catch every word: "The great betrayer has returned. And without his pretty whore mother."

And just, fuck it.

With Kessan's words still ringing in his head, Falcon launches his weight at Sunder before the heir can get a weapon or any magic free, his fist cracking cartilage as he lays Sunder out violently on the steps of the House of Bone, all to the chants of "*Jagerin! Jagerin!*"

As he's pulled off and shoved up the stairs, the veins in his neck swell with his thundering pulse. When he reaches Kessen, Falcon seethes, "The *stadhelm* then."

The valley seems to cheer louder, like the tournament's unofficially begun.

CHAPTER 33
NORTH & GRUDGES

KÚZLO IN THE NORTHERN TERRITORIES
11TH NIGHT IN THE NEW WINTER
OPHELIA IS ON HER OWN

Ophelia is struck by shouts and the slam of bodies, by an air thick with the scent of oils and sweat.

Ghastly's gone. She's faded into some cavern, where a foreign crowd in leathers and furs is throwing their fists to the air, chanting to a drumbeat.

Staggering against a rocky wall, hands tingling and heart thrashing, she angles her face to hide the soft glow of her skin and gives her body a moment to become fully corporeal.

With a glance around, she wages she's in the bowels of a mountain, in an arena that looks hollowed out of rock and ice. It isn't encouraging that anchoring to Trix's spellcloth led her here, where nightmarish sounds ricochet and there's no mistaking the crack of bones.

Hannah warned her Kúzlo was its own breed of rough.

Metal rings from the depths of the place, followed by a ferocious growl that sounds barely human.

"Kamfe! Kamfe! Kamfe!" the crowd shouts. *Fight! Fight! Fight!*

A fighting pit.

She trembles—not so much from the "fading," the dampness of the cavern, or even the northerners' call for blood and the wild intensity of *maether* pulsing at her—but from knowing Trix must be somewhere close. Which means Falcon could be here.

He could be here.

Peering between tall, sculpted bodies, she assesses women and men wearing raucous, loose smiles, their hair tightly woven in chignons or braids, the same way Ophelia wound hers after seeing her mother in the looking water.

At the time, she had no idea she'd been born with northern blood.

She blends in well, wearing Hannah's old garb: a brown hood scarf, leather pants and bodice, and gray-white pelts that drape her shoulders. Along with northern attire, she has a hand-drawn map and as much knowledge about the icelands—and what to be wary of—as Hannah and Isolde could impart before she traveled.

Searching through the throng, she's taken aback at the number of face tattoos, the likes of which she has only ever seen on Elora and Saira. Deep-blue symbols with delicate lines that speak to ancient traditions. She'd assumed the inking was tied to the Magie rule, but maybe the women were given the markings here.

Ophelia's scanning for anyone she might recognize when a shock of copper hair catches her eye. The female's back is turned and she's dressed like a northerner, but her physique is familiar as she perches near a ledge with no rail. Keeping this possible Trix in view, she shoves off the rock and into the masses just as the crowd erupts in a round of frenzied cheers and a brute of a man rears into her path. A woman hangs on him, devouring his mouth.

Ophelia grunts against their collective weight, catching herself on a table before continuing forward. She takes stock of other roaming hands and mouths—other couples tangled in open displays—and though she doesn't begrudge anyone expressing their love or desire, at present it's making her path difficult.

Pushing forward, she threads in a circle around the woman she hopes is Trix until she's able to catch her profile. It is the Spellcaster, standing beside another female with plaited white hair and a thin, muscled frame.

A blade flicks out of the crowd, halting Ophelia's step. "Nisht regen." *Don't move.*

Slipping into view at the other end of the dirk aimed at Ophelia's throat is a woman with narrowed eyes, elfin features, and braided golden hair that skims her waist. "How did you get in here?" Intrigue, not accusation. "Kúzlo is closed for the tournament. Are you a spy for the Drünkeldisi?"

Ophelia's gaze darts from the tip of the blade at her throat to the northerner's confident stance.

"I warn you," the woman says, "I am good with a knife."

Ophelia guides her gaze toward Trix, holding it there until the woman tracks it. Then she swipes Falcon's blade from where it's stowed in her bodice and flicks the tip into place.

Two blades. Two throats.

"I've never been to Drünkeld," she replies. "And I'm fairly good with knives myself, but I'm not here to fight. I'm looking for my friend."

Sapphiric eyes flash at Ophelia, then at her weapon. "Not a spy, but a thief." The northerner sounds impressed as she lowers her dirk. "Which heir did you steal that from?"

Heir? Keeping her own blade aimed, Ophelia takes the woman's full measure. A woolen dress the color of a jade forest, too clean for a fighting pit. Furs neatly clasped at the neck. She looks a couple years older than Ophelia. "I didn't steal this," she replies. "It was given to me—"

"Reya Lark!" At the unexpected booming voice, both women cut a look into the crowd.

A bear of a man with a full chin of auburn hair is shoving his way toward them, an open leer on his face and a dram clutched in his fist. Ophelia lowers Falcon's blade discretely to her side before the warrior approaches.

Ale sloshing onto his boots, the man peacocks before them, Magiesian tumbling out his mouth in a slur that Ophelia translates as best as she can. "Did you come to bet more of your betrothed's good furs, Reya? Or are you looking for some other fun tonight?"

"Drunken pest," she mutters as the warrior's glazed interest blankets on Ophelia a brief moment before drifting back to Reya.

"So many layers," he observes of her attire. "Too warm for the *stad-helm*. But I can help with that." Grinning, he waves a hand, stirring a swell of *maether* Ophelia can sense as he calls upon his affinity. A pointed rush of air poofs Reya's hair off her collarbone, giving the pig a clear view of her cleavage between pinned furs.

"*Fun,* it is," he determines, stepping closer.

The desire to pummel the man with his own wind comes so fast, Ophelia's stunned to realize she's latched to his *maether* as surely as it were her own. She has the urge to tug, so she does. Air rips from him in a small burst, drawing a grunt. When it funnels back at him, the warrior staggers in surprise, ale dousing his face and shirt to leave a foamy trail down his chest.

As satisfaction purrs inside her, the *maether* she roped snaps, disconnecting her from his magic, and she quietly gasps with its release.

She just did that.

While the warrior wipes ale from his beard, scowling in their direction, Reya eyes Ophelia curiously. As the pig starts to say something, Reya knifes a gaze to him. "You will leave us now."

Ophelia can feel the force in those words, see the discomfiting way they wash over the man. This woman—Reya Lark—is an Enchanter.

Waving the Bender away as if he's a terrible nuisance, she mutters a last remark about her dirk and his manhood. The moment he's gone, her focus narrows keenly on Ophelia. "Not a spy and not a thief," she agrees, glancing at the weapon Ophelia still knuckles. "But then who?"

Ophelia considers her next move. Falcon always says there's a time to run and a time to gamble.

Sheathing her blade, she steps forward, lowering her voice below the din. "My name is Ophelia Dannan. My mother was from Kúzlo; she went by the name Elly." According to Hannah. "I've come for information about her and to find my—the man who gave me the blade. Falcon Thames. I think he's here with a woman named Trix."

Reya's face reshapes with surprise, her curiosity melting to realization. "Beatrix and Falcon?"

"You know them?" Sweet, desperate relief.

Reya's head lifts to catch some movement over Ophelia's shoulder. The woman swears. Following her gaze, Ophelia notes a man who's entered the upper floor from a tunnel. He's handsome, blond, and dressed in white pelts that distinguish him from the spectators.

"My betrothed," Reya says. "He'd like to think I'm too delicate for the *stadhelm*. Come." Grabbing Ophelia's arm, she pulls her in the opposite direction. "I know where your friend is."

When the crowd parts, Ophelia's heart thunders an expectant moment, but there's no Falcon. Only Trix, watching the arena floor. Reya whispers in Trix's ear, and when the Spellcaster turns and spots Ophelia, she drops her arms, stunned.

Ophelia has no plan, though she does imagine hurling another knife at Trix's head. Instead of throwing her arms around the woman like she did last time, she crosses them. Betrayal frays trust in seconds, and a weakened rope doesn't mend so quick.

"Where is he?" Ophelia bites out.

"How...?" Trix scans the crowds, looking nervous. "Did you come alone?" She takes hold of Ophelia's arm. "You should be at Ghastly."

She shakes Trix off with a snarl. "*Where is he?*"

The force of her voice knocks Trix off kilter, as though fully seeing Ophelia for who she is. Not a woman afraid to wield magic. Not someone to trifle with. A goddess who could bring this whole arena to its knees.

"I'm not your enemy," Trix says quietly, angling herself sideways to gesture beyond the stone ledge where they stand.

Ophelia's stomach weakens.

Blood is spattered across the glacier-blue rock of the arena floor, the fighting pit dim and dirty. A warrior with a face as swollen as a plum is being hauled out by two guards. From the tunnel where they exit, three other fighters emerge—two males and a female—each bigger than the next. Wielding an array of weapons and lingering near the walls, the trio is focused on the fighter who still kneels in the center of the ring, his head bowed.

When the fighter's gaze lifts, Ophelia's entire center of gravity shifts.

Though he's covered in blood, she knows him instantly. She has thought of him nearly every minute that she wasn't training or discerning Kier's motives. She knows the muscled planes of his broad chest and how they flex when he thrusts a sword. She knows the feel of his stubbled cheeks beneath her palms, the way his eyes sharpen to steel in battle or deepen in lust.

He's alive.

Alive. Alive. Alive.

Ophelia tenses her fists as Falcon, weaponless, rises to his feet. Garbed only in leather pants, blood drips from his forehead and down his bare chest. He looks savage, his face empty of emotion and hard at every edge, and she can see what his past has molded him to be—a vicious warrior.

The nights Falcon tossed in his sleep tortured by dreams of his past... Anger mounting, she spits at Trix, "How could you bring him here?"

"We need the North's army," the caster says with a lift of her shoulder, her reply rising calmly above the din. "Falcon's an heir to Kúzlo. Did he ever tell you that?"

Heir.

It's the second time she's heard the word tonight, and it reverberates through her.

At her obvious surprise, Trix nods. "Figured." With a wave of her hand, she gestures to the arena. "Your boyfriend's still got clout in the North, but family drama, too. Apparently, this is how Kúzloan warriors settle their grievances."

Ophelia seeks Falcon below.

Heir.

The wildness in him, his fierce loyalty, the merciless way he slings a weapon to defend what's his... Falcon was born here, but not only that. It clicks into place—from the past he hates to talk about to Kier's adamance that the legion needs him alive. "Fighting tonight will get the Darkwielder an alliance in the war?" she asks.

Trix snorts. "No. *This* is just for fun. If he wants an audience with the high lord to beg an alliance, he has to train with them the next two weeks and compete in their tournament of heirs, all because that one's betrothed"—Trix loathes a glance at Reya—"refuses to help us."

"Kessan does not forgive easily," Reya says.

"Clearly," Trix grumbles, as Ophelia's frustration mounts.

"Forgive? What are you talking about?"

Trix glances at her. "Falcon's brother has a grudge against him and got the tournament rules changed."

"It was the elders, not Kessan," Reya amends.

"Who cares?" Trix sharpens a fiery brow. "Either way, Falcon can't bow out. He wins or he dies."

Ophelia goes cold, feeling as though the drums that beat in the cavern pound straight through her veins, even as they drain of blood. She looks to Falcon, who's standing down there in the arena weaponless, and catches sight of the warriors near the walls starting forward.

Refocusing on the fight at hand, she demands, "Who are they?"

"Idiots," Trix mutters.

"The older warrior is Yuli," Reya answers. "He was once Falcon's terichen." *Teacher.*

Ophelia studies the russet-bearded man with a club over a shoulder who doesn't look enthusiastic about being here. "And the other two?" Gripping weapons, their eyes keen, these opponents look more eager to fight.

"Our *volorost* took seven wives who bore him nine viable heirs. Many of them agree that Falcon has something to atone for." Reya motions to the pale-haired female who wields an iron chain. "She is Aris, daughter of the Seventh Wife, Delilah. And he"—Reya motions to the white-blond warrior who fists a spiked mallet—"is Argan, son of the Third Wife, Kahli. Argan is second favored in the tournament, behind Kessan."

Falcon's siblings. "Do they wield magic?"

"Of course, but not in the arena. We cannot see from here, but there is a ward below. Fighters cannot sense or use magic."

Trix blades a look at Reya. "He's fought two of those brutes already. If this is about settling grudges, he should take his beating and be done with it."

Reya looks pitifully at Trix and mutters, "Nast stärke al sersi. There is no strength in surrender. To win is the only way to earn respect in the *stadhelm.*"

"And where's your 'betrothed'?" Trix fires. "He's the one who got them all riled up in the first place."

Interest sparks in Reya's eyes as she looks Trix over. "Kessan watches tonight, but he may have a chance with Falcon in the tournament."

A battle cry steels from the arena floor as the warrior Argan takes a run with his menacing mallet at Falcon. Ophelia braces a hand on the leather of her bodice, every muscle coiled. But if Falcon fears, he doesn't show it.

The second Argan swings, Falcon grabs his elbow and knees him in the gut. The mallet flies from the warrior's grasp, but as he keels forward, a small blade in his other hand slashes Falcon's stomach.

Falcon doesn't even flinch; it's as though he's shut some part of himself off entirely. His fist cuts up like a brick to Argan's jaw, sending the knife clattering and the warrior to the ground, out cold.

"Behind you!" Ophelia shouts, but her scream is swallowed by the jeers of the crowd.

The second fighter—Aris—cracks the whip of her long, iron chain from where she's stepped forward. Falcon spins with a moment to spare, so that it glances a blow to his back. The third challenger, Yuli, shouts something to Falcon that Ophelia can't discern, but Aris is quick as rain, despite her heavy chain, singing forward with momentum.

This time as the chain lashes, Falcon catches it in his open hand. His jaw tenses at the bite of the iron against his skin, but he keeps his grasp on it and yanks.

Ophelia recognizes his next move: As Aris pitches toward him, Falcon catches her at the back of her head, then cracks his skull—hard—against the heir's forehead.

Aris staggers off balance, looking dazed. It's just long enough for Falcon to cast aside the chain she holds, get a grip around the heir's neck, and deliver a finishing blow to her jaw.

Ophelia can hear the gnash of teeth from where she stands. Though she's seen this side of Falcon before—fought her way out of trouble beside him—his violence is still chilling. Maybe because she's witnessed what comes after. The pain that creeps behind his eyes when she asks where he learned to fight or how he can stand the blood. The same faraway look he gets when she asks about his past.

However distant, whatever grudges, these fighters are some kind of family. This must be torturing him.

To the crowd's raucous approval, guards haul Aris and Argan out of the arena through the tunnel.

Falcon straightens, chest heaving, a hand seeping blood, his gaze swiveling to that of his third opponent. Yuli.

The audience shouts for a swift end to this fight as the man circles Falcon, but there's a difference in how the two assess one another—with less hostility and more emotion. With a strange sort of acceptance of this barbaric ritual.

Yuli nods, then charges at Falcon with his club raised. Just before Yuli brings his club down, he intercepts the warrior's wrist. The emotion is gone from Falcon's expression as he pulls Yuli's arm taut, bringing his own down like an axe on the upper part of the warrior's thick limb. An audible crack drops Yuli to a knee, and Ophelia's stomach rolls at how his bone sticks through a bloody break in his skin.

Yuli's club rolls across the floor of the arena, and the whole scene fills her with grief.

Falcon's eyes shutter for the briefest moment, and she wonders if anyone else notices his pain, the lack of triumph or malice as he faces Yuli and takes a fistful of the warrior's dark hair in his hand to force his head up.

A chill runs through her as Falcon cocks his arm and smashes Yuli's face with punishing force. This time, it's Falcon who flinches with every strike.

She can't watch anymore.

When the crowd roars definitively louder, Ophelia knows it's over. Falcon has won whatever respect he sought here tonight, but not without a price.

CHAPTER 34
WINGS & WOUNDS
VALLEY OF IRON, KÚZLO
11TH NIGHT IN THE NEW WINTER
OPHELIA IS ON HER OWN

"Where are they taking him?" Feeling the echoes of brutality, Ophelia walks beside Trix through an arched tunnel, the silent Shadowcaster, Ashë, ahead with their host.

As they break off into a second tunnel where blue walls are lit by spheres that look carved from bone, Reya glances over her shoulder. "Heirs have rooms in the *volorost*'s residence. I will show you."

Ophelia frowns at the woman's back. She's treating the three of them as guests, not prisoners, yet the woman is betrothed to a man who wants to see Falcon bleed. "Why are you helping me?" she asks.

Reya keeps her elegant stride. "I have a sense about people. And I never believed what was said about Falcon when we were children."

"Will he get a healer?" Ophelia fights against an image of him, spent, bleeding, hauled from the pit by two guards.

"Fighting in the *stadhelm* is not blessed by the elders. Warriors fight there at their own risk," Reya says.

No, then.

A well of emotions sifts to the surface. She has no trouble directing the angry ones at Trix. Quietly, she hisses, "I get why the Darkwielder would force Falcon to come here, but you? If you're looking for someone to punish for Cleo, you should be punishing me. Not him."

"You don't know what you're talking about."

"Do enlighten me."

Trix keeps her eyes forward, but her teeth stab her lip with the effort of containing her temper. "Falcon had a chance to escape in Ravish, just like you. He chose his fight, *like you*, even knowing the costs."

"What costs? What did you threaten him with to convince him to enter a tournament to the death?"

Trix looks at her then. "Everything he's doing is for you. You shouldn't have come here."

"*You* shouldn't have come here," she hisses as torches brighten the tunnel and illuminate a wide stone door, next to which a woman on watch has put the four of them in sight. But the guard doesn't question Reya's company.

"This is the families' wing," Reya announces as they breeze into an open foyer.

The walls are forged of a blue-gray rock. The floors, a smoother, lighter stone with grooves of ancient symbols etched in the slabs. It's late, but several females wearing dresses akin to Reya's are gathered in a sitting area by a fire, smoking from petite pipes and moving wooden pieces around a gameboard.

Reya makes a slow nod to them, but doesn't stop. In a low voice, she says, "I am supposed to spend my nights with the other betrothed, but I would rather watch ice melt." At a staircase, she leads them to the top floor. "Falcon's mother was the First Wife. This is where they lived."

Oh. "You knew his family?" Ophelia asks.

"His mother, Evangeline, was kind," Reya reflects. "She did not need a trade or to work in the inner valley, but she did. My family lived in a stone cottage on the outer fringe. Falcon and Kaitriona, here. But we were all friends—him, his sister, me, and Kessan."

Ophelia's heart frays like the threads in an old cloak. She wonders if Reya knows Falcon's family is gone. It isn't her place to speak of it, not in what feel like hallowed halls. She can almost hear echoes of the past through the open doors—from a room where dreamcatchers decorate a wall and woven baskets fill shelves, and from another where animal figurines stand in a row on a wooden table by a small bed.

It makes her throat thicken, despairing how small and cared for Falcon once was, and how ravaged he looked tonight. She felt the same empathy for Kier a few days ago. Maybe once for herself. But it doesn't matter how innocent a child starts; the world is so broken, they're all destined to be sharpened into something equally as harsh. At least, that's how it feels tonight.

Two men step out from a room at the end of the hall, their faces red from exertion. They're the guards who took Falcon from the arena.

"What?" one is saying in Magiesian. "We left him water. He's got a bed. He'll sleep it off."

Ophelia stiffens as they near, but the hulking pair slip past with only a curt nod at Reya. Either she is, truly, a skilled Enchanter, or her relationship with this favored heir, Kessan, affords her access.

As their host reaches for the door, it fully strikes Ophelia that she's about to lay eyes on Falcon. "Wait," she pleads. The last time she saw him, he was slipping out of their room in Ravish, swearing he'd be back, telling her to stay put.

And she left him.

She left.

There was more to it than that, but the reasons for going with Kier don't seem to matter now.

Tilting her head, Reya backs away from the door and looks to the other women. "Ladies, let us allow them some privacy."

Ashë looks to Trix, whose face carves a scowl.

Reya laughs. "You need a drink," she decides, looping her arms through each of theirs. "It has been far too long since I had the company of such interesting women. Let us see where the night takes us."

Falcon's room is circular and dim, lit by a small flame in a bone-carved sconce. But mostly, it's the moons and stars and dust limning through a large window in the ceiling that lights Ophelia's steps.

The hearth is regretfully cold. There's firewood on the grates, but the guards didn't bother to light it. In all, she notes few effects in the chamber except for a wooden dragon that rests atop a pine chest.

It's the bed she moves toward, set low in the middle of the room.

Eyes shuttered, Falcon lies on his side. A lump rises into her throat at the moans he makes. At the way he twitches, his brows troubled.

Ophelia crouches by the bed. Aching to touch him, she runs a delicate finger over the bruises forming on his cheek and jawbone while following the dried blood along his throat, his collarbone, his bare chest that's missing so many tattoos.

Hannah warned her the North confiscated weapons. She's fortunate she didn't have to pass through the gates and relinquish hers. Seems it saved her with Reya tonight.

With shaking hands, Ophelia calls *maether* to spark a fire in the hearth, then the warm, healing light within herself, letting it pour from each fingertip to the swollen, purple skin over his rib bones. Apart from his knuckles, they look to have suffered the most damage.

"Falcon." When he doesn't rouse at her whisper, she presses a kiss to his cheek, closing her eyes at the feel of soft stubble, savoring his warmth. He smells of blood and sweat, but also wind and leather. *Him.* "Falcon."

"Ophelia?" His voice is gravel, groggy, but a beautiful relief.

"Gods." Her breath escapes. "You scared me to death."

His eyes flicker, glacier blue. Then widen. "Ophelia." His undamaged hand rises to her face, sliding to fist in her thick, half-braided curls. "You're here?" It's a war between worry and unbridled relief.

She isn't sure who moves first. Their mouths collide in anguish. Tears mingle with the kiss—salty, sweet. *He's alive.* When Falcon pulls back to look at her, she is unmoored to discover his eyes well with moisture, too. That he doesn't blink it away.

"You're a fool," she says. "Five warriors? They could have killed you."

Falcon stares at her with disbelief and a depth in his eyes that makes it hard to breathe. Over what sounds like a lump in his throat, he says, "I never claimed I wasn't a fool. And you... I'm guessing the Darkwielder didn't let you out of a cage."

"No one put me in a cage," she admits.

His eyes briefly close. "Trix said as much." With a shift of his weight, he swears.

As the blankets fall a bit, she sucks a breath at the full view of his wounds. "They ravaged you."

His brows lift. "Battle wounds don't do it for you, Teacup?"

"How can you joke?" As he settles onto his back with a sigh, she rests a hand over his chest, gathering all the words she's been saving.

A shimmer of silver-blue ink appears. Skittering like liquid silver up from below Falcon's pants, it meets her touch. When her hand slides away in surprise, the ink follows, reshaping itself beneath her fingers. Her gaze locks on Falcon, who seems to breathe as shallow as she.

Is this like what she did earlier with the Bender of Air?

Careful, testing, she trails her touch along the unbruised skin of his side, focusing her senses on the fast, hot, trilling *maether* that sings between them—something far more intense than what she did with the air. Again, the ink follows her touch.

Even before the tattoo settles to form a curved, jagged blue line, Ophelia knows what's buried there, what's following her fingers.

A handle. Her broken teacup.

She and Falcon stare at one another while the past drifts by in fragments...

Stop calling me Teacup.

It's not that I think you'll break. Consider it a compliment. I've never seen a girl make fine china a weapon before.

You saved the teacup?

The teacup saved me.

He surrendered his weapons at the gates, but he hid this.

"I can feel your magic," she tells him as a tear slips, silent and warm, from her cheek to the bed where she hovers.

Falcon reaches to catch it, his thumb lingering on her skin. "Do my 'skin pouches' impress you now?"

She takes his hand. He's jesting, but as far as her abilities go this feels significant. As she lowers his palm, trailing eyes over every inch of him, she notices another tattoo with a lighter sliver of ink, peeking from Falcon's other hip. "What's this one?"

Tracing her gaze, Falcon's brows gather. "Just a souvenir from our passage into Kúzlo."

"A souvenir?"

"A piece off a stag's horn," he says. "It's sacred to the North for its healing properties." He doesn't elaborate, but seeming to notice her study of his injuries, he adds, "I know what you're going to suggest, but the horn's not worth wasting on me. I'm fine."

Shaking her head at his stubbornness, she removes Hannah's leather sleeves, the pelts, and her boots, then curls her legs up to sit beside him on the bed.

Fire crackles in the hearth as magic pools on her fingertips. In the soft glow of it, Falcon looks questioningly at her.

"I can heal them," she says.

With a look at his battered chest and arms, he frowns. "You ought to leave them."

"Why? Because heirs need scars to prove their strength?"

Falcon winces, no doubt at the mild venom in her words. But if she's honest, she's hurt she had to find out about his heritage from Trix. Chewing a lip, he says, "Scars are a good reminder."

Ophelia's hand pauses on his chest. "Yes, of what idiots men can be."

"Of what we're willing to die for." He holds her gaze. "I've missed your mouth, Teacup. But did you come all this way to fight with me?"

"I came..." She falters at that look, and fumbles to hold onto her anger, though it's a far easier emotion to wield than whatever is stirring here. "I came because I thought you might be dead by dragonfire, only to find you in a fighting pit trying to finish the job."

"I had to."

"Right, you're here for an army. Trix and *Reya* said as much." Ophelia presses her hand over split flesh on his abdomen, allowing her light to seep. It's not to the bone like Kier's wound was, but it's no clean cut.

Falcon clenches his teeth as the skin reweaves. "Should it sting like needles?"

"You took a beating from five warriors and now you're feeling sensitive?"

An intense, vexing look. When the wound fuses, Falcon releases a breath. "Tell me everything, Ophelia."

She knows what he means.

Hesitating, she feels the edges of her mind. She can't sense Kier, and it seems he can't reach her through the tether when she travels, at least not the same as when they're just physically apart, so as she heals the most damaging of Falcon's wounds, she holds nothing back.

Every detail spills out from the moment Kier found her in Ravish. Her plan to spy and win his trust, to try for the dagger. Her training, the golden dragon, the inner workings of Ghastly, the guilds. Kane the Morphist King, without a brain, but with a beating heart. Reluctantly, her tether to Kier.

A quiet flicker of rage ignites behind Falcon's eyes as he stares at the Shadow marking. "*Kier*," he intones. "You've been spending time alone with him?"

Ophelia trains her gaze on the bruised planes of Falcon's stomach, warring with her guilt over the mixed emotions she beheld for the man of shadows. "We share a bloody history and a common enemy. Besides, he knows what wielding the power of a god feels like. He's been helping me learn how to control it and I thought—I don't know. For a minute, I hoped he could be a true ally."

Falcon's expression is stone. "I've hated every second you were with him."

"I had a plan—"

"I know." Those eyes—*fury*. "I still wanted to kill him. Didn't want his Shadow—anything he's touched—near you or inside you."

She swallows. "After I heard he sent you to the North, I thought about killing him myself. But he has the dagger." *And we're tethered.* She looks at the blood on Falcon's chest. Some his, some not. "You went with Trix even after she betrayed us."

Falcon doesn't answer for it, only nods at her as if he knows there's more she needs to tell him. "What else, Teacup?"

Hating the sight of the blood that coats his skin, she reaches for the cloth and basin of water the guards left on the night table. In the dimness, she spends a silent minute cleaning Falcon's skin while he watches her.

Finally, her voice so dry the words hardly form, she says, "I found Rune and Hart."

Falcon wants details—every detail of the prison, how she traveled, where she saw Hart. While she divulges, she dabs the cloth to his skin, watching it pinken while his face darkens.

She expects more rage, a barrage of Falcon's opinions on how they'll reconnect with Hart and retrieve Rune amidst everything else. But he doesn't give it.

Intent on her, he takes the cloth, setting it aside. Without wincing this time, he shifts to make room for her. "Come here, Ophelia."

CHAPTER 35
SKIN & FLAMES

S he considers the space Falcon's made for her. A safe place. Letting the familiar pull to him guide her hands, Ophelia unstrings the leather bodice that cinches tightly over her cotton shirt, not caring enough to fold it, then slips into the warmth of the bed.

It dips as Falcon pulls blankets to her hip and settles his broad, muscled frame beside her. His scent washes over her, a heady salve, and in that moment she really does have to fight the overwhelming urge to touch him—her partner, her equal. But time roars, screaming that she has precious hours to do what she came here to do.

"I didn't just come to fight with you or because I worried you..." She can't say it; even the thought of it hollows out her chest. "I came because of my mother." Telling him what Hannah revealed to her, Ophelia shares her hope for clues about Elora's disappearance.

Falcon listens with a fraught brow, his eyes miles away. "You were born here."

"Maybe we met as children?" Hannah said a few thousand live in Kúzlo, most in stone homes or *yurten* in the Valley of Iron, some in patrol camps and cottages in the Valley of Bones, and the rest in cabins on the remote western fringe beyond the dragon nesting grounds in the Valley of Ice, where Elora spent her last years with Ophelia.

Falcon searches her face, quiet at first, then shakes his head slowly. "If we'd met, I would've remembered you."

His words shiver through her. Or maybe it's his stare. He looks afraid she might disappear.

She rubs the gold of her locket. "I can't dredge memories of this place or the people, but Hannah said there were seers who suspected who my mother was. Plus, she found love here. I can't shake the feeling that for both of those reasons, she would've come back if she needed help finding the other relics."

Falcon reaches for her hip, his fingers finding a slip of skin below her shirt, and the bed shifts again as he edges even closer. Absently—or not—his calloused thumb begins to trace little circles on her flesh.

It has the opposite effect Falcon usually has on her, which is to haul her back to the present and what she must do next. Instead, it makes her want to cast all that aside and steal this one precious moment that could be theirs.

She fights it, or tries to. "Falcon, I need to talk to people. Find out what they know. I need... I need the amulet." It's a breathless plea, as his fingers skate her skin.

"Tomorrow," he says.

She wasn't expecting that. "I don't have time." It takes focus, but she can feel the anchor, an invisible thread just behind her heart connected to the spellcloth she left at Ghastly. At least without her life in imminent danger, the way it was in the prison, it's a steady pulse—for now.

"Teacup, this late, you won't find anything out there but a bunch of drink-stupid warriors looking for a challenge or a woman's bed."

"And what will I find here?"

He holds her gaze. No—he *blazes* at her, undressing her to her core. It might unravel her completely. They are not a pair who lie still and hold one another with tender, aching gazes. They are flame and steel and fight. They are sparring and banter and keeping one another alive, ever avoiding the discomfort of things like feelings.

Something has changed between them.

She can't put words to it, even as a thought rises in her throat. She clamps her mouth shut for fear of what speaking right now might do, of what she could lose if she put it all out there.

As Falcon trails his fingers up her arm and the side of her throat, as his thumb skims her lip, the sheets where they lie seem to heat.

It's him. His touch is entirely distracting. "Falcon."

"Please—" The word breaks, such feeling in it catching her by surprise as he brings a finger to her lips. "No more talking tonight."

She stares dumbly at him. Kier still has the dagger, the Dark Shadow river still rages, and any day the Gray King could launch an attack straight at the heart of the Magies' territory. Before she's called back to Ghastly, they need to figure out how to locate the amulet, how to balance power long enough to bring the war to a halt, and how to keep Kier in check.

Falcon's expression looks so raw; she reminds herself what he's been through tonight, how violently he was made to tear down rivals who were once his family.

Maybe that's what this is.

Tracking the bruises along his jaw, she says, "I just want to take the hurt away."

"Shh." His eyes smolder, and that finger traces her lip again. "I told you. Reminders of what I'm fighting for."

At that look—so dark and needy—unfathomable heat throbs from her heart to her core, and she barely breathes. "Is it my turn to tell you not to look at me that way?"

A growl shudders out of him. "Gods, Ophelia. When I look at you, I think I'll catch fire. I... I didn't expect that we'd have tonight. I just... I want to look at you." His hand squeezes her hip to underscore his longing, and that's it. She relents to him.

As soon as she nods, Falcon sweeps an arm under her, flipping her to face away from him so fast that her breath catches—in surprise, in *pleasure*—when he presses the warmth of his front flush against her back, banding his arm across her breasts and tipping her chin back so he can trail his lips along her neck.

"I want to look at you," he murmurs again, and she can feel his eyes drinking her in from behind. "We have some unfinished business, yeah?"

Desire sparks its match, and at more of those maddening circles, she gives fully to the impulse singing through her, to the safety and freedom of Falcon's arms, to the words stuck inside her that pound with every heartbeat.

She writhes as though she can will his hand lower.

When Falcon's hardened length nudges against her behind, she gasps a little and arches against him. It elicits a maddening groan from him, and he stills her hips with a hand.

"What's wrong?" she breathes. "Are you still hurting?"

"The important parts work fine. I just... Not all in one night."

But as his fingers trace the slope of her breast, she can't stop herself from grinding her hips down against him.

He growls into her ear. "You're a terrible listener." When he drags his teeth over her skin, a moan escapes her. "What is it you need, Teacup? Tell me."

She needs to fuse the two disparate heat sources that seem to burn the sheets around them. She needs to keep Falcon safe, forever. She needs certainty there *will* be another night after this. She needs...

"You." *Only you*, she realizes with a little cry as his lips find the slope where her neck meets her shoulder.

Thinking Falcon was dead, watching him give up something in that fighting pit, knowing she has to leave him again, *she wants him*. Despite the world burning around them. Despite the other, different kinds of love she holds in her heart and how she hasn't had a chance to really speak with Rune or Hart since they were separated.

Despite what either man might think of her.

"You." She tremors at Falcon's touch, at his nose brushing her ear. Then his hand skims inside her shirt to cup her breast.

When his rough fingers graze her nipple, arousing one, then the other, until both peak and strain against her shirt, she makes a soft cry.

At last, *gods*, his other hand dips below the waist of her pants, and Ophelia is all sensation as his fingers trail just shy of where her ache for him pulses. His touch pulls a moan from the very depths of her.

Falcon curses as though the feel of her, wet and wanting for him, might be his own undoing, as he circles around the apex of her thighs, never quite grazing that spot where she is desperate to feel him.

"Falcon," she pleas.

A low chuckle rumbles against her back—an igniting, infuriating sound.

Ophelia arches her hips to feel the granite against her behind. When she grinds there, Falcon groans and, finally pressing down against that delicious spot, flicks his thumb.

Her body goes languid. Her head falls against his shoulder while her legs part to him. She savors his torturous stroke.

"There you go," he coaxes in her ear. The words tingle from her lobe to her throbbing center as his fingers glide through her slickness. Every sensation, every thought, every need narrows to the feel of them there, on the precipice of her core.

"Please," she begs.

He growls where his mouth meets her shoulder, then slides a finger inside her. "Ophelia—" He curses.

She can feel every one of his heavy breaths, feel his eyes watching as she starts to move on him, craving more of him, of everything.

There's no coldness in the room now, only the fire that's well and caught. Heat that she and Falcon have been trying to tamp since the first day they met, four years ago. Heat that comes out of her with a long moan that echoes in the silent, circular room.

He presses another heated kiss to her neck, and it's not nearly enough.

She writhes, twisting until she finds his eyes, hooded and lost to her. Capturing his mouth with hers, she drags his bottom lip between her teeth.

Falcon snarls, nipping her back. "Gods, you can't know. You can't know, Ophelia—" He swears, and a second finger slides to fill her, thrusting slow, deep—hard—setting a rhythm and hitting that delicious spot inside that makes her spine arch. His tongue sweeps into her mouth with such intention, Ophelia fantasizes the feel of it between her legs.

Everything—*everything*—at the periphery of them fades away, leaving only the taut ache that climbs with each of his thrusts, each mirroring stroke of Falcon's tongue against hers.

"*Ophelia.*"

Her name, moaned that way, is her ruin. She combusts. Her entire body aflame, her core pulsing like a sizzle of stars, she comes apart at the seams while Falcon holds her tightly in his arms to keep her there.

He shudders against her, his hand coaxing her through the waves and ripples, until she is utterly shipwrecked on his shores.

She struggles for rational sense, and to fill her lungs, as Falcon gently withdraws his fingers, painting her belly with a trail of her own pleasure before he brings them to his lips.

"No regrets?" she breathes, an echo to their too-short tryst in Ravish.

He holds her gaze as he tastes her. "I've thought about doing that since I hauled you against that tree," he admits. "Maybe a long time before then."

His length twitches against her hip.

"I want to feel you," she breathes. No, she wants to devour him.

When she pushes the blankets down, Falcon catches her hand. "Oh, no. I would need to be at full strength when you touched me." It's then she notes the condition of his pants—the slashing cuts in the leather.

"But—"

Falcon draws her chin up, his expression serious. "If I had my way, there'd be plenty more nights like this, watching you come undone for me." He presses his lips to her jaw. "Somewhere not in a house shared by jealous heirs who would hear you scream my name."

Heat paints her cheeks as his longing crashes through her, but his eyes grow distant and Falcon pulls her against his chest, his fingers making comforting strokes along her back. "Sleep, Teacup."

There is no way.

He's still aroused beneath her and...what was that look?

Somehow, though, her breaths sync with his, and as she relishes in the feel of his calloused hand on her back, a reminder that he's there, she feels safe enough to let the world fade away.

CHAPTER 36
PROPHECIES & REMEDIES

VALLEY OF IRON, KÚZLO
12TH DAY IN THE NEW WINTER
OPHELIA IS WITH FALCON

She wakes, warm, rested, and blessedly still in Kúzlo.

Rare sun seeping through a drift of the snow coats the window above, light speckling the bed and catching the amber shimmers laden in the walls of the room. It dapples Falcon's arms, too, which wrap around her from behind, as they have the entire night to keep the cold at bay.

His breaths draw long and even against the back of her neck. When she shifts, Falcon's arms tense, as if holding her tighter might keep her from vanishing back to Ghastly.

She checks the anchor behind her heart. It's there, humming steadily, but it does somehow feel...looser. Or maybe it's her muscles.

A rush of heat comes at the memory of Falcon's touch and what they did last night.

When she manages to twist in his arms, she finds him awake. For a long second, they look at each other.

The sun glints on silver, drawing Ophelia's eyes down to the ring she didn't notice Falcon wore last night. Etched wings. A blue jewel in its center. Quietly, she asks, "Are you really going to fight in this tournament?"

His eyes hold hers as he nods, and whatever she imagines he'll say, it isn't, "Because of the vision."

Unease slips into bed with them, a thief of warmth and comfort.

She pushes up on her elbow. "What vision?"

Sitting against the headboard, Falcon stretches out his legs. There's no blood, but she can tell he's feeling stiff. He says, "Cleo had a prophetic vision before she died. She saw the war before it happened."

"How... Did Trix tell you that? Falcon—"

"Trix betrayed us to help us."

A chill skates along her spine at the certainty in his tone.

Visions are sacred gifts given as warnings from the primordial gods. Falcon has never seemed devout, but his tone and the taut lines in his jaw say he believes this to be true.

"What did she see?"

Raking his mussed hair back with a sigh, he replies, "She saw you bringing the relics together and the North fighting on your side."

That should be a good thing, but his expression is grave—too grave. "Did you say *my* side?"

He hoists himself toward the edge of the bed, light dancing across the generous muscles of his back. "In Dwymore, you asked how we save Magus. I'd rather you not have to go back to Ghastly"—his muscles tense, at the thought of the Darkwielder, no doubt—"but you have to."

"Because the anchor—"

"Because you need the relics." He balls his fists in the sheets as if hating what he's about to tell her. "You have to keep playing the game, Teacup. Convince him that you choose him—"

"*Choose him?*"

"Choose him," he repeats, the two words seeming bitter on his tongue, as if he hates the idea but it must happen. "You need to do what it takes to bring the relics together, and I need to get the North in the fight." His tone is resolute, even reckless—a throwing of caution to the wind.

As Falcon rises to his feet in search of fresh clothes, her insides rattle with a warning. *Everything he's doing is for you*, Trix said.

She hardens a look at his back. "Do you think you need to fight in a tournament to the death because Trix said Cleo saw the North in the war?" He doesn't answer. "Falcon, this can't just be on you. There has to be more than one way to win. And the future can change. Isn't that the point of visions?"

He strides to a dresser she didn't notice in the low light last night, where clean leathers and training attire are laid out, and pauses with a tunic in hand. Quietly, he says, "Do you remember what I told you before your first reset?"

She's taken back to a forest on the edge of the Constelli grounds four years ago. Light was making a kaleidoscope of the colored leaves, and she was at her lowest after the Constelli had burned at her whim.

"You said hiding would be no vacation with you," she remembers.

He huffs an exhale. "And you said not to go easy on you." He turns, then, every line on his face carved with determination. "I didn't go easy, did I?"

Cons. Carriage chases. Beheadings. Between all that, stale lager and one-room inns and late nights talking about ships and the seas and how to tell whether to fight or flee.

No, he did not go easy on her. "I survived because you didn't."

Falcon chews on that a moment. "Rune used to go on about how you deserved a world that would bring out the life in you, not just the fight. I used to think he was too soft."

Her heart is a bruise at the mention of Rune, the one who was broken in that prison cell and squeezed her neck and alerted the royal guards. Also the one she gave her heart to between chapters of fairytales when she didn't know herself or what she'd done. When she was living his idea of her perfect story.

She'd loved Rune in that little bubble he'd created. The memories that flooded back to her in Dwymore were shiny, cast with a magic of their own. She felt the love that girl had for him. His Ophelia. Love heightened by the shock of discovering their past and the danger they were in as captives of the crown. But in the aftermath, in the settling of the dust, she didn't feel like Rune's Ophelia anymore. Theirs was a love that bled between resets and time and worlds, not quite something they could hold.

The room is so silent, she can hear Falcon's breathing.

"I was never very good at the living, outside the times with Rune," she confesses. "Since Wythe, sometimes I wonder if it would've been better had I..." The nightmare taunts her anew. The light, piercing her chest.

Fury on legs, Falcon stalks within an inch of her. "Don't finish that thought. Don't ever wish it, you hear me?"

He's shaking with something as he lifts her face to him. She can see a sliver of that rare fear that doesn't rear in Falcon often.

Something is wrong. Something that would make Falcon tell her to choose Kier.

"Cleo saw more than you're telling me, didn't she?" What did Falcon say last night before they slept? *If I had my way, there'd be plenty more nights like this...* Does he think last night was it for them?

His expression grows darker than she's used to, even from a man who's taken heads. "You have to be ready when the fight comes. It's going to be goddamn bloody and not everyone's making it out, but you have the teeth. The steel and fire. You always have. You're going to change the world."

Change the world. So his motivations still ultimately lie with upending the system. "What exactly are you asking me to do?"

"For starters, be who you were born to be." His piercing eyes hold hers. "When you go back to Ghastly, play the game until the last possible minute, then take what belongs to you. Bring the relics together, whatever you have to do—whatever the consequences—because in the end, that's what's going to save Magus. And whatever I have to do here..." Falcon pauses. "Magus will be free, and you're going to live."

It's a disconcerting vow, and she doesn't miss the slightest tremble in that last word. She doesn't miss his fear. *Live*, he said, as if that end isn't certain or even likely, but he'll move the moons to make it so.

Every muscle tenses as she stares at him, inferring this is what he omitted about Cleo's vision. He fears her not living, because Cleo saw her death.

She can't find the words to ask him to confirm it.

When he turns to draw his shirt over his head, she reaches slowly for her own clothes, trying to fathom how the primordial gods would allow one of their lines to die.

She straightens her shirt with extra force, hating the notion of visions and fate. Spoilers of joy, they feel only like chains—one more obstacle that threatens their freedom.

But, fine. If she's meant for death, she will go fighting for everything that matters—her mother's quest, Falcon's revolution, Rune's life, the family Hart longs for in his soul, and the freedom her kingdom deserves. She will make every second they've spent *surviving* in this world worth it, and in the process—this time—she will protect those she loves.

Fully dressed, Falcon turns. With a long look at her, he asks, "Are you ready?"

He asked her that same question in a safe house in New York. She didn't feel ready then, but now, fastening the furs over her shoulders, she keeps the complicated emotions at bay by avoiding his direct stare, and says, "I came for clues about my relic, and I'm going to get them."

When Falcon doesn't reply, she peers up to find him grinning. For a second, he looks like the man she's always known, a gleam of adventure curving the mouth that burned hot on hers last night.

Still her partner.

"All right," he says. "Let's work on that army while we're at it."

I t's the dead of winter, but Falcon finds the Valley of Iron alive with color. Maybe it's Ophelia.

He can't stop looking at her. Can barely keep his goddamn hands at his sides with this cruel, vexing, greedy need in the deepest sinews of his chest. He's been restless with the feeling for weeks, but with her here... It's a torture he's not used to, walking around with his heart in someone else's hands.

He didn't understand it at first. Now that he does, it only makes the bone-deep ache for her worse. He has half a mind to say fuck it all and throw her over his shoulder, trudge out into the Hunter's Forest, and splay her against another tree—take her right there. Beg her to let him make her his, for however long they have.

Glancing at her pinked cheeks, the soft slope of her neck... Shit. A growl simmers in his chest with the impulse to take her chin in his hands, then her hips, to seize her gaze and tell her what she does to him—how it broke him this morning to tell her to go back to Ghastly and choose the Darkwielder.

But he knows how this ends when Ophelia brings the relics together, a task she has to complete for the sake of long-term peace in Magus. For her own sake, too.

With a frustrated sigh, he forces his gaze up to where flags and banners are catching the wind from peaks on colored tents.

Ophelia weaves around a pair of kids in their path, brushing his arm on her return. "This is the festival?" she asks.

Falcon looks sidelong down to her and his heart slams. Thickly, he says, "It'll go a few weeks in all, ending with the tournament."

The tournament—that's what he needs to focus on.

Steering his thoughts to matters at hand as they dodge through the central part of the valley in search of Trix and Ashë, he scans faces. "The *volorost* should be making an appearance today. I'll be expected to train..." At the sight of a white banner sewn with a dragon and twin gray moons, Falcon trails off.

Ophelia's gaze follows his. "What's that about?"

He inspects the emblem tied above a small tent, inside which a small crowd gathers around an elder male draped in spotted pelts. A seer, sitting cross-legged on a wool with his hands folded, eyes stormy-white.

Falcon scowls. "It's a seer, predicting Snow Moons on the night of the Sanctioning."

They've witnessed the mortal equivalent of the moon event, a so-called gate between winter and spring. But in a world where seasons last as long as the gods please, Falcon can't remember seeing true Snow Moons in his lifetime.

"'A rare brightening of the twin gray orbs across the sky,'" Ophelia recites, as if she can see a tome in front of her.

Sometimes he forgets she remembers everything now.

Peering at the banner, she rubs her fingers together like she might feel a prickle of something, and once again it sparks a deep fire in him to think of her training with the Darkwielder, to imagine them sharing time and maybe meals, to know he's the one who stirs her light.

But it's made her more confident. It's opened something up in her. In Falcon, too.

Gods, he can't stop thinking about how she felt under his hands. An ache pulses in his groin like a bruise replaying how close he was to tearing off the last shreds of fabric between them and burying himself inside her the night before.

"I've heard stories," Ophelia says, snapping him back to the present. "About Snow Moons as a night of enlightenment. Seers think the veil between the primordial gods and Magies thins, right? What do you think it'll bring?" Watching the seer, she bites her lips in thought.

Lips Falcon can still see parted with the pleasure he gave her, his teeth grazing the sensitive skin of her neck.

He's staring so hard at her that a blush creeps into her cheeks. Groaning inwardly, he clears his throat as he adjusts his pants. "It's just one more thing to keep an eye on," he says, motioning to the crowds. "Moon events bring out the fanatics. Come on."

Salt-laced smoke wafts from outdoor cookstoves, and kids race across the tundra, gleeful as they chase their hounds and one another. For a second, it brings a smile as he threads the scene. The next, he's stopped cold in his tracks, overcome by sudden images: Himself with his chest bare and stained with blood; Ophelia in a golden gown, cold and unmoving.

The noise of the festival rushes in, but Falcon's feet won't move as he tries to catch his breath. His hands shake—his whole goddamn body.

He doesn't see visions. What the hell was that?

A hand touches down on his arm. "Hey." Ophelia, frowning. "You okay?"

He reaches for her without thinking, a hand cupping her face. Her hair, half-twisted with braids, lifts at the ends in the wind.

Blinking, he steals back his touch. "It's nothing," he lies.

The air is ripe with sweat and stew.

Ophelia wars between revolt and insatiable hunger as they pass a tent with long, slab tables where warriors twice her size are heaving down something lumpy and red. They dine in heavier northern leathers than most wore at the fights last night, with humps of dark fur pelts on their shoulders.

She does admire the bone-white spears and knives that fill their sheaths. She has the one blade from Falcon still, but one never seems enough these days. By the goggles around the warrior's necks, she surmises these are the ones who fly dragons.

"What do they do, exactly?" she asks Falcon of the flyers.

"*Seshen* patrol the borders. Other territories covet what's in these mines, but between the seers and the patrol, no one's ever penetrated Kúzlo's walls."

"Did you fly when you were young?"

He glances at her. "Yuli took me up a few times, before I left."

Falcon nods at the man himself, who takes up a spot at the table. She winces at the sight of Yuli's bruised jaw. Staring without malice in Falcon's direction, he wears a sling of hide and cloth on his arm. After a moment, the warrior returns his greeting.

The rest of the men at the tables gaze at them as they pass by, pausing mid-bite, allowing their breakfast stews to drip from spoons. She heard the jeers amid the applause last night when Falcon won. This morning, at least among these flyers, there are more nods of respect than hostile stares. It pacifies some of the tension in her shoulders.

A ring of swords clangs from across the Bowl.

In the center of three stone circles, a warrior in stunning white pelts is thrusting a sword. Ophelia recognizes him as the man Reya called her betrothed—Falcon's half-brother. He clashes with another northerner, moving like the wind. Weapons sing and breaths burn the air white as they grunt.

It makes Ophelia crave a sword to wield.

As they slow to watch, Falcon's hand brushes hers, igniting a rush of heat. At her ear, he asks, "Missing a good length of steel in your hands, Teacup?"

She rolls her eyes for his benefit, not hiding her smirk. "I see you're still a pig," she says. Though silently, she can't deny how she would've welcomed *his* length last night.

A cocky smile. "Guess some things don't change," Falcon says, shifting his focus to the training match. It looks set up for the crowd's enjoyment more than anything else. Perhaps to let the heir be seen. "Kessan's got himself a good mentor," Falcon notes.

In the circle, his brother spins and jabs—precise, quick movements that don't push a hair out of place.

She'd put Falcon just as quick on his feet, but wilder, less restrained. "You have two weeks," she notes. "Who will you train with?"

Falcon drops his gaze to her. "Let me worry about that, all right? Focus on what you're here for."

Because she's not here for long. In the light of day, the notion is its own looming shadow cast between them, tightening her chest.

Falcon points to a wide, red tent beside the training circles. Amid the warmth of firebowls, another breakfast crowd watches the parries, feints, and thrusts. Slouched over a table, Trix and Reya look half-asleep. Between them, Ashë is alert, chewing strips of bread she's torn off while her vigilant eyes rove between the training circles and the crowd.

As they approach, Ophelia and Falcon share a look at the trio's rumpled clothing. They wear the same garb from last evening.

"Well, you look positively wretched," Falcon announces. There's amusement there, but a grain of irritation.

Trix's head swivels from where it's resting on her hand to meet Falcon with a menacing glare. "*Volume*, smugger."

"Sorry, what was that?" His voice pitches as he points to the side of his head. "Bad ear."

She glowers. "In my next life, I'm going to come back as an oxboar and spear your ass with my tusks."

"Classy," he allows. "Why not go for a wolven? You can eat me, ass first."

Trix positively scowls at him, and Ophelia hardens her jaw. After the Spellcaster's treachery, their bickering is less a comfort than it was.

Curling a hand around her stone cup, Trix draws its contents to her mouth with a grimace, then immediately replaces it on the table. A sour, fishy stench wafts in Ophelia's direction, and it might be petty, but Trix's horrendous hangover gives her the smallest twinge of satisfaction. If this mission's so critical to winning the war, if Trix is helping them and not betraying them, what was she doing getting sacked last night?

"Was drinking yourself ragged a part of your strategy?" she asks.

Trix blades a look at Reya. "It was her fault."

But Reya merely sips from her own cup, unbothered by the smell. "I was under strict orders to acclimate our guests to northern ways. It is not my fault you cannot hold your mead."

Falcon grins, taking full notice of his childhood friend. His eyes soften on her. "It's been too long, Rey."

Reya's lips twitch. "It is good to see you, *jagerin*. Though I am disappointed you did not bring your sister. She was always the better company."

Ophelia's chest fills with heaviness at Falcon's small flinch, one he hides behind a smirk. "Can't argue that, but she's been gone a long while now. Mam, too."

Something snuffs in Reya's sapphire eyes. "Tragedy," she says as she downs the last of her remedy.

Falcon nods a look at the crowds. "Any word on when Ryke will address the valley?"

"You missed the announcement," Reya answers. "The *volorost* is abstaining from festivities today."

Falcon swears. "Kind of an insult, isn't it?"

"Between us, I am not sure our high lord is well."

Falcon leans over the table. "What do you know, Reya?"

She glances toward Kessan, then back, causing Ophelia to wonder how forthcoming the woman can be given who she's promised to. Quietly, Reya says, "Kessan has been more distant recently. I thought he might be courting a second already. But a few days ago, he confided he has been invited into the tribal council."

Ophelia tracks Falcon's features sharpening. "Any idea what prompted that?"

"No." Reya lifts a finger up at him. "And before you get ideas, *jagerin*, remember that my affinity is useless on Kessan. You would have more luck bleeding the answers from your brother than I would trying to enchant or seduce my *Amati*."

Ophelia's ears prickle at the foreign term, but she's more keen on the way Trix's gaze flicks up, then quickly tucks back to her cup. Ophelia takes notice of the red mark on the side of the Spellcaster's neck. A love bite.

Oh.

Reya hides a small smile, while Ashë signs something Ophelia doesn't catch.

"Ah, yes," Reya says, as if remembering something. She directs her attention to Ophelia. "We were not only playing last night. Beatrix met a warrior that Ashë and I worked information out of."

The wraith tears a piece of bread and chews it vigorously. For a small thing, she even eats fiercely, and Ophelia has the feeling she's a good one to have on their side. "What did the warrior say?"

"That he knows someone who knew your mother," Reya replies. At her slight smile, Ophelia realizes Trix must have told Reya who her mother was. There is reverence in that look.

"Who is it?" she asks.

Reya traces the rim of her empty cup, her expression wary. "The elder Kessan replaced on the tribal council. Northerners call her the Binder."

CHAPTER 37
LIGHT & KEYS

They weave beyond the din of the festival through the inner valley, where axes chop at carcasses in hunters' tents and fishmongers pick at ice blocks, scattering chips in deep tubs. Farther and farther they trek, passing the last white row of tents.

Ophelia notices how Falcon keeps stealing glances at her, and she can't shake the anxious notion of time slipping too fast, though the sky is still slung with a low sun.

They've been walking half an hour. "What did Reya mean her affinity is useless on Kessan?" What did she call him? Her *Amati*?

Falcon's long hair, half pulled back, whips across his face as he tenses a look at her. "It's just part of the ceremony between an heir and their betrothed. They take a blood oath to never wield against the other."

Ophelia frowns. "They need an oath for that?"

"Surprised?"

Nothing surprises her anymore, least of all about the North. But at a road where pillared cages stuffed with large, white rocks mark entry to the outer valley, she notices Falcon's side-eye for the hundredth time and finally asks, "What?"

"You still wear the locket."

She lays a hand to the shape of it beneath the cloak Reya lent her, arching a brow. "It's a reminder of what *I* fight for."

Falcon doesn't smile. His face is still as taut, if a little pale, as when Reya first mentioned the Binder.

"So, tell me about this woman. You knew her?"

"Everyone up here knows of her; she's been alive through a dozen shifting moons," Falcon says. Two-hundred-forty years, give or take. "I never saw her much in public. There were rumors, though."

The cold catches the wings of Ophelia's cloak. The effect is a few stolen breaths, but also a sharper mind, which she welcomes. "What would she have taught my mother?"

"The Binder kept a shop once, here in the Valley of Iron's outer fringe. Specialized in tricky spellwork—wards, small curses, poisons, locks."

They look at one another.

"Locks." Ophelia squeezes the shape of her locket. "Do you think...?"

"Don't get your hopes up. The Binder's always been a little off her rocker."

She sighs. "Perfect. Anything else I should know?"

Falcon looks wary as they edge to the fringe of the valley. "She trades in secrets. Whatever you do, look her in the eye. And don't let her see what you fear."

At the top of a hill, the Binder's home puffs like a chimney.

Under frozen limbs of northern trees that grasp at the house, a white-gray fog—like steam—smokes through the seams of the tight stonework as if in bursts of breath.

She feels the assurance of Falcon's hand on her lower back as they climb the hill. "You've got this."

"I know."

She survived capture by the Gray King, losing Grimm, and Kier's less than honorable tutelage. She's fine.

Fine, fine, fine.

Behind the clatter of her own heart, more distantly, she feels the rope of the anchor. Has it loosened? Hannah didn't say there were physical boundaries, or that Ophelia had to stay near Trix. The Spell-caster went with Reya and Ashë to snoop around about the *volorost* and whatever alliance the North is brewing.

At the door of the Binder's home, Ophelia feels the sting of the ward the same time Falcon goes rigid, laying a hand to his chest as though the pressure of the magic is too great.

It's not as intense as the ward that sealed the Morphist King's room, but it's layered. Ophelia senses its weave just as the blueprint of it appears before her, a complex threading of *maether* bound in hundreds of little golden knots.

They could wait, hope to be invited in...

She remembers Rune hunched over levers and shimmering switches when the moons wrought havoc on their carriage outside Galdur, when he solved a different sort of puzzle. Automatically, her hand rises, fingers plucking on instinct to work out the knots.

When the ward falls, Falcon groans as though a stone's been rolled off his chest and the door shudders open on its hinges. From inside the house pours the faint sound of humming...and a rhythmic creak-ing-scratching-tapping, like reeds being woven together or tiny beetles crawling over one another.

Then, the sounds stop.

"Who are you?" It's not so much a voice as a song. A high, rasping melody.

The walls waft another breath.

"Are you the child?" the voice sings.

Ophelia's pulse speeds as she and Falcon trade glances. After his win in the stadhelm last night, he was able to procure new weapons—two long blades carved from bone, one of which he lays a hand against on his hip. So she's not the only one hearing the song.

Peering into the cottage, Falcon says under his breath, "How bad do you want answers?"

"I'm fine," she mutters. She has the power of a goddess. She's not afraid of the Binder, nor the house. But the truth she's longed for about her mother all her life may be another story.

No—no, she can do this.

"You're the blood-red night..."

In a sparse kitchen, a black pot rattles and smokes on a flameless cookstove.

"...come to feed my bones."

A narrow window along the far wall fogs, then freezes, thaws, then fogs.

"You're the light..." the song goes.

A slab-wood table littered with bottles of colored tonics stretches the center of the room, and the walls themselves aren't stone. Softer even than wood, they seem to breathe like lungs.

"...come to steal my soul."

The floor creaks under Ophelia's weight. Every cell in her freezes as the song and humming cease and the chair near the small hearth turns itself around. When the front door slams shut, Ophelia jolts.

The Binder is pale as ash, her cheeks deeply creviced with wrinkles. Her eyes, though milky blue and clearly unseeing, seem to sharpen on Ophelia and Falcon.

"It's been ages since I met a god." The woman's mouth is open, but the words seem to sigh from the walls that contract.

She's blind and mute, Ophelia realizes. The house serves as the Binder's eyes, and her mouthpiece.

"Come in..."

Ophelia steps one foot forward, but no more, refusing to let fear turn her back now. "Hello."

The Binder's old hands move absently in her lap, fingers pinching and pulling in a manner that suggests the weaving together of long strips. *"Elly, Elly, Elly..."*

The pot on the stove rattles, and the house groans as the woman's mouth curves into a disturbing, knowing smile. Every muscle in Ophelia tenses.

"Goddess," the walls hiss.

"The daughter of Elora Dannan," Falcon clarifies, like a warning. "She's come for information."

"*Clever heir.*" The Binder's face lights up like a child's on Falcon, at whatever the house reads in him. "*Secrets, secrets.*" Ophelia fights the urge to turn away as the woman licks her lips.

"*Ophelia,*" the house breathes her name. "*Tell me, how does it feel to burn in the light?*"

She goes absolutely still. No—no, she will not talk about that.

On the table, a bottle of pale-pink liquid slides forward to her, but Falcon spreads a hand at her back. "Give us proof you knew her mother first."

The pot on the stove stops rattling, the lid settling as the woman's lips draw a taut line. "*Goddess...*" That hiss. "*Goddess with an amber jewel, her light as sealed as fate is cruel.*"

Amber jewel.

"The amulet," Ophelia murmurs.

Stepping out of Falcon's touch, toward the table, she's aware of him moving in sync with her. She takes the bottle. The liquid is sour and leaves a tart trail down her throat. Nothing happens, at first. Then, her mental shields vanish and her tongue unspools. "I will trade you a secret," she agrees.

The Binder's hands stop weaving. "*Tell me,*" the walls rasp, "*how you gobbled the darkness. Tell me how it feels to bathe in light.*"

She can feel Falcon stiffen.

Everything inside her rebels against the request. Reliving Wythe... She thought she put it behind her while training with Kier, but she can't... Glancing at Falcon, thinking of what he said before—she must do whatever it takes—her shoulders fall.

She just needs a breath, to think. Her nightmares have twisted everything.

Slowly, bracing, she lets her mind meet the memory...

The broken curse and blood and gunfire and screams from the temple—there were so many shadows. A platform shuddering under her feet, the Gray King escaping, the Darkwielder falling... How she didn't care if she died—*she didn't care.* She just wanted the innocents and people she loved to live.

She can feel the walls contract as the Binder's eyes roll, as if the potion is letting her see inside Ophelia's mind. Falcon watches closely, hand at his weapon.

But Wythe didn't break her. How it tried, but she is a golden dragon. She survived the nightmares.

She will survive this.

"I felt its call," she says, and Falcon's attention snaps to her. "I felt the curse break in the Gray King and darkness flood like a chilling river. It was unending but...not unpleasant." At the admission, she can't meet Falcon's eyes. "I didn't know which felt better, at first, or which scared me more—the darkness or the light."

She does glance at him then. It hurts to see pain etched on Falcon's face. Pain for the past. Pain for what yet awaits, perhaps.

The Binder leans forward in her chair.

Ophelia presses on with the truth. "The darkness was hungry and vengeful...and potent." Part of her liked it. "When the Darkwielder fell...it felt as though I'd fallen." Her words are a breath, and she sees Falcon shutter his eyes. Still, she makes herself go on. "Then there was terror. I was searching for the one—ones I love in the dark and dust and fire, and I knew. I knew that the darkness would take everyone I cared for and Magus would still be enslaved."

She unclenches her fists, drawing up her sleeve to bare the lumen ridges.

The house seems to gasp.

"In the cold of the darkness, I searched for the breath of magic. Then that's all there was, pouring out of me. It felt like a thousand suns, and...like I was destroying part of myself as it devoured the shadows. Then I was empty. So empty, I felt nothing."

"Did you die?"

She shakes her head. "I was cold, so cold, until..." She tries to remember after the light released, before she woke. "There was warmth beating into me. A different kind of light." She inclines her head at Falcon. "His *maether*."

"Where did the darkness go?"

"I don't know."

"Did it die?"

"I—" She thinks of Kier, of the tether it forged. "Darkness can't truly die. It more so...scattered. It's still inside me, wrapped up in my light." Though Ophelia keeps her eyes on the Binder as Falcon told her to, she speaks more for him now. "I fear it less than I once did. The longer it's inside me... I'm beginning to understand it. And light can be just as vicious—it burns, it destroys, it kills..."

"Enough," Falcon tells the Binder. "You have your secret and then some." From the corner of Ophelia's eye, he looks devastated, like he wants to rip the Shadow from her chest.

The walls exhale. *"Fair is fair. What is the secret you wish to own?"*

"My mother," Ophelia says, as calmly as she can. "Fifteen years ago, she set out from Magus to make sure the Gray King could never get his hands on her relic. Where did she go?"

"With the amulet?"

She stiffens. "Yes."

The Binder nods to the table of potions and spellbooks. *"Elly returned the first day of the new spring asking for an incantation to locate others like her. But there was not a spell that could find what was not yet discovered—power that had been trapped. I bade her go to the* volorost *and declare herself the rightful queen. It was not without its risks, but might have prevented the oaths Aksander was considering."*

"Did she go to him?"

"I never spoke to her again."

Ophelia pains a look at Falcon. His father might've been the last to see Elora.

"That wasn't the only time you saw her, though," Falcon says to the Binder.

Her ancient lips curl up. *"A secret, heir. Then I will tell you more."*

Ophelia braces for whatever truth the Binder would deem worthy, feeling a surge of protectiveness. Falcon's life has not been easy.

But he only shrugs. "You know, I can't hold my whiskey. Never could. Gets me surlier than a boarhound in heat and prone to reckless hands at the card tables."

Ophelia gapes at him, sure the Binder has no sense of humor for this. Then the house lets out a long, suffering laugh. *"Clever heir. I hope you win your tournament. To feel that power shift and see what deeper secrets might be risen…"*

The woman's face angles to Ophelia. *"Fair is fair,"* she echoes. *"Your mother spent a week here, seventeen years ago. That is when the secret of who she was became mine and I helped her cast a powerful lock spell she called 'insurance.' It was in case she were ever captured. The blood of a god does forge the best locks… The best wards, too, which is why only you were able to disarm my door."*

Her mother's blood. Ophelia's blood.

She doesn't interrupt as the Binder continues. *"Magus was hunting Descendants, that was no secret, but the monarchy was visiting our valley more frequently than many of us found comfortable. Elly stayed until she forged her locks, then fled the North with the pair of objects and her child."*

"Suppose you won't tell us what those objects were and where they are now?" Falcon asks.

The Binder lets her gaze wander between them. Her smile, toying. *"I will, if you tell the goddess a secret."*

"Thanks for your time." He takes Ophelia's elbow, turning her toward the door.

"Falcon." She tugs her arm free. "It's one secret." Her first thought is of his blade. She's gathered it's sacred to northerners. Whatever its purpose, it can't be as devastating as Wythe.

Pulling it from her sheath, she holds it out to him, the *A* greeting them from the hilt. At Falcon's widened eyes, the house draws another long, wheezing laugh.

"You said it's old," Ophelia reminds. "People keep saying it's special."

"It's"—he swallows—"It's just a blade heirs receive when they're born, made from *migth* and dragon bone. It has the blood of my first kill."

She digests his hurried answer, re-examining the memory of him slowly spinning the handle in their room in Ravish the morning they parted. He looked serious, handing it over to her.

"You want me to have your old blade?" she had asked.

He blinked at her. "Looks like a good fit." Then he turned away, as if it pained him somehow. Perhaps the sight of it brought too many memories. Perhaps he saw it as a way to give her strength, something to remind her of him the way her nickname and the teacup handle remind him of her. And it had. But was that it?

"So, you gave it to me for protection?"

Falcon grapples for a reply.

In the silence, the pot rattles on the stove. The walls huff. And the Binder tilts her eerie face. *"What do you fear, heir?"*

He glares at the old woman. "The rumors about you are true. You like to stir up trouble."

"My own secrets get lonely in these walls."

Watching Falcon struggle, it's clear there is more. He wouldn't look so at war with himself, so rattled. Ophelia suddenly doesn't want the secret of this blade—not this way. If there's more to it, she trusts he'll tell her if she needs to know, when he's ready.

That still leaves them needing information, though. About those objects.

Taking the blade back to sheath, she faces the Binder who cannot see and is trapped in her own dark place, surmising what the woman wants.

"The light," Ophelia says. "I did terrible things before I learned to wield it. It can be lethal, but that's—that's because I feared who I might hurt with its power. I was afraid of what it might show me...about who I am. But light is also hope." She can't help but glance at Falcon's bruises. "It heals. And when I draw it now, I don't feel death. I feel life...in every thread of light."

The Binder's face softens, her milky-blue eyes unblinking. *"You have one of the objects your mother spelled. You've had it from the beginning."* Unseeing eyes trail Ophelia's throat.

She goes entirely still. Then her hands are fumbling to tug the chain free from beneath her cloak. "My locket." She thought it spelled by Grimm. She thought it the key to retrieving her memories and magic. And maybe he did make it a token to help her remember, but it was something else first.

"As for its purpose," the Binder ekes through those walls, *"you know that, too."*

Elora spelled Ophelia's locket with her own blood and carried a green pouch with the second, locked object.

"We don't need a key to open my locket. My locket *is* a key," Ophelia tells Falcon. "It must open whatever holds the amulet."

"We've got as much as she's going to give us," he whispers.

"Do you know where she is now?" Ophelia asks anyway.

"Ophelia, no more secrets—"

The Binder tilts her head. *"Goddess with an amber jewel, her light as sealed as fate is cruel."* The woman's hands resume a weaving motion. Secrets, Ophelia realizes in horror, noticing the baskets by the hearth she hadn't before. The Binder is weaving their secrets into something she can hold.

The house fills with a humming again, and the creaking-scratching-tapping.

Falcon's hand clasps Ophelia's—firm, assuring. She's so lost in her thoughts, her body so suddenly sapped from reliving everything, that she barely feels it. They say nothing as they leave, not to a woman who took such pleasure in wringing out their truths.

Down the hill, Ophelia finally says, "The *volorost* has to know something."

Falcon nods. "And he's conveniently absent. Maybe Trix and the others are having some luck working things loose."

He keeps her hand tight in his, and Ophelia clings to his warmth as they trek back across the ice and pebbled paths toward the festival. Along the way, just thinking about the Binder's song and the secrets she learned, a shiver sets in.

Light as sealed as fate is cruel.

She doesn't think about how the woman knew, from the start, what they had come seeking.

LesyaBlackBird

CHAPTER 38
ARRIVALS & DEPARTURES

VALLEY OF IRON, KÚZLO
12TH DAY IN THE NEW WINTER
OPHELIA IS ON HER OWN

Ophelia sees no signs of their three co-conspirators, or the high lord of the North.

Worse, six menacing dragons perch in a half-moon circle around the inner Valley of Iron upon her and Falcon's return.

The sharpness of the beasts' natural shadows cast long across the Bowl.

Falcon's grip tightens once around her hand before releasing it. They edge into a crowd growing thick near the stone training circles, where in the center a behemoth warrior is commanding the crowd's attention, his chest inflated as though to make clear he's in charge.

It's the wing-plated furs and goggles around the man's neck that has her brow furrowed.

"Weshkamfen!" the warrior calls. *Competitors!*

Falcon swears. "It's time for the flight parade." At her questioning look, he adds, "It's tradition for competitors to circle the valleys from the air." Falcon scans the throng. "And my father still isn't here. He should be presiding over this."

Ophelia draws a hand to her temple, having to shake away a bit of light-headedness. "What about—"

Cheers erupt as the other heirs make their way toward the training circle. All male but two, she realizes, spotting one Falcon pummeled last night. Argan, she thinks. He seems to wear his bruises with pride.

Each heir bears a resemblance to Falcon in some way. Similar slopes of the nose or cuts of the jaw, or the way they move. But it's Kessan, whose descent from the House of Bone is turning heads now, who most resembles him. When the favored heir reaches the circle, it's only Falcon left to come forward.

Ophelia can sense the interest of the crowd drift to him—and by way of him, to her—as northerners begin to take notice.

"You have to go," she acknowledges, glancing at the winged beasts that surround the Bowl. Then, tension pulls in her chest. "You've flown just a few times?"

Intensity shapes Falcon's features as he faces her, the inches between them seeming a greater distance now than they did in bed last night, before he told her of the vision. As if he can feel it, too, he leans to close the gap, touching his forehead to hers, his thumb drawing circles on her wrist.

Her breath stutters when he dips his nose to brush her cheek. "Don't worry, flying's like riding a bike. And don't waste time watching the parade. Find the others. Tell Reya what we learned; it might trigger something she remembers. And if... If you're gone before I'm back"—his voice thickens—"remember everything I said."

"Don't say that like I'll never see you again."

Brushing a rogue strand of hair from her face, he starts to say something but swallows it down, merely holding her gaze with an unspoken plea.

When I look at you, I think I'll catch fire.

You have to be ready.

Keep playing the game.

Choose him.

With her heart trapped in her throat, she nods. "Tell me you'll find me."

"In every life," he breathes.

Ophelia cuts away from the main crowds, feeling every beat of dragon wing as the creatures and flyers prepare to take to the air.

A blood-red dragon—*drecora*, they call them—launches first to the cheers of a name that sounds like Sunder.

Ophelia wipes at her brow.

Though the wind snaps fresh and cool, she feels warm, still light-headed. And to her great frustration, she's fairly certain she's passed the same fishmonger's tent three times in her search for Reya and Trix and Ashë.

It feels like time is running out.

Nearly every northerner's gaze is trained on the sky except a pair of men taking their sweet time in front of her, blocking the way. She notes the matted, frozen fur of their coats and the amber-green sheen that sticks to their cheeks, shimmering in the sunlight. *Migth*. They must be miners.

As she walks, she thinks of the Binder, until her head starts to throb from puzzling at the riddle and how it's tied up with the high lord of the North.

Goddess with an amber jewel. It must be her mother. *Her light as sealed as fate is cruel.* But Elora was dead. Ophelia knew that because, years ago, the magic of Selene passed to her. Maybe Falcon was right and the Binder's mind has devolved. But...no. With trepidation, an instinct tells her that's not true at all.

Distracted, she nearly collides with the miners where they're paused in front of a tent. The seer's tent, from earlier. The one with the dragon-and-two-moons banner.

One of the men turns. His eyes saucer as he nudges his friend, then grasps his arm. "Ma aushna korpen!"

Apparently she looks like someone. Ophelia starts to inquire when the silhouette of another dragon slips over the valley and stirs raucous cheers: "Argan! Argan!"

Amid the din, the world seems to tilt.

A third and fourth dragon blink across the sky as she sways, feeling the simmer of heat in her body just before she flickers—her hand, her arm—fading out and in, out and in. With rising panic, she realizes two things: the anchor is waning, and people are staring.

The miners are calling others over, pointing at her. Their curiosity vibrates as wildly as their hope, as a small crowd comes to see. Drawing the hood of her scarf over her head, she tries to push through the people, to shut her ears to the rippling of a rumor that is spreading around her as fast as fire.

"Gosten," someone says. "Gosten!" *Goddess!*

"Ophelia!"

At the familiar voice, she whips her head. "Reya?" She staggers forward through the crowd, eyes on her new friend.

A bald man cuts into her path—the seer from the tent. His face slackened with awe, he looks at her as if she's the antidote to a great plague. "Gosten," he decrees. "Ost ma!" *It's her.*

Particles blink in her peripheral, bringing a deluge of high-pitched whispers that cry a warning and tick like a thousand clocks. The rope of that anchor gives a little more, and she feels the flicker again. This time, in her ribs.

Two men in the crowd drop to their knees before her. "Gosten!" Mutters about her and the Snow Moons get passed around like a dram in a drought.

A shiver passes through her as, one by one, more bend the knee. Like falling stars, they bow at her feet. Fanatics, Falcon called these people. Zealots.

"Please, get up," she urges as the seer joins them, a hand to his chest and eyes clouded an egg-shell white.

In Magiesian, he bellows, "She was born in fire and bathed in dragon blood! She will call them! She will call them from the dust!"

Murmuring assent undulates in waves around her, making her sway again.

"Ophelia!" Reya—just up the row of tents.

Dragging a quick breath, Ophelia lowers her head and pushes beyond the bowing crowd, holding the anchor as tightly as she can.

A fifth silhouette crawls across the valley, the dragon's brilliant white shape soaring above as a fervent chanting begins on the ground. "*Jagerin! Jagerin!*"

She casts a look skyward as she hastens toward Reya, hating that the rope behind her ribs sees to slacken with every step. She flickers—this time it's her legs, and they give. Landing on uneven ice, sharp pain splits in her hand.

"Ophelia!" Reya is on her knees. "Beatrix and Ashë are searching for you—" She gasps, taking Ophelia's wrist. "Your hand."

Nausea stirs at the sight of the deep gash on her palm, iridescent with blood. She draws it away. "It's fine. I'll heal it later."

But Reya's already extracting a blade, drawing her skirt up as if she means to cut a scrap of fabric, and Ophelia's vision tunnels to the weapon—to its winged hilt and the initial *A* carved in it.

Reya notes her intense interest. "Do not worry. Yours is safe." She motions to Ophelia's waist as she slices a scrap of cloth. "This is Kessan's dragonblade. He gave it to me the night he chose me for his *Amati*."

Ophelia's breath winds as that word spins in her head—her head that's growing too light from the struggle of holding the anchor in place. Everything tangles. Reya's words, Falcon's, the Binder's, the seer's.

A drumbeat pounds across the valley.

Sitting back on her heels, Reya cranes her head.

"What...is it?" Ophelia asks.

"The arrival drums," Reya murmurs gravely. "We have guests."

As the last dragons take to the sky, every shred of Ophelia's remaining focus shifts to a silver procession marching into the valley from the direction of the main gates. Led by warriors, there are at least twenty soldiers, all wearing the two-headed daw emblem of the Gray King of Magus. Kingsguards, a few Spellcasters, and...

Her eyes must be playing tricks.

As the procession draws near, her gaze locks on the man shielded in the center. A man in a gray doublet and finely threaded cape. His expression is dutiful, his shoulders are back, and his chin is tipped up in such a way that the sun catches on the seven-pointed crown pressing down upon the dark curls of his hair.

She can't make sense of what she sees.

And, yet, it's him. "Rune."

He's not imprisoned by kingsguards but protected by them.

She can hear the echo of his voice from the prison cell, feel his phantom hands tightening on her throat to suggest what the king's people have done to him—to his mind. What would happen if Rune turned his head and saw her?

"Reya," she pants, grasping for the woman's hand. She's supposed to tell Reya about the Binder, but what comes out is, "The alliance. Kúzlo already has a trade agreement with the Gray King. I think your *volorost*"—she clenches her teeth with the effort of staying, as though something pulls on the anchor. "Falcon's father," she tries again. "He must be allying with the Gray King in Magus's war. All that...*migth*."

Reya's eyes widen at the implication. What would ten thousand royal soldiers do with it? This is exactly what Kier has feared, isn't it?

"You need to tell Falcon. Tell him...Rune Ethera is..." She cries out as the rope in her snaps. And as Rune marches closer in that horrid crown with that unreadable look, there is only light, bursting and breaking through her.

FIVE

EN PASSANTE

CHAPTER 39
TROUBLE & ICE
KÚZLO
12TH DAY IN THE NEW WINTER

Trouble sits across the tribal council table from Kessan Aksander. He faces the prince of Magus with a steeled jaw that conveys his irritation, even as it belies his pounding heart.

The crown is not supposed to be here.

An hour ago, his father's personal advisor pulled Kessan from the applause of crowds gathered to watch the flight parade. In that sharp, harsh tongue of the North, Thorin informed him, "The king of Magus has sent his heir. You know what this could mean?"

On the surface, it meant delaying Kessan's enjoyment of the people's adoration. And his flight to the Valley of Bones for official training with the other heirs. More, it meant pretending. Convincing a monarch's new heir that Kúzlo's tribal council had nothing to hide.

Across the table, wearing a crown that must weigh more than Kessan's sword, the prince confers with an aide who looks about his age, with brown skin and eyes that cut like a gem.

Kessan sits arrow-straight in his father's chair, holding himself with the posture of someone who belongs there.

"Just be quiet and let them see the strength of an Aksander at the table while your father is unavailable," Thorin told him earlier, as they filed into the room.

A room that is uncomfortably quiet.

Kessan has always hated silence—time alone with thoughts and guilt and secrets. But it is customary for guests to have the first word, and this prince seems in no hurry to speak. Rather, he looks lost in thought as his aide talks to him in hushed tones.

After measuring the few kingsguards in metal armor who loom at the back of the room, Kessan trades a look with Thorin at his left. The man's an elder, hair spun in an old-generation knot, face wind-weathered and as carved as the walls in the room. Like the rest, Thorin says nothing. But Kessan can read his look. *They do not know,* it seems to assure. *This is merely the king's heir come to make himself known.*

At least, that is what Kessan tells himself.

Because the crown cannot know—*they cannot know*—that two weeks ago, he raised a body coffined in ice from the bowels of the sacred mountain, and it spurred a vision of trouble to come. A vision that—

Kessan swallows, remembering what came after.

"Tell no one of your father's state or what was found in the Virstone, certainly not before the tournament concludes and a successor is chosen," Thorin said grimly from the foot of Ryke's bed after the high lord collapsed. "Even with drecora, with gatekeepers, with the mountains themselves, the truth would make us vulnerable to attack. We do whatever we must do... You understand?"

"I understand," he said.

Kessan learned long ago what he could live with doing if he had to. Convincing the elders to banish Falcon. Circulating the lie that his half-brother betrayed him to protect his own position. Learning to fight and not be small. These things kept bruises off his face and disappointment off his father's.

In the room, the silence drags on.

Kessan squeezes his leg beneath the table, unable to take it much longer, when at long last the prince of Magus gives a nod to his aide, who then asks the obvious question: "Where is Ryke Aksander?"

Thorin clears his throat. They rehearsed this. "The *volorost* is elsewhere preparing for the Sanctioning, as we were not expecting you to—" Thorin's words strangle in his throat.

Kessan frowns as the advisor's eyes glaze. As the lie on his thin lips withers under the glimmering gaze of the crown prince.

An Enchanter. The prince is enchanting Thorin.

Kessan realizes this in that time-slowing way, with piercing dread, while their guarded truth begins to spill from the advisor's mouth in the same manner blood pours from a fresh kill. Too fast to catch.

Mechanically, Thorin says, "The *volorost* is dying."

Panic grips Kessan. "Stop," he demands. "This is not how we negotiate."

But it's as though the prince is in a trance, and Thorin drones, "The high lord is days from meeting the gods."

Fear spikes straight through Kessan. Fear the confession will instantly erode everything Thorin said it would—trade, neutrality, safety from the war. Kessan's future at the helm. He must stop this before he loses everything. He cannot... He cannot lose what he has been clawing his way to achieve.

But harming the prince of Magus would mean certain war.

Kessan sweeps a bone blade from his rib sheath. He was never the vicious one as a child, but he continues to learn what he is capable of when cornered.

Thorin goes on. "Recently in the Valley of Ice—"

Twisting in his seat, Kessan wrenches open Thorin's jaw wide enough to grasp his tongue. The elder does not fight as Kessan cuts it from his mouth.

It is bloody. Extreme. He can hear the other elders draw sharp breaths, but no one on the council challenges his choice. Desperate things are done when the North is threatened. A worthy Aksander acts.

Rivulets of red spill down Thorin's chest onto the table. The elder erupts from his stupor and clasps his mouth, shoving back in his seat with widened eyes before he falls from his chair to his knees.

Kessan lays the tongue on the table. "I said," he grits at their guests, "that is not how we negotiate in the North."

The prince's aide looks horrified. Guards start forward from the wall. But the prince himself holds up a hand with a deep frown and studies the scene as though he is just catching up on what happened.

He looks from Kessan's ashen braids to his white pelts, the ones reserved for heirs.

"You're a lord," the prince says.

"I am Kessan Aksander." His heart still pounds, but not with nerves. "I am the favored lord of the North, second son of Ryke Aksander, seer of the *Nomme Geseh*."

As Thorin is lifted by two elders from the floor, Kessan swipes the tongue from the table and hands it to them, his eyes attempting an apology for the advisor. It was a brutal show of strength, but necessary. Hopefully a healer can reattach the tongue.

In Magiesian, Kessan whispers to Thorin, "Ka ren nasmi has." *Whatever we need to do.* Understanding passes between them, and the advisor nods.

When Kessan faces the royal guests once more, the prince's face looks oddly vacant as he says, "I'm sorry to hear about your father, Lord Kessan. But you strike me as a man willing to do what's necessary to protect his people. This tournament. If you win, will you uphold the *volorost*'s previous agreements without fail?"

Kessan's thrown by the prince's amiable tone. Sheathing his wet blade, he slowly sits. "My father has already been mining *migth* for your weapons. It is being sent directly by passage into Prum, as requested."

"And when he dies?" the aide cuts in, those gemstone eyes pinning Kessan in place.

He glares back. These southerners. They speak so flippantly, as if the death of a high lord is something to strike from a chore list. Through his steeled jaw, he replies, "I have no reason not to keep my father's agreements."

This treaty is what Ryke wanted, and all Kessan has striven for is to make Ryke proud. He will not lose favor now.

Words are exchanged on the royal side, then the aide folds his hands on the table. "The prince would like to offer you his full endorsement as successor. He'd also like to stay for the tournament. It will expedite the transition of our arrangement when things...conclude."

Endorsement.

Kessan's anger fizzles. He hears the echo of the crowds chanting his name and it broadens his chest. This is the best outcome they could have hoped for. The trade agreement intact. Their truth, and Kessan's path, safe.

The rest of the tribal council wear tight expressions, but with their slight nods he can see they are aligned.

To the prince, he says. "Then we welcome you to the North."

The aide smiles. "Good." He slides a small, sharp blade from his robes. "Should we make intentions official, then, with an oath?"

That night in the Valley of Bones, where he is stationed for training, Kessan flails in the jaws of a nightmare.

An army of silver. Cannons of green fire. Drecora falling from the sky, ensnared by dark beasts that tear into their flesh. Walls crumbling, rock raining, tunnels collapsing in the Virstone. Two eyes staring from a block of ice.

"Kessan," a voice hisses. "Kesssss—an." His name echoes, echoes, echoes. "The river, Kessan... The river, the ice, the amulet."

He bolts upright in the dim glow of the *yurten*, heart racing like a storm, and his elbow catches a lamp still aglow beside his mattress, next to the notebook where he was mapping fight sequences. With a quick hand, he rights the lantern before flames catch his rugs.

He can't fill his lungs full enough.

The dream.

As a seer, the stories that weave in his mind in sleep are always vivid. The zealots also believe events like the impending Snow Moons can wake affinities one has stifled, or make existing abilities more potent.

When he smooths each fingertip across his thumb, they tingle the way they always do after a vision. One of them—his forefinger—still feels raw from the prick of a blade. A reminder of how his meeting ended.

He should be elated. Calm. Ready to begin training in earnest in the morning. But that dream pushes him out of his bed—a desperate, unfurling need for reassurance powering his movements.

In less than a minute, he is stepping from his *yurten*, staring out into the distance at the formidable blue mountain that divides the two northernmost Kúzloan valleys. The Virstone.

It is reckless, but irrational panic drives Kessan through camp on soft feet, goggles in hand, while the rest of the heirs sleep.

The night pushes two hours past high moons, and under the stark star-filled sky, puffs of smoke plume from tents warmed by fires. Stalking toward the very edge of camp, Kessan fingers the light-blue scale that hangs at his neck and feels for the vibration of wings as he calls for Rakúa.

Drecora patrol at all hours. It isn't unusual for one to land in the flight field. Still, Kessan makes haste to avoid being seen, distracted by the dream, desperate to make sure.

They land in the Valley of Ice without event.

Leaving Rakúa to perch, Kessan clips up the steep, shimmering tunnel that wends to the Virstone's sacred cavern while the dream—the vision—pounds in his head.

As he approaches the mouth of the cavern, he can feel the thick weight of the ward that was cast here. His most complex yet, thanks to the incantation he sourced from the Binder. A ward nary a Spellcaster but he can open.

He is cutting a small tear to slip through when a clatter of rubble in the tunnel makes him spin.

Pebbles crumble from a ledge along a jewel-blue wall. When they settle, the tunnel is silent save for the far-off drips of ice.

Expelling a breath of relief, he considers turning back. He shouldn't have come. He's smarter than this, and if anyone saw... But the need for assurance keeps his feet rooted. It will take only a minute. He has to see for himself it is still here, that the tribal council's second secret is hidden where it cannot disrupt agreements, the Sanctioning, or worse—bring the bloodshed and war that plagues him in visions straight to the North's door.

He steps with far more trepidation into the cavern than he would a sparring ring, and his neck pounds with his pulse when he sees it.

Like it did that day when the vision seized him, Kessan's heart beats to a trouble in three.

The river, the ice, the amulet.

The river, the ice, the amulet.

As the prophecy rings through his head, he keeps his distance, avoiding the frozen eyes that stare out from the coffin of ice.

In his periphery, something moves.

A flap of raven-dark wings cuts through the roaring silence, and Kessan spins to see a large, black bird sail through the narrow tear in his ward, slicing in a circle with its midnight glare showing Kessan his own horrified reflection.

His stomach bottoms as he realizes the creature is memorizing everything it sees.

As he frees a blade from his sheath, the trouble disappears as quick as it came, soaring back through the ward.

Saucer-eyed, and with blood beating between his ears, Kessan gives chase, bone blade in hand as he sprints down the sloping tunnel after those wings.

He let a daw into the sacred cavern. A pet of Magus aristocrats that rarely comes north of Jagst. A bird known for the secrets it collects but does not keep.

Hurling himself around a wall, his shoulder scrapes a knuckle of stone, but with a grunt he pushes harder.

A dark flash ahead, and the daw shoots out through the entrance of the mountain, into the night and out of Kessan's reach. Just before he breaches the mouth, he hears a pinching squawk. And the first thing he sees at the top of the ridge is a dead, feathered mass, bone blade driven clean through its breast.

Kessan redirects his weapon at the muscled silhouette coming up the slope, readying a spell on his lips that will make his blade sail true.

A face too much like his own hits the moonslight, and Falcon Aksander—*Thames*—bends to retrieve the carcass and the blade that cut it down. "Never trusted these bastards," he mutters, freeing the weapon.

Falcon's face is grave as he hurls the bird behind him. The sound of gnashing teeth tells Kessan a drecora is near, just down the sloping trail, and that the dead bird is dragon food.

Relief washes through him a moment before he fully registers his half-brother is here. He cuts a glance further up the mountain to where Rakúa watches the two of them with interest—and what looks like no intention of intervening.

Kessan grasps the scale at his neck, tugging on the bond between them, but she stays put.

Knuckling the weapon in his hold, he faces Falcon, cursing the furyskull drecora that took a liking to him before the parade—the beast is the only reason his half-brother was able to tail him here from the Valley of Bones.

"You are prohibited from leaving camp during official training," Kessan grates.

Falcon's brow jabs at him. "Thought that applied to all the competitors?"

Kessan looks him over. His half-brother wears the same white pelts Kessan does and flexes the hand that wears an heir ring. It chafes him. "Did you send that ugly bird to spy?"

"I still feel her." Falcon nods to Rakúa on her perch. "I felt her alight at camp and saw you leave. Thought I better follow to make sure someone didn't throw you in a trap. I hear that happens out here." A sardonic look. "What are you doing at the Virstone alone?"

As Falcon glances toward the entrance Kessan just came through, as if trying to piece things together, Kessan steps into his line of sight and makes a mask of the fear creeping into his eyes and rigid posture. But not fast enough.

Above the groaning night sounds and howl of wind, Falcon asks, "What did that daw see that's got you spooked?"

The concern in his voice as well as Kessan's own guilt make him lower his weapon a fraction, even as he scowls. "You killed the bird." *Why would you help me, after everything?*

Falcon slides his blade into the rib sheath under his pelts. "I've always been on your side, Kess."

Moonslight glints off the ice shelves, drawing Kessan's frown. He remembers the night Falcon shoved him, remembers looking up and seeing his brother palming that glowing scale, how the *seshen* lifted him to their shoulders as though Falcon had cemented his place at the top. Kessan knew, even then, that jealousy warped what he was seeing. That his brother was only trying to protect him. For a second, he wishes he could go back and do it differently. Wishes he could unburden all his secrets. Ask the only brother he ever trusted if he made the right choice allying with the crown.

But what Kessan did... The lies he told... He cannot believe Falcon returned only to warn the North. No one is that noble. More likely, his brother is looking for secrets he can use to get what he really wants—Kúzlo.

"Kess." Falcon comes closer. "We've got to talk about what's coming. I know there's something going on with Ryke. You said there are alliances in progress, but I've been trying to tell you, he can't make a deal with the crown. It's a trap, all right? I know the one the Gray King sent here as his prince." He says it like he can't stomach it. "I've known Rune for years, and I've got no idea how the hell..." Falcon runs a hand through his wind-swept hair. "Look, I swear to you. You make a deal with the monarchy and the North will be theirs before the war's over. There's another option—"

"And what is that?" Kessan spits. "You?" Falcon has always had grand ideas about a better world. There is no way he has come to the Virstone to help. If anything, he followed Kessan in order to take the favored heir out before the Sanctioning. No... If there is a threat to Kessan's future, apart from his father's secrets, that threat is standing in front of him now. "You say you do not want the title, and yet you return just in time for the tournament."

"I came because you're not the only one who saw a prophecy of war."

Shock jolts through Kessan, as Falcon takes another step to him.

"Do you remember when we were kids and you used to say the *trinūten* every time we caught a glimpse of this mountain?" Falcon asks, shaking his head. "I'd given up on the primordial gods giving a shit about us by then, cold and hungry as the valleys always were. But not you. That prayer wasn't Ryke's. You got it from Yuli, right? It gave you hope?"

Kessan clenches his jaw. "I am not doing this...bonding with you."

As he starts off, Falcon blocks his path. "It's the gods you worship who are waging the war against the monarchy, Kess, through their Descendants. You must've seen that in your vision."

Descendants? Like the one that made the river? Rumors are he used it to create Shadow-touched soldiers. "If you have anything to do with the one they call the Darkwielder, I should kill you now."

"I'm not here for him. Did you notice the fanatic and his followers after the parade? Waving signs about the goddess reborn?"

"Zealots—"

"Except it's true. The Descendant of Selene is alive. Her name's Ophelia Dannan and she was born in Kúzlo."

Kessan stills, thoughts pinging. *No. It can't be.* "Lies."

"It's true," Falcon says again. "She's going to change the world, Kess. Lead us to true freedom. She just needs the North's support."

He snorts a plume of white breath. "Get out of my way."

Kessan pushes past him, but Falcon grabs his arm. "What would you have our people do? Hide behind their iron gates? Cower in the mountains while Magies to the south suffer and die?"

"*Our* people suffer," Kessan snaps. "This is what our father has tried to stop, by staying out of Magus politics. This is the legacy I—" He cuts himself off.

Falcon frowns, and Kessan worries he has said too much.

"Kess," he tries again. "The title's yours. Just help me convince Ryke to let the drecora choose whether or not they want to support Ophelia. We either take the fight to the monarchy or let the war come here."

"The war will not come here," Kessan seethes. "I have made sure of that."

"What?"

Kessan whistles sharply, fisting the scale in his heating palm as he throws a harsh look at his drecora. Finally, the air shifts as Rakúa descends for him.

Face stoned at his half-brother, he warns, "Do not speak to me again of war, *jagerin*. In fact, do not speak to me at all, unless we are crossing swords."

CHAPTER 40
ENEMIES & FRIENDS

GHASTLY
12TH NIGHT IN THE NEW WINTER
OPHELIA IS ON HER OWN

I t's darkness that greets her.

With a wave of shadows crashing against her mental walls, Ophelia rouses after what feels like hours asleep, slumped in a wing-back chair near a languid fire, back at Ghastly but not in her room.

"She's returned, Kosost, as I said she would." The room spins, but the whisper sounds like Hannah.

"Leave us."

After a moment, a single click.

As Ophelia's vision centers, a chill grips her at the sight of dark-papered walls, bookshelves she's only seen in Kier's study from behind a near-closed door, and a four-poster bed where the dark king sits with his head bowed. His shirt is half-unbuttoned, and he clenches a tight fist.

The room is deathly silent.

She trembles, as much from the power Kier exudes as from the effects of fading across planes twice in two days.

"Where have you been?" His voice is quiet, cold.

Does he know?

Ophelia still wears northern clothes. Her hand has bled on the chair. Pulling it to her lap, she offers a modicum of truth. "I couldn't just sit here after discovering what I could do. I saw an opportunity to spy, and I followed a hunch about the amulet. What good it did me."

"You went to the icelands." Kier looks up, slowly.

She braces for the monster, but she's met with a darkness that only haunts his eyes. Sleep-deprived or tortured, he looks like he's traveled to hell and back. "What happened in the West?"

But Kier doesn't hear her, or doesn't wish to answer. He drops his eyes to his fist, uncoiling each finger until she can see the cloth that was balled in his palm. He dangles it, revealing the red stains.

Trix's old blood.

Kier rises from the bed, stalks straight to the fireplace, and wastes no time tossing the cloth onto the burning woodpile.

She tenses as the greedy flames devour her way to Kúzlo in a single breath.

Turning so the light profiles his striking face, he says with lethal calm, "Lesson three, goddess. If you intend to betray your allies, do it well. Never leave a rope behind for them to burn."

Though she quakes with fury, she forces an expression that might...convince him. Remembering the way Kier reacted in the cottage when he thought she stopped breathing, Ophelia pushes to her feet and creeps forward until she can feel the shield of his power within arm's length. "You were worried I wouldn't return." Kier's eyes narrow on her. She holds them. "But I left the rope so I *could* come back, despite the truth you withheld from me about Falcon Thames."

As if in agony, Kier's eyes shutter briefly. Breathing through parted lips, he looks at her. "Do you have any idea what it feels like when you disappear?" The question rings through her between sharp crackles of fire. "When I can't feel you through the tether, it's as though the sun's been shot from the sky."

Her heart catches at his confession. At his ravenous look.

Stepping slowly closer, Kier backs her in a half-circle. "I was fending off an ambush a mile from the Shadow river when another fifty royal soldiers came, guns firing with the force of *migth*. My own soldiers were falling around me, and as I drew on more power from the Shadow river...you disappeared. The connection went cold," he says. "I faltered, and twenty soldiers were lost before I pulled myself out of the darkness to unleash it at our enemy."

Her hand rises to her heart as if she's been speared clean through.

Twenty dead.

She's cost more lives without even being present—or because she wasn't. Because she was angry with Kier, so angry she denied her crown and went behind his back in search of her relic and Falcon.

She doesn't bother with telling him she's sorry. It would never be enough for the loss of life.

Kier's distant gaze recenters on her. "When I returned, your attendants were quite vague about where you'd gone."

"They only did what I asked. Tell me you didn't hurt anyone."

Kier prowls closer, and she has to steady herself against his power. "My Enchanters merely loosened their tongues. This time. But do not test the lengths I will go, Ophelia. Like you, I would travel to the ends of the world to protect what's mine."

The warnings Kier's mother dispelled bleat in Ophelia's mind.

"Are you telling me I'm something to own? A prisoner to cage? Or...or that you wish me to be yours?"

The flames lap.

"Do you love him? Your Falcon Thames?"

His question hooks a hundred memories and hurtles them toward the surface, but she has to cut the string on them, let them fall back to the depths of her mind, for she is certain, if her face shows a shred of the truth, she will make an enemy of Kier.

If she goes openly to war with him, it would be much harder to keep her promise to Falcon and do everything she still needs to do.

She lets her thumb bite the wound on her palm, lets the pain it causes distract from her heart, and says quietly, "I love all my friends. I'm sorry that's a bond you haven't known well. I'm guessing it wasn't for lack of wanting."

With the tensing of his jaw, a tendril of mist snakes across his neck. "It was imprinted on me from childhood that love makes one weak. Hatred and fear are easier to build armies and loyalty with." The look he gives dares her to contradict him, or convince him.

Her sympathy wavers. Kier was raised by the Gray King. She spent a terrifying carriage ride looking into Osiris Lestat's cruel gaze and, more recently, saw what he made of Rune. Though the sages were a nightmare at the Constelli, at least Ophelia had people she cared for, who cared for her.

But catching sight of the ashes in the fire, her pity for him strangles.

She's been forced to leave Falcon twice. Though he was adamant she return to Ghastly, she felt the pain in his plea. And then there was his blade, and the notion that giving it to her meant something. Something she can't yet fathom.

For using the anchor to call her back, before she had a chance to speak to Falcon about it, she wants to beat her fists against Kier's chest.

Holding him in her sight, she echoes, "Love makes us weak? Now that is a lesson you've been gravely mistaught."

Kier angles his head, seeming intrigued.

It may reveal more about herself than she ought to, but she is fire inside. "At my *Asenti*, my best friend attacked the testmaster to try to keep my magic from being revealed. I never told my friend what I truly was—not then—but somehow, he still sensed the danger I was in and was willing to sacrifice his life to keep me from being discovered. Had I not burned that hall to the ground and nearly everyone in it, he would have been executed." She draws a shuddering breath. "To love takes a strength like nothing else in the world. Courage and patience and trust and putting someone first—and sometimes sacrificing yourself. Love," she says for emphasis, "doesn't make one weak. My friends give me something to live and die for, and that is more powerful than anything fed by hatred or fear."

He looks at her a long moment, brows folded deeply. "And are *we* friends, Ophelia?"

She doesn't cower under that stare. "I thought we might be. But you said I could trust you, then you lied to me. You kept me in the dark." About so many things, according to his mother.

"Lies," Kier echoes, taking notice of how she holds her hand to her stomach. Gently taking her wrist, he turns her palm over.

The touch is unexpectedly warm.

Though her wound is hardly bleeding now, Kier looks transfixed by the shimmer in the cut. "When I came to your room, I intended to tell you of Falcon Thames. But you disarmed me by your declaration that you'd changed your mind about being queen. Now, I wonder if that was a lie." His eyes drift up. "It would not be the first time I was deceived by a woman."

Ophelia braces as a lick of shadow eases from Kier's hand. Cool as silk, he directs a cord against her wound, allowing the chill of its fingers to press there and lessen the sting. "Is Falcon Thames why you left?" he asks.

"I told you why I went."

"Spying," Kier repeats, letting her wrist go. "All right." Stepping around her, so she faces the fire once more, he commands, "What's your report?"

She thinks. They were supposed to find the relics together, but after Saira's warnings and Kier's lies, it seems smarter to keep the riddle to herself. *Just focus on the war.*

"You were right to be concerned about the Royal Army's arsenal. A party of the crown has arrived in Kúzlo." With effort, she staves off pictures of Rune. "I think the *volorost* intends to ally with Osiris to protect his trade agreements. Falcon is regaining support as an heir among the people, but he has strong opposition. He's being refused an audience with his father unless he survives the tournament of heirs." It's hard to keep the bitterness out of those last words, but she does.

Kier faces her, his expression dire, but unsurprised. The truth is there in his peaked brow.

"But you knew all of this already," she says.

"Ms. Farrow checked in with the legion."

Trix. Of course. Like Falcon, she's convinced of Cleo's vision. She would've told Kier what she had to in order to get Ophelia back here to play this game she hasn't worked out yet how to win.

Kier's woe sharpens in the firelight. "The West is still ours, but they're gaining ground elsewhere. Osiris found a blood heir to the Gray Throne to strengthen his house. Perhaps you saw him on your trip."

Ice, in her veins.

Kier's lips part in a sneer. "It seems the scholar wasn't the friend you imagined."

It's difficult to breathe as the image of Rune in a crown surfaces. Kier is telling her it's him. Rune is the legitimate heir to the Gray Throne.

The part of her that noticed how he wore that crown well, how there were no Enchanters present and no hint of pain or regret in his posture, knows it's true. But how does she reconcile that Rune with the boy born of a Crat and Magie who, like her, lived a childhood of running and an adolescence under the monarchy's swift hand?

Stories flit through her mind stitched by candlelight and quill, picnics and gin, pages of *Alice in Wonderland*. But right behind the make-believe that wants to deny he could be a prince of Magus is a douse of cold logic: Grimm Hermes did nothing without intention.

Did he take Rune under his wing at the Constelli all those years ago and send him with Ophelia as much to hide him as to hide her?

The first time Grimm introduced them, Rune's eyes shimmered like emeralds when he finally looked up from his shoes. He had a wise, worldly look about him. Smart. As though he'd seen things and had stories locked away. It wasn't until they were teenagers and Ophelia threw herself into learning about the gods that Grimm sent her to the library each night, where Rune was always scribing.

The truth is a stone falling toward the bottom of a dark sea.

Grimm knew who Rune was and meant to prevent who he might become. But it didn't work. Proof, perhaps, that none of them can escape their fates.

Kier watches her as if he can read her thoughts. At the moment, with her heart ravaged and walls buckling, he likely can.

Rune, an enemy?

Grimly, Kier says, "We cannot let them gain the upper hand. We need more than one iron in the fire if we're to strike where it wounds our enemy."

Thinking of the Shadow river, she's afraid to ask. "What do you have in mind?"

"Drastic measures," he says. "If you don't wish to be in the dark anymore, then we need to trust one another. So I will ask you this,

Ophelia, and do not lie to me." A shadow curls against her mental walls as Kier pins her gaze. "Have you returned to be my friend, or my enemy?"

The question pounds across the tether, darkness stretching out a hand toward her light and demanding an oath of its own. Nothing as binding as blood, but as dangerous.

Friend or enemy—nothing in between.

Be who you were born to be, Falcon urged. *Take what belongs to you.*

Thinking of him, the relics, her mother, the riddle, all who she left in the North, she says, "I came back to be queen."

At the decision in her heart, wood snaps in the hearth and heat flames in her cells.

The tether pulls taut between her and Kier as her world re-centers, like she can feel the declaration shift her very core. It brings a flood of responsibility that seems to strengthen the primordial magic that binds her—a Descendant—to the rule. And, as she looks at Kier, she senses something...more.

Something just out of reach. Something cold and infinite as the night sky. Something terrifying that she might like to reach out and hold.

Kier's satisfaction shudders through her like the pleasured purr of a cat. "You feel that, goddess? Your claim?" His eyes glitter. "Savor it tonight. Tomorrow, we take a trip, and I will show you the secret to crushing our enemy."

CHAPTER 41
PARTIES & PAIN

Hart would welcome a miserable night in the woods over this. Fumbling with dessert spoons—where to put them—he curses the damasked white table where plates glisten, chocolates sweat, and mosses lie artfully arranged.

It's taken him less than an hour to regret this whole ruse. He was trained to soldier, not present a seven-course meal at a Crat dinner party.

Amid servants bedecking Dorian Hobb's formal dining room, he catches a glimpse of Willow Winter leaning across the mahogany table to place a goblet. Unlike him, she moves with the practiced ease of an innkeeper.

Hart marvels at her.

The toughest men would break after losing their village, watching a friend die, having their people taken prisoner. Yet Willow manages to remember the wine glass goes to the right of the water.

She works her way down the table to stand beside him—the *him* he's shifted to be. A man of thirty or so with fumbling hands and fair hair pulled into a tail at his nape.

A butler who apparently can't buttle.

Adjusting a plate, Willow's arm brushes his. After glancing at the other servers, she looks at him with knitted brows. For a second, Hart's sure she can see he's not the capable man she needs.

"Are you having second thoughts about this?" she murmurs.

His snark almost replies, *which part?* Sneaking into the manor with the new staff this morning? Not being up to strength enough to shift both him and Willow? Having to bank on the fact that it was dark enough in the rebel camp only the grunt who shot Shepherd saw their faces, that no one will remember a "mortal" girl in a cage? Or perhaps the ploy they devised an hour ago, wherein Hart slips the true butler a heavy sleep tonic and takes the man's identity so they can spy at a Crat party in hopes Hobb reveals everything—namely where, exactly, the prisoners are located and why they're at this estate.

Before Hart can answer, a pair of servants approach the table to set chairs.

He and Willow each make a show of inspecting the centerpieces.

Over winter-white fernroses woven with spikes of black lunar thorn, Hart notes Dorian Hobb and *Lieuten* Price talking privately in the hall. It feels like tempting fate that the last man whose likeness Hart stole—Price's—is within eyeshot.

He and Willow have kept cover in the woods for three days, memorizing guard rotations and sleeping in a deserted old shed on the edge of the property. Last night at high moons, Willow woke him brusquely from a dead sleep. Hobb, Price, and a man who clutched a box were leaving the tent by the river. This time, with their prisoner. It was no one Hart knew, but they weren't dead.

He didn't know what it meant, but urgency eddied in him, reflecting in the wide hazel of Willow's eyes.

It was time to make a move.

When a guard strayed to piss, they took a chance. With the right pressure to his neck, the man folded like a sack and Willow read his memories. Brushing snow off her skirt to stand, she relayed in a rush, "He didn't see what happened in the tent, but the prisoners are in a lower level of the manor, somewhere doors are numbered. I couldn't see where or who's still alive. Hart, we need to get inside the house."

And they did.

He feels stabby as a fork now, waiting for servants to stop fussing with the chairs near them. Wagging his head, he motions Willow down the table to mutter, "This is dangerous."

"Think that goes without saying," she replies. "But...?"

Hart looks at her—really looks—for the first time since they put on these clothes. It hurts. He didn't realize how much he wanted to help her. How deeply Willow has burrowed under his skin these weeks. All the traveling together by siegehorse. Sharing blankets for warmth. Her unfiltered probing about his past (grim), his love life (pathetic), his family (dead), even his favorite food (buttered figs) and favorite color (blue like the sea).

Their mundane conversations snuck up and gave him something dangerous. Hope.

It's reckless to do in this moment, and it's not even his true hand, but Hart can't seem to stop from gently brushing a thumb across the vee between her brows. His heart does things it shouldn't, and a memory jiggles loose of just after Wythe. Willow in her half-burned cottage, leaning over him at the side of the bed to pour Cibus in his mouth as he sweat like a beast and moaned like one, too, about his shattered knees. She'd stayed with him after the metalsmith reforged them. Tended to him while she made salves for others who'd been injured when the king's second wave came through.

She sang to him, her voice angelic as her ashen hair.

"You're vulnerable tonight," Hart tells her, hating the taste of the words.

He is four years into mastering his affinity—barely any time for Magies—but if he hadn't made a certain oath to spend his life fighting against his magic and who he was, maybe he'd feel more capable tonight.

Willow shows no worry. "I've had a lifetime blending in, Hart. They won't recognize me."

"I'm not sure that's true," he says regretfully. "I would recognize you anywhere."

He can feel her breath catch, just as a plate clatters down the table.

They break apart.

"Some dirt there," Hart feigns, motioning with a knuckle at her forehead as he hands her a handkerchief. "Make yourself presentable."

"Of course." As Willow makes a show of dabbing her face, other servants glance over but go about their lists.

She looks meaningfully at him. "Do I look all right now, sir?"

"You look beautiful," he admits, dragging his eyes back to the damn silver.

He can practically hear her faint smile. "Spoons on the right," she advises, then lowers her voice to whisper. "And Hart?"

When he glances up, she motions to a carafe. "Rich people like to talk at parties. We're going to find them. All of them."

He nods.

They have to.

He can't shake the dread that their enemies are closing in, that the next time rebels and the monarchy meet, it will be so much worse than Wythe. Worse still if he can't get to Ophelia.

At the thought of her, he feels a phantom echo of the tug in his chest. But he doubts Ophelia Dannan is anywhere near a city filled with Crats.

At eight bells, they've relocated to the front of the house, where string music starts in the great foyer. A melody of torturous anticipation.

Stiff as a penguin, Hart stands in a black suit near the footmen, bowing a welcome to the small horde of guests arriving in sharp dress.

He can smell the money on the Crats, though tonight they don't wear a shred of gray to represent their royal ties. He's careful to keep his gaze lowered, directing other staff to whisk coats away as flutes of sweet wine are divvied out.

Soon, the foyer teems with conversation. Nine guests turn the room—two representatives, who Hart has to remind himself won't recognize him in his shifted form, and other wealthy tradespeople and influencers.

They all mingle, admiring Hobb's tacky paintings, the gold furnishings, the chandelier dripping in crystals. None look surprised at the rebel soldiers posted near the walls, so clearly they were given an explanation. What, Hart infuriatingly can't say.

Hobb has just pounced on his second glass of wine when Officer Price checks the hall clock and angles near the door, announcing, "Our final guests arrive shortly!"

Hart raps a finger on his pants, impatient. Between the rebels and the Crats, they're in the lion's den. He'd prefer to get this over with.

He keeps one eye on Willow, who's serving wine across the room. In the time it takes her to empty her tray, the door opens with a cold breeze.

Striding in on the gust is a Magie that Hart doesn't know. He tries to place the familiarity though, if it's in the blond hair teased to a slight peak, or the slender build beneath a uniform that matches Price's, with shoulders black as a daw.

Rather than blade his throat, as he'd have done in the king's Special Army, Price snaps a bow. "General Salt."

Hart instantly tenses.

Rivmere—also known as Jasper bloody Salt.

Anger flares so fast that Hart fears he'll break shift to take a far less civilized form and launch himself straight at the prick.

"Price," Salt returns, sauntering into the room as if it's he who owns the manor.

Hobb falls all over himself to greet the "general," snapping his fingers to beckon Hart.

Tumult tightens his limbs. If anyone's likely to suspect Hart in shifted form, it might be the man who used Hart's affinity to move around Magus inconspicuously when they were both undercover in the Special Army.

Biting a cheek, Hart lumbers toward them. "May I take your coat, Captain?" He immediately curses inwardly. "Excuse me, *General*."

Salt's eyes narrow at the slip of tongue. Lowering his chin, Hart counts the seconds until someone calls Salt's attention and a coat lands in Hart's arms.

As Salt joins Price, Hart hears him mutter, "I trust our guests are being well cared for?"

He strains to hear the reply as he fills his lungs, pulling air laced with the putrid perfume cloy in the room. They're too far away now. Hart hands off Salt's coat to a footman and works to regain his composure, considering what it means that Jasper Salt is among the evening's guests.

He doesn't mull long before the front doors open and an invisible force keens in his chest, causing his lungs to lose air again.

The music quiets, and a monster stands on the steps in raven black. Feathered guards on his shoulders give the illusion of wings, and the Darkwielder's face is calm as surprise at his presence ripples throughout the foyer.

All business, Price comes forward to make his bow. At his heel, Dorian Hobb dabs a brow with a kerchief and thrusts his wine glass at a server, announcing, "Our surprise guest of honor! Friends"—he waves an arm grandly—"we are in for quite the evening. May I formally introduce you to the Descendent of the Witchists' line. The Darkwielder!"

Hart's mouth tastes like metal, he's bit his lip so hard.

The Darkwielder is still as stone, but the power that beats from him... Palpable. Hart finds his gaze calculating as it drifts around the room.

Guests clutch their flutes, but Hart is likely the only one bracing against this *pull*. The same that woke him in that cave weeks ago. The same he felt on the dais in Wythe. The thing he's never spoke of because he can't, because the blood oath he made with his parents put the truth in chains.

Hart captures Willow's attention across the narrow room. A look of flight or fight, knowing they can do neither, not if they're to have hope of leaving here with Willow's family. A hope growing smaller by the minute, with the knowledge they are well in the lion's den.

Willow lowers her head in a show of respect with the rest of the dinner guests.

When the Darkwielder's gaze lands on him, Hart realizes he—the butler—is the only one not bowing. Feeling the pinch of his tight collar and the weight of the Witchist king's eyes, he drops his borrowed face to the thrum of blood rushing in his ears.

"Good evening." Addressing the room, the Darkwielder's voice is cool silk. "I know Representative Hobb has told you little of tonight's agenda. Your curiosity will be rewarded." At the Darkwielder's faint smile, the room breathes.

Except Hart, who's straining to see past the door to where that call is pulling him.

"I hope you don't mind," the Darkwielder says, "but I brought a guest of my own."

He steps away from the door, and Hart's chest might explode when he sees her, garbed in a gown with bursts of gold to offset the black. A waterfall of gilded leaves hugs her breasts, travels her shoulders, and drapes her back.

Hart can't process what he's seeing. She looks nothing like the woman he was separated from in Wythe. His heart pounds and pounds and pounds—so hard it takes him straight back to that moment when he and Falcon and Ophelia were escaping the wreckage of that battle, leaping from Grimm's tree toward the passage.

He's falling all over again.

She's here. *Here.* With the bloody Darkwielder.

Through the pulsing of his blood, Hart barely hears the Witchist king say to the room, "May I introduce the only living Descendent of our goddess Selene, the true queen of Magus, Her Majesty Ophelia Dannan."

CHAPTER 42
CLAWS & ENVY

*Q*ueen.

The title she didn't want resounds through Ophelia as Kier hurls a serpent-like shadow at her in a premeditated, grand display. A party trick, meant to prove who she is to a room of aristocrats who have served Osiris Lestat for years. Crats not yet on their side.

The small crowd gasps, stilled by the burst of light she emanates from every pore to swallow the darkness.

Daughter. Orphan. Fugitive. Matterist. Spy.

Queen.

For a woman taught to hide all her life, being seen is both freeing and incredibly uncomfortable.

Pride tingles across the tether. "You'll get used to the attention," Kier promises quietly as he stands beside her.

While her skin dims, she traces the faces in the room. Some twenty. "I'm not sure 'attention' is the word I'd use."

It's more...realization that dawns among the guests. They're mortals at a dinner party with two Descendants of the primordial gods who've waged a bloody war with their monarch. One led the attack and wields a godly relic. The other just unleashed a burst of light. Both are sworn enemies of the crown the Crats have served all their lives.

Though some guests seem to consider the distance to Dorian Hobb's front door, Ophelia's heartened to see a few looking enthralled. The rest openly pin the royal representative with a look she recognizes well—a look that says they've been swindled into coming here.

At least Hobb is on their side. He raises an arm in his brilliant purple coat to cut the murmurs, mercifully calling the dinner party to follow him down a wide, checkered hallway.

Ophelia lingers with Kier at the back of the group. Better to observe.

The narrow, twisting hall spills down a set of marble stairs to a lower level of the manor.

The home is an ode to peculiar tastes. Boarhounds, birds, sea creatures—all manner of hunting trophies—gawk at them with glassy, dead eyes, their heads mounted on jewel-green walls. In gothic frames, paintings depict wild beasts in coitus with mortal lovers. And a few dim halls give Ophelia pause for the sequentially numbered doors.

A sense of something at her fingertips. A prickle of magic, like someone's tapped her back.

With a sharp look over her shoulder, she catches midnight eyes. For the way she's reminded of Hart, Ophelia's thrown down a rabbit hole of emotions and memories.

"Everything all right?" Kier's low purr ropes her attention back.

Stupid. It's only the house butler. "Of course."

Shadows curl against her mental walls. Reluctantly, she dips her shield.

"They look well on their way to drunk," Kier observes of the guests.

Ophelia wends a gaze through their stiff suits and elaborate gowns to see what he means. Some sway, but the way a few cast anxious glances back at them, she doubts it's from the wine. *"I think it's more that we make them nervous."*

Kier's mouth curls, all too pleased. *"Tonight, they'll beg for an alliance to spare their regions from the worst of the war."*

She doesn't want to think what Kier will do if they refuse an ally-ship. He was vague about that as they passaged from Ghastly and took a phaeton to the Bruxo countryside.

In the carriage, moonslight bathing his pale features, he looked serious. "With Osiris's emissaries in Kúzlo, we need more levers to pull. A secret weapon."

"What do need me to do?"

He took her in from across the cabin. "Disarm them, as you have me."

Her cheeks heated, self-conscious in the extravagant frock he'd picked for her. She'd never worn anything like it and felt like a fraud.

"I want you to pay attention to their fears," he added. "Their weak-nesses."

"An Enchanter could do that for you."

"I don't trust just anyone these days."

Her stomach keened with the secrets she was keeping. Secrets about the Morphist councilman Lokin and the list of names, Kane in the Witchists Guild, the Binder's riddle, her true feelings. "And if the Crats refuse to jump sides, what then?"

Kier's thumb caressed the black crown ring on his finger. "So long as we stay united, they won't."

Echoes of that earlier conversation ebb, replaced by expectations and unease that rise with the swell of violin music as she and Kier enter Hobb's impressive dining hall.

The room is blood-red, bathed in the waxing and waning glow of gas lamps. A crystal chandelier flicks a softer candlelight over an elaborate table. Just beyond, a lavish tapestry shrouds a wide window.

Ophelia snags on the statues strewn about the room like odd sen-tries. They look a science experiment, fusing humans with beasts—the chests or arms or legs of men and women, with the wings or horns or hooves of myth-like creatures.

A savory scent drifts. But Kier, keen on the guests, looks as though he's preparing for a wholly different meal.

It only adds to the tension in the room.

"You might try smiling," Ophelia suggests. "I know you prefer to toy with everyone, but I think half the room is waiting for the Witchist king to shake them down with his shadows."

As a tray passes by, Kier plucks two long-stemmed glasses of crystalline wine. "You make me out to be a child."

She accepts an offered glass. "If the tantrum fits."

"'Tantrum'?"

"That's war, isn't it? Manchildren throwing fits when they can't have everything they want?"

A dark look. "And would you let me, Ophelia? Have everything I want?" She shivers at the way he invades her space, at the faint wisp of darkness circling his wrist as he raises a finger to lift a curl off her shoulder and twist the ends. "Would you stop me?"

She feels want, need, *desire* from the other end of the tether and shudders as it seeks to consume her. There's momentary worry as she wonders how long she can tow this line with Kier, but for now, she holds her own.

"Don't be vile," she manages, as a voice cuts in: "Careful now."

Recoiling from Kier's reach, she finds Jasper Salt wielding a wary look, a glass of amber liquor nested in his palm, long fingers tapping at the side.

Her eyes catch on the black polish painted on his pinky finger, something he never wore as Rivmere.

Glancing between her and Kier as if he can feel a palpable tension, he says, "It would be a shame to end the party early on account of wayward banter." Though there are daggers in her gaze, Salt nods a faint greeting. "Kososten. You look much recovered since the last time we saw each other."

Behind a party smile, she replies, "No thanks to you." *Traitor.*

Deep within, her raw magic snarls like the golden dragon she cast forth against Kier's serpent shadows, and Ophelia remembers the way that manifestation of her power seemed to appear to her in the mirror outside Kier's study, how her eyes also threaded with golden light.

They seem to do that when the goddess in her rouses.

Maybe Salt can see those threads of power now, because he steps back, tension obvious in the planes of his jaw, in a slight crease of his eyes.

Raising his glass to Kier, he says, "Think it's time to mingle." Then he's strutting to a delicately gowned female, a middle-aged Crat woman, alone near a sculpture.

"Exquisite form," Salt remarks as he works a dimple. "You, that is, Ms. Hobb. Not the art." He laughs, a sound the woman echoes as he kisses her hand.

Ophelia practically feels the blush as she tells him, "Call me Celia."

Kier rounds into Ophelia's glower. Taking her wrist and elbow, the dark king positions her arm between them gently so all she can see is the light humming to life there, and him.

"She's Hobb's sister." He glances at Salt's would-be conquest. "When her partner recently died, she took over trade for all of East Port. No small route."

"A route cut off by the Shadow river." Ophelia feels a surge of protectiveness. "You...You'll call it back when the war's over?"

Fixated on her arm, Kier trails a cool touch along the lumen ridges. Her skin pebbles as her light snuffs.

"Let's focus on the present, shall we?" Kier captures her eyes. "And hate Jas if you wish. He can be an arrogant prick, but he's been a good counsel to me and his life also began in Osiris's clutches. He fights for freedom for his own reasons." Kier threads a lip through his teeth. "Besides, charm can be a powerful weapon." His gaze glitters over her meaningfully.

Seduction, he means. So there's nothing off the table when it comes to winning.

Extracting her arm from Kier's hold, she says, "He's still a murderer."

A perfect brow peaks at her. "As are we all."

She loathes that she can't argue the point.

By the fifth course, half the table is drunk.

The only Crat currently amenable to allying with them raises his wine glass. "The way I see it, a return to Magie rule would infuse more skill into the trades." The man savors a drink, then re-curls an end of his bowtie mustache. "If, that is, the magic-born are permitted to pursue interests beyond serving the crown."

Beside her, Kier rests one arm casually on his chair and swirls the wine in his own glass. The apricot-glazed oxboar sits untouched on his plate. "I assure you"—his voice stretches like a slow shadow down the length of the table—"all who survive to see the new Magus may use their talents as they please."

Ophelia's fork idles in hand, her shoulders tensing, at the thought of magic with no leash.

It harkens to dark, dangerous streets of the Underbelly. Decrepit buildings, poverty, and Magies succumbing to addiction, left to fend for themselves.

The supposed sacrifice Kier made to keep Ghastly secret.

Is that how he thinks the whole kingdom ought to be run? As the sole Descendant who's been molding the new rule all these years, Kier's had no real opposition in forming his political positions. He's had the Council of Guilds to himself.

But no more.

"And what about passages?" the representative from Easton cuts in from down the table. "My family's owned six ports in the south for a century. The king swore to expand routes along the Lost Sea a decade ago, and he's only done the opposite—closing passages to keep control of the magic-born—to the detriment of fine, good mortals."

"Here, here." Another tradesman raises his glass.

"Indeed." Jasper Salt's voice blades above the chatter, and faces turn to where he splays an arm over the back of Celia Hobb's chair. "But perhaps you should think bigger. For instance, imagine what's beyond the seas yet to be discovered."

There's a flicker in Salt's gaze as it meets Kier's across the table.

"Ridiculous." A second tradesman waves him off. "The monarchy says there's nothing out there."

Despite no love for Salt, his words rouse adventure in Ophelia. She and Hart used to pretend they were sailing high seas, using sticks to fend off imaginary pirates in the boughs of the bounty woods.

Kingdom maps all stop at the fringes of the Lost Sea in the West and the One Sea in the East. The only cartography she's glimpsed otherwise were the parchments in the black tent in Wythe, where the rebels were holding Grimm. At the time, those maps were the farthest thing from her mind.

"Well, the general's half right," allows a portly businessman as he hands his plate off to a servant with ashen-blond hair that Ophelia finds familiar.

But the businessman blocks her view as he shifts to extract a coin from his pocket and holds it up. It's blackened, but still rimmed silver.

"Royal patrol ships have brought back loot like this and stories about the Lost Lands," the man says. "Land long dead and blackened from war before our time."

Ophelia finds herself leaning forward. "An impressive relic, sir. Have you seen the Lost Lands yourself?"

Attention shifts to her.

The man lowers his coin, avoiding Ophelia's eye. "My brother guards the passages in East Cirque. The wards at sea, too. He wouldn't lie."

Salt frees a grating laugh, spearing the tension. Offering Celia a charming smile, he says, "'Lie.' No, surely the Gray Throne would never do something as heinous as lie."

In a dreamer's voice, Celia says, "I've always believed there must be more. When we were little, Dorian and I were told tales of marauders who fought for an enemy king, supposedly split from the Magie rule."

A throat clears. A Crat in a blue tweed suit sets down his wine glass. "Well, I, for one, am more concerned with retribution than the promise of exploration. We've all been at the mercy of the monarchy's strict laws. Felt the tightening of routes and purses. But who will be punished for the sins of the crown if the magic-born take charge? Decades of... Well, do we think Magies will just forgive and forget once they're free? Or do we think they'll take it out on us?"

Ophelia can almost hear Falcon curse, *Richie bastard.*

Unclenching her fists in her lap, she reminds herself even Crats must know struggle. No one's life is without, though high-born mortals bury their strife better beneath pretty clothes and placid smiles.

Still. It's hard to forget the miserable nights at the academy, hands and backs bruised, children sobbing. Or the sickening taverns where Crats trade Magies. The countless magic-born made to fight for sport, just for a chance to be free.

It's hard to forget her mother setting inns on fire so they could escape royal soldiers.

As Ophelia's own anger simmers and the table argues, she wonders if peace will be possible.

"A council ought to rule." The suggestion flies like a challenger's blade from Kier's left.

The weight of the conversation shifts to a robust woman with burgundy hair, who's been quiet until now. She says, "Is a monarchy our only option? Why not a government chosen by the people to represent us all?"

Across the tether, Kier's power tenses, but Ophelia feels an immediate kinship. It's the same idealistic wonder she's had all her life.

"That's heresy, Madam Berg," Hobb balks from the head of the table. "Magus has always had a monarchy—the primordial gods themselves ordained it. But think of the opportunity a shift in power would bring."

If Ophelia despised politics before, the next half hour cements it. Her head throbs as conversation battles on, Crats so plied with wine that they speak freely. She has to admit, she's impressed at Kier's restraint. His silence.

When dessert comes, he prods for her opinions of the room.

"Most of them would betray or kill us if given half a chance," she surmises.

Kier's mouth hovers at the rim of his wine glass. *"What of their weaknesses?"*

She's already assessed them. The way they fiddle with expensive rings or pearls, smooth their coats and mustaches. *"I thought it was obvious. They're worried about their futures. Their wealth."*

"Dig deeper."

Prick.

She studies them further, even while loathing that Kier would treat tonight as another lesson, and notes a pattern. Little glances, stolen in brief interludes. Looks of longing, of imagining, at her and Kier. The same emotion on nearly every face.

"Envy," she tells him, surprised. *"They envy what we are."*

A thin smile carves his mouth and stays there, even as conversation devolves to woes over land, legacies, propriety, the safety of mortals, and the plague of winter. In fact, Kier looks vexingly at ease.

When conversation breaks into smaller chats, she notes his focus land across the room on an officer called Price. Draining his wine, he says to her, "I need to check in with my legion. Keep your wits, Kososten." Then he lifts her hand, pressing a slow kiss to it.

Stunned at the gesture, her mouth falls slightly open in surprise and Kier leaves her with a smirk.

She drinks a steadying glass of water, then reaches for a carafe to refill it. A hand gets there first. The butler looms, pinning Ophelia with a look of perplexing urgency. She tilts her head at a familiar prickle—frantic, strong, beating with her heart.

As the butler starts to bend forward, Madam Berg slides into Kier's empty seat and takes the water pitcher from his hand. "I've got it."

Ophelia frowns, about to apologize for her rudeness, but Berg cuts, "A word, Majesty?"

The butler's urgency lingers, but he reluctantly backs away, and the woman nods. "Mikaela Berg."

Ophelia shifts to focus on the woman. "Representative." It sounds like the question it is.

Berg eyes her a moment. "Have you ever heard the saying that 'opinions are like assholes,' Majesty?"

Ophelia peaks an amused brow. The woman's no conventional Crat. No air of self-importance. No high-bred manners. "I might have heard that somewhere. Dare I ask what you mean, Madam Berg?"

The woman pours water for herself. "I've heard a lot from Representative Hobb and your Witchist king about a freer Magus. I'd like to know about you—a fugitive who King Osiris chased to the ends of our world."

Of course. Berg would know about the bounty the Gray King put on Ophelia. Perhaps she'd even encouraged it.

"Farther, actually," Ophelia points out. "What do you wish to know?"

"For one, your stance on things. You've been quiet all night."

Ophelia casts a thoughtful look at the rest of the table, tucked into their chocolate mousse and squabbling. "I'm not sure much good comes when sovereigns talk more than listen." Rune said that about the monarchy once.

"Fair." Berg sips. "I'll be frank, then. I never agreed with King Osiris's...education system, or the indentures. I'd say it to his face if he wouldn't cut my tongue, but after fifty years, I'm fond of it. I need my voice to speak for citizens in Vils who don't have the protection I do."

"Do you still have that protection? Communication with the Gray King?" Could Berg know what Osiris is planning in the North and elsewhere?

The woman snorts. "Haven't heard a peep since the war started. Sent my daws to Cirque to check on family in Bowery. They didn't make it back."

The Shadow river.

Ophelia hasn't seen it up close. She's been distracted with training, uncovering secrets, pursuing the relics. But that river's cut off trade routes in the middle of a harsh winter. It's killing daws... Yet, Kier has not used it offensively. Not yet.

"What about summoners?" Ophelia wonders. "I'm guessing you employ Witchists to keep you in touch with the crown." That could be useful, were Berg on their side.

"I did. They deserted when the war started." Berg glances around the room, eyes pinching with unease. "I wasn't keen on coming here. It leaves my city without its leader."

"Why did you, then?"

"Because Hobb said he found a solution. And without a solution, all I've got is hope that Vils doesn't burn in this war. I don't know about you, but I've never found hope a comforting strategy."

"No," Ophelia agrees, thinking of Dwymore—that second when she hoped Willow Winter might be the one who could free what was locked inside her. That was but one time in her life hope was all too cruel.

"But," says Berg, "what your king said? I can't support magic running wild. It'd be no kind of good for mortals."

"For anyone," Ophelia agrees quietly.

Surprise slackens Berg's jaw. "You don't intend to torture our kind the way Osiris has yours?"

Ophelia considers her own deep anger. "Revenge may be satisfying for a night. But in the end, it'd change nothing." It wouldn't give her what she truly wants—those she loves back. "Magic isn't so different from the weaponry the Gray King wields, Madam Berg. Or the influence you hold. It all comes with great responsibility. To protect, not harm."

Would Kier agree? *One mountain at a time.*

"Maybe we won't entirely persuade you tonight," Ophelia acknowledges. "Perhaps with time and action and healing on all sides. But if we don't try for better, what will you do in Vils instead of hope?"

Berg shakes her head. "I didn't want to like you."

I didn't want to be queen, she thinks.

The woman downs her water and slides the glass away. "If it were just you, I might not hesitate. But him?" Ophelia follows her gaze to Kier, who's in the hall with his officer. "If I loosen my purse and give you the private little army I've got up in Vils, is that river of his going to bury all my people in the end?" Fear flickers in the woman's eyes.

Ophelia starts to assure her Kier wouldn't dare use the river to decimate a species, but she can't get the words out. Instead, she inspects Berg more closely—her lack of jewelry, the simple plum dress. Ophelia sensed envy in others at this table, but her own empathy recognizes the same "weakness" in Berg. She fears for innocents, as Ophelia does.

She can hear echoes of what Falcon said about the North fighting on *her* side. Envisioning that hungry, dark river raging at innocents, she holds Berg's eye and swears, "I won't let that happen."

CHAPTER 43
WEBS & PEACE

Bruxo, West Magus
13th Night in the New Winter
Willow is with Hart

Better a fly on the wall than in the web. Willow tells herself this as she flattens against the wainscoting near the dining hall entrance, blatantly ignoring the plates that need taking to the kitchen.

She strains to hear the conversation between the Darkwielder and his officer in the hall.

"... so Philo finally did it."

"Last night, Kosost..."

A growl of acknowledgment. "...then all the torture wasn't in vain."

"What, Kosost?"

The Darkwielder glances over his shoulder, and Willow ducks her head away.

"Ghosts of the past," she hears him answer. "Tell him it's time."

Willow springs for her trays just before the Darkwielder enters the room. With a quick glance, she sees he's headed straight for the table, from which Hart is leaving.

She waits with bated breath for him. But when his path crosses the Darkwielder's, Hart halts mid-stride as the dark king approaches him.

Crikes.

Willow's only been assigned to clear dishes and stack trays—not serve the main table—but none of this is going to plan anyway. Ophelia here. The Darkwielder in their midst. That general, Jasper Salt, who knows Hart, loitering about.

Role be damned, Willow grabs a fresh carafe and beelines for the table, her heart thundering with the force of twenty Dwymorans pounding fists on her old slab bar.

There, she asks, "More water, sir?" but keeps an ear on the exchange between Hart and the Darkwielder, a few feet away.

The Darkwielder is saying something about entertainment, clearing the room of nonessential staff. Butler things.

Relieved, Willow starts to walk away, but a chair being shoved from the table catches her leg, sending her backward to collide with something firm.

Swift as a serpent, a hand catches her wrist.

At the cool touch, Willow perceives a dark tower. The moons shine pink through an arched rose window. It's snowing, and strange, dark mountains climb the distance. A gray-haired man is folded over bubbling vials at a work table, pouring silver liquid into a cup.

"This could change the world," he rasps, a nervousness in his voice.

From natural shadows, the Darkwielder emerges in a tunic and pants. "My father's life work," he muses, resigned, running a finger over the lip of a glass tube. "Get it done, Philo. Perhaps I won't gut you after all, for your experimentation on Delphine and serving the wrong king so many years."

Philo? Delphine?

Willow snaps into the din of the hall, head a whirl. She's sitting on the floor.

Oh no.

Hart hovers near her, carafe in one hand, the other supporting her back. The Darkwielder looms, his gray gaze like a deadly blade on Willow as she gets to her feet.

Her chest's a ball of panic. Seers slip unnoticed into most minds. But under the Darkwielder's inspection, she's convinced he somehow knows. Willow's pulse spikes.

"Kosost," General Salt interrupts. "They're ready as they'll be..." he trails off as he notices Hart and Willow, wet from spilled water.

Hart bows. "Apologies, we'll clean ourselves up."

The Darkwielder bends to whisper in his general's ear, and Hart hastily grabs Willow's elbow.

As they rush toward their trays, she asks, "Did you talk to Ophelia?"

"No. Damn Crats."

They make themselves busy, dabbing wetness from their clothes. Willow's thoughts race. "I saw into the Darkwielder's mind."

Hart freezes with a towel in hand. "What did you see?"

When she relays the memory, he casts an urgent look toward the dinner table. The Darkwielder is seating himself but Willow doesn't see his general.

Hart's attention lingers on Ophelia, who radiates like a golden sun in her gown. Willow looks away, trying not to dissect the feelings that pinch his brows. There's no time for *feelings* at all.

Straightening her uniform, she whispers, "They're planning something. Things are going to change tonight, Hart. I can feel it. We're almost out of time."

With a deepening frown, he sets down the towel he's holding. "I should've put it together sooner. I was...distracted. On the way downstairs, we passed halls with numbered doors."

Willow grasps his arm. The numbered rooms from the soldier's memories. Rooms where they're keeping everyone. She didn't see them earlier because she took the servant's hall down.

"That has to be it," she whispers. "Hart, after all these weeks, Ophelia's right here. You have to keep trying to get her attention. I'll go—"

"We'll go." He tallies something around the room. "All the soldiers from the foyer are here. I can't get to her. But your family... Now is our chance."

Hart heaves like an anvil against the first door they come upon, numbered twenty-one.

He still can't believe it. Ophelia is here. How the hell is she here with the Darkwielder? How did Falcon Thames let this happen?

An explosion of his frustration rattles the wood and reverberates down the halls, where dead animals stuffed on the walls watch their attempted heist.

The door stays stubbornly shut, one more thing determined to stand in their way.

At a voice that pleads from the other side, Willow splays a hand on the wood, saying into the seams, "We're going to get you out."

The desperate look she gives him cuts Hart to the quick.

"This isn't working," she says. Facing him, Willow shucks the apron from her servant's garb, letting it fall to the floor as she rolls up her sleeves. "I used to use magic to pick locks around the village with John." She shakes out her hands, then rubs her fingertips together. "It's been a long time since I dabbled with spells, but maybe…"

By the moons, it's unlikely. Not on a lark. Seers are Spellcasters, but unless sight and spellwork are equally trained, one skill thrives and the other withers.

But Willow isn't every girl, Hart thinks. "Try." He nods. "I'll look for another in." Searching the taxidermy on the walls, he stalks down a second hall, then a third, until he finds an elken head with an impressive rack.

An antler will do for a prybar.

He strains for a grip to haul the head down, cursing the shorter borrowed legs he still inhabits. Cursing this whole damn mess of a situation, in fact. Willow's people behind not one, but dozens of doors they need to open. Ophelia here on the arm of the Darkwielder.

Two of the three Descendants reunited.

Hart was so close. She was right there.

His fingers just brush the nose of the elken head, but slip off the fur. With great effort, he corks his frustration but glares at the dead animal. "I never wanted this," he growls.

Eyeing the rack again, this time he leaps. And when a finger catches at the base of the antlers, he grabs and reefs.

The head groans off the wall, crumbling bits of mortar to the floor as he catches the trophy in his arms. Chest heaving as he lays it out on the floor, he dead-eyes the mount.

"I didn't want this," he bites at the thing as if it can hear him.

With a firm hold of its rack, stepping a boot to its forehead, he wrenches against one spindly antler. Wrenches until it breaks free and his heart is an engine overheating in his chest.

Gripping the spear-like horn in his hand, he stills. Staring at him from the mount's glazed eye is his own reflection—rather, that of the man whose likeness he's stolen.

How the hell did I get here?

Five years ago, he and Ophelia were going to suffer through Asenti, get through their requisite years of service, then find their way to something better. That was his plan. It failed, miserably.

"I just wanted peace," he tells the man he's become. A man, he realizes, who walked away from Ophelia tonight, rather than make a scene as he did at *Asenti*. Because it would've left Willow and her people on their own.

From behind a closed door comes a murmur. The plea has the rasp of Old Pete.

Spearing the antler into the seam of the door, Hart shoves and pries, the collar of his butler's coat cutting at his neck.

He doesn't hear the footsteps behind him, doesn't have time to turn and thrust the antler, before a crash of wind hurtles him down the hall, where his back slams a sideboard. The antler careens across the floor in a ringing echo, stopped by a thick, black boot. It scrapes the marble as someone picks it up.

Pain spots his vision, breaking the hold he has on his shift, and a bone cracks like ice.

"Peace," an amused voice mocks, and Hart centers on a man in black, bending over him with muddy brown eyes. "Still clinging to that dream, *Privfir* Aurum?"

E yes closed, Willow pictures herself at the bottom of a well. Cold, smooth stone. Counting *one, two, three.*

She's ten again, trying to shut out the world. Shut out the horror of John just outside the well in town center, giving himself up to the Special Army so she can stay free. She hides like he told her to until they're gone, counting, *one, two, three.*

"Someone has to take care of Cora and Mammy," her brother told her as he helped her crawl down. "Anyone ever asks you, it's me with the magic, hear? Me who fabricated those wagon locks open. Let your magic go, Willow. No more dabbling."

"I won't, John. Just come back. Promise?"

"I promise."

I promise.

One, two, three.

Standing at the door numbered twenty-one, her hand on the knob, Willow counts to calm her mind and lets the memory go. In the quiet, she mutters a dusty spell, surprised to find the words come and her hand warming the knob.

She can see John's upturned smile, same as the time an incantation got them into Pete's shed, where John found the material to forge Cora a butterfly hairpin for her birthday.

The knob clicks.

Willow barrels into the room to find Laurel and Nezra, two women from her village. She only takes long enough to assess they're all right, but scared. "Come on," she urges.

Picking lock after lock, she frees four more Dwymorans and a pair from Inri. When she shoves through the last door in this hall, she nearly collapses in relief. "Mammy."

Willow rushes to embrace her, but Mammy catches her arms, the look in her urgent eyes as dire as death. "They took her, child." Opening her hand, Mammy reveals a small object she's been clutching so hard it's bit her skin. A butterfly with a broken wing.

The pin John forged for the girl he loved, long ago.

Taking it, Willow's heart hikes to her throat, and with utter dread she recalls the prisoners being trekked to the river.

The Darkwielder's memory loops in her mind as Willow pulls Mammy from the room. They already lost John. Tuck's blood stained her inn. Shepherd died in her arms. Half their village is gone. She will not lose another.

She's leading them around a corner, gripping the pin, praying Hart's there and had luck freeing others so they can make a plan, when a crash sounds down a distant hall. The deep groan that follows makes Willow instantly halt.

Hart.

By the time she hears the echo of voices and bootsteps, it's too late. She's not a fly on the wall anymore. Instead, the halls themselves become a knot of spiders' webs and she can feel the strands of silk tremble under her feet, as vengeful black widows—soldiers in rebel uniforms—come round the corner hunting for a meal.

CHAPTER 44
ARMOR & SILVER

K ier is disturbingly quiet. Broody, since he returned to the table.

When the hall suddenly dims with the douse of a few gas lamps and the staff hastily leaves the room, only soldiers remain at the walls and Ophelia looks questioningly into the dark armor of his eyes, unease pressing against her chest.

She nudges Kier's mind, but it takes longer than usual for him to lower his wall so she can ask, *"What's going on?"*

He fingers the stem of his wine glass, a cord of muscle clenching in his throat as he glances at her. *"More than I suspected, it seems."*

Abruptly, he signals with a brow across the table to Hobb.

The representative dabs remnants of mousse and merriment from his face, his expression growing serious, and sets his napkin aside. "Ladies. Gentlemen." Chatter dies. "We've emptied my wine cellar. Our bellies are full. Most importantly, our every concern has been heard by the Descendants of our gods. Now, let us turn our attention to a special demonstration to conclude the evening before we make our decisions regarding support."

Murmurs spill across the table.

When Kier rises, the force of him—his mere presence—quiets them all.

The gas lamps that flicker on the table shadow his striking features and feathered shoulder guards. Even without his mist or a crown, Ophelia finds him the picture of the kingdom's most powerful.

Candles crackle from wicks in the pregnant pause before he intones, "What if I told you that despite the harshness of war and winter, you could keep your wealth, your land, and your influence—in fact, you could even prosper. And without need of the Gray Throne's protection. Without fear of the magic-born's reprisal." Kier surveys every face, including hers, which must look utterly confused. "Without the limits," he emphasizes, "weak mortal bodies are bound to."

A chill climbs the column of her spine as guests trade whispers.

Kier inclines his head toward the wall in another signal.

With the grating of metal, the grand tapestry just beyond the table slides open to reveal a large set of windows, and a rush of reddened moonslight pours into the room.

Frowns deepen around the table, cutting creviced vees between guests' brows.

On the other side of the windows, not a dozen feet from where they sit, is a crisp white tent Ophelia can see clearly into. Its interior is dim but for the suffusing glow of a lantern that hangs from its center, offering enough light she can note a table set with flowers and an empty chair.

The scene has the look of a little stage. Around the exterior of the tent, there's space enough she can see a snow-laden garden with frost-bitten hedges and a glimmer of curious particles.

"Honored guests." Kier draws the words out. The room is so quiet, he needn't raise his voice. "We heard your reservations about siding with a Magie rule, but with the endorsement of Representative Hobb, we're able to show you firsthand how we intend to make mortal citizens safer in this war."

With no further explanation, Kier reseats himself to mutters around the table, but movement in the garden calls Ophelia's attention toward the window.

Two silhouettes are trailing toward the tent. As if magic is at play or there are vents somewhere, sound filters into the hall from outside. She hears the crunch of boots and a man's voice nudging someone to walk.

When they enter the tent, the lantern light ebbs and, with mounting dread, Ophelia realizes it's Officer Price. He guides a young woman who wears a long cloak, her face lowered, toward the empty chair.

One more silhouette slinks into view.

Coming to stand behind the girl is an older man in a leather cape. He's silver in the hair and humped at the shoulders, as if he's stood too long pouring over work. His severe aquiline nose profiles in the glow, but it's the silver box he holds and the way he smiles thinly at the window that chills her to her core.

"Who are they?" she asks Kier.

The same question is passed around the table, to which Hobb simply assures the room, "You'll see."

Irritation spawns in her, hot and lashing. Despite her declaration, despite Kier's insistence they be united, he has kept her in the dark again.

She scours the tent beyond the window, trying to discern what's at play. By the prickle of *maether* alone, she wages the man with the silver box is a Spellcaster. But the young woman in the chair... She's mortal.

Snatches of conversation between Kier and Stolm at breakfast rush back to her:

A report on our little project in the West yet?

The first will arrive soon.

Project?

Measures to make mortals in the West safer during the war.

Measures. Drastic measures. Naively, she thought Kier meant the allyships.

She steels a look at him, so stoic, so unreadable. *"Tell me what this is, Kier."*

He glances down his raven lashes at her. Calm, cold—the dark king. *"Our secret weapon."*

Death is in the air. Though, there's been no bloodshed and the snow beyond the window is yet pure—pristinely white, in fact.

As shadows lick across the tether, soothing through the marking on her chest, Kier lulls, *"The girl won't be harmed."*

Still, Ophelia's stomach sours. She can practically smell decay, or something hungry for it. Something sharp and sultry reminding her of the curse she pulled from Osiris Lestat. She can't look away from the tent, where the young woman has just looked up.

With a start, Ophelia recognizes her. An innocent girl who used to serve drinks at the Weeping Bell in Dwymore. Cora—her name is *Cora.*

The girl clutches her cloak and looks with frightened eyes at the window. Ophelia starts to raise her hand, to call upon her magic, but stops when she notes the shimmer of the glass. It's a mirror. One way.

Over a shoulder, she catches Berg's eye, finding the same wariness guttering in her expression.

"What—what am I doing here?" Cora asks the silver-haired man. "Who are you?"

"Don't be afraid." His voice is as creaky as the box he props open. "You may call me Mr. Philo." He crooks his head at her. "I once had a daughter like you. Golden and tall. Beautiful, unmarred skin..."

Beside Ophelia, tension radiates from Kier. As if Philo, too, can feel it, he flinches and draws a hand to his neck where Ophelia notes the mark of the Dark Shadow—slashing lines like the ones Falcon once bore. Like all the legion soldiers wear. *Protection,* Kier called it.

Philo clears his throat. "You're going to do your kingdom a great service, Cora, and be rewarded for it."

Hesitant, the girl asks, "Then we can all go home?"

All? Ophelia glances in surprise at Kier. *"There are more mortals here?"* When he doesn't respond, she scowls at him before returning her attention to the scene.

In the tent, Philo looks to where Officer Price stands back as he replies, "Once we're finished, 'home' will seem far less important to you, my dear."

"What do I have to do?" Cora asks, her voice small.

Philo reaches into the silver box, plucking with care a thumb-size vial. "You will drink, then follow simple orders."

She takes it between her fingers. "Is it...safe?"

"You'll survive," he assures. "I've nearly perfected the dosage after...some difficulty." Philo's gaze flicks to the window and back. "Now, drink."

And Cora does.

When she lowers the vial, her entire body shudders. Clasping the sides of her chair, her head falls back, her eyes flinging wide as dinner plates, and Ophelia watches in horror as the girl's irises flood with liquid silver.

They glimmer like the moons.

Cora relaxes into her chair, examining her hands in wonder. "Mmm," she purrs.

Philo keeps his distance now. "Cora? How do you feel?"

"I feel..." Her eyes center on the mirror window. And she laughs. "I feel powerful."

CHAPTER 45
BREAKS & GLASS

Magic strikes Ophelia like a grating chord. Something dark and smoldering and *other* rolls inside Cora, with no breath of life. A force beyond the gods' creation. A force not bound to the magic of the moons.

It's unnatural.

Aghast, she cuts a look at Kier. *"What is this?"*

Sipping his wine, he gives no outward sign he's heard her. Then, *"Watch, goddess."*

Philo is nodding. "Good, good." The man motions to the side of the tent where a gun gleams an amber-green in Price's hands. "We shouldn't need him, but the officer will remain with us to ensure our demonstration proceeds safely."

The room seems to hold an eager breath. As if tonight's all been a production and now comes the thrilling third act.

Ophelia's fingers clasp her locket where it hangs between the golden leaves of her gown.

"Something simple first. The flowers," Philo points to the vase on the table in the tent. "Focus the power you feel and crush them."

Cora doesn't ask how. Some innate knowledge or instinct makes her keen to obey, and her silver eyes center on the bouquet. When her palms close on her lap and her knuckles whiten, the stems flatten, every petal compressing as if strangled by invisible force.

The girl's fists spring open and the buds plume to dust, sending a tremor of horror through Ophelia. The magic in her bolts to attention, and she spies a cloud of particles gathering above the tent.

Where Cora slumps, the girl's breaths sound slightly strained.

Ophelia peers harder, trying to be sure what she's seeing is real—a trail of liquid-silver, slipping like a single tear down Cora's cheek, though she tries to smile.

Philo hands her a cloth. "Well done," he says as the dining room erupts in excitement and disbelief.

"Did you see that?"

"The power!"

"But how?"

"Turning a mortal girl Magie?"

"No." The correction resounds from Kier. "The power the girl wields is *other*. Temporary, for now. You all may experience it yourself, if you choose to ally with our rule."

So this is his game.

Ophelia bites her cheek to keep from openly fuming. In secret, for who knows how long, Kier's been brewing dark magic to fortify their army, testing it on mortals in case the North doesn't come through. And at what cost?

The girl looks pale. Tired. As if she hasn't just spent up the magic in that vial, but part of herself as well.

Kier looks pleased.

Kier is not the boy who found his mother under lock at Gray Castle, nor is he the man who freed me later. I see his father in him. The ruin he craves for all who threaten his power. The dark lengths he will go.

As Saira's words taunt her, Ophelia hisses across the tether, *"What is this? Do you even know the consequences of it? How to control it?"*

He ignores her, or doesn't hear, his attention diverting across the room.

Tracking it, Ophelia bristles to find Jasper Salt leering in the entrance, his gaze darkened on Kier. Salt's a Matterist and thus cannot summon, but they seem to exchange a report with just a look. After a decisive nod, he disappears into the hall.

She grasps Kier's arm, forcing his attention to her. But at the cold, dark storm in his eyes—a squall devoid of amusement or flirtation—Ophelia drops her hand.

Something's happened elsewhere.

Before she can demand to know, Kier inclines his face to where Philo stands beside Cora, a stoic sentinel trying to straighten the hump in his back as if expecting important company.

It's a tense moment—tenser when four silhouettes darken the side of the tent.

For the benefit of the room, Kier says, "I've just been informed of a traitor in our midst." As he spins his crown ring, murmurs elicit around the table. The tether is taut as wire, quivering with Kier's anger. "Shall we see what this special power can truly do?" he asks the room. "What it would allow you to do on behalf of the Magie rule to anyone who seeks to undermine our cause?"

Only Berg does not sit eagerly forward.

Into the tent, two legion soldiers haul a slacken figure—a large male, judging by the physique—whose hands are bound at his back and whose face is fully covered with a dark hood.

The dust above the tent grows agitated, and it's difficult to control the light that squirms for release beneath Ophelia's skin.

Uneasy, Cora asks, "Who is that?" Whatever she drank has worn off, and only fear colors her eyes.

One last silhouette slips into the tent. "He's a criminal," Jasper Salt answers, his coiffure of blond hair forming a misleading halo in the glow. "A dangerous man. A betrayer of his people. He"—Salt jabs a hand at the prisoner—"has killed a mortal."

It's impressive how fast the dinner guests gasp and fume, calling for justice.

Salt eyes the table where Cora's crushed the flowers. With a wave of his hand, a sprig of wind releases to blow the remnants off the table. He looks at the girl. "There's no place for traitors in the new Magus, is there, darling?"

Hesitating, Cora shakes her head.

Philo dips a hand into his silver box once more, producing a second vial. This one, longer and fuller than the first.

Cora licks her lips.

"Drink it all," Philo says as the girl snatches it from his hand.

When the dust dives in an anxious circle outside the tent, Ophelia braces for an onslaught of whispers. But whether it's her power sharpening or the dust trying a different tactic, only a single, urgent message seizes her.

Death... it screams.

Is... it screeches.

Coming... it shrieks.

Kier must feel the sear of her magic—the call of it. In response, a deep chill ekes into the marking on her chest and spools inward. Then, his challenging words fill her mind: *"This punishment is for the greater good, Ophelia. Prove to this room you are queen. Prove you are ready."*

"Prove it to me," he doesn't say.

Ophelia is ready. She swore to Falcon she'd take her place. The Gray King has a foot in the North, and if she doesn't wish to level Magus fighting with Kier, she ought to concede tonight and deal with the dark king and this terrifying power he's created after, in private. Carefully. Because a queen must be smart and practical. If this demonstration could deliver justice to one deserving criminal, convince the Crats to support them, and keep Kier in hand, how can she interfere?

The dust swarms in opposition to her decision, but one thing is true: *"We cannot react like Wythe,"* she tells it.

There's no making the same choices, no reaching emotionally for her magic out of fear. She has to match Kier's calm and learn when to sacrifice the battle for the war.

Though it pains her to the bed of her bones, she nods her silent agreement to him, despite the dust's frustration as it vibrates mid-air.

In the tent, the prisoner is rousing, head and neck still shrouded in that hood. With a grunt, he seems to realize his hands are bound, that soldiers clasp his arms. He thrashes in a grand struggle.

Cora's eyes spark silver with the magic she's consumed, and that blissful smile buds again on her mouth.

This time it's Jasper Salt who runs the show. With no emotion at all, he says, "Break his hand."

Ophelia's own bones quiver in protest.

The dust nudges, willing her to latch, rivaling the echoes she can hear of Kier's lesson: *Let empathy slow your sword with the wrong beast, it's you who will end up on the pike.*

As if she's unable to disobey Salt's order, Cora doesn't hesitate. With a squeeze of her fist, there's a visceral crack as the prisoner's hand jerks at an impossible angle.

A cry of pain, ebbing to a growl.

Ophelia flinches, her breath catching, and Salt tilts his head at the prisoner, his expression turning bitter. "Now his legs," he commands. "Which he is so fond of using to run."

This time, the cracks are so loud they seem to cut right through her. *"Kier, is torture necessary?"*

He doesn't respond.

At the man's cry of agony, Salt's gaze slides to the window before he grimly tells Cora, "Perhaps our prisoner requires a bit more remolding. He is so adept at it."

A chill drapes Ophelia's skin at those words.

She bores a look at the man's hood, suddenly needing desperately to know who's beneath it. But under the jolting force of Cora's next wave of power, the prisoner curls forward in that hood, his likeness indiscernible, his protests muffled. He must be gagged.

She reaches across the tether. *"Kier, that's enough—"*

"It will never be enough," cuts his cold reply.

She can't understand what he means, why his anger sounds so personal. She can only feel the prisoner's desperation through a flood of sudden *maether* as familiar as her own.

The prisoner riots while Philo coos to Cora, "You're doing well."

But she's trembling with concentration, sweat slipping between her brows. With a gasp, she sags into her chair and the prisoner slumps, blood dripping from beneath his hood to stain the snow.

"Now," Salt commands. "End it."

But the girl looks spent. More than that, she looks sick.

With renewed vigor, the prisoner reefs against his captors and his arms break free from whatever was holding them. A faint light begins to glow under his hood, and Price trains his gun, finger hovering at the trigger.

Ophelia doesn't realize she's stood from her seat until she's already moving toward the window. She doesn't check to see if Kier follows, but rushes to lay a hand against the cold glass, her vision narrowing to the prisoner's forearm.

It's far too muscled for the white shirt he wears—a butler's shirt—which is split at its seam.

Her focus, her magic, her center of being spindles to the ebony skin that bears a starburst scar. The evidence of her choice in Wythe to save innocents like him.

"Hart." His name is a fiery breath off her lips.

It's impossible. *Impossible.* Yet, it's him.

Her lightdragon doesn't wait to be tamped by shadows or explanations. It is ancient magic drawn from the strength of her alabaster moon, and there are no dinner guests, no manners, no proving who she is, no attention of Crats.

This is no party trick.

She is queen, gilded and feral, unfurling the force of a thousand suns in the name of saving her best friend. Consequences be damned, losing him is a sacrifice she cannot make.

Her magic roars so loud she hardly hears the shattering of glass.

S hards glitter like frost.

When the storm of light ceases, the window between the dining hall and garden is gone and cold rushes in, biting Ophelia's cheeks, pelting her bare arms with snow. The wind snuffs more gas lamps, plunging the hall even dimmer. Somewhere, Hobb is trying to calm the guests.

She cares nothing about that, though.

Shoving to her feet, she's paralyzed at the sight of six bodies lying prone in the tent. It drags her back to *Asenti*. To the moment when soldiers seized Hart and she erupted.

Has she done it again?

Killed them?

Price and the legion soldiers are utterly still. Then, it's like a slow chain reaction... Jasper Salt stirs. Cora coughs. Finally—*finally*—Hart rolls with a groan to his back, his ravaged hand clutched to his chest and his legs still mangled, the hood fallen away to reveal his beautiful, bruised face.

It's like she's careening again through the Glow Woods in the aftermath of the shadow beast attack, after her light scathed Hart's stomach.

Picking up the hem of her golden gown, she starts forward to him.

A hand clamps down on her arm and whirls her against a wall. Kier's arms cage either side of her face, his cool breath an angry hiss as a black mist emanates, rising thickly around them to make a shield—a private veil.

Ophelia's arm still glows, letting her see the granite eyes that skewer her from inches away. *You failed*, they accuse. *Failed to prove yourself, failed to win my trust.*

She burns right back at him. "How could you do this?"

"*Me*?" The word is vicious. Kier's chilling breaths, a serpent's strike. "You would ruin the future of our kingdom for a boy who wished to sabotage us? A boy who has only ever tried to hinder who you are?"

There's a stinging truth in his words that she can't examine now. Through a sliver in the shadows, she catches movement in the garden. Salt, groaning to his feet. She has to fix this—before he ends Hart.

What might convince the Crats...and Kier?

Swiftly, she cups his cheek in her palm, noting how instantly surprise softens Kier's eyes. In a rush, she says, "I wanted Hart to live because he's family, but I didn't break the glass to save him. I did it for you, Kier. She was going to die. The magic was burning her up inside."

A flicker of doubt in the flex of the hands that still cage her in.

"Kier," she implores, softer, though urgency is a writhing worm beneath her skin. "If that power killed the mortal girl, every Crat would turn on us. You know how that would play out, don't you? If they refused to ally?"

Kier's expression glazes, murderous, as though he's watching it all unfold in his mind. "I would leave their heads on the floor."

Bile sours her stomach, for the fact that she can picture it.

"I know." With a hand, Ophelia urges his gaze back to her. "And we'd make enemies of every city in the West. We'd be faced with revolts and having to send soldiers to force alliances—"

"And I would," he seethes.

She shakes her head, something in the tremor of his lip making her sure of her next words. "You don't want that, or you would've done it at the start."

Searching the depths of his eyes, imploring him, she latches on to what stares back—the tragic belief he has held about himself maybe all his life.

"Kier," she whispers. "You don't have to be what he made you." His jaw flexes beneath her hand. "You—you're not Osiris."

Kier's brows fold, and his hands fall away from the wall one at a time.

She doesn't let his face go. "We can salvage this. You've demonstrated the power. You've delivered...justice. Tell them I stopped it to protect the girl—she was drawing too much, too quickly. The Crats will see that you care about mortal lives, which makes you the better king. And..." She swallows the stone in her throat, swallows the pain and her anger, her aching heart, and tucks away sounds of cracking limbs and sinking dread at the thought of the dangerous magic Kier's manufactured. She is queen. "And you can spare Hart," she says.

Kier's eyes lace with a gleaming flare of jealousy. "What?"

She draws his forehead down to hers. Stifling a flinch when his nose brushes her own, she says, "He's all the family I have left. I know you care about that more than you'll admit. Apart from that, he'd do anything for me. His abilities might be useful to us. Just...take him to Ghastly. Put him in a cell if that makes you feel better." Alive is better than dead. "Let's get what we came for tonight and go home."

Kier's lips part with an audible breath. His hands find her waist. "Home," he rasps, pulling back from her with clearer eyes. That slow, ghostly curve returns to his mouth. "Very well, goddess."

He straightens and his darkness peels back.

She's won, and her relief is profound, but it by no means feels like a victory.

It's devastation, as Hart is hauled away before she can heal or speak to him, and it festers as plans are laid with the Crats—even Madam Berg—for mortals to be culled and taken to the Belly for training. It deepens when she and Kier are escorted back through Hobb's halls, toward the foyer, and while he's engaged in conversation with his soldiers, she sees other mortal prisoners being lined along the walls for transport.

She stops in her tracks, sick at the sight of a young woman with ashen hair and wild, hazel eyes hugging her mother close.

Willow Winter—one of the "mortals" caught in the crossfire of Kier's desperate measures.

Feigning inspection of the prisoners, Ophelia approaches the woman who nursed Hart to health, who clearly cares for him. As she turns to command the soldiers to release her, to take her to Ghastly as well, Willow's hand lashes out, grabbing Ophelia's.

Memories flood into her, those of a young girl hugged tightly by her mother as her father is beaten by a master in wealthy garb. The memory flits, and Ophelia sees the same girl galloping through a little town on bare feet beside a boy, laughing as villagers look on with grins. Then there's Willow and those same villagers, older and far more serious, dragging a slacken Hart through a snow-heavy wood back to the safety of that village. There's a man using shining metal to heal Hart's legs.

Ophelia exhales sharply. Willow saved Hart. Her and her people.

"Hey!" A legion soldier barks, breaking Willow's hold and snapping Ophelia back to the moment.

Willow stares at her, an arm tightened around her mother. By the gesture, Willow is not a woman who will be separated from her people. Not willingly. Ophelia can understand that.

With the smallest of whispers as she turns to leave, she promises, "I'll find a way to help you."

She should have put together why Hart and Willow were chasing legion phaetons that day, but she had no idea Kier's soldiers had taken the Dwymorans captive to experiment with a dark magic that would allow Kier to grow his army.

And Ophelia showed him where Hart was, when she agreed to his game of trust and let him into her mind. Kier knew, or had a hunch, that Hart was here at Hobb's, and he sent Jasper Salt to look for him.

All the way back to Ghastly in the glittering dark, she replays what Kier told her: *It will never be enough.*

Weeks ago, he swore it wouldn't serve him to harm her friends. And yet, tonight, he nearly let Cora kill Hart, just for trying to free his captives.

As Kier spirits them back, she's speared by it all. If he is true to his word, Hart will be locked away and the mortals will be given power, but at what cost? Ophelia did feel Cora's life start to fade. And what of the Binder's riddle and the unreachable relics? Rune, conspiring with the Gray King? Falcon, about to compete in a suicidal tournament?

She saved Hart's life, but she's no closer to freeing the magic-born. She hasn't won. In fact, it feels more like she's losing everything.

Still, under the heavy cover of night as Kier crests the mountain with her in his hold, there's a faint whisper.

Not the dark king's.

It's probably her sorrow, seeking comfort. But the whisper sounds an awful lot like Grimm, reminding her, *Those with nothing to lose are the most formidable.*

SIX

RULE OF SPIES

CHAPTER 46
RUNES & RIOTS

A gasp tears the prince of Magus from his vacant thoughts.

In the *yurten* they supplied him in the Valley of Bones, the northern woman who's been readying him for dinner rears away from his dressing table, gripping the razor she's been using to shave his face.

For a few seconds, his head's too clouded to understand why fear blooms at him—a sharp, biting emotion—contrasted by another that's duller, pitting.

Remorse.

The woman falls to her hands, begging, "Firsi!" Her white hair is a fountain of repentant braids as she tosses the razor aside, bowing her head at his feet.

Distantly, there's a sting on his chin as he slips out of his chair, seeking the glinting blade. Not yet dressed for the evening, the prince wears only breeches and a tunic. The shaving cloth draped at his chest falls away as he crouches over a pile of furs, which the northerners covered his *yurten* with.

Between the rugs, the thick canvas walls of the tent, and magic-fed fires that burn, his skin is flush with warmth as he idles there, retrieving the razor.

How red the wet edge of it is. He half-thought this body he shares with the old Rune had no blood left, that his insides were ashen by now.

Eyeing the razor, he realizes the northern woman must have cut him. As he rises to his feet, he skims his neck with deft fingers, but only finds a scab—rough, thick, and spanning the width of his carotid artery. He's been picking at it since he left Gray Castle, so it keeps growing back. Even now, its texture conjures a phantom bite of the siphoner's blade in his king-uncle's hands—one last session to fortify the prince for his mission.

The advice his uncle gave him before he came to the north plays in his mind: *Let every scar be a comfort, reminding you what it costs when you let yourself be ensnared by magic.*

To himself, the prince mutters, "Magic is corruption."

At his voice, the young woman looks up, her brows threaded with confusion. "Firsi," she says, softer, holding out a hand at the prince as if to mollify a dangerous animal.

Amid the candlelight bobbing on waxy stems around the furnished tent, the prince recenters on the northerner at his feet. The old Rune tenses at the sight of her bare throat and all that unmarred, ivory skin; it makes him anxious, particularly when the prince tightens his grip on the blade. *She thinks you might harm her,* he worries.

When the prince's gaze hooks on his reflection in the dressing mirror, the female's fear makes sense. There's a great deal of blood dripping down his chin.

Pressing a palm to the wound, it coats with warmth and...so much red. "You did cut me," he muses in wonder. He didn't even feel it. "It's interesting," he tells the woman, "how you don't feel the nicks when you've been bled almost dry." Another gift from Osiris.

Worry stares back at the prince from the woman's widened eyes. He presumes she doesn't speak modern tongue, but she watches him carefully.

"You can't imagine it," he murmurs, which only deepens her frown.

The woman edges forward on her knees, until she's right below him. "For—forgive me, Prince. I make...you want...feel good?"

His gaze fastens on her cheeks, the tattoos that wink like stars. Like freckles. Distantly, his chest aches. They remind the old Rune of the goddess the crown still hunts. Ophelia Dannan.

A slender hand reaches up, curling around the prince's exposed calf.

The touch makes the old Rune jolt, causing his chest to pinch rictus-tight, holding the air in their shared lungs captive.

The prince grits for a breath. *It's okay. It's fine.* The old Rune is just not used to being touched this way, with the suggestion he's owed pleasure and not pain. This—a woman on her knees—is what Osiris predicted after the prince's aide, Jura, told the king what occurred at the tribal council meeting.

"Going forward," his uncle conveyed, "the north will bend over to make us happy, now we know their high lord is heading fast toward death and Kúzlo is vulnerable."

Vulnerable, the way Osiris had always wanted it.

It's frustrating that the memory of the meeting with the elders is still so fragmented in the prince's head. He remembers sensing tension in the room, the nerves and fear around the table, Jura taking that to mean the council was hiding something—that Kessan Aksander was hiding something. Learning the *volorost* was on his deathbed explained why, after years of dealing with the king directly, the North's leader stopped taking Osiris's summons. Which is why Osiris had been eager to send Rune to Kúzlo personally.

The north is vulnerable.

In the council meeting, Jura reminded the prince of the king's instructions. But that rioting voice—the old Rune—must have screamed to the surface for a few seconds, enough that the heir Osiris so painstakingly carved had slipped away.

These lessons take time to stick, nephew. But this is your chal-lenge—overcome who you were. Consider whose blood flows in your veins, and seize who you are meant to be.

There was red blood in his veins, the blood of a half-breed prince, and no Enchanters guiding his thoughts any longer. He earned that much freedom. But there was still Jura. Witchists were the only guild able to send and receive summons, thus Jura had become a true shadow—the bridge between the prince and Osiris—constantly in the prince's ear with the king's reminders about their mission.

Looking down on the northern woman, he thinks, *that's all we need remember—our mission.*

Deliver the North, and Osiris's lessons will cease. As will the king's constant checking in. When the war's won, the North's in their hands, and the broader kingdom's safe from rebels, they'll settle into a new normal. *One where we have access to your family,* he reminds the old Rune. *That should make you happy.*

The prince relaxes into the northern woman's touch, her hand skimming up his thigh. She hesitates before sliding it farther, before cupping him.

At the contact, the prince is pulled deep into the mind he shares to a beautiful face basking in the sun of an old Rune memory. There, Rune's hand brushes a thumb across a soft, bronze cheek as he leans down to let his lips playfully skate over hers...

Reveling in the feel of skin and sunlight, the prince moans as the woman strokes him. He's just getting lost in it, feeling a rising within, when the sound of his own pleasure brings a swift summer storm in his head, causing that warm memory to churn.

Osiris's stern face replaces it in his mind. His likeness chides, *The northern woman cut you—the prince of Magus! Make her pay!*

The prince looks down, taking a fistful of the woman's braids in hand. She cries out a little when he tugs her head back, and inadvertently the blood that was smeared on his palm mars her hair.

Stop!

The prince's grip on the razor shakes as the old Rune wrestles for control, using memories as his own weapon, showing the prince more blood. Blood on his hands. A blade clattering to a dais. A needling string of commands that seize him. And Ophelia Dannan, slipping a stone into his palm.

The muck and sand at the bottom of his mind churn, and in front of the prince is the vibrant, if brutal, dregs of more memories. They empower the riot in him—that naïve old Rune who survives on strings of hope, whose heart bleeds out yet refuses to stop beating. The riot that has to be quashed for good.

But the old Rune lashes through the murk, clawing for a grasp at the prince's throat.

In the tent, the prince's hand rips away from the northern woman. Eyes glimmering like emeralds, jaw clenching, the old Rune emerges, fighting to grit out, "This never happened. Leave now."

Glassy-eyed, the female rises and goes.

Rune looks wildly around—feeling the urgent need to warn someone. Warn Falcon Thames. But the prince is strong, thrashing in his head so hard that something snaps, and he's pondweed in the murk again, his claws slipping off the prince's throat as a chain around his ankle catches.

In the tent, the prince staggers, grasping for his dressing chair to steady himself, blinking to find the northern woman gone. The fire spits. Outside the *yurten*, voices murmur. As the prince studies his blood-streaked palm, it takes a few breaths to comprehend how quickly the riot got loose without Jura here to keep him focused.

Maybe he needs the aide, after all. The prince had felt himself...drowning.

Snatching a cloth off the dressing table, he's wiping the blood off his palm with extra force when the tent flap lifts.

Jura frowns at him, moonslight spilling on the leather shoulders of his red cloak. The twilight kisses his brown skin a soft pink.

"Your Highness." Jura's concern swings from the razor the prince still holds to the cut on his chin. "I thought they sent someone. Were you attempting to shave yourself?"

It seems easier and less humiliating to say nothing.

Jura rakes over every inch of him, his mouth open in exasperation. "Dinner is in an hour and you look savage."

Taking full stock of himself in the mirror, the prince sees it's true. He didn't notice earlier, but blood has wrecked his fine tunic.

While Jura gets a towel and steeps it in a pot of hot water, the prince peels off the soiled shirt. When Jura turns back, he pauses at the sight of Rune Ethera's bare chest, his citrine eyes softening with sympathy on the swells of lean muscle marred by pink scars.

The prince turns away from the pity, studying the marks himself. They remind him of notches in tree bark that a mother might carve to measure the ever-climbing height of her child. Maybe, once, Rune's mother marked out the years her son survived in her care that way.

The prince must wonder long enough about it. When he looks up, Jura's eyes are clearing of a milky haze and he's muttering, "Yes, Majesty." There's a note of irritation in the aide's tone as he ends the summons. Or maybe the prince imagined it.

Jura motions for him to sit. Dabbing the hot towel to the prince's chin, he holds it there, assessing him in the mirror. "The Sanctioning begins in three days. Your uncle wishes I make certain you understand the stakes. Kessan Aksander is his insurance the Royal Army will be integrated into the *seshen* patrols that guard the valleys. If we're to take the North, the favored must win."

"I know." Through Jura, Osiris has told the prince as much every day since the council meeting.

"Your uncle's been courting the North for decades. He's counting on you, Prince."

"Of course."

The other Rune flinches when the towel in Jura's hand touches down on their throat again. He cradles the back of their neck with a hand, pausing to angle a gaze at the scab. "The king should've given you more time to heal."

For as shrewd as Jura can be, his touch is careful, even kind, like he understands the conflicting emotions touch brings for them now—the prince who wants to please and explore and be taught, to pay penance for the things the old Rune has done, while Rune wishes only to be loved and curl in on himself, where no one can see the broken pieces.

Slowly, their tight muscles uncoil under Jura's hand.

As the blood stains disappear from his throat, Jura asks, "What did you learn from Kessan Aksander today? Was his mind malleable?"

The prince considers his ride with the heir to the Dragonwood south of the Valley of Bones. The pair took two of the valley's red stags. Kingsguards trailed within earshot, while Jura stayed back to keep an eye on the heirs in training. Namely, Falcon Thames.

The old Rune hadn't been quiet when he discovered his friends were in the North.

Enemies, nephew, Osiris reminded through Jura. *Whatever they were once, they are our enemies, sent to Kúzlo on behalf of rebels who wish to see this kingdom fall into chaos and corruption again. Do not let them get to you.*

The prince let the words be his guide and managed to keep Rune at bay as he rode with Kessan Aksander across snow-glazed terrain, shoulders weighed down by heavy furs. The sun shone as they neared an open river where the shores were cut by rifts of ice. For a second, its beauty stirred colors—a summer's sweetness and light.

But summer was a lie. A lie Grimm Hermes orchestrated. There was only winter now. Winter and war and what must be done to secure Magus's future and get Rune—and himself—back to what they lost a long time ago. He's yet to see his mother and sisters, but soon. Osiris promised.

Holding Jura's gaze in the mirror, the prince admits, "Kessan wasn't easy to enchant but he told me about the patrol. The drecora and welded speak mind to mind, though it's the *volorost* who wields the most influence. The patrol will stay close to the Valley of Bones during the tournament. They've also been talking about Snow Moons."

"Veils and gods," Jura scoffs.

"You don't believe?"

"That on a single night, those worthy can speak to the primordial gods, and the gods will gift them knowledge? The only gift the gods have given us is birth, death, and war. They abandoned us long ago." Jura pauses. "The monarchy is god now." He sets the pinked towel aside and inclines the prince's face to inspect his chin. "This will sting."

We're used to it, the prince thinks. His skin warms and tingles under Jura's hand as it zips together.

"The North's superstitious streak is all the more reason the king needs the tournament to go our way," Jura says. "The people will believe the gods ordained this alliance." He goes to stand behind the prince, assessing his mending in the mirror. "We lost our daw the other night. But from what I've observed in the heirs' training, Falcon Thames is the only threat to our ends here."

From Rune, the prince gathers images of memory. Mocking blue eyes. A rasping laugh. Shifting tattoos. Limbs and lips tangled in a pink wood. This weaker Rune's heart breaking and a storm in him rising.

Before the riot can make sound again in his consciousness, the prince finds the scab on his neck and runs a finger over the comforting ridges. "There's nothing to worry about," he assures Jura. "Kessan Aksander will win."

KOIJIX.

CHAPTER 47
DRINKS & LEDGES

I can still keep him in line.

Ophelia tells herself this as she and Kier embark to the West on a tour of the region that's been shielded, thus far, from the bloodiest brunt of war, but not from winter's cruel embrace.

With Crat cities cut off from the hand that's fed them for half a century, there is evidence on every street that food is scarce and hope is waning, even in the wealthy regions. Phaetons loaded with food and supplies, bannered with the Darkwielder's sigil, have been sent ahead to grease the wheels of the allyships they're going to cement.

With every mile, Ophelia tells herself she can change Kier's mind about using mortals to fight this war. It's one reason she allows herself to keep playing his willing captive. There's also his continued advantage in possessing a relic. The fact he has remanded Hart to a cell at Ghastly. That the more entrenched she becomes in kingdom politics, she grows increasingly incapable of only *playing* the queen.

By the second night into their trip, in Mikaela Berg's city of Vils, Ophelia's sick of forcing smiles and stringing every word with care, pretending she isn't horrified by the unnatural power Kier has created—the silver elixir he calls *stärke vas*, which translates, roughly, to *strength unseen.*

Representative Berg is no eager supporter. After much negotiation, she agrees to send just a quarter of her city's able mortals—less than four hundred—off to the Belly for training.

After their tense dinner, Kier is a storm on the verge of unleashing. His agitated shadows yank open the doors of Berg's manor, and he stalks past the legion phaetons with the punishing stride of a god who means to take a forest down.

He isn't privy to Berg's parting words at the door, which are for Ophelia alone: "I gave you any of my people at all, Majesty, because you assured me you won't let that river be our destruction. If it is, Magus's blood is on your hands."

Cursing, Ophelia hurries down the steps after Kier, her light already pulsing, ready to spar if he does intend something rash.

"Kososten." From behind her.

She spins.

Jasper Salt is descending Berg's front steps, hair windswept, hands clasped at his back in his black general's uniform. As the leader of Kier's legion, Salt has joined them at the dark king's bequest. He hasn't apologized for Hart and she doubts he means to.

Just the sight of him spurs veins of angry light into her palms. And when he dares to continue toward her, she can't help it—she flicks the surge across the snowy gravel, close enough to singe the tip of one of his boots.

He stalls in his gait.

"*What*?" she bites at him.

Brow raised, he lifts a smoking boot to examine it, then shrugs his chin. "Weren't my favorite pair, anyway." Salt nods over her shoulder to where a driver waits outside a phaeton. "You should return to the inn, Kososten. Take the night off." His interest drifts to the distance, in the direction Kier went. "I'll look after him."

There's resignation in the offer, as if this isn't the first time he's had to coax Kier from the edge.

On the verge of giving his other boot a matching look, she says, "You think I trust you to keep him from doing something irrevocable? You who tortured—"

"There's a time for retribution, and a time to let off steam." Salt bats snowflakes off the sleeve of his coat. "I'll take him for a drink."

"A *drink*?"

She stands there, exasperated, as Salt marches past her. But because she will do something she might regret to the legion general if she follows him, she storms in the direction of the phaeton.

I n town, the lakeside city of Vils is coated with shining frost, yet it carries the faint spring smell of brine. And sweet bread, which is waiting for Ophelia when she enters their shared suite alone.

She can't sleep.

After dressing for bed, she paces the planks of her private room, burning log after log in the hearth until the sound of muffled voices makes her perk.

Something crashes. Then come slow, staggering steps before a long creak.

In the main room of their suite, she finds the balcony door ajar and a cold waft of night reaching fingers toward her robe. Tugging it closed, she creeps outside.

Kier lounges lazily on the stone wall of the balcony, his back to her, a glass of something dark curled in his hand and a decanter beside him. A shadow-raven perches at his other side, its hollow eyes tracking her. Once, she found the creature terrifying. But in a short time, she's come to see shadows as an extension of their wielder.

This one feels...somber.

Kier drains his glass. "I can feel you there." The words drawl.

She's conscious of keeping a few feet between them. "So," she assesses tightly, "to keep you from razing Vils, Jasper thought it wise to ply you with liquor."

"Jas has learned how to bring me off a ledge."

"And apparently put you on another." She eyes the precarious wall and curses inwardly. These men with their devastating power, acting like entitled children. She'd like to push them both off the balcony, but Salt's not here and she's not up for discovering what happens if Kier is gravely injured, given the inconvenient tether that links their lives.

Looking for a place to dispel her irritation, she steps up next to him, surveying the sky that's dipped dark-pink under the triple moons. She sees no signs of anything different there, nothing to hint that Snow Moons are coming.

A crisp breeze toys with her hair as she studies Vils, sprawled below. Its tidy rows of streets are dotted with gas lamps, and the twin Mirror Lakes that mark the border of Magus shine a silvery-rose hue in the distance. She can see why Berg would wish to protect it. Here, magic rolls above the lakes, but there's hardly any dust in the city or blanketing the sky, what with no full-time Magie residents to draw its interest.

She observes Kier's glazed eyes, hunched posture, and dangling legs. "You're drunk."

He chuckles—dark, sad. "I'm brooding."

"Same difference."

"I could take her head," he says suddenly. "Berg. Then have all the rest of her mortals." He pours another drink and holds it out to her. "No?" He takes a long swig.

She's never seen him like this. Then again, it's the first time she's spent nights this close to him. With quiet strength, she points out, "Not every war has to be won with brutality."

He gives her a patronizing look. "Tell me you're not so naïve."

It's enough to cut her composure—his tone, his antics, his methods, her lingering anger over Hart... All of it. "We have a number of options at our disposal," she snaps. "We're gods, as you've repeatedly pointed out."

"I told you. We can't contend with ten thousand at once when they bear guns that best magic. Not without obliterating Magus." He looks at his glass. "And I'm not interested in ruling a kingdom of corpses."

"Well, there's comfort in that, at least." She stares hard at him. Where is the overconfident Kier who came for her in Ravish? She tugs her robe tight against the breeze. "I'm not talking about battlefields. This is a war between rulers. Why should it be fought by innocent men? If you want me to spy, as you say, then give me an anchor—something you have from Gray Castle. I'll steal into the walls and scout a direct way in."

"Osiris has earned my brutality." Kier looks between his drink and the shadow-raven, a sheen in his gaze that betrays an old, deep hurt—a flash of the boy the Gray King broke—then swallows the liquor down.

So appealing to Kier rationally will get her nowhere. Her own long breath expels a rush of white air. Softening her stare, she asks, "Are you going to brood all night, then?"

The smallest lift of his brow, as he pours more.

"Because I've never explored the city, but you seem to have gotten around. Where might I go 'blow off steam'?"

His head lolls to her. "The bookstores are closed at this hour."

She'd be insulted if she didn't love to read. "I was thinking somewhere people like us can get physical."

He looks at her a long moment, his lips grazing the edge of his glass, his gaze traveling darkly over the curves in her robe. "*Physical.*"

Her face heats when she realizes the mistake in her phrasing. "I mean I miss wielding steel. Though"—she eyes his dark creature—"I forget that weapons aren't your specialty. Were you ever trained to hold a sword?"

Kier abandons his glass, and she edges back to make room as he swings his long legs to her side of the balcony. His fingers trace the spine of his shadow-raven, and its form unravels beneath his touch, misting eagerly into his skin.

"I was taught things you can't imagine. Things that...burrow. How fragile steel can be under the pressure of darkness. How armor buckles and splits with the flick of fingers." He holds his up, inspecting their tips, not seeming to notice the cold that tousles his hair, or the fact that his coat and shirt collar are open to welcome it. "How betrayal can carve out a heart the same as steel," he says, and she flinches against the stab of pain that drives across the tether.

"I hated my shadows as a boy," Kier says. "In my room at Gray Castle, I'd stare at a mural of the gods and vex at how Erebus could gift a power so monstrous. I wanted to be normal."

Ophelia barely breathes as his shoulders sway, enough that she readies her hands to grab him, fighting against the memory of Kier falling into the chasm in Wythe. She remembers how terrifying that felt. They'd been newly tethered, and she didn't even know.

He looks at her, gaze turning predatory. "When I led Osiris's Special Army, I learned why Erebus made me what he did. Because it takes a monster to kill a monster."

He half-leans, reaching for the carafe and glass. Ophelia intercepts them both. Pouring a finger's worth, she takes a full, burning drink of it.

She looks upon Vils once more and thinks of the secret she gave the Binder—her once-fear of her own light. "I understand why you became the Darkwielder. Why you're willing to go to any lengths to make Osiris pay and steal the kingdom back." She gazes between the alabaster moons, the crimson between them. Perhaps she was wrong before; they do seem to bear a frosty sheen at their base.

"But?" Kier asks, leaning closely, intent on her.

Her breaths quicken as his hand inches along the wall toward hers, as his power pulses across the tether.

"But," she says, "the path you want to take only leads to more pain. Coercing people to fight our war, making more enemies, destroying the land and anyone in the way of your wrath..." She shakes her head. "You'll become something worse than Osiris, something you will loathe to live with for eternity."

"And what is that?" he growls.

She chooses to ignore the bite in his words. "A man who hates himself," she answers. "A man who thinks he doesn't deserve to be loved. What a tragedy that would be to a woman who could one day care for him."

Kier stares at her, the sharpness in his features softening. "Love," he murmurs to himself. His face—such a ravaged, beautiful face—twists in pain.

As if on instinct, her magic ebbs to the surface, leeching gently toward him. As it glows, soft and warm, Kier tips his head back, lips parting as his fingers brush hers on the wall.

"Thank you," he sighs, and for a quiet stretch he looks so unguarded, so at peace.

Gazing upon him, Ophelia frowns, her own words echoing: *A woman who could one day care.*

It's hard to tell if she's pretending or if it's somehow become the truth.

The next morning, Kier's put together before she is—hair in place and folding a newspaper where he sits on the sofa—when Ophelia comes out of her room toting her bag.

She doesn't know what to say but, "Good morning."

Standing, Kier bows his head a little. Nearly sheepish, he replies, "I want to thank you for last night."

"You did."

He sets the paper on the sofa table. "Properly, then. Maybe I could find a better means to deal with my...ghosts." He seems to chew on a thought. "Perhaps I've also been rash about the mortals."

Cautiously, she sets down her bag. "What are you saying?"

"I intend to bring Gray Castle down. But I'll consider using mortals as a last resort, if you have other ideas about how to infiltrate places I can no longer reach."

Kier said there were places his shadows were warded. He must have meant the walls at Gray Castle. She wonders if it's true of Kúzlo, too. He did send Falcon in his stead and didn't billow himself into the North to bring her back when he discovered where she'd gone. Granted, he had her anchor, which clearly sufficed.

"I do have ideas—"

A pound at the door. "Are you decent, Kosost?" Jasper Salt.

Kier's gaze instantly traces Ophelia's shape, which is tucked in deep-green silk that spirals into a layered skirt. For her ears alone, he murmurs, "I'm rarely decent."

At his seductive tone, she rolls her eyes, about to quell the innuendo by calling him *vile*. But his expression grows serious. Intense and hooded, like last night when she was drawn to the heart of him, to the man Kier could be when stripped of his dark armor and hunger for revenge.

"I could try, though," he says, his tone so low and deep she imagines it's what he'd use in bed. "For you, I would try."

Her heart pounds at his earnestness, at the veil of intimacy he's managed to lace the moment with, so thick that she startles at another knock on the door.

Without taking his eyes from her, Kier calls out, "We're coming."

"Well, don't let me stop you," Salt mutters in the hall.

Her face burns to think what the general imagines they're doing, that she herself wondered about Kier's tone in the same way.

"We work well together, Ophelia," he says, bending to take her bag. "A monster and...a woman who might *care*."

She swallows at his inflection of the word—at how he seems to be holding her to it as though she made a promise.

Feeling no better than Salt, who used seduction to charm Dorian Hobb's sister, she gives Kier a smile without correcting him. Because being direct didn't work last night when she implored him to consider less brutality, but being his friend seems to keep him in line.

For the next few days, things seem to go better.

There's no news from the legion camps about more skirmishes. The borders and Magie possession of the Constelli hold. And Kier tells Salt that the mortals will be trained only in case they are needed. There are no more drunken nights or threats of a rampage with his shadows.

It's something.

But there is being Kier's friend...and there's this. The way he looks at her and offers her his arm, how often he talks of books she might like, and how, in the quiet nights that follow unsavory dinners with allies, he opens up about being molded by the Gray King. His lack of friends, his tutelage under Grimm, the time Osiris chained him to a wall for raising a shadow to him, the many Magies he was made to kill on the king's behalf as captain of his army.

He lets her see the parts that make him a tragedy, parts that tell her he is haunted by as many ghosts and bears as many scars as she.

Two of the same.

Ophelia has to remind herself this friendship isn't real. As they travel south, she does this by forcing herself to picture Hart's broken limbs.

Passing through Bruxo in Hobb's region, an area still inhabited by mortals and Magies, civilian unrest slows their phaetons. In the street, curses fire between the two races, and Ophelia gathers, from inside the carriage, that mortals are protesting the war, denouncing the gods.

With a tense jaw and flashing threat in his eyes, Kier orders their caravan stopped. He moves for the door, but she gets there first. "Let me," she says.

Exiting the carriage with light spilling from her fingers and magic straining against her skin for release, Ophelia casts a blanket of starlight to the sky in an umbrella of peace. It vibrates with power until, one by one, the crowd slows their shoving and shouting to stare up at it, and then to her. As if they didn't believe in the gods until now.

Some fall at her feet.

Hearing Kier behind her, she braces for shadows. Instead, she's stilled at the sight of him helping up a young boy—a mortal boy—who's been trampled.

I'm rarely decent... I could try, though. For you, I would try.

That moment echoes in her head, even nights later as they walk around Inri, a hilly valley filled with snow-covered wheat fields and quiet grain mills that reminds her of Dwymore. Only, it's three times the size and colder, being within a half-day's ride to the Lost Sea.

Since Vils, they've kept up their mental walls on the off chance a seer on Osiris's payroll might cross their path, and Ophelia is grateful Kier doesn't know how often she'd been thinking of him.

He is pointing out constellations, wondering aloud at what might happen when gods die, where their ancestors went, what realms exist that they cannot reach, and all the while, her gut twists in mortification to find herself enlivened by the conversation. To enjoy being in his presence. To know that in another life they might have been true friends. Maybe more.

Amidst the snow, it feels good to walk. It reminds her of her mother, though with every passing year the memories of Elora lose their sharpness. They walk so long, they slope a hill where Kier treads off path, his entire focus trained eastward toward something vast and dark on the horizon. He seems to bask in it—how it catches the glow of the moons and goes on and on.

Her Shadow marking pulses. "Is that the river?" she asks, bristling at a faint hiss.

Kier nods at the gaping reminder of the darkwielder he is.

"Why did you create it?" He must have done it shortly after she and Falcon escaped Wythe.

He turns to her, eyes dark as night. "So my enemies would know I'm coming."

CHAPTER 48
DESIRE & DISTRACTION

Days later, the morning sky paints a cheery yellow that contrasts Ophelia's dark mood.

Across from Kier in their private phaeton, she stares a hole into the chess board that hovers, suspended by his shadows, between them, while counting the miles and trying not to think about their last night in Vasgale. Lest she heave this game at his head. Instead, she channels her fresh fury at the dark king into their chess match.

Unsurprisingly, he's a worthy opponent.

But I will beat him at this damn game.

Edging her queen forward, then diagonal, Ophelia narrows the box to which she's banished his black king.

With a lazy hand, Kier moves his piece a single square, then settles back against the dark-velveted seats. His irritating smirk mocks her, even as she tangoes her white queen forward, devouring the space to further corner his king.

That granite gaze locks on her, impressed. "You dance well, goddess."

Fingers stalling on her queen, she's drawn back to a rooftop—to a summer sky bursting with stars above the stink of New York streets. There was a song on her lips that night, and after some encouragement, Falcon's broad hands in hers. She can still feel the tepid wind of the mortal world, Falcon's touch on her back, the graze of his cheek, her heart slamming in her chest.

She loves dancing. But it's a wholly different game with the god of darkness.

I should have known he'd never keep his word.

Retracting her hand from their floating game, she fashions a tight smile for Kier. "Chess is one thing. You don't want to see me actually dance."

His gaze glitters. "I intend to do more than see it, goddess. And I doubt you're inept at anything."

She shivers at the way he says that—*goddess*—as if he wishes to worship her in other ways. He has some nerve after last night.

Kier returns his study to the board, his chin bracketed in a hand. "You did well in Vasgale," he notes. "Representative Bale was taken with you."

Her forced smile vanishes. "As beguiling as I am, I think he was more taken with what you had to offer."

At her tone, Kier's brow edges up. "You're in a mood today."

"*Mood*? You make it sound like I'm upset you changed an outfit and not our entire war strategy. You said you'd listen to my ideas."

"And I did."

"You allowed Bale to imbibe the elixir—"

"It kept him committed."

"And if he'd died?"

Kier's long fingers hover at his black king. "Then my legion would take Vasgale and the city's cooperation would go easily."

"*Go easily*... And what about the mortals? You said you'd try to be decent, then you let Bale in your head with his talk about potential for the elixir's power in the war and after."

"I'm not only a ruler, Ophelia, but a business man. Bale made good points. *Stärke vas* will help us end the war, and the demand may be profitable as we rebuild."

She shutters her eyes, the image of silver streaming from Bale's irises haunting her. "What's even in it?"

"This and that," he says vaguely.

Only when she grinds a look at him does he relent, drawing his hand away from the game.

Where his legs cross at the knee, a finger absently traces the dark leather of his pants. "*Migth* is coveted for powering carriages, guns, and remedies...but it's never been forged with the marrow of a Descendant's power—our essence— twisted and reformed under the right spell."

Twisted to something unnatural.

"Whose marrow?"

His eyes grow distant, his ringed fingers trailing to touch his chest through his shirt. "The experiments began half a century ago with my father's. But everything of his, apart from books, was destroyed long ago."

Horror washes through her. "It's your marrow?"

As he studies her, she can feel him at the other end of the tether, probing, as if trying to decipher her concern. "It was the only option, until recently."

She swallows, smoothing her gown at the thighs as she processes what he's saying. What it ultimately means. "So we're back to sending mortals to their deaths."

"As leaders of the guilds, we're obliged to do what's in the best interest of our kind. Tell me you don't hate me for that."

"What I think seems to matter very little to you."

"Everything about you matters to me," he snarls. The mix of anger and regret seething from him throws her off-center, and he drops his gaze, nostrils flared. "The mortals aren't meant to be a failsafe. They'll be far more effective as martyrs, paving the way from the Belly into the East, targeting Royal Army camps along the Shadow river." He looks up. "In their wake, I'll follow into the capital of Cirque with experienced legion soldiers at my flank and, with the Dark Shadow Dagger, fork the river straight to the heart of Gray Castle, all while knowing you're safe at Ghastly."

"Ghastly? I'm not staying—"

"You have no relic. It's better you stay there with a sky of dust, the mountains, soldiers—"

"Kier—"

"—and our people, who will need your protection," he finishes.

She bites her reply at the reminder of citizens she's meant to meet in two days, when Kier intends to fill the throne room at Ghastly with them and their new Crat allies for a coronation—the official beginning of the new rule.

"We'll mount an attack within the week," Kier says, the decree a slamming door on the subject.

She shoves through it. "You said the mortals would be a last resort."

"I said I'd consider it and I have." His eyes darken. "I won't send you into Osiris's clutches. I'd sooner slay ten thousand mortal lives than risk yours." His shadows quiver, and her white queen topples on the gameboard.

Reaching to right it, she gets ahold of her emotions. If traveling with Kier the last ten days has taught her anything, it's that fighting him head on gets her nowhere.

Hating herself, she resorts to flirting. "Fine," she sighs. "So, dancing. That will be a highlight of the coronation for you. And is that all?"

His shoulders relaxing, he regards her a moment, a wisp of a smile returning. "I'm also eager to see how exquisite you look beside me on your throne."

The idea only stirs thoughts of the secrets she's harboring. "Do you...ever think about the Morphist throne?"

"What of it?"

She shrugs, gauging his reaction. "The stability it would offer having three rulers, as the gods intended. Wouldn't you welcome the balance?"

Kier cracks a knuckle with his thumb, his attention returning to their game. "Some would argue three's a crowd."

Her hand travels to her Shadow marking. In the pit of her stomach is a swelling suspicion that Saira was right. Kier wants to restore the rule, but in a way he can control.

She motions to the game. "Do you intend to resign anytime soon?"

With a long look as he leans forward, Kier slides his king to a corner square without glancing at it. Baiting her. He wants her to chase him into a stalemate, but she hardens her stare. No draw. She will have checkmate.

Grimm always said chess was a test of patience, as well as strategy. *Think of the wild panthera and water beasts and wolven. From the trees to the seas to the mountains, they still themselves to stone before attacking, just as your queen must wait for her moment to strike or risk the king's escape.*

Ophelia does still her white queen. Then walks her white king forward, holding Kier's gaze.

Back and forth it goes.

Kier vacillates between two squares while her king creeps in, until it's directly across from its enemy and she can see several ways to put him in check.

As she plucks her white king between two fingers to end the game, a side-swiping sensation flares across the tether. With it, Kier's eyes go hungry, trailing to her neck and dipping to the swell of her breasts where they're constricted by her gown.

Desire is a serpent coiling around her core. *His* desire. She's wholly distracted as he asks—sultry, soft, "Will you strike the final blow, Ophelia?"

Another pulse of yearning breaks through her mental shields, leveling her focus.

She coughs to hide a whimper, knowing without a doubt that he's flooding the tether with his emotions to distract her. She hates that it works. Absently, she slides her white king, and it's a full moment before she realizes she's moved to a position that affords his black king an exit.

Kier's mouth curves in pleasure as he reaches for his game piece.

A loud *rap* knocks against the front window. The phaeton slows.

Yanking his hand—and desire—away, the dark king's smirk withers to a glower. His raven hair falls over a brow, but he doesn't smooth it back, lost in whatever unwelcome thought has occurred to him.

"We're nearing the passage," he mutters, a pained gaze settling on her. "I'm overdue to see to training efforts in Ravish, then there are military advisements and meetings until the coronation. And after..." With a thumb, he cracks another knuckle. "I'll be away as long as needed to take Osiris's head."

Her senses sharpen with a glance at the Dark Shadow Dagger. He hasn't removed it from his belt at all this trip. At the thought of the wreckage it will cause, given his amended plans, Ophelia's jaw tightens.

Lives sacrificed. Their kingdom resurfaced.

"I thought you were eager to get back to Ghastly," she says, motioning to the board. "By now you must tire of these games, and my company."

With a sudden wave of his hand, the shadows beneath their game rip away. As pieces crash to the floor, Kier sweeps to a knee before her, bracing a hand against the back of her seat while the other slides up her thigh. "The games, perhaps," he growls. "But never you."

Inches from her, his slate eyes lock on her mouth, and a shiver climbs the bones of her ribs. After all the walks, the conversations, and the flirting, is he calling her bluff? Would he try to take her here? She can practically hear him reply: *Would you let me, Ophelia? Would you stop me?*

She can't deny the simmer of something between them. And Falcon told her to choose him, told her it was vital. But in choosing Kier, in convincing him, how far did Falcon mean for her to go?

Kier doesn't advance. In fact, his eyes shutter as if he's savoring her proximity. When the wheels of the phaeton slow and the carriage lurches to a halt, his eyes flash upon her, pained. "It will be a torture to be away from you," he admits.

At the confession, at the way his hand flexes achingly on her thigh, at how vulnerable he looks on a knee for her, her breath catches and holds.

Though voices stir beyond their phaeton from his entourage, Kier holds her gaze, looking lost and needy.

With conflicting emotions, she slides a hand between them, pressing gently to make a little space. "Admitting things like that might ruin your reputation as the Darkwielder," she breathes, her focus pulling, unbidden, to the peaks of his mouth as aching need pummels her.

Edging closer to her, his eyes eddy a dark-gray. "If I'm to be ruined, Ophelia, let it be by you."

Her throat dries, the warmth of their mingling breaths sending an ache to her traitorous core. "That sounds catastrophic," she whispers. "But I'm too exhausted to ruin anyone, least of all before breakfast."

As if undone by the idea she is ravenous—as *hungry* for something as he—Kier emits a low growl. Then he does advance. He *devours* the hair's breadth between them and claims her mouth in a wicked kiss.

She startles back with a gasp, but his hand on the seat is quick to catch her up and draw her against him. When his tongue slips against hers in a sensuous stroke, it feels like drowning in a cup of cibus. Before she can process what he's doing, his hand on her thigh is working her skirts up, enough for his knee to part her legs so he can settle between them, closer to her still.

Kier deepens their kiss, his mouth as shockingly soft as it is desperate on hers. Waves of dark desire ribbon from him, and soon shadows cloak the cabin, filling it with a heady sweetness that steals her reason. When his competent fingers trace her cheek and skate along the edges of where their mouths meet, a shiver of pleasure she should not be feeling drives down to her belly.

His kiss isn't giving. It's greedy, mind-shattering. And when the hardened length in his pants rubs against her center—*damn him!*—her hips pitch to meet him, as if coaxed by a will that isn't entirely her own.

This is so much more than flirting. This is dangerous. This is…

"Kosost?" A male voice beyond the phaeton pierces the fog of lust that's caught her in its trap.

As the veil of desire smokes, their kiss stalls and Kier groans. Inching a breath back, he calls out to his legion in irritation, "A moment!"

When his hooded gaze lands on hers, though, taking in the flush she can feel on her face and neck, Kier chuckles. Lingering between her legs, he runs two knuckles over her cheek, then trails the touch down her throat. "Ruin me now or in a hundred years, goddess," he says, his voice the velvet of bedsheets. "But will you keep me at arm's length?" His gaze darkens, sultry and imploring. "You feel this between us."

She does feel him, still aroused and wanting her. Is the desire only his?

"I've taught you to harness your power," he coaxes, fingers skimming her collarbone. "Think of what I could teach you elsewhere."

She shivers as his thumb traces the exposed lines of her Shadow marking. A radiating chill draws her shuddering breath—one that makes his mouth curve in satisfaction.

And there he is. The dark king.

Across miles and between dinners, Kier has been waging a subtle warfare with her, slowly punishing her with his fervid emotions across the tether. It's hard enough that god calls to god, but this connection may be the death of her.

Mind clearing, fury rising, she presses against his chest with her palms and says, "I need time, Kier. I can't think about us when our people are threatened, when my own friends are in danger and imprisoned."

His smile vanishes behind a stone wall, and he studies her a moment. Shoving back to his seat, posture rigid and angry brow peaked, he straightens his collar. "So you're only thinking of your soldier."

"Of course not," she says, smoothing down the skirt of her dress. "I told you, he's like family."

"Is that all?" Casting a loathing gaze at the mess of their interrupted game—a game she should've won—Kier says, "Lesson four, goddess. Those who master the art of distraction always win."

When he leaves the phaeton, her mouth, still bruised from that stolen kiss, forms an angry line at his back. *Perhaps, finally, a lesson we can agree on.*

T wo days. She has two days to change what Kier means to happen after the coronation.

On return to Ghastly, staving off thoughts of that kiss, she's relieved to find Hannah and Isolde in her chambers. The latter stokes a fire that warms the room while the other contends with organizing fabrics on the dining table that's been pushed aside to make space for dressing curtains and long mirrors. The women cease their tasks when she enters, cutting bows that stir the moted, sunlit air.

Tugging off her cloak as the door clicks shut, Ophelia heads straight for Hannah. "Did she—" Snapping her mouth shut when she notices Stolm near the window, she gives him a courteous nod. "Officer."

"Enost, Kososten."

The sound of his northern accent stirs an unexpectedly swift ache. For Falcon. She splays a hand on her bodice to quell it.

"Are you well?" Stolm asks her.

"Of course." She pulls a smile, taking note of a plate of food set on the sideboard, and her attention drifts to pastries filled with dark berries. The ode to her first breakfast with Kier gives her whiplash. Perhaps he planned for them to be sent up before he stormed out of their phaeton. She cuts a look to Stolm. "Don't tell me you've been assigned to see to my stomach again?"

He keeps his hands clasped at his back. "I am to remain with you and your ladies at all times, as a precaution."

While she bites the inside of her lip in irritation, Isolde beams at the news. "We're fortunate to have your protection," the girl says as she crosses the room.

By her smile—thank Selene—she doesn't appear to have lingering trauma from being questioned by Kier's Enchanters. She moons over every slip of steel sheathed in Stolm's baldric. "Were you a *seshen* in the North, is that how you became a soldier? Was the training intense?"

Flustered, he babbles, "I... That is... My family..."

Ophelia bites a smile. Hannah is the pragmatic of the women, but Isolde is an idealist wrapped in a daydream. It's a sight to see Stolm in that severe legion uniform, fidgeting under a woman's attention.

She didn't put Isolde up to distracting Stolm, but it gives her ideas.

While the girl has him stammering, Ophelia thinks of Hart, imprisoned somewhere at Ghastly. A deep pang fills her and she eyes the writing desk where her belongings are still stowed, suddenly wanting nothing more than to read the letter she's tucked way. The one he gave Falcon to give to her.

Dropping her cloak atop the chair, she glances over a shoulder while she works the bottom drawer open. When her fingers graze the square of paper with the wax seal, she slips it discreetly into a fold of her dress.

Rising, she says, "By all the fabrics, it seems we have the critical task of fitting me for another gown?"

"The most splendid yet," Isolde affirms, her attention fastened like a patch on Stolm.

Ophelia lifts the slush-coated hem of the dress she's worn since last evening. "Then I should freshen up before we start."

"A wonderful idea, my lady," Hannah encourages as she spreads a swath of golden tulle out. She gives Ophelia a long look. "I took the liberty of starting a bath. There are *towels* set out for you."

Towels.

She nods, but as she eagerly turns, Stolm steps away from the wall as if he means to follow. For a second, the sight of his hair making a white halo in the sunlight strikes her. Now that she's been to the North, from where he hails, she finds a new familiarity in the shape of his face.

With a perked brow, she asks, "Is some privacy all right, Officer Stolm? Or does our king require you watch me bathe?"

Stolm blushes a furious shade of pink. It's a very un-north-like reaction, and it warms her to see a shred of the kindness he showed her en route to the library, when he fed her information about the North and didn't mention their conversation to Kier. At least not to her knowledge.

Alone in the washroom, the scent of jasmine calls from the bath, but she hastens for the towels by the tub instead, finding a note tucked in the folds.

The message Hannah scribed is short:

She will meet you in the library, high moons.

Ophelia feeds the paper to the lantern flame, then retrieves the other letter she recovered from her effects.

CHAPTER 49
BLUE & HART

GHASTLY
21ST DAY IN THE NEW WINTER
OPHELIA IS ON HER OWN

I t's not a letter.

Since Falcon left the sealed paper for her in Ravish, Ophelia has braced herself to read a long speech from Hart. She imagined it would contain all the things he might have wanted to say when he thought he was about to meet his end, the Dark Shadow curse spreading up his hand. But working the wax seal open, she unfolds the thick paper to find a child's drawing.

An ache spills like rain through her.

How many pictures did he draw for her in this same blue chalk when they were five or six? Always blue. Always bold, exaggerated lines. Pictures of their families, mostly—Ophelia with her aunt and uncle, Hart with his parents.

"Why do you always draw us blue?" Ophelia asked once.

"It's my favorite color."

"How come?"

"I—" Frustrated, Hart shrugged. "Because."

"Maybe you like the sky or the sea," she suggested, gazing at the night. "Like me."

When she looked back, Hart was staring at her. "Like you," he agreed.

In the picture Ophelia holds, Hart is wearing his favorite childhood shirt—the one with a button missing in the middle. Only, there are no moonberry stains on the chest from the day they met, when Ophelia smudged her fingers on it during a game of chase, which means Hart must have drawn this before she met him.

In his hand is something round, colored a lighter blue. It appears to be smoking, or glowing.

Her heart ticks.

She draws the paper closer, feeling like she's circling an answer to a question she never thought to ask, when her eyes fall to two words chalked in the corner. In the spot where her best friend always signed his drawings *Hart Aurum*—so everyone would know the artist—is another name.

She braces a hand on the tub, shock and disbelief and betrayal pulling her, like warring hands, to drag her to the floor, where she sits on her heels and reads the two words again—twenty times more—to make sense of what she's seeing. Of what it can mean that Hart signed a name on this drawing more than fifteen years ago that matches the one she found on councilman Lokin's stationary, circled as if that kin of the Morphist king were still alive.

A name that conjures three thrones as a hole in a gaping puzzle slides together. *ISAAC VALORAN.*

That night, Isolde leads Stolm down the east wing hall, saying, "Hannah was sure she saw rats. They scurried this way."

With the watchful officer away from his post, Ophelia sticks her head back into her room from where she hovers at the threshold, nodding at Hannah. "I'm going."

"Stay near the walls, my lady."

With the stealth of a mouse, Ophelia darts in the opposite direction of Stolm and Isolde, her pulse ticking against her neck, her silk robe and nightgown swishing. The flats she wears softly skiff the marble as she glides down the grand stone staircase to the landing and veers for the hall that leads to the north tower.

Isaac Valoran.

Every time the name pounds through her, it feels like a stab. Can it be true?

Determined to reach the library by high moons, she picks up her pace, keeping close to the walls lest she end up in one of the wards Kier sets at night. No one is awake. The halls are pinprick quiet save for her breaths, the gentle groans of the dark mountain, and tinny pelts of dust and snow pattering against the window panes.

She's watching the ceiling slope as the walls grow bumpy beneath her hand when her flat catches on an invisible lip. Her shoe rips cleanly off her foot and, half-barefoot, she staggers to catch herself, spinning so the wall is at her back.

Her shoe is suspended mid-air, caught in a clear, globular net. A trapping ward.

She exhales a tight breath. Backing away, she loosens her other flat and sets it down, moving at a more careful speed. As the halls grow darker with fewer windows, the natural shadows close in and Ophelia risks allowing light to seep into the ridges of her arm to guide her. It feels as though she walks forever.

The only sound is the name in her head.

Isaac Valoran.

Hart is like her own blood. Could he really have been keeping this from her?

The outlines of twin arched doors come into view, marking the end of the hall at last. The library.

She has just grasped the cool iron handle, when footsteps echo at her back and a voice calls out, "Kososten!"

Ophelia shutters her eyes a moment, cursing the ward she triggered as she turns to see Stolm, his palm already aglow and sparking fire. He hastens to a darkened sconce, lifting the glass to let the fire catch. She squints at the breath of sudden light in the dark hall.

"What are you doing here?" He sounds exasperated.

Her back to the library doors, she notes the shoes he holds a moment before he extends them to her. She takes his measure as she slips them on, registering once more the slope of his jaw, the way he holds himself. He's dignified, but she has no doubt he would draw up fists at a moment's notice, if necessary. Just as a *seshen* of the North would to defend their kin.

Straightening, she watches his reaction as she says one word: "Reya."

Stolm takes a full stride toward her. "What did you say?"

"I said *Reya*. You told me you had a cousin you missed in Kúzlo. That's her name, isn't it?" If Ophelia's wrong, this won't work.

It takes a moment for Stolm's rigid demeanor to melt. He drops his voice. "You saw her? Is she well?"

Ophelia nods, quickly. It must be nearing high moons. This might be stupid—certainly, it's no small risk, as Stolm wears the mark of the Dark Shadow and she can't be certain she can trust him. But Falcon has always told her to listen to her instincts.

"Mathias," she says softly, and the use of his given name widens his eyes. "Reya has been helping me and my friend Falcon Th—Falcon Aksander."

Stolm's gaze drops to the floor, searching. "Falcon?"

"Yes." Just hearing his name breathes strength into her. "You knew him?"

Stolm refastens his gaze to hers. "As children. Everyone in the Northern Territories did."

"So you didn't know he was sent to the North to do the Darkwielder's bidding?"

"I have been more involved in what happens here, and in the West."

Relief unfurls like a soft wave through her. "But you know what our king is planning now for the East, after the coronation?"

Stolm's fists flex at his side. "I am informed."

"Then," she says carefully, "you know how many innocents are likely to die."

Thoughts battle between his brows so long Ophelia gets restless. At last, he says, "I owe the Kosost my life."

Her shoulders release a breath of frustration. "And he will gladly take it, Mathias." Ophelia steps to him. "Look, I care for Kier, too. But he has been left alone to make his plans so long, I fear he will sacrifice more than he intends. I need to find another way, and I don't have much time. If you want Reya to be safe, you won't tell him..."

Stolm looks startled. "Tell him what?"

On a long breath, she says, "What I'm going to ask of you."

At high moons, Ophelia enters the library alone.

The space is a wonder—silent, yet emanating with the power of knowledge. Two entire floors are filled with bookcases. The marble floors are etched with runes. And along the circumference of the room stand pillars the color of midnight, which Ophelia walks quietly between, inhaling the steadying scent of lignin and glue. With every step, she feels the tomes call out, as if they hold living, breathing worlds.

Soon.

But tonight, books are not why she's come. It's the far wall that captivates. Beneath two rows of stained glass windows that look out onto a dark, snowy wilderness, there waits a figure in funeral black.

As Ophelia approaches, a voice rasps, "Clever girl."

Saira Balcombe holds a candle dish, its small flame casting over the short veil that covers her face. Not to hide her likeness, as Ophelia doubts anyone would mistake Kier's mother, but perhaps to keep them from admiring the teardrop tattoos beneath her eyes that beckon to another time.

Fear doesn't strangle Ophelia as it did last she saw the woman. In separating from Falcon, seeing what Osiris made Rune, witnessing her best friend's torture, and discovering that Hart is more than she ever knew, Ophelia has carved a strong spine.

When she slows within a few feet of Kier's mother, a brow draws up like a bow at her. "You have me intrigued," Saira says. "Having your attendant summon me, arranging a late meeting here. Finally heeding my warnings, Kososten, and seeking more truth?"

The sharp corners of Hart's folded drawing press into Ophelia's skin where it's stowed in her nightgown. "I'm not sure I trust you, honestly, but you know every inch of Ghastly and how to hide people here." *Kane, for example,* she thinks. "I need your help finding someone. It would benefit the rule."

Behind her veil, Saira's lips curl in curiosity. "The particles lead you, do they not?"

"I tried. Kier must have him somewhere the dust can't sense."

"Hm. And on the eve of great war and your imminent coronation, who is it you seek, Kososten?"

"Someone he's imprisoned. Someone he might see as a threat to what he envisions for the two of us, if you're right about what he would do to Kane and the Morphist line."

Saira closes the space between them. In a hush, "You found his kin?"

Ophelia only has to raise a brow to confirm what she strongly suspects—that she has located the long-lost Isaac Valoran, the Descendant Saira and Lokin have been searching for in order to keep the guilds intact.

"Come," Saira says quickly, leading her away.

They're ghosts then—the mother of the god of darkness and the queen of light—disappearing through a panel in the wall. This time, Ophelia's not surprised when the ground falls out beneath her.

S he should have expected tunnels.

This one is made of stone, not dirt, but it makes Ophelia's hair stand on end how it wends like the one in her nightmare about the golden dragon and serpents of shadows.

Every few feet, she holds her breath as she and Saira pass by doorways carved in stone. The cells are empty and clean, as if someone's been down to tidy them or the tunnels themselves were recently hewn. But for how closely they still remind her of the Shaft at Gray Castle, where she found Rune in a cell, Ophelia shivers.

"Why would Kier recreate the prison here?"

Saira sets an urgent pace, looking disturbed to be underground. "We all pick at wounds to relive the things that scar us, punishing ourselves for our regrets."

It rings true. She saw Kier punishing himself firsthand that drunken night in Vils. But she needs to focus on Hart.

Glancing at Saira, she considers what's next. "When we confirm my friend is Kane's descendant, what then? You'll let Kane go so his power can pass down?"

Saira pauses her stride, taking a moment to peer into yet another empty cell before continuing on. "Let's worry about confirming his identity before making plans."

A scratching sound echoes through the tunnels, and they halt. Saira's frozen like a stag, listening, while Ophelia's own ears strain to identify the sound: *sous-sous, sous-sous.* The tenor of bristles striking canvas—flicking, scraping, weaving against its grain. She knows that sound.

Spotting a small light that's ebbing from the end of the tunnel, Ophelia starts toward it.

Saira grabs hold of her forearm to stop her, then tugs the collar of Ophelia's nightgown aside to reveal her bare shoulder. Defensively, a current of energy rages through her, sparking her lumen lines to life with a warning flash that prompts Saira to let her go.

"Your Shadow marking," the woman says, resting a palm over her own chest. "It's spreading?"

Taken aback, Ophelia casts a slow look at the whorls that have started to climb from her heart to her shoulder, and also down her arm. She's tried to ignore its growth the past few weeks. Though, every gown Kier procures for her seems fit to show off the evidence of their tether.

She admits, "It seems to flourish the more time I spend with him."

Saira chews on that. "Severing it won't be simple. I never managed to break mine—not on my own."

Ophelia looks anew at the way the woman's fingers dig into the skin of her chest. "You?"

Saira lets go a long sigh. "Me." She paces a few steps and stares into an empty cell. "Long ago, I loved a man from a distance. Then Lucius Balcombe returned to the Magie palace after academy. His power was seductive, and so persuasively did he speak of fate and futures. I was naïve, and easily convinced the man I loved would never return my affections. Lucius... He made me feel special. And I was. With two affinities, I was the best available prospect he could hope for to produce powerful offspring. He convinced me," she says again, "that rather than pine for love, I would do better to seek power in the rule. As his vowed *viclumeni*."

The walls grow deeply claustrophobic. "*Viclumeni*?"

Saira drops her hand away from her chest, turning. "I told you to look into it."

"Let's pretend I've been busy."

"Bonds of the gods, Kososten. A Descendant's chosen mate—a sacred, eternal bond that is blessed by the guilds and gods alike to ensure their line."

Pressing a hand to her stomach, Ophelia forces her body still. The tunnel seems to echo with her heartbeat.

"'Mate,'" she repeats. "Please tell me you don't mean the gods have chosen someone for me? Like some curse of fate?"

Saira scoffs. "Stories always paint the gods' will as stone, but it's not as simple as fairystories, where 'fate' means we don't have to do the hard work of choosing. I'd gather the moons have been nudging you to one who'd be a worthy match." Ophelia's face heats at the physical memory of Falcon's hands on her. She doesn't know how to name what she feels with him—vital, perhaps. And what about Kier? She can't deny that he calls to her.

As if sensing her conflict, Saira says, "A Descendant must choose their fate—unless, of course, you remain tethered. Then it becomes near impossible to identify one's true mate, let alone choose them."

"How are *viclumeni* bonded?"

"It begins with a ceremony."

"Like a marriage?"

"If a match is for love. But bonds of the gods play a bigger role—ensuring heirs, harboring secrets, and sharing the very *maether* that breathes between them and a Descendant. It's the epitome of vulnerability—trusting one to share your life."

The warning gongs through Ophelia, striking a chord of realization. "Kier said our lives are already linked by the tether. If one of us dies, the other dies. But Lucius is dead and you're still here. Was Kier lying?" Hope swells.

"No," Saira says gravely. "*Viclumeni* do not die when they lose their bonded—the tether would be responsible for that. I would've died had Osiris not captured Lucius's power with the Dark Shadow Dagger, but doing so called the Shadow from me. It broke the tether as well as the bond."

"The tether and the bond are separate things," she digests.

Saira nods. "The tether links your lives and your minds, allowing you to sense one another's magic. The viclumeni bond enables the drawing upon and sharing of your magic."

"But the tether's also eternal if it isn't broken," Ophelia realizes. "And it could hinder me from sensing my true match."

Again, Saira nods.

Her heart drops. "But no one tethered me. I pulled the Shadow into myself, and I've tried, but I can't command it out. You think the dagger could?"

"I can't say with certainty. But the Dark Shadow has a true home—in its master or the relic that can hold it."

Kier or the dagger.

"Even if the relic could sever our connection, Kier won't just give it to me." Ophelia vividly recalls how he savors the closeness of her light. It won't be something he simply agrees to.

"No." Saira bows her head. "He won't give up access to your mind, or to your power."

The blood leaves her. "But you just said only *viclumeni* share magic." Absently, she presses the tips of two fingers together, remembering how Kier's shadows sometimes felt within reach. Is that how her light is for him?

Watching her, Saira cants her head. "Light is naturally called to dark. He's probably realized that with the tether he can *provoke* your magic, though not wield it against your will. Not like…" She trails.

"Not like what?"

"You," she finishes. "I'm told your mother could do it. How long have you been capable of manipulating magic?"

Ophelia falls through time at the question, back to New York when she felt so much life pulsing between her broody keepers. Then to Ravish, where she sensed Falcon's unique essence so keenly. And last to Kúzlo, where she made his tattoos move.

A progression of power.

"I didn't realize what it was," she admits, her thoughts a knot. "You're saying I could manipulate Kier's shadows, tether or not."

Through the veil, Saira purses her lips. "One more reason to keep you and his dagger close." With a long inhale, she says, "You would need to create an opportunity to get to it. Until then, don't share your new knowledge widely."

Saira throws a sudden hand to her temple.

"What's wrong?"

"Seems my son is looking for me. He's been…checking in more recently. I suppose it would be suspicious if I answered here." Motioning up the tunnel to where they heard the *sous-sous*, Saira says, "We'll worry about tether troubles tomorrow. Get answers about your friend's identity. Before it's too late."

CHAPTER 50
LOVE & VALORAN

H art makes Ophelia many things.

Angry, as fast as she can throw a knife. The way she marched into that Galdur tavern determined to prove she could procure a Crat's key. *Riled*, to the point of recklessness. So unwilling was she to let Hart die that she burned an academy to the ground. *Devastated*, to the brink of disaster, unsure how to mend the hole in her chest where he'd been all her life, after her hand couldn't find him in the passage out of Wythe.

She can't seem to hold onto feelings of betrayal at the sight of Hart standing there, wearing a smock and...painting in a room that's nothing like the other barren cells. It's been furnished with tapestries, lanterns, a bed, a smoldering hearth, a table bearing bread and cheese, a faux window in the ceiling spelled to show a forest canopy, and canvases that line easels and the walls. Painted furiously over the ten days since she saw him writhing in pain, each shimmers blue as the night sky, cerulean as the sea.

There aren't even bars on the room, only a watery veil acting as a ward.

Ophelia can sense the threads that knot together and knows she could pick it apart. The notion it's a simple spell both gives her pause and fills her with relief, the latter because Kier must not know Hart's identity. Her best friend wouldn't look so healthy if the dark king had that knowledge—not if Saira's instincts are to be believed and Kier would do such a thing as cut down the Morphist line.

The moment Hart sees her in his periphery, he turns, brush lowering in his hand, the dark pools of his eyes locking on her as though she's an apparition, a ghost he's been chasing across the kingdom.

The ward distorts the fine lines of him she longs to see. He's framed by lantern glow, and still—so still that Ophelia searches for signs he might be broken by what he endured at Hobb's—if not physically, then emotionally.

Time seems to rush forward, and the brush rolls from Hart's hand to clatter on the stone floor, smattering paint as it lands.

"Lia." It's a thick plea.

Relief waterfalls in her springing tears as Ophelia positions herself at the edge of the clear veil separating them, a barrier she wants to obliterate. But she's certain if she brought it down, Kier's soldiers or Kier himself would storm the tunnels in a minute.

Be smart.

She forces herself to stop just shy of touching the ward, scouring as much of Hart's exposed skin as she can make out to assure herself he's really healed. She can see the faint gold lines on his neck—the mark of a Morphist that allow him to shift—but no obvious cuts or scrapes or evidence of broken bones.

Covering her mouth with a palm as a stream spills down her cheeks, reality hits how close she came to losing him. How easily it could have gone the way of death.

"You're okay." Relief drags a full, unrestrained sob from her chest. "*You're okay.*"

The mystifying breath of energy that was tamped when Hart was in shifted form at the party is there now. Even through the ward, it calls to her, stronger than when Ophelia's own magic was buried in her mind.

The energy skims along her bones like a current she could tug the threads of, just like with Kier. Yet, different. If Hart is Isaac Valoran, his magic isn't of the crimson moon, but one of the gray spheres made long ago by the goddess Luna, Selene's scheming partner when it came to forging the relics.

Ophelia and Hart aren't blood kin, and he's always been reluctant to scheme with her, but they're family in all the ways that matter.

She chokes, "I didn't know."

Stalking to the other side of the ward, Hart flexes his hands at his sides as though he itches to reach out and dry her face. The burn of the veil between them must make him think better of it. He soothes, "It's all right, Lia." And the four little words are a sword flaying open her chest. All the anxiety and fear she's been holding inside spills out in more shed tears.

She didn't know how much she needed to hear it was all right.

That he is all right.

Midnight eyes as familiar as her own hold hers. "What happened isn't your fault," Hart says. "I knew the risks of aiding the Dwymorans, and I regret nothing. Willow's become—"

"No..." Ophelia palms her eyes. "No, I don't mean the party." Hands shaking, she retrieves his drawing and flattens its creases. She turns it around. "I didn't know *you*."

His whole body stills, his gaze seeming to fix to the drawing. "Falcon gave it to you."

"I thought it was a letter, or the drawing you did of me that 'Rivmere' found. I should have opened it sooner. I have a million questions." She tries to keep the hurt from her voice, given what he's endured, given he's a prisoner. But it finds its way to her spine, stiffening her posture. "Is it true?"

She can feel him wrought with tension. "I..." He groans. "I can't tell you."

"Hart—"

"I need *you* to say it, Lia. Out loud."

Confusion tempers the hurt as she tries to see him clearly. But it's like peering through water.

She doesn't want to do this here. There have been too many walls between them, for too long. Glancing at the drawing, she wars with her options.

It's a risk—but she isn't going far, and she'll be quick. Maybe Kier won't notice.

"Hold on," she tells Hart. "I'm coming to you."

Folding the drawing—something of Hart's—she hunts for a place to stow it in a nearby cell. After she's tucked it behind a lip of stone, she rights herself and concentrates, already feeling the hum of her raw magic storming to life.

She's never traveled so near the subject of an anchor. It should be less taxing.

Picturing Hart clearly, she lets her magic swell until it bathes her skin in golden light and she seems to fold together, time slowing as her body becomes lighter than air and she is funneling across space.

When she fades into herself again, Hart rears in surprise. But he's there. And as the light and tingles fade, Ophelia traces the muscle of him, the strong velvet brows over earnest, coal-dark eyes. He wears the same eager expression he did when they met as children. Like he's been waiting.

When her limbs feel steady, she says, "You're Isaac Valoran, the missing grandson of Kane Valoran. Descendant of the goddess Luna."

An audible breath punches from Hart's lungs. He sways like a man cut loose from his own anchor. Hart looks at her as he slowly removes his smock to cast it aside, then faces her in a clean tunic and pants, his large frame straining against the fabric at every seam.

His *maether* undulates between them.

Ophelia launches herself into his embrace, engulfed by his firm chest, thick arms, the scent of paint, and old memories. No walls. No secrets. No space or time. She whispers into his shirt, "How long did you know?"

His arms squeeze tighter, his chin atop her head. "The name was trapped in me before we met."

She pulls back, extricating herself but staying close. "You lied to me."

"I had to."

She shakes her head in disbelief. "We could've left the Constelli. Two Descendants?" Turning to gather her thoughts, she whirls back with a finger aimed at him. "We could've searched together for the relics if you'd told me from the start. Maybe I wouldn't have set that fire to the academy and none of this—"

"No."

She drops her hand. "What do you mean, no?"

Hart sighs. "I couldn't tell you. I took a blood oath to keep the name a secret." He holds out a palm.

She takes it between her hands, tracing a faint white line that crosses the center, a scar she overlooked because it could have been any childhood injury. "A blood oath." A vow that's nearly unbreakable. "Why? Who?"

"My parents." Hart grits a sharp breath, reaching for his knee as if it's flared with pain. It dredges echoes of that horrible cracking and has the instant effect of dousing her frustration.

She reaches for him.

"I'm all right." Straightening, he says, "My parents thought like your mother. Hiding was safer. The truth was chained in me a long time, Lia. You cut the lock on it when you said my name aloud. I feel like I..." His throat bobs. "I have so much to tell you." He glances at the wards. "We don't have much time. A guard comes every few hours."

"I'm listening."

Hart paces, bursting with the bloody need to vomit everything. Yet, he grapples with how.

The secret's been under lock so long. For the first time, he feels free and it's unmooring. As is the idea of speaking the words, accepting who he is.

Ophelia's eagerness reflects in the wells of her eyes.

"I'm sorry," he says, taking a seat on the bed. "I drew that picture before the oath. It was based on a dream I used to have of a hand reaching out of a tree. A hand holding a rock that glowed."

"A rock," she echoes, sliding the painting stool in the cell over to sit across from him. "You've had that drawing this whole time?"

"I found it at the Pyre a few months ago, in a box of things from the Constelli. I stuffed it in my coat, then..." He shakes his head. "I let it eat at me all the time we were apart."

"So you knew what you were."

"I didn't know Isaac—" At the sound of his given name, no longer caught on his tongue, he's a man set free. "I suspected what my name meant after *Asenti* when I realized what you were. But I shoved the possibility down in the deepest parts of myself," he admits. "I threw myself into being Rivmere's pet, doing what I had to do between your resets." His fists ball the covers on the bed. "But I had a lot of time to wonder while you were with Falcon and Rune. I overheard more than I cared to about our histories at the Pyre and worked it out. Still, I rejected it."

Brows folded, Ophelia studies him. "You never cared about the histories. All the stories I'd tell you about the original rule or the relics, you always changed the subject. You never wanted to know who we were, and you didn't want me to either."

"No," he agrees. "But it started to make sense why I was so drawn to you."

Before he can see the effect his words have on her, he rises from the bed and removes a canvas from the easel to show her the painting behind it. There's a soft inhale as she registers the blue girl he's painted. A girl balanced in the boughs of a twilight forest with magic spinning all around her.

"I knew enough to surmise we were different from the start," he says. "And different was dangerous. When I put together my guild line, I was furious. It felt like a sick joke, Lia. A boy who never wanted magic, who had everything taken because of it..." *I hated it—hated myself.*

He rakes a hand through his cropped hair, feeling it all anew as the confessions continue to spill. "I was glad for your resets in the mortal world because it meant you'd be safe. Both of us. You with the spell to forget, and me with my oath. We'd lost everything. I didn't care about relics or your plan to save the kingdom. All that mattered was I didn't lose you." His heart's an unrelenting animal in his chest. "I was afraid." He looks at her. "You were everything to me. I—I loved you entirely."

She blinks at him with parting lips. "You loved me?"

"Always." *Every night, yours was the face I saw when I slept.* "You were my home."

As she shifts to face him, he has to look down to meet her eyes. She says, "You almost got yourself killed for me at *Asenti*. I was so focused on my plans, I didn't see you... I didn't see what was in front of me." She touches his arm, sparking that little shock of breath that used to confound him. Staring at the touch, she says, "I felt you. I never thought to ask why, but you always felt like home to me, too." She looks up. "'God calls to god.'"

His heart constricts.

Without thinking, Hart moves aside the soft tresses that've sprung loose near her face, tracing her freckles and long lashes and lips that softly perk, as familiar as his own harder details.

Then he steps back. She didn't say she loved him, too.

He braces to feel the gutting pain of rejection. Once, that pain would've come swift as a punch. But now... While it stings, he feels relief more than hurt.

It feels like a door closing, but also something new beginning between them.

"I was wrong," Hart admits. "It took Rune and Falcon and that bloody curse to show me, but we need what we are now, every bit of it, don't we?" His insides darken, the delicate moment giving way to the anger he's been tamping in this cell, anger steadily building with every stroke of his brush. "When Jasper Salt delivered me here, he implied mortals were rounded up at Hobb's and taken to the Belly to train some new power. That includes Willow?"

Reluctantly, Ophelia nods. "She wouldn't leave her people to come with me here."

His teeth stab his lip. "Of course she wouldn't." *Which means I failed her.*

The last glimpse he caught of her was in Hobb's halls—Willow, with her unfiltered questions, disarming honesty, and resolve to protect her family. A woman who pulls confessions from him without even trying, who sees him and needs him in a way he's always wanted to be needed. Who makes him yearn for the simpler life with a family that John Winter dreamed possible.

Hart realizes the truth, and it feels too late—the dream's always been his, too.

Eyeing the gold-threaded robe Ophelia wears, the fine nightgown, every muscle from his fists to his back tightens. "Tell me you had nothing to do with the Darkwielder's plan for mortals."

Her eyes flash with venom. "Of course not."

"Then what are you doing with him? Where the hell is Falcon?"

And she tells him.

Hart paces as he listens, growing angrier with every highlight, from the time the Darkwielder apparently tracked her to Ravish, to her discovering Rune was the godsforsaken heir to the Gray Throne, to finding Hart's drawing.

"We need to get out of here." He stalks to the ward, contemplating its design. For the first time, he wishes he had the full magic of his line. Perhaps he'll try, anyway.

Ophelia catches his arm. "I need a couple more days."

He scowls at her.

"You don't want to be a king, do you? Any more than I've wished to be queen?"

"No."

"You want... You want Willow. Free," Ophelia says.

He can't deny the feelings he's developed without even trying—not anymore. Hart nods.

"Then we change things. Truly," she says. "Make a world Magus has never known before." She sounds just like she did when they were twelve, telling Hart they could make it out in the world on their own.

"How?" he asks, full of doubt as always. "With the army Falcon Thames is going to kill himself to procure? It's a long shot at best."

"Hart, the gods chose us for a reason. Maybe it's to rule, maybe not. How will we know if we run and don't try?"

"You're suggesting we stay?"

She keeps a leash on his gaze. "I'm suggesting we have faith in Falcon...and Trix...and try to mount our own rebellion."

"I've no god power, Lia. You've no relic!"

She holds his impassioned gaze. "I'll figure it out. I just need you to trust me, Hart. Believe in me."

His weight settles on his back leg as the slap in her plea hits. He has always doubted, and worried, hasn't he? Never believed things could turn out happily or that he and Ophelia were strong enough.

Because that's what the monarchy told them.

Disgusted with himself, he glances from Ophelia to the girl painted blue on the canvas, both always eager to lead him into the unknown.

She led you to Dwymore and Willow. She forced you to see who you are.

Ophelia said somewhere in this castle his grandfather is being kept alive by a spell, and that when he dies, his power will pass to Hart. Could he use that power to create something new?

"A better Magus," he says, jaw ticking as he takes in all the parts of her he still recognizes—her empathy and heart. Plus others that are new—her confidence and the sheer power he can feel blazing inside her.

Yes, she was always something, always stronger than he cared to admit. Always his friend. And now...a queen.

With a growl, he says, "I trust you with my life, which apparently means more now."

She squeezes his hand. "You have always meant more to me." With a whisper, she adds, "You were my everything, too. Just... Not every love can burn. We may not be the romantic kind, but we're the enduring kind. Two of the same, Hart. You're my greatest friend, my counsel, my family. I will always need you."

Somehow, his cheek has wet. She needs him. Albeit a different way than Willow does. Willow, who deserves the better world Ophelia dares to imagine.

Hart curses, knowing it's futile to keep denying what he is. He has to become whatever he must—go to hell and back if that's what it takes—now that Ophelia's gone and made him hope.

CHAPTER 51
RITES & LIGHT

GHASTLY
22ND DAY IN THE NEW WINTER
OPHELIA IS WITH HER ALLIES

B etrayal begins at the edge of the shadow woods, where a thick fog marshes the inken trees and an unexpected accomplice with a large muzzle and white fur has seemingly anticipated their arrival.

A collective gasp gales behind her.

Before Hannah, Isolde, or Mathias can stir a defense of magic, Ophelia holds out her arms. "It's all right. He won't hurt us."

In the golden mirror of the wolven's eyes is a trio of shocked faces, ridged with the outline of the palace from which they've just snuck.

Stepping forward into the calm of the wolven's steady *maether*, she nods to the creature. The towering beast bends its head the way a subject would greet their sovereign, allowing her to press a kiss to its wide forehead.

"It appears we're to be friends," she whispers into its fur. "I ought to have a name for you."

"Dirigo."

The unexpected reply makes her head jolt up. It doesn't come in the modern tongue, but in a wild tenor that races like wind—a growl registered by an innate part of her that's apparently capable of deciphering the sound.

First, unreadable whispers on the dust, which she's still figuring out. Now, a language of beasts.

"Dirigo," she echoes. "You already have a name."

The wolven's wise eyes glow at her, as does the leg she healed of his weeks ago. He bays.

Glancing back to her friends, she says, "This is Dirigo."

"How did you make friends with a wolven?" Isolde asks in awe, pulling her long cloak tight around her. She keeps a safe distance near Hannah and Mathias.

"It's a long story, one we don't have time for." Ophelia urges, "The tomes, Mathias."

Recovering—if not his unease, his shock at her taming the creature—Mathias clears his throat and slips cautiously past her. "This way."

He bends flame to scorch drifts of snow, and they wend along a narrow path in the still, fog-laden forest, heading opposite the road that leads to the passage hidden in Ghastly's front gates and away from anywhere Kier has billowed Ophelia to train before.

"We're certain we should be doing this?" Isolde asks.

"It is a risk," Mathias says, not for the first time tonight. "The Kosost will not want us here."

"But you can lead us there," Ophelia prompts, and he nods. "Then we have to."

They spent the day scouring tomes Mathias squirreled from the library and Kier's study, looking for anything that might reference an "amber jewel" or "light as sealed," so she could solve the Binder's riddle and pinpoint where her mother took the amulet after her likely meeting with the *volorost*. But despite Mathias's great personal risk in aiding her, there were no useful clues and Ophelia felt the tightening of time as the sun sank out her chamber window.

"Kier's still in the Belly," she reminds them.

He must've left shortly after Ophelia emerged from her visit with Hart, which she believed escaped notice, as Kier didn't come seeking her before he left or even knock on her mental walls. He'll return soon, though—for the coronation tomorrow night, and the attack he's planning a few days after.

As they trek deeper among the black boughs, there's little sound save for the swinging lantern Hannah carries between her and Isolde, the crunch of Mathias's boots, and the rumble of the wolven's breaths as he scans the forest.

Dirigo keeps a protective flank near her side. Absently, she lets her fingers comb the fur at his shoulder while keeping her own vigilance, half on the tether and half on the still, dark woods.

An early moons' glow claws through crevices in the dense foliage. She doesn't miss that the frosty sheen is climbing their face now, like icy fingers up the spheres. And she's relieved to see the dust sweeping in its usual, rhythmic pattern above the canopy of trees. Clouds of it would only draw unwise attention, what with the legion soldiers Kier left at the palace who may not be as keen to support her as Mathias.

A burble of water interrupts her thoughts, and, moments later, the trees break into a small clearing. Ophelia goes still.

Before her squats an intricately carved stone structure. Blackened moss weaves a vice-like embrace around its crumbling edges, and half its façade is buried in dumps and drifts of snow.

As Hannah and Isolde draw beside her with wide eyes, Mathias mounts its short steps, red flames cupped in his palms.

When the drifts obstructing the door melt away, Isolde vocalizes what Ophelia's thinking. "The tomes are in a crypt?"

Mathias lets his flames die. "There are chambers below. The Kosost comes every month or so to work with his Spellcaster."

"You mean the one called Philo?" The creator of *stärke vas*—the one Kier lets perform experiments on him.

Grimly, Mathias nods. "Philo has gone with Kosost to Ravish. The crypt should be empty, and there are very old tomes inside. I saw them once, when I was called here to entice Kosost to use a healer."

There's a flash of grief in Mathias's eyes—grief that mirrors her own. But Ophelia shoves it down. *Books. They are the reason we're here.*

With Dirigo prowling in the snow as if he doesn't like this plan, she steps to the door. It's not warded, but there's no handle.

"There," Mathias motions to a flat plate. "Only a Descendant can open it from outside."

She doesn't need to summon light. The door is imbued with an old, ancient magic that calls to her own unending well. Laying a palm against the frigid stone, it heats instantly beneath her touch—as if it knows her—and something shudders through her before the door groans open.

Paper-white moths flurry out from the dark.

In the tangle of wings, it's Isolde who stirs a swift wind, and it's the first time Ophelia's seen her use her affinity defensively. Albeit, against insects. Picking one from her hair, Ophelia sets it free while Hannah holds up her lantern so Mathias can dig free the torch he's packed.

But Ophelia pays little attention. She steps into the darkness of the crypt with light in her lumen lines, called to the edge of stairs that spill down, down, down.

She feels it then—the smallest pull of god magic.

The stairs descend to a flagged floor that's been cracked and chipped over centuries. In a circular vestibule, Ophelia peers at vases entombed in cobwebbed stone.

She'd stake her life on there being ash in those vases—she can feel death in them.

Through a preserved archway unfolds another room, this one with a vaulted ceiling and a small alter hewn from blackening stone. The flagstones are worn in here, covered with soot, except for a trail where boots have scuffed recently.

Ophelia tries not to stare at that alter, where a blanket is folded beside bowls and unused vials, and an apparatus she's never seen unsettles her for its long, protruding needle.

A cloth lies on a stair. Before she can stop herself, she's picking it up, inspecting the ash that films one side. Blood coats the other.

"Look at this!" Isolde calls.

Ophelia whirls to find her balancing a large, dusty book in her arms, while the others bend over cubbies where yellowing scrolls and fraying tomes rest undisturbed. Absently stuffing the cloth in her cloak, Ophelia goes to peer over Isolde's shoulder at the same time Hannah takes up her other side.

"*Rituals of the Relics,*" Isolde reads aloud as Mathias trails over. "It's hundreds of years old."

As she cracks it open, Ophelia devours the details of each drawing until a scene catches her eye. She clasps Isolde's arm to hold the page on what appears to have been a meeting between a northern warrior and Magie rulers. They wear crowns and...

At the sight of the primordial relics, her hands tingle. "Where is this?"

Mathias's brows fold together in recognition. "I think it is the Virstone, in my homeland. A sacred mountain where ceremonies such as baptisms are performed."

"Let's lay it over there." Clearing space on a second table, Hannah sets her lantern to bathe the book in light and the four hover around it, careful not to touch the ink.

Hannah looks up as if incredulous. "This isn't a baptism. It's the First Northern Rite—the initial bestowal of power on the *volorost* title, using blood and relics of the gods."

"You don't mean Falcon's father?" Ophelia asks.

"No—the very first *volorost*. Five hundred years ago, in response to enemies attempting to infiltrate the icelands, the rule empowered a guardian of the North. Each high lord since has wielded the power of the Great Sight, along with a telepathic connection to every drecora that lives."

"The power that's passed to heirs," Ophelia realizes. This is what Falcon stands to gain if he wins the Sanctioning—the same thing Reya's betrothed fights for and Osiris Lestat covets. Control of the North.

In the sketch, the amulet is broached on a chain and held in the palm of a Matterist queen who bears the vaguest resemblance to Ophelia's other ancestors with her tumble of wild hair. The legacy in these pages is so potent and visceral Ophelia's lumen lines heat. She skims fingertips over the swelling ridges of her arm with the strangest notion that those women who came before her are close. Queens with immortal magic who must have died fighting for freedom at every crossroad in their history.

Isolde uses careful bursts of air to loosen the next page, then squeaks, "Is that a coffin?"

Ophelia bends to take in the scene where a *volorost* convenes with two of the same rulers from the first drawing. Somber and slightly aged, the men kneel as if in prayer within the walls of the cavern. The Virstone. Between them, a young girl is laying a hand upon the body of the third ruler. The Matterist queen.

"Why does she look frozen?" Ophelia murmurs.

Hannah raps a finger on the table. "This is a Transference, an old ceremony where the power of a fallen Descendant was transferred to kin."

"I thought that just...happened." She doesn't remember Elora ever transferring anything to her.

"A Transference is not required, but it's a sacred honor and tradition. It serves as the death rite and offers greater certainty a Descendant's power will find the next in line. When I served your grandmother long ago, she insisted on wearing the amulet for this reason. Were she alone at death..." Hannah swallows, as if struggling to keep memories at bay. "If she were alone, she said the relic could cast a shield around her body to keep it from disintegrating, preserving it for this honor, until kin arrived to claim their legacy."

"I thought the relics amplified or siphoned power. How do they preserve a body?"

"Messandra called it 'continual amplification.' The relic would fuse with the heart of one's power and continuously flood the body with its own *maether* to keep the vessel intact," Hannah says, then shakes her head. "I never fully understood it, but I am not a Descendant."

Ophelia's veins alight with the knowledge. "So it was sacred to hold a Transference at the Virstone." Studying the sketch further, she notes the people in official-looking furs and pins on the periphery of the drawing.

There is such detail that whoever inked this must have been there. Her mind flits to the Binder, and answers beat against Ophelia's sternum, drumming to the sound of the riddle. In the drawing, the fallen queen wears the amulet around her neck. An *amber jewel* once passed to Messandra and later Elora, who was the last to possess the relic.

"So it's not a coffin?" Isolde asks beside her.

"It's not a coffin," Ophelia echoes, her hands trembling where they're splayed on the table. *Light as sealed…* "It's ice."

Ophelia's heart caterwauls as it all coalesces: Her mother returned to the North for help. At the advice of the Binder, she went to petition the *volorost* for support. Whatever happened, her mother's light was sealed.

A horrible little instinct tells her where Elora may have taken her last breath.

She was candid earlier with Hannah, Isolde, and Mathias about her mission and what she intends for the relics. Trading an urgent look with them, she says, "I think my mother took the amulet to the Virstone. It might still be there."

"You need to go," Isolde pipes, the same moment Mathias cautions, "You cannot leave now."

A sharp chill draws Ophelia's hand to worry near her heart. In the distance, she swears she hears a howl. "We need to get back to the palace."

Tucking the book away, they depart the crypt in haste, the weight of the tome and the scent of pain following her back into the woods. Dirigo is waiting, and like shadows fleeing sun, the five of them steal back the way they came.

From Dirigo's side, she glances over a shoulder to Hannah and Isolde. "Mathias is right. If I go before the coronation, Kier would sense my absence and take it as betrayal. I was lucky he didn't feel me travel last night."

"It's because you stayed within Ghastly, my lady," Hannah says. "Within the wards around our realm."

"*Realm?*" she asks, a little jolt crashing through her at the reminder of other information Kier's withheld.

"It does not exist to the known world," Mathias explains from where he leads.

Nearing the edge of the forest, Ophelia looks to the sky—to the colors that eddy that eerie purple-green-amber. "That's what Kier said," she mutters, recalling the dinner conversation at Hobb's, the tradesman's blackened coin, and the look between Kier and Jasper Salt across the table at the mention of other places out there.

She whips her head down. "Is Ghastly... Are we in the Lost Lands?" she asks them all.

Mathias doesn't miss a step. "I thought he'd told you by now."

"No," Ophelia replies. "He didn't."

It was Celia Hobb's tale at dinner that planted any seeds at all. How before Kier's time, hundreds of years ago, there was a Descendant who broke from the Magie rule to occupy an island palace in the Lost Lands. An enemy king who sent marauders to attack Magus's shores by sea. A sea now guarded by the Royal Army.

It's unreal.

Kier may have rebuilt the Magie rule at Ghastly, but its bones were already here, scorched by war and awaiting the next conqueror to take it up. The chill in her deepens as she comprehends how long, how intricately, Kier has been plotting his revenge.

How history dares to repeat.

It's almost an hour before they're back in the east wing. In her chambers, cloaks hung to dry, she faces Mathias, Hannah, and Isolde. "You have two choices if you wish to be safe. Leave my room right now and have no further part in anything I plan..."

Mathias folds his arms, his golden hair still wet with snow. "Or?"

"Or when the time comes, go to the North with me. I'll do everything I can to protect you, but you would need to be certain about your loyalties."

Mathias tugs aside the collar of his uniform, slowly drawing out a silver chain. "I once wore a drecora scale at the end of this," he says with a hint of sadness.

Ophelia's lips part in surprise. *Seshen.* Brave, stoic, heartfelt Mathias, cousin of the courageous Reya—of course he once flew a dragon.

"My loyalty is not to land or castle, but to cause," he says. "I think the gods led me here so our paths might cross and I could be part of protecting their creation."

Emotion wells in her throat, choking off words.

Mathias shares a look with Isolde and Hannah and, one by one, all three lower to their knees right in front of her, their faces carving with reckless grins and unflinching loyalty.

She shakes her head, a laugh bubbling up. "Mounting our own rebellion?" It's what she proposed to Hart last night. "It might be madness. *Suicide*."

Hannah scoffs, traces of formality gone. "I was with your mother the day you were born and baptized in the Virstone. I will follow her daughter back again."

"So will I." Isolde beams, looking expectantly at Mathias.

The officer bows. "As will I."

She has nothing adequate to convey her gratitude, that they would risk themselves and follow her—pledge to her—when all she has is a hope of a plan and doesn't yet wear a crown.

And escaping Ghastly is only a start.

The amulet will even things between her and the dark king, but it may not solve every problem. The tether, for instance. Or the imminent attack Kier is planning.

"The dagger." At the whisper in her mind, Ophelia darts a look to the window, where a sweep of particles is blinking at her through the pane.

"My lady?" Hannah asks.

"The dagger," she echoes. Before games and feelings that grew complicated, the dagger was why Ophelia came as a willing captive to Ghastly. In everything, she lost sight of that goal. "Kier is practiced with the dagger. If he takes it to war, I'll be too late with the amulet to stop the wreckage."

If she possessed the dagger, she could bide more time, test Saira's theory about the tether, and keep Kier from wielding it further. But asking to hold it would only stir suspicion now.

She's shooting holes in unformed plans when a knock rattles the chamber door.

The three jolt up off their knees, joining her in shoving library tomes out of sight. When Ophelia straightens, Hannah is gripping a bed post, her spine rod-straight. Her eyes, white.

"Yes…" she mutters. "She has, Queen Mother… Yes, I will tell her." When the color returns to her twinkling eyes, Hannah motions toward the door. "I told the queen-mother you confirmed your friend's identity. She cannot meet us now, but she has sent you a gift, 'as to your other matter.'"

The tether.

There's no one on the other side of the door, only a small box set just beyond the ward. Retrieving it with haste, Ophelia cracks the lid to find a card that reads: *Find your opportunity.*

"What is it?" Isolde asks as she, Mathias, and Hannah drift into a line in the middle of the room, looking expectant.

Under the card, Ophelia finds a red velvet pouch. When she peeks inside, her thoughts whirl to the chess game Kier destroyed, and she pictures him on his knees. *If I'm to be ruined, Ophelia, let it be by you.*

Falcon, who's about to risk everything to win the North for her, told her to play the game until the last possible minute. Hart is waiting. Rune may be lost to them forever soon. And she made a vow—no one else she loves falls because of her.

Time is nearly up.

Fisting the pouch Saira's given her, a phantom chill brushes against her mental shields, aching through her chest.

Kier is home.

Guilt wrings her from the inside out as his shadows curl against her walls—as if he's missed her.

He's done unspeakable things, omitted so much. But there have been moments when he was the only one who could understand what it is to be who they are.

It's going to hurt, what comes next.

"This is the plan," she tells her accomplices. "But there will be no going back."

CHAPTER 52
KING & QUEEN

Ophelia's nerves seethe like the heat of a hundred torches when the doors to the throne room thrust open. Hope burns back at her from nearly three hundred guests that fill the great hall for the coronation.

Even Kier, who wanted this night and looks the part of the formidable king in his elaborate black garb, tenses beside her under the gawping.

She thought she was prepared for it. But all the *maether* emanating in her direction from Ghastly's citizens kindles to a point that her magic squirms for release.

There's also the pouch strapped to her thigh, waiting for the right opportunity.

From within the crowd, murmurs drift about saviors, the goddess returned, the Shadow marking that sprawls her arm, and her spectacular gown—a monstrosity of sequins, glitter tulle, and mesh lace that Hannah and Isolde tailored to hug her form and trail, with golden bursts giving way to shivering black tendrils, like a stardust river.

She can feel Kier's eyes and his power across the tether. *"They're going to love you."* The words sound nearly pained.

"You'd rather they feared me."

There's too much to decipher in his gaze, and in the flutter across the reaching cord that binds them. *"Perhaps they'll fear how much they love you."*

Swallowing, she faces forward, shoving her mental shield up and fastening her attention on the crowd as an unseen orchestra starts—the signal for her and Kier to step into the throne room.

She didn't expect such a soft glow. Despite so many guests, the atmosphere in the grand space is nearly cozy. A mood created by so many candles and torches along the walls that any bare skin of hers catches the warmth.

The room is also lit from above with chandeliers. Dark flowers waterfall from gilded planters, their buds shaping a path across the marble that cuts through the brimming crowd. At the end of the walk, those black-carpeted stairs await like a parapet, ascending to the royal dais. There, in the light of the triple moons that drop through long, arched windows, gilded statues spire to the vaulted ceiling. And, below them, sit the three ornamented thrones.

It's a travesty one is meant to remain empty tonight, its rightful occupant in the bowels of Ghastly.

Just get through the ceremony.

The orchestra plays a low, epic ballad as she and Kier stride together, close but not touching. From the candelabras in every corner, flames lean on their wicks as if to watch their procession.

Near the front of the crowd, Ophelia is relieved to spot Mathias in his raven uniform. She wonders what he thought when he put it on tonight, if it's harder to wear now. He stands with the other legion soldiers flanking Saira. The queen-mother is unmistakable in her spider-black layers and veil.

It gives Ophelia pause to see soldiers at every exit, but Kier would have the room well-guarded with all the guilds present and important aristocratic guests passaged in from the West.

She's even less comforted to spy Representative Bale from Vasgale, just behind Saira. Stuffed in a suit half a size too small for his frame, he's rubbing elbows with two tradesmen she recognizes from Hobb's dinner. All three men look uncomfortable. Guppies in a room full of sharks. But they're so desperate for power, they're willing to brave it—and send their own mortal citizens to die.

Not if I can stop it.

As she walks alongside Kier, Ophelia's gaze threads the horde of citizens. Men, women, and young people who've known hardship and, for it, look all the more grateful to enjoy the safety they've been given at Ghastly. Her eyes catch on a pair of young men wearing high-collared blue coats studded with golden buttons. They can't be more than fifteen and their eyes shine with emotion at her. When they each make circles on their foreheads as she passes, her heart swells at the motion.

Nodding at them, she feels the weight of her cape grow heavy.

How many years did she pray to the gods to set her and Hart free?

She's overcome by a surge of protectiveness for the citizens in this room. For all who bow their heads before sleep with a plea on their lips for freedom. In the mortal world not long ago, she herself remembers sitting in a dusty washroom while Rune pulled off her boots, telling him, *I just wanted a little freedom.*

Even in resets, she ached for it the way her people do. Now, tonight, a queen who never wanted the title will take her throne for them. Then do what she must to preserve their future.

With a steadying breath, her nerves fall away.

There's only the gentle tug of the golden veil that capes her shoulders. The soft weight of her locket below her collarbone. The tings of gold-and-black jewels that twine on her arms in delicate cuffs. And Kier's audible breaths, beside her.

He isn't adorned tonight with his shadow perch, but his onyx-jeweled doublet and mantel with its wing-like feathers are intimidating enough, as is the Dark Shadow Dagger that taunts her from its sheath. He looks...pale. More than usual. If she didn't know better, she'd think he's also fighting nerves.

He's used to living in the shadows.

But he knew what to expect. He orchestrated this event—the guest list, the ceremony, the masquerade to follow.

Ophelia's relieved when they near the dais, eager to be over with this part.

From where a consortium of the guilds is taking their places, three members in robes threaded green or blue or red greet them with reverent bows. Two hold small, regal pillows that bare three-pronged, silver-plated crowns. They are symbols of such magnitude that her skin pebbles with gooseflesh, the full weight of the moment washing over her.

This is the first time she's faced members of the Council of Guilds. She expects to see Lokin, but he's absent. With a quick glance, she does find Stasia, who seemed to be his confidante, among the legion soldiers with Mathias.

As she and Kier take their places, his shadows brush like knuckles against her mind, beckoning for admittance. *"You'll need to keep your mind accessible during the ceremony,"* he tells her. *"The guilds want assurances their sovereigns have honorable intentions."*

She finds it discomforting his voice lacks its usual snark. But before she can question it, a door slides open left of the throne stairs and sucks the room's attention.

Dusked in hooded black robes, an acolyte emerges, moving with a slow, somewhat sideways creep across the marble floor. He carries a book in the crook of his arm, and as he comes to stand before her and Kier, he waves a hand.

The stairs shudder. With a start, Ophelia watches them slide open to unveil a golden altar that bears a statuesque cross with triple circles.

She steals a glance at Kier, who doesn't meet her gaze but...fidgets. Has she ever seen the dark king fidget?

The acolyte takes his place before the altar, and as he lowers his hood, she's taken aback to see it's Aman, Kier's personal seer. She's spied him a few times with the dark king's entourage, but Kier must keep him busy elsewhere; he's never in the east wing and didn't accompany them West. In fact, her only interaction with him was their first, when she somehow survived him reading her intentions.

Tonight, the seer's eyes are the same bone white. Her thigh burns where she strapped the velvet pouch.

Stay calm.

As they're instructed, she kneels next to Kier before the altar, forcing her mind clear of absolutely everything but the morsels of truth that will matter in this ceremony.

I love my people.
I will fight for them.
I will end this war.

"By the gods!" With surprising voracity, Aman's shrill voice pierces like an off-tune bell, shredding any whispers in the room. "Amid great turmoil in Magus, this eve we come to witness the anointment of our realm's unquestionable king and queen, who bring before us their intentions."

Aman turns his sightless gaze on Kier. "To resurrect a united rule," he assesses. "And defend the kingdom against all enemies."

Ophelia holds her breath as his white eyes shift to her, unsure why she instinctively reaches across the tether for assurance. Strangely, there's nothing to grasp. Kier's walls are not down; they're hard as onyx.

She frowns between him and the acolyte, so distracted that she misses half of what the latter has just said. She snaps back to catch him say, "...here to welcome a new kind of rule that ensures the future of the guilds." Without warning, Aman reaches to clasp Ophelia's hand, then Kier's, joining the two together. "A rule"—the acolyte punctuates—"that is united in every way."

A chill crawls the length of her spine when Aman shifts focus to Kier, who's reaching for an object beneath his mantel.

The music noticeably shifts to a lulling melody, one that raises the hair on her neck.

This isn't part of the ceremony.

With pounding in her ears, she whips a gaze at the attendees, bedecked in their finest threads and gowns, then to the guild members waiting with the crowns, and to the acolyte again. To Kier.

It isn't just nerves now; she's *unnerved* at the scene. This is more than a coronation.

"Ophelia."

It takes a moment for Kier's soft voice to cut through her swelling unease, to realize he's drawing her to stand with him, to face him. Her body pulses with little bolts of panic at the square box he holds in a palm.

Letting her hand go to snap the lid open, he retrieves the small object inside. At the sight of it, half the room shares her gasp.

It's a ring. A gold-leafed black band that Kier gives a long look as he rubs its face delicately between his fingers.

She's stilled by shock, unable to search for Hannah or Isolde or even Saira for counsel, while Kier takes her hand in his.

"I hope you'll forgive the surprise," he says quietly. "I told you it was torture to be away from you..." She can't breathe as he threads a lip through his teeth. "We're the same, Ophelia. Tell me you finally feel it, too."

"What"—her whisper catches—"what is this?"

When Kier replies, it's for all the room to hear, but still he looks at her. "Since Ghastly was forged, I've vowed to learn from the past and pave a stronger way forward. As we take our oaths tonight, I ask you to also build something new with me, for all who stand among us." His eyes glitter, unreadable as dusky starlight. "A world safe for us all," he says. "A rule stronger than what our ancestors failed to hold. A kingdom that protects those who are different...and rewards those who seize their own fate."

She trembles at that word—*fate*.

Kier shifts closer as he hovers the ring at her finger. Softer, he says, "You hate my methods, and often me. But you've been talking to my mother..." Ophelia's spine stiffens. "She's led me to hope that hate isn't all you feel for me."

"You spoke to Saira."

A nod. "This was her ring. Her idea," he admits. "She thought it might be the gesture to finally earn your trust."

Too many thoughts climb atop one another as she claws to make sense of what he's said.

Though the music in the throne room is meant to soothe, the chords break against her as she stares at the ring Lucius must have given Saira—its cutting gold flecks bursting into onyx.

How history does repeat.

In a fury, she searches her last conversation with Kier's mother for a sign she's been played. Through clenched teeth, she says, "I don't like surprises."

He leans down, his lips brushing her cheek. "When we win this war, we'll have eternity to forgive one another, as *viclumeni*."

A thunder of darkness claps around them, swallowing her reply, the music, and the candlelight, and throwing the throne room to utter blackness. It's like nothing she has felt—not a threat, but an urgent call. A question that demands an answer from the power within her.

Lightning sweeps through her veins as her magic thrusts from the depths of her. Her lightdragon roars to the surface, breaking her open to throw spindles of pure sun to every corner of the grand room, like fireworks or a thousand roots of a lumen tree. She feels like she is *bursting* as her light reignites candlewicks already dancing with the veil of Kier's darkness.

As their magic waltzes, the tether between them tightens with such force that she staggers straight into Kier's chest.

Aflame with golden threads that shock her, the dark king's starlit eyes seize hers.

Awe fills the throne room as the magic around them swells, and Ophelia's every thought and sound and need narrows to Kier.

She's aghast to find that threads of her light are seeping from her palms where they press against his chest. That his misting darkness is also skating over her flesh.

What did Saira warn? *Light is naturally called to dark. He's probably realized that with the tether he can provoke your magic...*

"What did you do?" she asks him, hating how her voice tremors.

As their magic dances above the throne room, Kier's lips part at her in wonder. "Enemy, ally, friend... Bond," he breathes, gazing at her hands—at her magic—like he can't drink his fill of it or her. Eyes lifting, he says with reverence, "*Viclumeni.*"

With a surging flood of raw anger, Ophelia yanks her hands free of him, stealing back her light. The dance above them fizzles like the smoky embers of a fire. It's only then she sees he's slipped the ring on her finger.

koillx.

CHAPTER 53
VILLAINS & VOWS

GHASTLY
THE CORONATION
OPHELIA IS WITH THE DARKWIELDER

She is bonded to the dark king.

Not only tethered. *Viclumeni.* Bonds of the gods. A Descendant's chosen mate.

Horrified to the depths of her soul at his betrayal, she stares at the ring he's placed on her finger in disbelief. Kier has truly mastered the art of distraction, for not only has he coaxed her magic out in front of everyone, he's called her bluff and made her his.

You don't believe in him, she accused Saira once.

Oh, I do. I think, without question, he sees you two left in the end and he'll risk a great deal to be sure of it.

Ophelia took those words as a warning, but what if...*what if* Saira has been the mastermind, plotting from the Witchists Guild? Has the queen-mother been fearing what her son is capable of, or counting on it?

Ophelia thought she'd gambled well, trusting her intuition, begging Saira's aid. But Kier's ring is an icy vice on her finger and her thoughts delve to dark places.

Saira's ring. Saira's idea.

Surely the guilds won't recognize this...marriage. Descendants don't bond one another. Based on Saira's accounts, they each seek their own *viclumeni* to continue the lines.

With the eyes of their people watching, counting on them—on her—Ophelia boils with silent fury at the dark king. He doesn't seem to notice. The guild members are already stepping forward with two crowns, the acolyte raising his palms above the two of them as if to bless their union.

This isn't how they were meant to restore the guilds. This is how one would *collapse* them.

With the thought thundering in her head, she stiffens as Aman's belling voice decrees, "By the laws of the gods, bear witness! Valkieran Balcombe, sole Descendant of the Witchist line, rightful king of Magus, and our queen Ophelia Dannan, sole Descendant of the Matterists, have initiated the bond of *viclumeni*."

The word is a dagger in her heart.

I have chosen nothing, she wants to scream. Yet if she were to unleash what she truly feels, it would start a war at Ghastly tonight and raze the very symbol of what she is meant to save.

How she would love to beg the goddess of her line to tell her how much she is meant to bear.

Aman shrills, "The Magie Order has been split across three guilds since the dawn of our kingdom, balanced by relics that have been sought and killed for. While no Descendant before has had the courage to unite our lines, our king has seen the way. Tonight, we become one people in the fight for freedom."

Cheers—*cheers*—as a flame rages within her.

The room is entirely swept up in Aman's rallying speech, and she can see why, can hear Kier's compelling logic in the words. Kier's, or those of whoever has long counseled him.

"Citizens and guests of Ghastly," Aman forges on. "You will have questions in the coming days, but tonight we pledge our loyalty. Tonight we celebrate the new rule—a single line that will produce our most prolific gods and reign infinitely." Ophelia's blood curdles. "Then"—Aman drawls—"we will take the war to the East!"

Fists raise with the swelling cheers.

Ophelia clings to the few faces that look unsure, those who remain quiet and as shocked as she. But Aman deems the assent enough to carry on, and a crown is placed on her head. Then Kier's.

As they're led to speak their oaths, Ophelia imagines spearing her crown like a dagger at him. But he has built something at Ghastly over many years and warm meals and the erection of safe walls, and these people don't yet know her. They haven't been shown another way.

It will take time—time I don't have right now.

She takes her vow. Not for Kier, but for their people. And when the acolyte declares them sovereigns as well as *viclumeni*, she stands stoically as the altar is tucked away beneath the stairs. Taking Kier's offered arm, they ascend to their thrones.

"You're angry," he observes.

She focuses forward. "Anger is a weak word for what I feel. Yet again, you kept me in the dark." *You ambushed me and stole my choice and I hate you.*

She can feel him studying her, but she doesn't deign to give him her eye to see if they hold a shred of remorse.

"We have time," he says softly. "I can bear your anger for now."

I hate you, I hate you, I hate you.

The words pulse like a new vow as they take their thrones, until hate is all there is and her nails bite the iron beneath her hands. It intensifies as the room is transformed, as masks come out for the masquerade and, in the dimming radiance and rising music, guests begin to dance for their sovereigns. All of them in blissful ignorance of her woe.

She's only glad she doesn't have to greet them just yet. She couldn't hide her anger. She's not even sure she can stand the celebration, not without releasing some pressure, when Saira ascends the stairs to bow before them.

"My king." The queen-mother's gaze is unreadable as it lifts to her son. "Wouldn't your father be proud."

"Mother." Kier regards her warily, but then his head tips to the side, his focus intent on someone else mounting the stairs. "Jas."

Ophelia tracks Kier's general, flanked by several other soldiers, who goes straight to the Witchist king's side and ignores her entirely.

In hurried Magiesian, Salt offers an update from the front lines: "Osiris appears to be pulling back his units from camps along the river."

Her anger splinters. The Gray King's retreating? The legion hasn't even attacked. It's days from mounting an offensive. She opens her mouth, but Kier slips from his throne to follow Salt somewhere more private while the other legion soldiers fan out across the dais.

"Kososten."

That voice pulls her steely focus back. Ophelia's spine stacks to see the queen-mother approach. "That's far enough."

When light bolts to her fingertips in warning, Saira wisely halts a few feet from the thrones.

Through a force of calm, Ophelia says, "You know, Kier was right about one thing. No one sacrifices what's good in them without being provoked. I've worried so long about hurting people with my power, but I'm feeling particularly provoked tonight. So if you don't wish to see what a queen is capable of when she's cornered, crawl back to your spellshop."

Saira holds up her palms in peace. "I've been watched. There was no way to warn you."

"Was this your scheme?" she hisses. "Pretend to help me and all the while you're working out your plan to take power through your son? You have the Morphist king's heir locked in a cell, and now me, tethered for eternity and *viclumeni* to your son! Well done. I was a great fool." She'd like to burn the woman where she stands.

Saira has the nerve to smile as if with pride. "I knew I sensed a fierce queen inside you. How pleased Messandra and Kane would be to meet her. I do wish they could."

With a hardening brow, Ophelia watches Saira glance past the thrones to the back of the dais, where Kier and Salt confer near the windows, though the music drowns whatever they're saying.

Seeming satisfied, Saira bows once more in a show of reverence. "Don't trust me, Kososten. Trust what motivates a mother. One whose every unappreciated move for nearly a half-century has been to prevent her son from becoming who his father was, not to mention the monster Osiris was bent on raising."

Ophelia is struck by the emotion Saira manages to fill her voice with. It reads earnest, if she's not being fooled. She searches for a sign of cunning—any a wicked gleam in Saira's eyes—but there's nothing. In the tattoos painted on the woman's cheeks, she's only reminded of Elora and the sacrifice her mother had to make in letting Ophelia go.

While she studies Saira a moment more, trying to decide what's true, the queen-mother holds her gaze, fingering the dark lace on her sleeve. "Nothing has been done tonight that cannot be undone. The night will be long, Kososten. Guests will drink. And no one will miss newly bonded sovereigns who take an early leave."

Almost unconsciously, Ophelia skims a hand to her thigh, to the shape of the velvet pouch Saira gifted her hidden in the tulle.

"When he returns," Saira advises, "seize your opportunity."

CHAPTER 54
FIRE & SCALES

VALLEY OF BONES, KÚZLO
23RD NIGHT IN THE NEW WINTER
FALCON IS IN THE SANCTIONING

S omething's not right.

In the arena, a tournament master is calling the opening ceremony to start. Falcon's been paraded like a prized steed with the other heirs to the center to face rows upon rows of northerners piled into the stadium seating.

He rubs his chest, where it feels like an artery's been shunted and blood can't get through. A strange, needling sort of numbness.

But he can't be distracted so he sharpens his focus on the arena, a formidable location for the competition. Carved from dragonbone, stone, and ice, the outdoor colosseum squats at the northern edge of the Valley of Bones and probably hasn't been used since the last tournament of heirs.

From one of two lines where all the competitors face the crowds, Falcon hardly hears the introductions before the tournament master is raising his symbolic weapons—a bone staff and iron mallet. From sky to ice, the warrior slashes them down in a clanging arc.

"Anfi kamfe!" he cries. *Begin the fight!*

At a resounding roar of the crowd, amber fires around the highest points of the colosseum flame to life. Cheers thunder through the stadium. And in a cold northern wind, banners in colors that match the scales around the heirs' necks wave at them in hues of red, gray, blue, white, and yellow.

As the lone heir with no scale and no drecora of his own to lend strength in the tournament, Falcon feels the emptiness of his bare neck. All he's got is the fire and focus that's kept him alive all his life, a prophecy that suggests he'll live at least through the tournament, and the last mental image of Ophelia always in his head.

There's his mantra, too: No soul.

He glances at his half-siblings, strapped to the teeth with leather armor, like his. Donning heir rings that glow ice-blue with waiting magic. Trading grins that suggest they're eager to beat the pulp out of each other. The sight of them makes a bitter taste coat his tongue.

For the first time, his mantra feels like a lie, and it's unsettling.

As the heirs are instructed to march back out of the arena, clearing the ground for the first match, the melee in the stands lowers to a tolerable decibel and the wind hurls a name from the stands: "Kessan! Kessan!"

Falcon's surprised to find no trace of satisfaction on his brother's face. Instead, Kessan's keen on the crowd, like he's searching for someone.

Falcon traces the section of seating designated for the *volorost* and heir families. Ryke's wives have all arrived, and the betrothed who wear the colors of their heirs. Falcon spots Reya in marine-blue and for a split second wonders what might've been, had he and Ophelia stayed in Kúzlo as kids and he found his way to her sooner.

Would he have vied in the Sanctioning?

Would she be wearing Rakúa's colors in support of him?

"Fool's dream," he mutters to himself.

The past is past, the war is coming, Cleo saw what she did. Falcon can't have what he wants, so he lets the wind take the what-ifs, grinding his gears instead on the fact that the great high lord is still absent.

Ryke was a question all the heirs except for Kessan finally seemed to be asking at training. The tournament masters always had the same answer, though; Ryke had other business. He'd make an appearance at the Sanctioning.

Unease climbs the ladder of Falcon's spine, and he rips his gaze from his father's still-empty seat. He barely feels the snow nettling his face as the heirs leave the arena and enter the tunnel that will take them to the hold, an old dungeon used to cage fighters in order to prohibit any pre-match interference.

As the ground slopes down, Falcon's boots find purchase on flat stone. Torches lap from the rocky walls and heirs cluster, guarded by *seshen*, while the iron door into the hold is opened.

In front of him, Sunder's long nose snarls in distaste as he complains to Xakai, "Richen wast hundin." Falcon translates: *Smells like wet hound.*

Xakai grunts his agreement. "Hanas ren brut. Ren wist drecora, nast hundin." *They treat us like animals. We are like dragons, not dogs.*

Their whining reminds Falcon of when they were *nakommen*, getting lessons from the *seshen*. The two were always pissing and moaning about things being fair, like life ever was, then took their frustration out on Kessan.

Beside Sunder, a lethal female leans in. "*Woof*," their sister taunts, throwing a smirk over her shoulder that lands on Falcon.

He raises a brow in acknowledgment.

Falcon was civil with the heirs at training, hoping to glean information from them about Ryke or what's going on with Kessan. Only his half-sister extended an olive branch—not that Serinna knew anything—and his trust in her only extended so far, given she's Sunder's twin.

The gated door groans open in front of them. "Innen!" A *seshen* motions them inside.

Serinna gives Sunder a long look, advising something mind-to-mind before cutting ahead.

Conversation ceases as they file through the door into a narrower tunnel that faces the fight arena. Ahead, along the right side of the tunnel, are viewing windows carved into the wall, giving a glimpse of where the matches will unfold on ground level. Falcon notes the crowds still waving their banners. Spread out in a row on the left side of the tunnel are compartments—veritable kennels—where the heirs will watch with their mentors.

Falcon doesn't see Kessan among competitors heading to their cages. When the tunnel door behind him clangs shut, he turns, coming face to face with his brother. Falcon is broader, Kessan an inch taller. They haven't spoken since the night at the Virstone, and each takes the other's measure.

When Kessan steps forward as if to pass, Falcon cuts, "You're really going to make me fight you? You know the rules. Once I get in that arena, they won't let me stand down."

Resolve stares back at him, Kessan's shoulders broadening like he means to fill Falcon's shadow. "You mean if you make it to face me, *jagerin*." Kessan slams Falcon's shoulder as he stalks by him toward the cages.

"Kess."

His brother halts, but doesn't turn.

Falcon lets go of a hard exhale, his thumb rubbing over the heir ring he wears. "If I fight you, I don't plan on losing." He lets the warning deliver its weight, but it half sounds like a plea.

Cleo saw Falcon fighting in the war from the back of a drecora. He intends to see that much comes true.

Lowering his voice, he tries once more. "Tell me where Ryke is and I'll withdraw. Whatever you've gotten into, I can make him and the council see what's at stake—"

Kessan swings around, bitterness sharp as a blade in the flare of his nostrils. "After tonight, there will be a new high lord of the North, and he can grant you nothing."

Kessan backs down the tunnel before Falcon can press about what the fuck he means. The Sanctioning decides a successor, but a *volorost* takes months or years to prepare that successor for the title and relinquish their power.

A new high lord after tonight...who can grant Falcon nothing?

There was malice in Kessan's tone. Maybe regret.

A slew of suspicions circle Falcon like vultures as he stalks past several compartments, when a copper head sticks out from one.

"There you are!" Trix looks exasperated as she grabs his sleeve, pulling him into a cage. Iron doors slide automatically to lock behind him. "They're announcing the first match soon."

At the back wall of his hold, Ashë's laying out lightswords and vambraces, along with cloths and salves for after. Compared to other heir teams, which have two mentors minimum and several healers standing by, Falcon's team is small.

The sheath of his skin under all his leathers grows antsy, hungry for steel.

Eight heirs. Each of them fights at least once, four victors battle again, then the final competitors face one other.

And now Falcon knows with certainty that Kessan won't surrender. If they fight, one of them wins, the other dies. He braces as the tournament master takes center ring to announce the first two competitors. "Serinna, daughter of the Fourth Wife! And Ronan, son of the Sixth Wife!"

His lungs release their tight grip.

The compartments rattle as two doors slide open, and jeers from the other heirs echo as Ronan and Serinna leave the hold.

When the crowds catch sight of Serinna brandishing her battle axe on a shoulder and Ronan—broader, moving slower—gripping his scythe, another eruption of cheers shakes the stadium.

Falcon watches the pair square off in the arena while the master lays out the rules already burned into his mind: It's weapons-only until the first in-match knell. Then, magic's on the table, including use of whatever finite spells have been imbued in their heir rings. Plus, the strength of their drecora, which is moot for him.

The second rule is that no interference from the crowd will be tolerated.

And the last: Heirs fight until someone's knocked out, bleeding out, or taps out. There's a strategy to surrendering in the Sanctioning, unlike in the *stadhelm* where warriors fight for pride alone and surrender is seen as weakness. Here, an heir who can't win must surrender to stay in the line of succession, in case a victor's killed before producing heirs.

Not that any of that matters for Falcon. He can't surrender.

"We need to get you ready," Trix says, motioning him to the back of the hold where there's a stone bench, some treewater, and a pot to piss in if need be.

He draws up one of his swords, inspecting its pristine edge as he settles on the bench.

While Ashë moves to the front of the hold, eyes on the match to study weaknesses, Trix comes to loom over him. "What was that with Kessan?"

"A last ditch effort." Falcon seethes at his own reflection in the steel of his sword.

"You're more annoyed than usual, so I'm guessing that got you nowhere. You still think he knows something?"

Falcon hesitates. He trusts Trix. She's been at training with him. In every pep talk or piece of intel she's gleaned, he's sensed her motives are true; she wants justice for Cleo and revenge on Crats. But his conversation with Kessan at the Virstone still has him chafed, raw and charged with feelings he needs to keep at bay, if he's going to win tonight.

"I should've gone back to the mount to see what spooked him," he finally says, keeping an eye out the viewing windows, where Serinna and Ronan await the starting knell and the silhouettes of their perched drecora cast over the arena.

Trix sits beside him, facing forward. "You tried to reason with him. Your brother's bullheadedness doesn't change why we're here." She passes him his vambraces.

Resting his sword against the bench, Falcon pulls one over a wrist. "I know."

He hoped laying the truth out for Kessan about Ophelia's identity would shake sense into his brother, but it seemed to do the opposite. The trauma of their *nakommen* days and the need to be Ryke's favored must be too deep-rooted. Or maybe it was whatever Kessan saw in the Virstone. Gods, he'd rushed out looking panicked as a stag in a rifle's sight.

Falcon yanks on his second vambrace in frustration.

He wanted this to go a different way—one where he wouldn't have to spill his brother's blood. Kessan's supposedly got their father's ear. He sits on the council...

The war will not come here. I have made sure of that.

Falcon pauses the hand fastening his vambrace, suspicions sharpening with every thought.

A clash.

Glancing at the arena where Serinna and Ronan are lunging, Falcon peers up into the stands, searching. Sure as hell, he notes the glint of silver armor now in the *volorost*'s box. Royal guests of the Gray Throne have arrived.

It's hard to make out faces, but he'd bet by the commotion and formation of all that armor who's at the center of it—Rune Ethera, made a symbol of Osiris's crusade to keep Magies under the blade. And in leaving Rune behind in Wythe, Falcon was a party to the monarchy getting claws into him.

It hits him like a runaway carriage.

"Fuck," he exhales, his elbows sliding to his knees. "Kessan won't listen to reason because he's already made a goddamn deal on Ryke's behalf." Probably paid for it in secrets—whatever Kessan wouldn't tell Falcon the other night.

Trix's gaze is unwavering. "Then you know what you have to do." She motions to the sword beside him. "Win, whatever it costs."

No soul.

He slips a look through the side bars of his hold, past Xakai's and Sunder's compartments, spotting Kessan with his mentors.

Falcon still sees the small boy who was afraid to take that scale. But if it's the last thing he does, he's getting Ophelia an army, one that's outside the Darkwielder's control. And with a look at the monarchy silver that cuts through the northern colors in the stadium, Falcon is confident it's more than his soft spot for Kessan he's up against.

"This won't be an easy win," he murmurs to Trix.

"Maybe not." A knell sounds across the colosseum and, where Serinna and Ronan are weaponless now, flames arc across the arena, followed by a guttural cry from Ronan.

Trix nudges Falcon. "I have something for you." Her cloak and furs cover her hands as they pick something from her pocket to palm.

Falcon feels a match spark the second he sees the scale. It shimmers, same as the night he cut it, held it in his hand, and inadvertently claimed Rakúa.

This scale's not marine-blue like the one Kessan must've clipped later from her leg. It's a light ocean-blue that matches Rakúa's lethal ironspade tail.

He stares like he's seven again, his hands itching to take it. "Where the hell did you get that?"

The council made Falcon relinquish the scale in front of the whole valley before he, his mother, and Kaitriona were sent out of Kúzlo. It was humiliating.

They gave the scale to Kessan. Had he saved it?

A smile buds in the corners of Trix's mouth. "Bow to me, heir," she quips suddenly, sitting straight. When he frowns, she lowers his head for him and settles the chain around his neck. As he inclines his face, she snorts. "If someone told me I'd be helping Falcon Thames become a leader of the North... Just don't think I'll ever bow to you, smugger."

"Still waiting for another arrow in my chest."

Trix grows quiet. "We've all suffered enough, I think." She motions to the scale. "Reya said, 'right is right.' You should have it."

"Reya?" Gods of Magus, Kessan will have her tossed out of the House of Bone. At least, it'll spark a good shouting match between the two. Reya could always hold her own.

"If and when you face Kessan, it more or less puts you even."

"Kess claimed Rakúa."

Trix shrugs. "She accepted you once. And don't forget she iced half our unit on arrival. She could've made you a pin cushion, but she didn't."

Falcon considers the truth in that, the scale warming on his neck as a flare of something wild shudders through him. A *hreeeee!* cuts above the colosseum. The sound reverberates deep in his chest, though he can't yet see Rakúa in the sky.

He wants to ride her. Maybe he always has.

Feeling a stare as sharp as barbs, Falcon glances up the cages again, somehow unsurprised to see Kessan glowering in his direction, as if his brother senses something amiss.

Forcing his attention to the arena, Falcon tucks the scale under his fighting leathers, against his heart, and lets the fire in him grow with the force of everything he wants—even the things he knows he can't have—until he can't fathom how he lived without these parts of himself.

His family. Rakúa. And Ophelia, though he might never get to tell her.

The tournament master calls the fight for Serinna, while Ronan's carted out of the ring to a pounding cheer. Then Falcon hears his own name and Sunder's, and the bars on his hold slide open with a clank.

SEVEN
RISE & DEMISE

CHAPTER 55
MASKS & HATE
GHASTLY
THE CORONATION
OPHELIA IS WITH THE DARKWIELDER

In the middle of the throne room, Ophelia spins in a blur of stardust sequins and tulle and fury, orbiting the dark king as they dance.

It's horrible enough he stole her choice. Having to sell her agreement to it with this obligatory show makes her blood heat.

The energy in the room is frenetic.

Masked guests stand on tip toes around the edges of the floor, every eye watching as Kier pulls her into his frame, closer than necessary. But when his cheek skims hers, and his lips—below the jeweled, midnight mask he dons—graze the lobe of her ear, a loathsome shiver of desire snakes through her.

When Saira told her the ceremony was only foreplay, she should've been relieved. Though the guilds consider them united, the *viclumeni* bond must be consummated to form a full, lasting, soul-level hold. The queen-mother didn't tell her how, against her will, she would ache deeply for Kier until the bond was satisfied.

"I'm glad you changed your mind about dancing," he lulls in her ear.

"Because you gave me a choice."

A dark chuckle.

She braces against the tingles it elicits. The elaborate plume on the side of her crown-metal mask bobs as Kier makes them graceful, despite the weight of their iron crowns and her cumbersome skirts.

"As I predicted," he says, spinning her, "not inept at all."

The harkening to their banter over chess is an irritating reminder of what a fool she's been, believing some flirting could keep him in line. "If you're so easily impressed, perhaps you need more partners."

"I've had my share, Ophelia."

She pulls back. "Just none you felt like forcing to be your *viclumeni* until now."

His expression withers as the music crescendos, and Kier drives her across the floor in a dramatic flourish to a punishing symphony and clash of violins. They whirl until the room becomes a blur of candlelight and champagne glass toasts.

Stealing subtle looks into the crowd, she finds Mathias. He wears a thin, raven mask that matches his uniform and stands near the two-story main doors of the throne room. Through the criss-crossing traffic of server trays, the queen-mother appears, free of her legion guards. A few whirls more and she spots Hannah and Isolde, masked in their guild patterns, waiting near the throne stairs where she left them.

Four allies. *Four.* While Kier has the guilds, the guests, his legion, and the dagger.

With a final epic twirl, her dress a fire of gold, Kier catches her in his arms and they halt under the grand chandelier, him holding her as their breaths rise and fall and applause fills the hall.

Her heart flutters as she catches sight of Saira in the sea, slipping through the exit Aman used earlier.

Cool fingers on her chin gently steal her attention. "You've caught a lovely flush," Kier observes. "Still angry, goddess?" At his dark stare, wretched need blooms inside her. He smiles. "Or...perhaps something else?"

"We've made a show of your treachery. What now?" she asks, hating how breathless she sounds.

His thumb skims her bottom lip. "I think it's time for bed, Kososten." But his focus drifts elsewhere.

Following his gaze, she braces to see Jasper Salt among a group of guests at a table. She catches on that pinky of his, painted with black polish, where it hugs the drink he sips as he watches the two of them.

With a single nod, the general seems to communicate a point to Kier, and as another song starts up and guests crowd the dance floor, the dark king takes her hand.

As they wade through people, she asks, "What was that?"

Kier glances at her. "Plans have changed. Jas and I leave for Ravish at dawn to ready our forces."

Leave. "The assault isn't for a week." Her stomach bottoms. "You're expediting it?"

Masks glitter in the crowd as they thread through, guests bowing in their direction but keeping a careful stride's length away.

Kier lowers his voice. "We leaked false plans into the East and it seems it has the Royal Army retreating. This is our chance."

It feels rash, and an instinct niggles that moving hastily against the Gray King isn't wise, but she has other problems at the moment, if Kier intends to leave Ghastly early—with the dagger.

As they approach the throne room doors, Mathias cuts a deep bow at them. "Goodnight, Kososten," he tells her, holding her gaze a moment longer than necessary.

Following Kier through the door, she feels more eyes on her back. Over a shoulder, she glimpses Salt again, standing at the edge of the crowd.

His eyes meet hers. Hard. As if he suspects she has plans of her own.

Ophelia smiles at him, as if to let him know he need not worry. She is queen. Kier has made her his. She will see to the dark king tonight.

CHAPTER 56
BONDS & BEDCHAMBERS

The bond is unbearable in Kier's bedchambers. Ophelia excuses herself to the washroom, and when she emerges from a private moment, the smell of cloves and books and the fire already burning are a sultry poultice.

Laying her crown and cape on a sideboard, she can't look away from the velveted four-poster bed. It's been turned down already and looks as dangerous as a serpent in the brush.

Before the fire, Kier is unfastening his mantel and looking up beneath dark lashes, his striking features still half-masked behind that jeweled cloth. His profile cuts like marble in the glow as he meets her gaze.

She doesn't bother with removing her own mask. It feels fitting as she attempts to hide every emotion, every thought, every sensation that pulses through her under his stare.

Slowly, he loosens the collar of his doublet, then deft fingers start on the buttons of his shirt.

The sight of his full tattoo sprawling his carved chest pulls a small gasp from her. The pattern is like dark, combing fingers—a mirror of the whorls covering her heart and half of her left arm. It feels like further evidence he always intended to make her his. That he did risk Magus with his curse just to draw her out of the mortal world to him.

I would have done far worse to get your attention, goddess.

He looks ravaged with need—dark, desperate, dangerous.

Despite herself, her breathing hitches as shadows sift from Kier's chest to disappear beneath the fabric of his half-fastened shirt. They coil in a chilling mist at his wrists. Like cuffs. Like they're ready to play.

Ophelia's lips part—and tingle.

Bracing as the masked dark king stalks the width of the room to where she hovers near his desk, she tries to keep her spine straight and her chin raised, even though she's conscious under his intense gaze that her gown leaves little to the imagination.

She tries not to tremble with that damn budding desire as he brackets her chin between his fingers, inclining her gaze to his. Her heart pounds with every second he looks at her, and she's certain he will kiss her.

Smiling, as if he knows how she's anticipating him, Kier reaches up instead to make easy work of freeing her masquerade mask, then casts it to the floor. It feels as if he's removed something far more scandalous, the way he appreciates the sight of her.

"*Viclumeni.*" He relishes the word. And like a firm stake in the ground, his smoldering eyes seem to claim her. "I will have you, Ophelia. Then tomorrow, I'll unleash the full strength of the gods and *stärke vas* to crush our enemy and secure our future."

His knuckles brush a slow, cool trail from her cheek to her neck, down her shoulder and along her side where it's exposed in her gown. When his thumb grazes the edge of her breast, she jolts, her pulse thrumming—the bond *desperate* to let him ravish her.

His pupils dilate with arousal as his exhale rumbles like a purring growl. "How I've wanted you," he whispers, drawing her flush against him, eyes dropping to her lips.

Her mouth flames in anticipation, knowing all it would take to change everything between them is for Kier to kiss her like he did before.

She allows her walls to fully fall, lets a wave of his desire and hers make the tether taut as rope. Still Kier doesn't bring his mouth to hers.

He hovers at her cheek, punctuating, "How I've thought of your skin beneath my hands." His touch alights on the side of her thigh. "Burying myself inside you." Her breath catches as the shape of him presses into her belly. "Claiming your love."

With a flick of his hand, shadows ensnare the tether and manifest from Kier's skin, rising to envelop them and deprive her of every sense—everything but him and the bond.

She's caught in the tempting darkness of his power, but somewhere in the tangle of desire, what Kier said cuts through. *Claiming your love.* Not power, not light. He wants her love.

As his nose brushes hers, his mouth descending, she pushes against his chest. "Wait," she breathes, light unfurling from within her to dissipate his darkness.

The bookshelves, the bed, the fire rush in—and Kier, whose gaze is flecked with confusion and a touch of irritation at her pause. But as moments of training, scheming, and late-night strolls flit through her mind, she searches his eyes in the fire glow for a flicker of goodness in him. For the man on his knees for her. For a shred of hope she can still turn all this around, before it's too late.

"Before we..." She swallows. "I need to know... Is there no changing your mind about the mortals?"

"The mortals." At a wave of his anger, she steps back, her waist bumping his desk. "We've discussed the mortals. There's nothing more to say."

She grips the edge of his desk. "Do you think winning this way—forcing people—will make them love you?" The temperature plunges between them. His chest rises in a ragged breath as he stares hard at her. But she forges on, clinging to hope. "For as much as you talk of sacrifices and heads and pikes, you don't want to be the monster. Please. Tell me you don't." *Tell me tonight was not your idea—tell me you regret it.*

His eyes are cold. "Anything but the monster in me died long ago."

A bitter breath leaves her. "With the woman you loved and supposedly killed? And what would she think, Kier? Would she want you to become this man?"

He devours the space between them. A hand lashes roughly to the base of Ophelia's throat and squeezes, tipping her head back. "She can want nothing. She is *dead*," he snarls. "And I will have Osiris suffer. He will see me coming, and the fear will drive him mad. He will *quiver*"—he seethes the word—"with the knowledge I am taking his kingdom, the way he took everything that meant something to me. Piece by piece," Kier vows. "And he will be the last to fall, so he can watch me do it."

The pulse in her neck pounds under his grip.

The Lost Lands. The Belly. The West. The Northern Territories. Piece by piece. The way Osiris broke him.

Despite his hand on her throat, an ache spills out of her to river aside Kier's pain. Slowly, she reaches up for the mask he wears, pulls it free, and casts it aside.

Her heart lurches as she takes in the pale planes of his face, noting the darkness that rims his eyes. When the pressure on her neck slightly loosens, she asks, "What did Osiris do to her? The woman from your memories."

Kier's eyes slowly soften and glaze. His hand eases a breath more on her throat. "Her...her name was Delphine," he rasps.

Across the tether, something flickers. Music drifts, inviting her in. Then Ophelia is there, sucked back in time.

CHAPTER 57
HEIST & HEARTSICK

GRAY CASTLE
15 YEARS AGO

G lasses clink as laughter chimes in a grand ballroom filled with chocolate fountains and opulent spreads.

Kier dislikes the perfume of aristocratic women in their pretty gowns, how it hangs in the air the same way the women hang on arms of greedy men wearing knuckle rings with the symbol of the crown.

Plastered across every tapestry in the room is the Gray King's two-headed daw emblem. At a cocktail table where he stands among four Crats wielding their egos, Kier glances at the clock above the main doors, tugging on the sleeve of his Special Army uniform in frustration. *Where is Osiris?*

Kier rolls his shoulders under the traveling cape he still wears. Fortunately, the men at the table don't notice, drunk as they're becoming.

Representative Boyle, of Cirque, lowers his voice and leans across the table. "We just traded for a pair of Benders, pretty little flame-throwers with fine asses to boot." At the wicked gleam in the old man's eye, the table of despicable men cackles. "I tell you, I tell you"—Boyle gets ahold of himself—"get yourself a pair of twins. Twice the heat in a cold bed."

At more resounding laughs, Kier's teeth stab his cheek, drawing the taste of blood. As Captain in the Special Army, he's endured years of these horrid conversations. A few more hours. A few more, and he will take this entire city and rip the spines out of men like Boyle.

A red-faced Crat barrels out from the crowd to join the table, a spittle of champagne clinging to his mustache as he bellies up. "Captain!"

Kier forces a smile that dies short of his eyes. "Brigham."

Vesh Derringer's father still doesn't shake Kier's hand or even clap him on the back. But the wine has made him more at ease.

Peacocking, Brigham tells him, "Vesh is around here somewhere with those entitled cousins of his, making plans to use my money to construct a business district in central Magus; you ought to say hello, sway them the money's in the Magie trade, what with *your* connections."

Kier cuts a glance to an array of seats where the slender Vesh swirls a wine glass, looking the part of a Crat's son in his fine suit, indeed.

For a moment, their eyes meet.

Kier hasn't forgotten the offer made in this room twenty years ago, when Vesh, Wyatt Kercher, and Arkimen Proffit promised the newly appointed captain their fealty, should Kier get the courage to topple the monarchy from within.

"Yes," Kier answers Brigham. "I really ought to catch up with them."

Brigham raises his glass to the table. "Well, gentleman. It's been a long road, but here's to us! An academy full of heathen children and, at long last, indentures fully legal!"

"Here, here!" Toasts all around. *Toasts* to that.

Tightness coils Kier's jaw, arms, and hands, and his shadows ache to release. His lips part in a slight sneer, a momentary slip, when a flash of golden hair pulls his gaze across the crowded room.

Delphine wears a crown of braids and a long, autumn-red gown.

His heart pounds, and he straightens when she looks his way, catching his eye and holding it a long moment before she makes in the direction of the doors to exit the ballroom.

Kier glances at the clock—just shy of high moons. But there's still no Osiris. Delphine is supposed to be among the king's attendants tonight. What is she doing?

Setting his glass on the table, Kier nods to the men. "Excuse me, gentleman." He waves a placating hand. "Do keep enjoying yourselves." *Filth.*

His gaze darkens as he steps away, cutting through the throng toward the main doors. Before he can reach them, a series of *pops* reverberate—soft and far-off, like distant fireworks. But Kier knows the sound of gunfire by now.

While guests at his back celebrate, oblivious, he slips quickly into the halls of Gray Castle in the direction he thinks Delphine's gone.

Servants mill, frowning and muttering in confusion at the distant spattering.

"Get out of the halls," he orders them, then rushes toward the fire.

At the threshold of an iron door blown off its hinges, panic claws into Kier's stomach, and he looks with horror into the chamber that leads to the king's vault room—at the bodies that litter the floor. There are some in silver livery, but most wear Special Army uniforms.

His men are all dead, their forms already folding to ash.

Rage unspools with a stir of menacing mist, thick as black smoke in his wake, as he steps past the bodies and surveys the full destruction. Every tendril is sucked back again, though, when from the vault room ahead the Gray King steps out—with her.

Kier blanches. "Delphine?"

Behind the king, royal guards shouldering guns step from the vault room, where Kier can just glimpse three glass cases that look alarmingly empty.

Air struggles into his lungs, thwarting his understanding of what's happened—what's *happening*—here. Then the biting truth rushes in. The king has discovered his plan. He's foiled Kier's long-planned heist.

As his blading eyes seize Osiris, a toneless voice beside the king says, "I had to tell him, Kier."

His gaze preys to Delphine, where it falters in confusion at the look of guilt churning in the hazel of her eyes.

"Did you think," the Gray King says, as if amused, "that all your scheming over the years went unnoticed by this crown?"

Kier stiffens.

"Did you imagine," Osiris pitches, "that you could confide in a lowly servant and she would keep your secret?"

The king shakes his head. "Turning my soldiers, infiltrating my prison tunnels, distracting my guests, and breaking into my relics vault—I suppose you thought when everyone was good and drunk, you'd slip away from the party with your *love* and your birthright and what? Kill me, as you failed to do when you first discovered I seized the dagger?"

Undone by his horror, Kier traces sorrow and regret in Delphine's eyes.

"But," Osiris goes on, "Your prey was late to the party, wasn't he? Because he—I—was with your love..." He brushes ringed knuckles against Delphine's cheek, and Kier snarls at the truth. "Yes," the Gray King spits, gripping Delphine's arm. "Your precious love led you here to die. She told me of your plans from the start."

Rage simmers along his bones where his shadows curl. How long ago had he confided in Delphine? How many months? And Kier didn't see it because he was blinded by her—has always been blinded by her—by his love.

With guns trained on him, Kier edges forward, looking bitterly between the king and Delphine. Fury edges his voice. "I loved you," he rasps at her. "Since we were children!" His shadows quiver inside him.

Delphine doesn't cry or struggle or deny what she's done. She simply says, "Jasper."

Kier's whole body goes taut as a chill plunges through him.

"Ah, Jasper," the Gray King echoes, harshing a glare at Delphine. "It's been difficult to be patient where the boy is concerned, but the satisfaction of thwarting this siege was worth delaying the acknowledgment of my son."

Son.

Kier steps to the brink of his rage as Jasper's young face appears like a snapshot in his mind. The child born of a coupling against Delphine's will, years ago, that she refused to speak about.

"Lies," Kier grits.

"Tell him," the Gray King beckons her. When she doesn't, he squeezes her arm. "Tell him!"

She lifts her chin to Kier, her eyes a well of pain. "Jasper is his son."

No. Anyone but him.

The king smiles. "You were away a long stretch at my bequest for trade talks in the North. A woman gets lonely."

Kier's anger flares—even as he sees it. Sees himself return to the castle after months away to discover Delphine with a baby at her breast. A baby that could not be Kier's.

Yet, he loved her still. And he loved her child because he was hers.

"How could you?" he whispers.

Hurt flashes in her eyes. "I didn't. It was him—"

"You hid my son away!" the king roars. "And you"—he whirls at Kier—"helped her keep him from the fruits of his noble birth, masquerading him as some servant's child!"

"We kept him from the fate awaiting him as Magie," Kier snaps. "Your brutal academy, your indentures. Worse."

Osiris shoves Delphine at a guard and widens his broad chest, taking Kier in with distaste. "I gave you an army. I made you who you are! All these years, plotting to bite the hand that's fed you. What a waste. But, then, you were always weak for love." Kier flinches. "Now you'll die for it, and I will have a true heir."

With a nod at the soldiers shielding him, the Gray King steals out of the room, leaving Delphine and Kier amid a vault of executioners.

The guns aim.

But so does Kier.

Bullets and darkness rain.

K ier stares at the severed heads and bodies in scorched armor.

There's piercing pain where bullets have grazed his side, and he sucks sharp breaths. But far off is a drum of bootsteps, a clang of more armor.

Then, a moan from the floor where Delphine lies on her side, bleeding from a wound Kier recognizes for what it is. A scathing of his mist that's ribboned her abdomen.

"No," he breathes, the word barely audible as he falls to his knees beside her, the room spinning around him. He lays a palm to her forehead. "No!" Searing agony rips through his own wound, maddening his cry with every beat of love and pain that guts him.

He falls to his side, woozy, a hand clutching the wound to come away red. The room tilts again, but there is sudden warmth. A hand on his skin, making it tingle. A touch he knows well from all the times before that Delphine has healed him.

When Kier swings his head up, her outstretched fingers are pressing to the lesions in his side, his skin already mending under her touch. "Stop!" he cries in panic, because he can see how it depletes her further, and he will not let this be the last time Delphine mends him.

As her hand falls way and she rolls to her back, Kier draws his shadows. Seeping cool tendrils, he intends to bandage what he can so he can move her, get her out.

She shakes her head at him. "You have to let me go. Salvage at least part of your plan." She chokes, and he moves closer, taking her face in his hand.

Her eyes shutter, and every muscle in his jaw feels ready to snap. "I will not!" he cries. "Stay with me!"

Her eyes flutter open. "I—I never told Osiris that you knew about your mother. Get her...and Jasper. Don't let... Get Jas away."

Like he should have gotten her brother away, long ago. Rhodin, the golden-haired boy wrenched from sleep, drained by the king right in front of them until he was ash. Because Kier didn't listen when she asked him to help. Because he feared losing her too much.

Delphine's eyes harden. "I said go. Go *now*!" She shoves at Kier, and blood is a river now at her side.

Armor rattles in the hall.

He lets the fury that unfurls with his darkness swallow him as he presses his lips to Delphine's paling forehead. He didn't listen to her before, but he will now.

Love makes Valkieran Balcombe rise to follow her wishes. But as soldiers tunnel in, hate makes his shadows scream from his skin and carve a bloody, merciless escape from the room.

He disappears into the walls of Gray Castle, shedding his gray cloak and becoming the phantom as he steals his way to Jasper. He rouses the child who is small for his ten years, but defiant and smart. Then his shadows pave a path to Saira in her prison tower, where an explosion of Kier's darkness breaks the stone walls open.

"The dagger?" Saira asks.

He can hardly stomach to say, "It waits for another day."

He doesn't speak of Delphine, instead allowing shadows to nestle where love once pulsed, as he, Jas, and Saira slip into the prison tunnels that are laden with more of his ambushed men.

It's inconceivable how his wrath grows with every step they flee into the Magus night.

CHAPTER 58
RAPTURE & REDEMPTION

Ophelia is thrust from the memory and back into her own mind to find the grip on her throat gone.

Kier braces two hands on the wooden desk beside her, his shoulders cowed, his shirt still hanging open. She fights the instinct to comfort him with a touch on his arm, reeling at what he showed her, what he endured—more than any man should have to.

And the truth of Jasper Salt's identity... He has Osiris's blood, like Rune.

The looks of disdain Kier and Jasper shared in Wythe take on new meaning when she thinks of how the two faced off with Osiris and Knight Commander Jory Dagon.

All these years, Kier has protected Jasper, lifting him up as his proxy and his general. The two have been fighting to reap the same revenge against the Gray Throne.

"This was always personal," she says quietly. "Osiris destroyed the woman you loved."

Shoving back from the desk, Kier straightens, hair disheveled. "I couldn't even be with her when she died. Couldn't say goodbye," he bites out. "And after...Jas was all I had of her. Embers to my hatred."

He looks upon Ophelia with that broken gaze. "What else could there ever be for me—a man with darkness for a soul?"

It's like sunlight rising over a hill, her realization of what Kier has wanted since his heart was irrevocably shattered. The thing he lost and never thought he'd find again. The thing he sees as a weakness but secretly craves.

"Love," she tells him.

At the word, softness bleeds into his eyes, his mouth, framing his face with something like hope as he leans against the desk. And maybe...maybe *hope* could be the light to finally tame his vengeance.

Maybe things could yet be different.

She studies the ring she wears, seeing it for something else now, admitting, "I was furious with you earlier. When you forced the bond, I was afraid that I"—she shakes her head, finding it hard to say the words—"that I would never know if the reason I feel so deeply connected to you is because of the tether, or because there's something real between us."

Kier hangs on her words.

"But if we broke the tether—"

He pushes off the desk, looming darkly over her.

She holds his narrowed gaze, laying her hand over the tattoo on his chest. His heart pounds against her palm. "If this weren't forced between us, we could know what's really here."

Please, she wills him. *Please change your mind. Tell me this is real and it will change everything.*

"Love?" he murmurs, an echo to earlier.

"Love," she breathes. And it's a devastating idea, because it could be true. If he agrees to break the tether. If she chooses him—really chooses him.

His gaze falls to the Shadow marking at her collarbone, his hand absently brushing the Dark Shadow Dagger at his hip. His reach for it is confirmation, and she sucks a breath.

"You can break it," she says. She didn't know for sure until now. "You could've broken the tether from the start." When he says nothing, a hand still poised on the relic's hilt, she presses, "Kier?"

At his name, a cloud darkens his face. He studies her a moment more, the edges of his jaw growing taut—distrustful. Forgoing the dagger, he seizes her hand on his chest as the other pulls her tighter against him.

He radiates intensity as his gaze pins her in place. "We are greater than love, Ophelia. Greater than mortal emotions that perish with the slightest betrayal. From tonight, we are *viclumeni*, and you are mine."

As his fingers skate up the slope of her neck and fist in her long hair, her stomach clenches with the truth. He wants her—she can feel how desperately—but not enough to relinquish control, not until he has obliterated her own.

The truth sinks like lead to the bottom of her stomach. This is obsession. A poisonous fixation—so intense, it's nearly impossible to resist. Yet she knows how it would end if she succumbed to its pull and allowed it to grow between them. It would burn the world to nothing and destroy them both. She would try and try to save him, and he would take and take until everything she ever was or loved in herself was gone.

However much she wants to, whatever she feels for him, she can't fix how he's broken.

I can't fix him.

The notion unfurls in her with a weight of sorrow. She nods to herself, accepting the anguished truth. But Kier must mistake the motion as encouragement, because his hand squeezes in her hair and he waits no more.

With a fervent tug, he lays claim to her with a crushing kiss that cuts to her core. Power and lust explode in tandem as his tongue steals into her mouth.

The intensity of him is unmooring—a match of desire that strikes a furious dance between their magics, in her bones and across the tether.

His hands reach greedily for her thighs and he hauls her onto the desk, scattering her thoughts and the contents of his workspace in a fluid motion. His lips destroy her composure, her reasoning, and stir a need so deep from that thing that wants this bond cemented that she grips his shirt in her fists and wonders if she was wrong—if maybe they could get there, someday. If maybe he could be her fate.

She shivers at the feel of his hand searching under layers of fabric. So consumed is she by his need for her, she lets him deliver those mind-wrecking kisses. Lets his tongue taste her lips. His power is everywhere. In her veins. In her mind. Caressing skin. She struggles to want to stop what the bond yearns for, even as her lips burn from his kiss.

Before she can comprehend the hunger, darkness's cool, silken touch is skating along the flesh of her thighs, higher and higher, seeking her apex, rubbing its cool fingers over the fabric that shields her core.

Unbidden, a moan rips from her as those coils slip beneath her undergarment, against bare skin, and set to relentlessly flicking and teasing her sensitive nub, priming her for the shadow king himself.

The touch coaxes a climbing swell of her pleasure and spurs her light to the surface, while Kier's arousal grows firmer against the thin fabric that stands between him and the center of her.

He leans her back further, letting his darkness toy with her, a hand still tugging in her hair, his lips punishing hers.

In the frenzy of desire, her arm knocks something from the desk. The clatter spikes a moment of vital clarity as she's struck by what she's doing—gripping his shirt, digging her heels into his backside to urge his mouth closer.

Kissing him.

As his fingers skim just below the edge of her undergarment, Ophelia presses a palm against his half-bare chest a little to gulp air, to steal back her reason. Kier's gaze is utterly ravenous—but it's his mouth she scrutinizes.

She imagines his lips must be heating, tingling, like hers. Starting to swell. In fact, they look faintly purple.

"Goddess," he purrs, starting to work down the fabric of her underwear. But as Kier's lips brush hers again, he stiffens, drawing sharply back with brows furrowed, his expression slowly twisting in confusion.

His pale hand crawling up his throat, Kier pushes off of her, and she sits up, lost for breath, searching for the floor with her feet.

That hot tingle has started to spread down her throat, too, but she fights against it to keep her focus on Kier—on the grimace marring his face.

He staggers back, looking horrorstruck. One of his legs nearly gives out, and he lurches off balance toward the bed, a shoulder catching one of the posts. He grabs for it—tries, but his arms start to fail and his eyes round on her. "What"—he rasps—"have you done?"

Around the pounding in her heart, she whispers, "I didn't want to. I never wanted to, but you forced my hand." She waits only until his legs buckle and he falls backward on the bed before her hands fly between the layers of her dress in search of the pouch tucked inside a hidden seam.

Ignoring the empty vial she drank from in Kier's washroom earlier, she extracts the second—the antidote—and swallows every drop.

"It's risky," Ophelia remarked to Saira from her throne chair tonight, while Kier was still speaking with Jasper Salt. "Won't it kill us both?"

Surveying the masquerade crowd as if they weren't talking treason, Saira said, "It's spelled to activate with a kiss and won't encumber you, so long as you drink its cure within a few minutes. Just don't get carried away."

She almost did, because of the bond and the memory Kier shared with her... And because of feelings that don't matter now, feelings that nearly made her change her mind about this whole plan. For compassion's sake and for the friendship they'd forged in between the game and the lies—for so many reasons—she wanted to be what he wanted her to be. She wanted to *be able* to be that. But she couldn't. Maybe partially, or maybe completely, because he took the choice away from her, again and again.

When she creeps to the bed, every muscle in Kier is twitching as if he's straining to move, but his arms are useless at his sides. Guilt swells, but she avoids his gaze as she heaves his legs up to angle him fully atop the sheets. When she tucks him into the blankets, he makes a muffled grunt, but doesn't move.

"What will it do to him?" she asked Saira.

"He'll be paralyzed for a few days, until I 'come up with' the antidote. Able to breathe, but not wield magic or speak."

"They'll know it was me."

"Hopefully it won't matter after the Council of Guilds receives the missive that awaits them, detailing how the Morphist Descendant was imprisoned so my son could collapse the guilds."

Ophelia hates to her core that she's resorted to treachery. But this is what Kier has driven her to.

You wouldn't break the tether.

The Dark Shadow Dagger seems to watch her from the sheath on his belt. It's time. With a long breath, after four years of waiting, she readies herself to possess it, then with every shred of confidence she can muster, she reaches for the relic.

Power slams through her, nearly sending her sideways.

Gritting against it, acclimating to the feel of its intense, chilling energy, she commands her breath even, until she feels steady enough against the hum of the ancient magic that she can slip the dagger from its sheath.

A strangled moan from the bed.

In her hands, the relic is as solid as stone and just as cold. She stares at the runes etched in its hilt, put there when it was forged. This dagger, like the amulet and lightstone, have the power to make gods of gods. To amplify. To siphon. She doesn't know what the symbols mean—they're not like anything she's seen before—but the energy that vibrates along her bones is potent.

With the dagger firmly clutched in her hands, she backs away from the bed while Kier's desperate fingers strain at his sides.

She can't waste time with more regret; she needs the next phase of their plan to go off without incident. And while she's confident the party still goes on, dawn is creeping ever closer and Kier's legion is bound to come for him.

Hastily stowing the dagger, she retrieves her crown and cape and mask. Then she turns her gaze to the bed, a war of emotions playing through her. As she approaches one last time, Kier's eyes attempt to track her, still frozen in that gutting look of horror.

She can remember every time he used the tether against her. Every time he manipulated her emotions. Yet as she stands over him, the thing she feels most is regret.

"You could have trusted me," she tells him. "You could've broken the tether tonight, and I would've told you everything. I...I might have been yours, and we could have worked together to chart a new path. But you left me no choice. For the sake of Magus, I ought to take your power and end you."

His eyes blink rapidly at her from the bed where he meant to take something more from her tonight.

"But I will not," she says, leaning close so he can see the earnestness in her eyes. "Lesson five, Kier. The only difference between men and monsters is mercy." Biting her lip, she twists off the ring he forced on her finger and closes her palm around it. "We are the same, you and I, with our betrayals and broken pieces, but we don't have to be who our enemies would make us. We can choose to be decent. To love. We can choose redemption, even now. Still." She lets the tear that falls stay on her cheek. "I tell you this as the woman who did care."

Along with her crown, she places her ring on the table beside his bed. Then she leaves him—a broken king, her almost-*viclumeni*—to stew in her words, praying her instincts to spare him were right.

CHAPTER 59
DAGGER & FIRE

Mathias is waiting like a statue in the darkened library.

When he sees her, he springs from the wall by the windows, anticipation causing his brows to cut a deep vee.

"Is it done, Kososten?"

When Ophelia lifts the flap of her cloak to let him glimpse the Dark Shadow Dagger, she can see the full realization of what they're doing wash over his moon-kissed features. He brings a hand to the back of his neck, and Ophelia furrows at the bandage there, almost like a scarf the way he's tied it inside the collar of his uniform. Drops of blood have seeped through.

"Gods, Mathias, what happened to you?"

His hand hovers over the cloth before it falls away. "You said there is no going back. I did not wish to be the reason we might be tracked. The Shadow his soldiers are marked with is only skin deep."

Nausea rolls through her. "You cut it out." When he only shrugs, she adds, "So there's northerner in you after all."

They slip through the panel in the wall, Ophelia silently cursing the gown she still wears, but she refuses to let it slow her. When the ground passage spits them into the tunnels, she asks, "So everything went as planned on your end? Hart?"

Mathias scans their surroundings with military focus. The temperature in the tunnels is much cooler. "Saira and the Morphist Descendant have gone to Kane to perform the Transference."

"Good," she says as they wend, wondering how difficult the ceremony might be emotionally for the queen-mother. "I think Saira and Kane were close friends. It won't be easy for her to let him go..." Though, technically, Kane's mind has been gone a long time.

"They were more than friends once," Mathias amends.

"More than—oh." Their breaths and stamping boots echo. But, of course. Ophelia should've read it in the groove of the floor where Saira probably stood often at Kane's bedside, or in the woman's wistful speech. It was Kane who was her true *viclumeni*. The one she would've chosen had Kier's father not interfered.

When they pass Hart's empty cell, the ward's been shattered, Hart's paintings of the blue-chalk girl left behind. At a dead end in the tunnels, a temporary passage stirs to life as planned, right where Saira cast it when she slipped away during the masquerade.

A stone weight lifts off Ophelia's chest the second they're out of the palace.

They come out at the farthest edge of the shadow woods, farther than she's gone without Kier since she got here and close to the gates of Ghastly.

Right away, the moons catch her by surprise. They've taken on the full, frosty sheen of Snow Moons. In the pink-silver bath of their light, she breathes in the humming energy she can feel, the sensation that something is near, and wonders if the original gods are close.

That's the myth. Tonight, the veil is thinner.

Trekking alongside Mathias, inspecting the moons, she points to one of the gray spheres, noting how its glimmer seems to pulse and that it looks almost larger. "Do you see that?"

Mathias angles his head. "The moon of the Morphists."

As they trade a look, she thinks of Hart and knows in her bones that the moons have sensed his awakening. A Morphist Descendant rising.

When Kier seized his power from the Dark Shadow Dagger, where it had been trapped for decades, the very act sent the moons into a Darkening and instigated the season's turn to winter.

How will Hart stepping into his power change things?

The air is absent of its cold sting. Ophelia peers at the trees as they trek through the snow, which is seeming wetter, heavier. A few chunks from the branches above drop at their feet. But moons aside, her focus must be singular now.

They follow a whirl of dust and starlight on the cloudless night that's painted with streaks of amber and green—and purple, like the color of Kier's lips when she left him.

Don't think of it.

Soon, rising before them up a small hill is the monolithic lumen tree she sensed on her first ride though Ghastly's gates. Its limbs are thrown out like its entire reason for being is to shine amidst the dark. Waiting at the base of several stepstones that lead to the lumen is her great, white wolven. He bays when he sees her, giving her side an eager nudge.

"Dirigo." Scratching his neck, she agrees, "It's time." After savoring a long breath and the feel of his thick fur, she faces Mathias. "Maybe you should stand back. I'm not sure what will happen when I use the dagger."

He gives her room as she mounts the stepstones and follows the pulsing energy of the tree. Amid the glowing spindles, the ridges on her arm mirror the lumen's light. As the Shadow marking protests with a pricking chill down her arm, she greets the tree and thinks, *Yes. A fitting place to exorcise one's demons.*

Kneeling before the lumen, between bulging roots, she takes another full breath, then extracts the Dark Shadow Dagger and takes a moment more to acclimate to its thrumming energy.

A desperate ache jabs along the tether. Maybe even from his chambers, Kier knows what is coming.

She can't think of him and do this, so she thinks of after. What she wants when this is all over, if she can change Cleo's vision and she lives: A vast horizon, a calm blue sea, shores bright with ships and trade and peace, and the scent of leather and brine in the air as strong arms slip around her waist and she feels the soft scruff of Falcon's cheek on hers.

Ophelia turns the ancient dagger around, letting the inky tip of a relic forged in deceit slowly press to her skin.

Darkness sings out of her from where it pierces.

Like an echo, a shower of lumen light rushes down the tree, limbs to roots, cascading like a waterfall around her and bathing her in warmth.

It's nothing like her nightmare, where she felt the sear of her magic under her own hand just before her light exploded, when she worried it meant she wanted to end it all. It was never death she craved, however deserving she might be. It was about the peril of the power Ophelia ached to tame. Power Kier hoped to amplify and take for his own through a *viclumeni* bond.

I am no one's pawn.

Pressing down with the dagger, Ophelia stifles a cry as it parts the skin over her heart. She bites against the sting that comes with every inch she drags the dagger up her shoulder, then down her arm. When she's done, she holds the relic out before her, meeting the eyes of the runes on its hilt, and frees a single commanding thought: *"Take the Shadow home."*

The pull is violent, wrenching, as the dagger answers her call and darkness leaches from her chest. From the nooks of her bones, from the blood in her veins, the shadow breaks through skin with a force so chilling, a scream rips from her lungs and she braces against a root to grip the relic with all her strength.

Mere pain would be a mercy.

This is hell. A hell echoed in the scream of her name across the tether. *"Ophelia!"*

But tendril by tendril, the Shadow extricates. She struggles to keep hold of the relic as the darkness rips itself from her and tunnels into the blade. And then she can't tell whose cry is whose, as every last icy claw the Shadow has on her magic and mind retracts.

With her own name reverberating in Kier's angry cry, the past few weeks streak through her mind in flashes of smirks and glares, break-fasts and training, chess games and power struggles...and pain.

She can feel the moment the bridge between them cracks.

Her mind is pierced with a guttural scream—Kier's scream. It's agonizing and seems to go on forever, and ever, and ever, until she might die in the shadow of his hurt.

When the tether snaps, the cry is swallowed. But the mercy is short, as everything goes dark.

Ophelia falls to her hands like a hollow shell, a terrifying void blanketing her mind and rendering her that ravaged ship she became after Wythe. This time, she has no anchor and sees no shore.

Vaguely, a call. "Kososten?"

But she's lost, her own breaths hard and rough in her ears as she seeks a steadying landmark. A true north.

And then she's not alone. There's a glimmer of light, like sun on rippling water, and a swath of heat at her back as, in her mind's eye, someone comes around. His face fades slowly into her view, bearing a heart-wrenching white scar that speaks of his heart and courage, and a smatter of stubble below crushing blue eyes that have seen their share of horror.

"Told you I'd find you," Falcon says. His voice echoes in the fringes of her mind, and a sob of relief shudders through her. She can hear him will her, "Now come find me, Teacup. Open your eyes."

Open your eyes.

Heat floods to the places where the Shadow was burrowed. When she blinks, the darkness is gone, the last tendrils of mist slipping into the Dark Shadow Dagger lying at her knees.

Cold be damned, she searches the skin under her cloak and finds the Shadow marking gone, replaced by long, raised threads that climb up her arm and shoulder, stopping shy of a faint, dark scar that resembles half a heart near her collarbone.

Scars are a good reminder... Of what we're willing to die for.

She'd die for freedom, for true love, for friends who are her family, though she has no intention of resigning herself to Cleo's vision.

The scar is also a reminder that betraying Kier is bound to come with some consequence, not the least of which is that Ophelia will never be the same person. But maybe that's good.

Tipping her head back, gathering the cold night air into her lungs like a blanket, she peers past the lumen tree and the vast, dark canopy above to savor the hope that beats like a pair of golden wings inside her. *Her*—the Matterist queen, the daughter of Elora, the goddess of light.

She's regaining her center when the dust that has been hovering suddenly perks and dives. A sheet of particles sails down through the canopy to circle the lumen, just as a powerful shot of magic turns Ophelia's head.

A deep voice booms, "Lia!" His boots already mount the stepstones.

"Hart."

She grabs the dagger to sheath it and has to brace herself as *maether* with the strength of a new god gales through her. A swift, grounding power as pure and strong and unshakable as the mountains that shelter Ghastly—a power she can feel because god calls to god.

Hart's tall frame fills her view, somehow bigger and broader than before. The gold in his light lines shines from under his collared cloak. Looking at him is like marveling at the fabric of the universe, there's so much to discover and she can now, somehow, see into the depths of him. At once, her soul recognizes who he's been all along—a creator, a molder, a transformer. Both a Shifter and Fabricater, like the Morphist goddess he descends from.

Like Ophelia is to the Matterists, like Kier is to the Witchists, Hart is now the last living Descendant of his guild. It was a possibility that never crossed her mind. A sight she never would have wagered she'd see.

Taking Hart's offered hand to stand, she shakes her head in awe. It makes sense now that the moons would notice this shift.

"Don't look at me like that," he commands, surly as ever.

"Like what?"

"Like you told me so."

Stepping over roots, she bites the smile he manages to draw. "I would never."

A throat clears below. "Majesties, time is of the essence."

Ophelia turns. Waiting at the bottom of the stepstones, Saira is cloaked in black, like the widow in mourning she has been all along.

Just behind her, Ophelia's relieved to see Hannah and Isolde, dressed for the coming journey and carrying bags.

Isolde looks pink-faced under her heavy furs, her pert features cast moonward, her fingers teasing the element she's so attuned to. "The air is turning," she mutters.

Ophelia's more concerned with what's next—getting out of the Lost Lands.

Five allies now, and it will have to be enough.

Dirigo paces in front of her. With a whimper, he nudges her side before bolting down the stepstones. At the same moment, Ophelia catches a faint prick of magic on her neck that whips her gaze into the trees. After a cautious scan, she finds nothing that doesn't belong. Perhaps she's feeling her allies, only it's hard to tell alongside Hart's overwhelming energy.

When the strange vibration persists, she asks aloud, "Do you feel that?"

"Feel what?" he asks, but she's already descending the stepstones, casting another look around as Hannah comes to meet her.

"My lady." The woman nods, motioning to the bags in tow. "We brought the things you asked for—all the personal effects from your chamber."

"Thank you." Ophelia squeezes her hand, letting a moment of warmth—a moment of home—fill her. She couldn't be more grateful to have the woman who raised her mother here for the next part of the journey.

But Hannah's presence doesn't banish her unease. "Do you feel that?" she asks again. "It feels like shadow magic." She turns to Saira. "It can't be Kier? The poison...worked."

Saira's gaze tenses as she surveys the woods. "It's not him, but others bear the mark of his power." She looks sharply at Ophelia. "If you're to seek the amulet, we must open a new passage swiftly."

They fold in the direction of Ghastly's gates, the mirage that Kier's soldiers always use to passage between the Lost Lands and the Underbelly.

Only, the Belly is not their destination.

"We'll use the mirage's energy to open a second passage, just inside the gates," Saira tells her and Hart. "I'll get you as close to the icelands as possible."

"You're sure you can handle things here?" Ophelia asks.

"I'll have to. Someone will need to steer the Council of Guilds when they receive the missive Lokin prepared."

"That will be enough evidence?" Hart asks.

Saira considers him. "Enough that they'll order Kier imprisoned while they investigate. Though even imprisoned"—she glances at Ophelia—"my son will need help seeing reason."

"You think he's capable of seeing reason?" Ophelia hates to imagine his fury, or consider whether the words she spoke to him before leaving his room will have any effect.

Maybe this is too risky—both her and Hart leaving Ghastly. How can Saira and the council alone contend with Kier? Yet...Ophelia must go to Kúzlo. The fate of their world depends on her bringing the relics together. And she can't fathom going without Hart.

Saira looks grimly at her. "I will do my best to give you a few days."

The closed iron gates loom into view then, and Ophelia stiffens, her skin filling with goosebumps. It's too quiet.

"There are no guards," she mutters. Given added security and legion presence for the coronation, they expected they'd have to deal with a few.

"Quickly," Saira says, then she and Hannah slip through the mirage. For efficiency and strength, they'll open the passage together.

Hovering just off the road, Isolde makes certain extra furs are tied tightly to their bags for the journey. And while Hart and Mathias talk of drecora and getting into Kúzlo, Ophelia paces a short distance on the long, long road that dips and winds all the way to the palace.

The trees rise on either side of her like dark sentries, obscuring her view into the woods they just left. Glancing upward, she notes with pervading unease that the dust is gathering thickly above the woods across the road.

"What do you see?"

She fastens her vigilance to the horizon. With Kier's relic in her possession, perhaps she's more attuned, but she can't shake the feeling of shadows. That something is watching.

She wills a handful of particles to descend and fill her palm, same as she did in the Glow Woods with Hart. With the touch, her mind's eye shoots above the woods and she can feel what the particles do—the silky nip of the wind, the veil of the moonslight.

From the higher vantage, she scans.

Wind rustles the dark foliage and small creatures rove under, but nothing shaped like people move. And yet, *maether* goads.

"My lady!" Hannah calls. Ophelia's vision snaps to the ground, the particles in her palm scattering, to find the woman ducking through the gates, signaling. "The passage is nearly ready!"

But that strange niggle begs her attention.

With the gates still at her back and the dark sea and palace before her in the distance, Ophelia shuts everything out to isolate the hum of shadow she has come to know until she pinpoints the pulsing *maether*.

It's in the woods.

There's something—

In the split second she reaches for her magic, silhouettes spring up in the dark, Dirigo howls, and a cracking gunfire explodes.

CHAPTER 60
BLOOD & SNAKES

GHASTLY, THE LOST LANDS
23RD NIGHT IN THE NEW WINTER
OPHELIA IS WITH HER ALLIES

Too fast, there comes a sickening thuck of bullets landing marks. At the force of something swiping her shoulder, Ophelia staggers back and stumbles to a knee as claws of pain sear across her arm.

Someone is shouting. In the melee of smoking gunfire, Mathias careens toward Isolde who lies prone just off the road but is lifting her head.

"Lia!" Hart's shout is swallowed by another burst of shots from across the road, and as bullets whir by, she sees him fall—or roll—in the opposite direction down a sloping embankment.

No. No no no no no no no.

Ophelia lurches up after him, but another round of shots veers her sideways. Catching herself before falling, she scrambles, vision tunneling on a slight female form that lies still.

Time slows at the sight of Hannah, unmoving.

With adrenaline powering Ophelia toward the gates, she lands at the woman's side. Hannah's silvery hair has come undone from its clasp and covers half her face. Ophelia moves it away and is met with umber eyes seized with shock. A gasp is frozen on Hannah's face, and a gaping, bleeding hole has tunneled straight through her throat.

Ophelia's heart beats too fast for reason.

Willing light to spark on her palms, she presses them against the wound, commanding it closed. Forcing it. But Hannah's eyes stay stubbornly vacant, the woman limp in her hands, her skin already losing its luster.

It's too late.

It's too late.

The horrible, unconscionable notion is a bomb going off inside her—paralyzing, crippling. It's a full moment of distantly hearing muffled shouts and shots before she can fathom this is real. It's only when Hannah's skin begins to ash and someone screams Ophelia's name that she can summon a clear thought. If *rage* is even a thought.

Swallowing everything else down, she faces the woods just as Hart leaps to his feet from where he's rolled, his eyes flashing in the dark.

"Lia!" he shouts in warning. Light flares inside her, but he's already throwing out a hand, acting on some new instinct of his own.

Sheer force sings past them both toward their attackers, and a sea of bullets aiming straight for them slows mid-air. The pointed metal spheres glistening with *migth* instantly melt, then drip to the road.

She meets Hart's eye for a fraction of a second before a whoosh of heat spears her focus to the woods. A funnel of flame spirals for them.

The dust is a vortex above and inside her, and she no longer fears it. She doesn't push it away like she did on the cold Ravish washroom floor weeks ago. Instead, she welcomes it, grasping each speck of *maether* she can sense.

Then she explodes.

Fed by every thread of light on the dust, the raw magic within her charges forward and her feral golden lightdragon roars awake. Scorching magic lightnings skyward, and its wings balloon in a vicious display as a shield blades down from her snarling beast to form a dome that drips protective magic, blanketing her friends.

Under the shield's crushing weight, Ophelia quavers while peering through the brilliant orb to seek the faces of those who've come for them.

It should be no surprise to see the legion's severe black uniforms, or the unmistakable, arrogant general who wields a wild, seething look from where he commands the attack inside the dark woods. Still, the sight of Jasper Salt shocks her.

He knows, she realizes. *He knows what I've done to Kier and that I have his relic. He's been watching me all night.*

"Kososten!" the general barks beyond the veil of her shield. "You are still a clever little fugitive. But I must insist you relinquish the dagger, or I will fill this wood with a hundred more Shadow-marked soldiers able to draw from the power of their king!"

"Never!" she shouts at him.

"Pity," he calls back, then nods to a soldier at his side, a female Bender toying with a flame on her fingers. Ophelia braces when she sees the general stir a gale of wind to feed the fire—fire that blazes wildly in her direction from the Bender's cupped hands.

Mercifully, her shield holds against the surge, but she can't count how many legion soldiers Salt has brought—some wielding guns, some advancing to draw on their affinities.

He's come not to threaten, but to maim or kill. What was it Kier said about Salt? *Jas was all I had of her. Embers to my hatred.*

Embers.

Salt was the one who became someone else—"Captain Rivmere"—to infiltrate the Special Army. He killed Knight Commander Jory Dagon, knowing the blow that murdering the kingsguard would deliver to Osiris Lestat. Salt let Grimm be seized and murdered. He oversaw the torture of her best friend, then had the audacity to smirk at her in Vils before taking Kier *out for a drink.*

Salt's scruples tick through her as she strains against the flames. In that suspended split-second, she's struck by the likely truth. While Kier has been manipulating her, Salt has been doing the same to the dark king. Inciting him. Coaxing him. Steering him to vengeance.

While she watched the Darkwielder, Salt watched her. By incapacitating Kier, she didn't just stoke the embers—she lit the flames.

Salt's assault of fire sizzles against her shield, her light flickering with every lance, her arms shaking.

Isolde and Mathias join her and Hart on the road. While her shield blocks the onslaught, it allows her allies time to mount a defense. As

Mathias sparks fire in his palms, Isolde draws wind to feed it, and they launch an echoing inferno at the legion.

Ophelia grits to keep that golden lightdragon aloft, letting its pure power thrum through her and back out as she calls deeper into her well, when a *wheesh* of energy unleashes behind her near Ghastly's iron gates.

She wrenches her gaze in their direction, her shoulder throbbing at the stretch. With profound relief, she sees a rippling burst of energy.

"The passage!" Ophelia shouts out to her allies. "Go! Now!"

She can see their hesitation, but finally Mathias takes Isolde's hand and they flee. It's only then Ophelia realizes she doesn't see Hart. That she hasn't heard a thing from him.

For a long, panicked moment, there's only the legion's assault and her flickering shield—the knowledge that breaking the tether, casting this barrier, and whatever wound she's suffered is starting to sap her. But she refuses to stop. She can still end this. She has Kier's relic and she can feel what her light could yet do, even without an amplifier as dangerous as the dagger.

Salt counted on surprising them here, and maybe also counted on her surrendering to avoid a fight, as she did in Vils when she let him walk away with only a singed boot. He is so arrogant and cocky, he doesn't think she will kill them.

The idea spurs her to throw more power behind her shield.

Maybe he and Kier had a laugh about her empathy. Her guilt, her nightmares. Poor little goddess, afraid to wield real power. Afraid to put her enemies' heads on pikes.

A command is on the edge of her lips as she finds Salt's face in those dark woods again.

I can live with his death, she tells herself. *I can bear it. It doesn't matter he was a boy whose mother was murdered. I can end him... I can... I...*

"Ughhh!" She heaves a scream of frustration at herself straight into the woods with such force that her shield flares outward and shouts of surprise ring as her attackers scurry back.

She can't kill soldiers she will need to fight Osiris's army when the time comes. Soldiers doing what they think they must because they've never been shown another way.

There are too many rulers with little regard for life. Too many who mistake mercy for weakness, when it takes every ounce of courage and strength in her to hold back the power that roars for release.

She digs for the faith still inside her—the belief there are different means to the end.

Then show them, she can hear Falcon bark, a challenging brow perking at her. *Show them a different way.*

Catching sight of three soldiers in a cluster who fire at her shield, Ophelia sucks a breath, then calls upon a level of magic she's not touched since the day she surfaced out of reset with Hart, when she misfired and made objects disappear.

Words aren't enough with this power. Intent is everything. One unspoken motivation means death for them all.

She visualizes the guns—only the guns—with their copper barrels and shimmering bullets fed by a pure source of magic. Tugging on the intricate threads of her power, she commands, *Make the weapons disappear.*

Gunfire fades, all at once, and instead of bullets, gasps reverberate in the woods. With simmering triumph, Ophelia imagines the shock of soldiers wielding weapons that vanish from their grasp. A tide of relief swells when her shield lightens, but she can only count on one breath before the legion turns to casting and wielding magic.

With a whip of a glance, she checks on her allies. Mathias and Isolde hover near the gates. And Hart? She finally sees the shape of him, crouched off to the side.

"Hart!" Is he hurt?

His eyes draw to hers just as she notices the lines on his neck spark gold. With a nod, he lifts an elbow up. Then, as if the road isn't made of gravel, he slams his fist straight to the ground.

The earth trembles under her feet.

As a shower of fire and ice and shadows batter her shield, Hart splays his palm flat to the road and his intent becomes clear. The trees beyond the shield wrench up like plucked dandelions, the earth heaving beneath them, and those shadowy sentinels fall sideways with the opening of a shallow crevice between them and Salt's unit.

Hart is fabricating a moat. Cutting off the legion.

From the distance, a snapping growl cuts to her ears. She knows Dirigo's rumbles instantly—can feel the clash of the wolven's teeth as he fights someone.

He is on the other side.

As the ground separates and a barrier mound thrice her height rises near it on the legion side, she scans for her wolven, who rips out an agonized cry.

For a moment, fear climbs her spine. Then, a flash of white as he leaps down the barrier to scale the widening crevice Hart is fabricating between road and forest.

The barrage of magic against her shield slowly ceases, and when it stops altogether, her shoulders sag and she finally allows the shield to flicker out. Leaning forward, straining for breath, her muscles shake like pudding and her head floats, light as air.

In the wake of a battle she didn't expect, Dirigo sprints toward her, clutching a claw-shaped object between his teeth. A hand, she realizes, as he drops it at her feet. Her stomach sours when she sees the black polish on the pinky finger.

Dirigo took Salt's hand.

Her lips part, her head shaking as she catches a breath. "I know a smugger who would like you."

Then, under a sky tipped with those ultra-bright gray moons, the air feeling oddly warmer, vertigo takes hold.

"Lia." Hart jogs to her, magic humming about him. His eyes are full of murder as he sweeps a last vicious look in the direction of the woods where Salt had stood. "*Snake*," he spits, and Ophelia imagines how personal this must be for him. He was at the side of "Captain Rivmere" for years in the Special Army.

Hart allows her to lean against him. Pain spindles from her shoulder down her chest and arm, and she sucks a hissing breath against it.

Inspecting her, his gaze laces with concern. "Your shoulder."

She dares to look. Her cloak is shorn just above her clavicle, where she bleeds. A bullet must have grazed muscle. "It didn't hit bone. I'm fine. We have to go."

But grief stabs once more as Ophelia's attention meets the empty cloak and dress that lie on the ground, where she had to leave Hannah. All that remains are ash, a metallic fragment, and the woman's rubied sleeve cuffs.

Gone are the twinkling eyes, the pert smile, the silvery hair—and any other remnants of the woman who drew Ophelia a bath that first night, who tucked her in bed and healed the welts on her neck that Rune left, who safeguarded the knowledge of Ophelia's past like a precious gift she had been waiting to give Elora's daughter.

Ophelia will remember Hannah's kindness. Her selflessness and love. She will not let Hannah's death be in vain. In her honor, she retrieves the sleeve cuffs, rubbing a thumb over a ruby, then stows them gingerly next to the Dark Shadow Dagger.

Hart takes her elbow and they rush toward the gates where she can feel the new passage Saira hid just on the other side of the mirage, so that the moment they step into the Belly, they'll find themselves in the North. It roars through her with urgency, and she's relieved to see the queen-mother popping through the gates to meet Isolde and Mathias.

But Ophelia frowns at them. "Why are you still here? You should have gone!"

"We stay with our queen," Mathias replies firmly.

Isolde holds a hand to her mouth, covering a sob.

Reaching to squeeze the girl's shoulder, Ophelia looks between her allies, feeling the determination of her mission return. "We lose no one else."

"No one else," they agree.

Ophelia half-steps inside the mirage to glimpse the passage where the North unfolds in a prism of winter and the next phase of their plan awaits. Where Falcon awaits.

Her heart sings at the thought.

"Go!" A breathy voice on the wind—or in her mind.

Ophelia whips her gaze to the sky, the breeze through the gates lifting her hair off her shoulders.

"Kososten!" This time it's Saira, shouting above the din. "The passage will hold for two trips through! Go before the legion breaches that divide!"

Turning to take Hart's hand, Ophelia finds him distracted, his stoic focus diverted toward the moat he's made. The way he studies his hand, flexes it, it must be sinking in what he's capable of.

"Hart," she prods.

"I can't leave with you," he replies.

Ophelia stills, unsure she heard him right over the roar at the gates.

He looks at her. "I need to stay at Ghastly."

"Hart—"

"Willow's in the Belly under legion watch," he says, as if he's processing his decision aloud. "She's safe enough within those walls for now, but only so long as someone's here to keep the Darkwielder's forces in check. Someone to provide physical proof to the Council of Guilds that he imprisoned the Morphist Descendant."

She opens her mouth to protest, when Saira cuts in, "He's right. The missive that went to the guilds is paper. Having the new Morphist king at the council's table will ensure a more thoughtful approach to this war." Ophelia can see the woman's mind turning, as if ideas are already forming about next steps.

Ophelia can recognize how it would keep the mortals safe. How it would buy her time to get to Kúzlo and find Falcon, her amulet, and the last relic—the lightstone.

But *dammit.*

As if Hart can read her face after all these years, he steps beside her. "It all hinges on you bringing the relics together. Before they're destroyed, we might need their power to end the war. And Salt cannot be allowed to do *this.*" With a sneer, he casts a glance at Hannah's remains, then back. "I have the power now. It's time I embraced it."

On an exhale, she studies him as Dirigo prowls anxiously around her. "I just found you and it's already goodbye?"

A suffering sigh. "Not goodbye, not forever. But we all have our parts to play."

Ophelia bites her lip, thinking of Falcon and hating that Hart is right.

"Kososten!" Saira urges.

Ophelia nods, then launches herself at Hart, shoulder be damned. In the warmth of his neck, she says, "I hate us all being apart. Someday we go together through one of these things. Promise me."

He pulls back. "We crush the monarchy, then we go anywhere we like."

"Somewhere there are strawberry cakes."

"Strawberry cakes," Hart echoes with a smile.

She nods, then another for Saira. "Go," she tells them, though her stomach tightens when they do, when the Morphist king follows Saira into the dark wood, away from the direction of danger.

Trust means letting go. Moving forward. Doing what she was born to do.

I am the light.

Brushing a hand against the shape of the onyx blade buried in her cloak, the weight of the next part of her quest settles over her as she stands at the gates, feeling the pull just beyond.

She motions Dirigo to lead Isolde through first.

The brightened moons shining in Mathias's eyes, he says, "Our turn, Kososten."

Teetering on the edge of the mirage, she replies, "You really have to stop calling me—"

Shrill whispers of alarm cut clear as starlight in quick succession—voices that come from dust, ringing familiar as they scream:

"Ophelia!"

"Goddess!"

"No!"

Then a crack echoes in the night. A second, and a third. Something bites her back at the shoulder blade, siphoning her breath.

One more.

Searing pain makes her vision swim, and she staggers, turning toward the source of the gunfire.

Jasper Salt stands on the barrier Hart's magic made with an arm tourniquetted above the wrist and a sneer etched on his mouth, holding a pistol aloft in his remaining hand.

Before he can fire another shot, Mathias's weight falls slack against her. Time slows as the pair plunge through the mirage into the mouth of the snapping passage, where Ophelia is swallowed by a spinning haze of winter light and crimson blood.

CHAPTER 61
STORMS & FATE

F ate is cruel.

As Falcon enters the arena from the tunnels, he's struck by the changing sky—the frost-bitten faces and venerable hum of the triple moons. Spinning the sword in his hand, he thinks how the gods have a shit sense of humor.

It's not enough that fate whittled eight heirs down to two tonight and it's him and Kessan in the final match of the tournament. Now, the moons.

Under their glare, the sky veins with rare lightning.

Shrieks follow the crack as a massive silhouette with sleek white wings soars, unsettled, in a circle over the stadium. Rakúa ought to be perched on the eastern lip of the colosseum where Kessan's banner waves, but she's agitated. Falcon can empathize. The lightning's a current in his Animater blood, riling him up. With his lightsword in hand, every synapse inside him thrums like the steel could channel the storm straight through to his soul.

Another bolt, bright and eerie, crackles its spindly knuckles.

Falcon eyes the sky with suspicion. If the original gods are watching, he wonders what they're up to, why the hell the crimson moon looks suddenly dull and small beside the others. He's taking a long taste of the night air that doesn't smell like snow, but the promise of rain and a faint tinge of thaw, when a wet sleet starts down, slapping his bare chest.

At least he runs hot.

To Trix's irritation, he left his shirt in the heirs' hold in favor of having quick access to the weapons in his skin sheath. Now the moons are a siren's call on his ink. The way it writhes, Falcon has a hunter's sense there's more going on than Snow Moons.

Something's shifting again.

His first thought is of Ophelia and what's happening at Ghastly, which only conjures her face and brings a swift, punching ache to his heart.

"*Jagerin! Jagerin!*" His focus snaps back to the moniker the crowds levy at him. Despite the storm, there are thousands of Kúzloans packed in the stands and their chant catches fast. By the time Falcon reaches center arena, half the stadium echoes it.

Yet, dread fills him. In the final match, the heirs who used to beat Kessan as kids will watch from the hold as the one brother who got banished for giving a shit has to strike the favored down. It makes him sick, but there are only two things that could stop it: Kessan changing his mind about helping him, or the gods intervening.

Neither is likely.

His brother stands with his back to Falcon inside the bounds of the fight circle. Twenty by twenty feet or so, its outline is well marked by the scorch of flames from the previous battles.

When Kessan turns, he's wearing leathers and wielding a billhook in one tight fist. In the other, a sickle with a long metal chain and weighted spike, still bloodied from his fight against Serinna. That's northern superstition for you. Warriors on a winning streak never clean their weapon.

Falcon's chest glows silver, beckoning him to take a second blade. He thinks of New York—the heat, the stench of those alleys, and Ophelia all riled up. "Don't call me Teacup," she said, and he loved it.

He chooses a sword he's lent her before, swinging it up against his left shoulder and back down, letting light sing to life in it. Repeating the motion with the opposite blade, he relishes how the strength of the steel courses through him.

The crowd's volume—their hunger—is a mirror of the moon's energy as he and Kessan circle one another. Falcon can see a flicker of Kessan's own irritation with their fate, and a sliver of reluctance. But it doesn't matter now, not with what stands between them: fifteen years of resentment and the same unwavering goal to win.

Still, as the tournament master waits for Rakúa to perch, as is tradition, he can't help trying one more time. Over the crack of lighting, he bites out, "You sure about this, Kess?"

Kessan scowls, then rotates his wrist to send his chain with the spike spinning in a vicious warm-up, its wide reach driving Falcon back a few steps.

Falcon's nostrils flare like their own weapons. "How the hell did we get here?" he calls, and Kessan's gaze pins him with a warning that says they are not going to talk here. That chain splits the air as it whirls. Still, Falcon presses. "The crown has some shit on you, don't they?"

A flash of those mirror-blue eyes, Kessan's whip circling faster.

"What was in the Virstone, Kess?"

His brother seethes as if he's about to lunge, but lightning cracks an egg in the sky and a fit of rain slaps in earnest. In Falcon's periphery, fabrics raise over heads in the crowd. Almost instantly, the ground under his feet grows slick.

He shouts above a gale of tepid wind, "Everything I told you at the Virstone was true! You see the damn moons? Just tell me what's going on, and I can help! It's not too late!"

For a flicker, doubt seems to seed in Kessan's eyes as he briefly glances to the sky, his hand lowering a fraction with his weapon. Water drips from his braided, bunned hair. Then Rakúa, dipping below the veins of lightning, breaks the moment, at last choosing a perch. It's not on Falcon's bannerless side, but not on Kessan's, either. To their surprise, she makes her own on the roof of the colosseum, her talons crumbling rock down to a few alarmed yelps in the crowd below.

She's perched above the *volorost*'s empty seat, right in the middle of the arena.

Quick as the storm, any moment between brothers is gone.

The scale around Falcon's neck plumes warmth into his chest, funneling it down his arms and legs to ease the sting of the sleet. A gift. And by the way Kessan takes a full, savoring breath, his chest expanding under his leather armor, he's being treated to some encouragement from Rakúa, too.

So, she won't take sides.

Like the ironspade heard his thought, Rakúa bows her impressive head and frees a shriek that makes Falcon's ears sing. With that, the tournament master takes a step between the heirs, grunting at them to clang their weapons.

Kessan angles his billhook forward without a word, not deigning to answer Falcon's earlier pleas.

Rain slaps in the pause.

"All right, then," he mutters, letting his sword fall against the billhook. "At least tap out if it comes to it, will you? Sei braven, nast ruchsi."

Daring, not dumb.

Kessan blinks, his hand tightening on his weapon. For a fleeting second, Falcon sees the boy who used to beg his help with bullies. But as the crowd beckons for blood and the sky demands nothing less, Kessan turns away to face the stadium where his name's gaining fervor above Falcon's. But he doesn't seem to bask in the admiration. As Falcon noticed earlier, it's more like he's looking to someone.

"Nast," he finally answers Falcon. "There will be no surrender, even if I wished it." He looks at him. "My blood has made its oath."

Falcon's knuckles tighten on his lightsword as the sleet pelts, and he struggles to swallow his brother's words down. This truth isn't something he wanted to know, and he pushes it away with a shake of his head.

A blood oath means his brother is in deeper than his pride. That it has nothing to do with the past yawning a divide between them, but that Kessan is compelled.

Falcon knew he'd made a deal, but a blood oath? Oaths are till death unless they're broken through a loophole. And without knowing the words spoken when the oath was sealed, Falcon can't help. He's been barking up the wrong tree.

Vaguely, he hears the tournament master take up the ceremonial weapons—the bone staff and mallet. But his fury searches the stands for silver armor and the prince that the Gray King has made a symbol of oppression.

Falcon doesn't spot Rune. He does see a ripple of movement in the rows above, and with that, he almost drops his lightsword.

In the *volorost*'s section, where wives and betrothed hold rain shields as they rise to their feet, a sacred white chair is hoisted and being carried by two warriors toward the spot reserved for the high lord of the North.

Sideways sleet pricks Falcon's skin like talons.

Ryke has come. Their father's finally here, and Rune Ethera walks beside him.

F alcon harbors no love for Ryke Aksander.

The high lord had been all too willing to believe Kessan in order to please the council, and Falcon's last memory was of his father's remorseless expression as Evangeline Aksander took her twins out the gates with little to their name.

Falcon can't make out the face he inherited from the man, only the *volorost*'s thin frame and the suggestion of a spellstaff Ryke appears to be trying to raise.

One of the warriors has to help him do it.

Like a thunderhead, it hits Falcon why the Sanctioning was moved up. Reya was right. His father isn't well. In fact, Falcon would bet the council's been saving up his energy just for tonight.

What did Kessan say? *After tonight, there will be a new high lord of the North.*

So, Ryke isn't here to watch his successor named. He's here to pass his title to one of his sons and watch the other die. Cleo's vision suggests it won't be Falcon, but that might be a fate as cruel, because it means he has to kill Kessan, just like he feared.

A rumble tremors the sky as the storm flashes hot, the hum of the moons deepening.

He'll count his brother's death among his sins, the way he counts his knives—every day until he becomes ash in the wind himself. But there are things you die for, and things you kill for. He will take lives—even his brother's—to be sure it isn't the goddess of light who goes to the moons in the end.

With a last glance at his father's shape in that white chair, Falcon swings his gaze to the tournament master as the warrior raises his bone staff and mallet, then slashes them down. "Kamfe!" the warrior shouts. *Fight!*

Despite the sleet, fire flares up from the boundaries of the fight circle, creating a barrier. A second of remorse passes between brothers, then Falcon charges.

He's got one opening before Kessan gets that chain going, and he doesn't waste it. His swords flash with light and, as he slashes across his torso with his left blade aimed at Kessan's billhook, his right starts an arc for the whip his brother holds.

Kessan blocks with the handle, but Falcon rips the billhook from his grasp with ease.

Before Kessan can retaliate, he whirls with a speed he's honed well. Nimble, agile, he dances around his brother at the edge of the amber fires. Spinning back, raising his swords up, Falcon has an opening to swing them down. In a flash of lightning, he can see the move play out in his mind—the silver glint of his blades as they arc on either side of Kessan's head to slash cleanly down, taking his brother's life and his blood oath. He can see his own likeness in Kessan's face—see his past—fall with a thud like a tree lopped off its stump.

Do it fast. No pain. No torture. Kill him with mercy. Kill him quick.

The stadium splits with a deafening roar of anticipation, but before his blades lash, a stab pokes Falcon's brain that he is not prepared for.

"Miss your mark."

His swords jerk to the side as if his body's not his own, his arms leaden against the quicksand grip of an Enchanter's hold. A hold that should be impossible if there are wards around the arena. A hold he fucking recognizes as another command comes, before he has a chance to fight it.

"Take his blow."

Rune. It's Rune, who sits beside Ryke.

The tournament's supposed to be guarded against outside interference. If the Enchanter can breach the *migth* fire around the fight circle, someone allowed it.

With Falcon's hesitation, before he can thrust up walls of iron and ice to shield his mind the way his mentor, Yuli, once taught him, Kessan draws closer amid the blaze, circling his whip like a propeller.

Their eyes meet again—Falcon's maddened stare flush with Kessan's look of...regret. *Cheats!* Falcon thinks.

"You know...what the prince...is doing," Falcon grits as he fights the hold.

Iron. Ice. Iron. Ice.

He's been less than honorable in his life at card tables, but apart from a couple escapades, his deception was for the good of spreading Crat wealth to struggling folks and taking care of his niece. Few men get executed over poker, but politics?

He watches Kessan's whip spin and is so close to freeing his mind as the crowd thunders for its victor, as his moniker blades on the wind—*"Jagerin!"*

"Aghhh!" he growls, feeling the snap of the hold just as Kessan's whip lashes down, its weighted spike singing against Falcon's head.

Warmth.

Heat spears through his skull, pulsing in the scale on his neck. Rain and blood roll down his face as he staggers to a knee.

No, he pleas as the world spins. *It doesn't end like this. I get the North. I win... I...* Unless something cataclysmic has happened to shift the vision. Something they weren't counting on.

"No," he grits. He doesn't die tonight. He walks out of here with Ryke's gifts, sway over the council, a connection with the drecora, and the North in his goddamn hands to give Ophelia.

I don't fucking die, not here.

Falcon lurches to his feet as Kessan stalks the circle around him. Keeping a healthy distance, his brother's profile is outlined in the lap of the *migth* fire. A knell must have sounded, because Kessan has sheathed his whip and is clenching a fist, heir ring pulsing with pale-blue light as he calls a spell forth.

An echoing light throbs from Falcon's ring. As his head clears, he can feel the magic the Gatekeeper imbued—two offensive spells and one shield.

Kessan's fast. A buzzing storm unleashes from his brother's ring that brings a swarm of northern jaw-bees—teethy hornets with a venom that freezes blood to ice in a few pumps of the heart.

Fuck. With a quick call, Falcon's forced to waste his only shield straight off. A glowing globule springs up around him, and the torrent of icepick-sharp insects hits the blue hum of the shield with audible pops, cracking and exploding one by one like smattering crystals.

Northerners are on their feet in the stands, but Kessan's already calling his second spell.

A cold bucket of irony spills over Falcon when the ground under him yawns open and he's sucked into a narrow ice trap there in the center of the arena. As his feet and arms fan out for purchase, his cheekbone and one of his bare elbows scrape the sharp wall. He kicks, and when his boots catch a groove, he digs in, bracing against the sides eight feet down the fissure, before he can fall any deeper.

Kessan looms into view over the trap, a haunted look in his pale eyes. Not the look of victory Falcon might expect, but one with a modicum of conflict. He knows the years of jealousy built up in Kessan's head and the crown's influence over him, but there's got to be a shred of love buried deep for the only brother who ever cared about him.

Still Kessan reaches for his whip as if he has no choice.

Neither does Falcon.

He's wedged tight, his nose nearly pressed to the ice in front of him, but he manages to get his ring knuckle up. Manages to sharpen his thoughts enough to tap into the pulsing of his heir ring, then starts to call an offensive spell.

The ring's blue jewel glows like an eye. Falcon keeps Kessan in his sights.

Oddly, his brother's hand has gone still on his whip, his head darting suddenly up and left. Kessan's face slackens from something happening outside their battle.

Falcon hears distant voices. Someone calls, "Talvi kamfen!" to stop the match.

But the spell Falcon started calling is already coming. His heir ring flashes, then a blast of force shoots from the jewel, knocking him against the wall of the trap. He catches himself as sound flies upward like a siren, loud as the night Rakúa took his hearing, only this time it's aimed at Kessan, and Falcon is the one "safe" in the trap.

His brother wails, lumbering backward out of Falcon's sight. Distantly, more shouts. Screams.

He searches for a handhold above his head, then climbs, muscles on fire, stabbing one foot after the other up the trap until he's pulling himself over the ledge to...chaos.

In the center of the circle, Kessan's on his knees, clutching his head between his hands, contending with that siren of Falcon's spell. The arena's darkened, but with a glance up to the moons he notices a horde of winged silhouettes cluttering the sky, and more on their way, as if some great event is calling the drecora to gather.

There's only one thing Falcon can think of that would summon all hundred-and-sixty-eight—their connection to the *volorost*.

He stalks to the edge of the circle where the *migth* fire still pens him in. Rain matting his hair to his face, he spots the tournament master meet two warriors who've rushed into the arena. "Ren *volorost*!" one cries. *Our high lord!*

Falcon cups the scale on his neck in his fist. It's beating like a frantic heart. Like a warning. *"Rakúa?"*

An answering shriek tells him she's up there amid the wing and that Falcon was right—something's happening with Ryke. In a flash of lightning, he sees a swarm of northerners in the stands who've surrounded the high lord's seat, and he could swear he sees his father's form being lowered to the ground.

The match falls away.

Falcon never begged at Ryke's feet for approval. But he didn't know until now how much he wanted to look his father in the eye and show him the anger in his heart. Anger for letting Kessan be beaten, for ingraining violence in them so young that it's been a crutch Falcon's whole life, for not giving a single fuck when his first family was cast out.

He's debating how fried he'd get leaping through the *migth* fire to face Ryke when he sees a flash of the tournament master's serious expression on the other side. "Kamfe!" the warrior barks at him, and the fires surrounding the circle flash hotter—forcing him back.

The master wants them to end this, fast.

It can only mean Ryke is dying, and dying now. The North needs an heir to claim the power when Ryke goes.

Chest heaving, Falcon turns back with a pit in his stomach to find Kessan still on his knees, vulnerable. It doesn't feel right, not when he can't defend himself.

An anguished scream rips from the stadium, and another. Screams that domino and sound like death.

CHAPTER 62
WINDS & LOSSES

From the stands of the arena, a force of energy explodes like a busted dam. Falcon whips to see an avalanche of pale-blue magic tearing toward him, picking up speed and wind and sleet, dousing a trail through the *migth* fire of the fight circle in its rampage.

It slams him like a brick wall.

Back arching, he's snatched by a wave of ancient power—the *volorost*'s power—and knocked off his feet. His hand braces on the ground, and he hears a second echoing thud. As the gods-granted power possesses him, he feels like he's drowning in a supernova. Everything goes quiet in his head—so quiet.

Then come the dragon winds.

It's a hissing, primeval tongue he's only heard about secondhand from his father, long ago. The tongue of the drecora, coded in the shrieks of the wing that circles above the arena.

Their voices flood all at once:

"This is wrong."

"This is not the way."

"It is what the gods choose."

"Trust in fate."

"They will never accept it."

"There will be danger now."

"But there is hope in the North tonight. Can you feel it?"

"We must warn the wild one."

The words climb over one other, but there's more going on in Falcon's head. A glimmer of gateways and cliffs and doors rises up, and he has the innate sense they open to endless futures. Visions he wants no part of.

The Great Sight.

Ryke is dead—he's *dead*. This is his power for the claiming. One breath, and Falcon's on the precipice of it, then like a glacier struck by lightning, the power freewheeling inside him cracks and splits. The gateways, cliffs, and doors slowly vanish and what's left are the wild winds—the drecora in his head—and the scale around his neck pulsing with heat.

A scornful, raging cry rings out.

The attention of the colosseum shifts as he shoves back on his knees to find the owner of that fury. Kessan guns toward him, charging with the billhook, eyes hollow. But Falcon's quicker, lunging to catch Kessan's arm as he barrels forward. The billhook flies as the two clash and topple heavily to the ground, Kessan landing over him.

Before he can get hands around Falcon's neck, Falcon takes hold of his leather cuirass and yanks, flipping Kessan to his back. With a knee to his throat, Falcon pins him to the slushy ground, then shudders. There's no mistaking the power Kessan radiates. It's the same sharp flow of energy that courses through Falcon.

Two halves that were supposed to be whole.

Ryke's power came for them both. It knows Aksander blood. It honors tradition and can sense which heirs lost their matches and surrendered their claims. Ryke died, and his title came for a successor, but there were two remaining heirs, so now they share the title.

Falcon pants, keeping his knee in place as Kessan tries to buck up. The crowd thunders, sounding thoroughly unsatisfied that there are still two heirs left in this.

Falcon's not sure how the hell the title split, but Kessan must have the Great Sight, while he lassoed a telepathic connection to the drecora.

He did it. He got the influence on the North's army without killing his brother. His heart pumps double time. He can sense and understand the drecora. He'll be able to command the patrol.

It's almost too good to be true.

The crowd jeers on. If they don't keep fighting, they'll incite a mob. How the hell are they going to get out of the arena?

"Kess," he grates against his brother's struggle. "Enough. Enough! No one needs to die here."

"Kamfe!" he hears the tournament master shout from beyond the circle.

"Don't listen to him, Kess. Look at me. We can walk out of here together."

Kessan goes still under him. Cautiously, Falcon eases his knee back. It's a mistake. Kessan's hand, long at his side, flies up with a sharp, glinting object.

Falcon barely catches his wrist before the hidden blade Kessan worked free can meet his chest.

The crowd swells with deafening cheers.

"I must kill you," Kessan seethes, his eyes looking frosted as the moons. Falcon knows that look—the look of an Enchanter's hold.

Rune again.

Above the colosseum, the drecora shriek, their voices breaking through the noise of the crowd. There's a collective gasp as attention shifts skyward.

He's not sure how speaking to the beasts works, but he's got a scale and instincts. *"Rakúa? What's happening?"* He searches for her, but every winged beast looks black as night from this vantage.

"Rumors that she has come," intones a resonant, but vicious voice in his ears. He's never heard Rakúa speak, but innately he's sure it's her.

"Who's come?"

Kessan bucks his hips, throwing Falcon halfway off him.

The crowd seems to like that, but Falcon's got size on his side and works his knee up again, pinning his brother, seizing Kessan's glazed gaze.

"This isn't you," he grates, not risking a glance to search for Rune, but it's got to be the prince messing with Kessan's head, trying to secure his victor. "Kess," he implores, "we've been taught since we were *nakommen* how to fight enchantment—snap the hell out of it!"

It takes two hard shakes before Kessan blinks. When he takes Falcon in, his jaw goes slack. His limbs, languid. Falcon can see the realization pass over his features.

"Ryke is dead," Kessan mutters. "And we..."

"It's a goddamn plot twist, I'll give you that. Let's work it out later, huh?"

Everyone in the stands is on their feet, shaking their fists, a fresh round of, "Kamfe! Kamfe!" starting up. There's another buzzing chant, too—fainter, farther off. Falcon can't quite catch it, but it pulses on the periphery of the arena.

The zealots, maybe, out at the festival that awaits in the village, piping on about the moons.

Kessan's gone slack beneath him. His eyes stare out, white as bone. "Kess—"

A hiss between Falcon's ears cuts the question off, and overhead Rakúa flies low—too low.

"We can feel her, jagerin," the drecora roars. *"The one who will call them from the dust. She who will save the Magies and dragonkind!"*

Under his hold, Kessan mutters, "Gosten."

Falcon's seized. Taking Kessan by the arms, he shakes him, demanding, "Ophelia? You see her?"

He yanks his brother up with him to stand, as Rakúa takes another low lap over the stadium. When it sends the crowds scattering, Falcon finally realizes what she's doing—creating a diversion. Distracting the ones who call for their blood.

"Get out of the stadium," Rakúa hisses for Falcon alone. *"Find her."*

"Find who?"

But Kessan jolts in Falcon's hold, his vision clearing, and with it, traces of the arrogance and jealousy he's wielded these weeks are gone. "She is of the dragon, of our blood," he mutters. "I—I did not believe you..."

"What are you talking about, Kess?"

Kessan wipes the back of his hand over his brow. "You tried to tell me Ophelia Dannan would save the North, but I feared you only came to take it from me."

"Never," Falcon swears. "I don't want the war to come here, Kess, but it will if we try to stay out of it. Then every drecora, the sacred mountains, the *migth*, your home—it'll be gone or belong to Osiris."

"I have seen it," Kessan whispers. "Freedom. I have seen the gosten here."

All the breath whooshes out of Falcon. "You mean she's—"

The air vibrates.

The stone of the colosseum quakes under their feet.

Same as Rakúa just did, four more drecora sweep low, their crocodile jaws unhinged, shrieking an urgent song in overlapping voices as they scare the living hell out of the crowds, forcing them out of their seats, to duck, to rush toward the exits.

"Born in fire..."

"Bathed in blood..."

"She who calls the dust has come..."

Falcon lets Kessan go as a fire relights inside him, in the spot where numbness took hold a couple days ago.

Ophelia.

The drecora must sense her, and Kessan just had a vision of her. She's here. Ophelia's come back to the North.

Tearing his gaze over the half-empty stadium, he sees no wives, no betrothed, no council members. Ryke's chair is empty—his body surely ash and taken to urn. A few royal guards on the lowest level of the stadium still linger and he can imagine what they're thinking: Kessan was supposed to win.

Falcon takes Kessan's arm. "Listen to me. If you saw Ophelia, there's a good chance the zealots did, too. They'll be spreading rumors the goddess is here and Rune Ethera will be after her. We've got to find her first."

Kessan lets Falcon drag him through the circle, through the path Ryke's power paved, extinguishing some of the *migth* fire. With every step, his northern blood simmers and the warrior in Falcon returns.

He doesn't reclaim his old mantra, though, not when it feels like he's got more of a soul than he ever had before. Maybe a new one will come to him.

In the tunnels, Kessan slows his pace. "No." He shakes Falcon off. "No, you need to stay away from me. I cannot help you," Kessan warns. "I cannot disobey my oath. I am not...strong."

The light of the village pours into the tunnel ahead as Falcon squares off with his brother. "You're wrong. You made a choice to change your lot, to claw your way up and become someone they can't beat down, Kess. You made wrong turns like we all do, but you're still my fucking hero."

Kessan's eyes soften. "But I cannot disobey—"

Falcon takes the back of Kessan's head and draws his brother's forehead to his. "I can, and I will. Sei braven, Kess."

Their first mantra, made new.

When Falcon pulls back, Kessan's brows are folded, his eyes distant. Softly, he echoes, "Sei braven."

F alcon and Kessan emerge east of the colosseum on the single road that carves through the central village of the Valley of Bones.

Here, it's even clearer the moons have a shift in mind.

The night is warming. No one even wears furs. The air is tinged with the smell of melting snow, mingling with the scent of smoked meat, and northerners who weren't at the match man stalls along the street where music plays.

It's a ready celebration for the final night of the festival. There's even a dais where the successor's meant to stand and address the people.

These villagers haven't gotten the message yet that Ryke is dead.

Soon enough.

The drecora still soar over the colosseum, and the crowds start to funnel out of the main entrance as silver-armored soldiers come up along the other side of the road. Rune is right in the middle of them, protected as always, his keen eyes searching the crowd.

Fuck! If they're seen, this comes to blows. The Gray King wants one *volorost*—the one who swore a blood oath to support the crown. Hopefully the northerners come around, but Falcon's not picking a fight with "Prince Rune" tonight.

His heart pounds an incessant rhythm: *Find Ophelia.*

With Kessan at his heel and his chest still slick from sleet, Falcon veers left to keep behind the carts. He pauses at a fabric trader, motioning Kessan to slow, then rifles in his skin sheath for two silver *dunai*, old northern coins that hold their value in trading cities like Jagst.

The cart proprietor, a thin man with silver braids bound like crossing swords at the back of his head, is busy with a villager. Leaving the coins, Falcon swipes a tunic and slips it on to cover his ink.

The faint, buzzing chanting he heard in the stadium is louder here. It's the zealots. He can make out their words now, and he was right. They're spreading gossip of a goddess's return.

"Rakúa! Have you spotted her?"

"No, wild one."

With a sharp nod at Kessan, he says, "This way."

Following instincts that tug him toward the *seshen* camp and flight field, he cuts around the fanatics under pine garlands and blinking magelights that hang from the eaves of inns and small taverns.

At the center of the village, warriors are laughing into their mead mugs at ale stands, while northern children toss bone spears toward targets to win sweets. Near the end of the road, Falcon catches the faint rattle of the bone chimes where they're strung up on two posts that mark the entrance to the camp.

A few minutes' walk on a clear day.

The path is thick with bodies. There are thousands here for the tournament, in a village that normally houses a third that many. He and Kessan are weaving by ice sculptures of drecora that dew in the moonslight when Falcon picks out a familiar tenor in the crowd.

"Have you seen them anywhere?" At Reya's voice, Falcon peers around a pair of warriors. "Falcon and Kessan? Did they come out?"

At a flash of her golden braids and the marine-blue dress that matches Kessan's scale, Falcon nudges his brother, but Kessan doesn't seem to see or hear his betrothed—he's quiet, flexing his hands at his side.

Falcon cups his mouth to call Reya's attention—her enchanting could help—but to his mounting irritation, a march of zealots mars his view. They hold signs and burn incense, chanting, "Gosten! Gosten!"

A bald-headed seer leads the group, and Falcon translates the decree he makes to anyone listening: "The moons say she brings a new season upon us! She brings salvation!" The zealots tip their faces to the sky, as if the gods—through the moons—are speaking to them.

But Ophelia isn't here.

Falcon is a thread away from losing his mind—needing to get through this crowd, needing to find her—when northerners start taking notice of him and Kessan.

"It is them."

"Two?"

"The *volorost* is gone!"

Falcon shoves in the direction he saw Reya, reluctant to push too far across the road where royal soldiers still scan the crowds. But the news that they're here is spreading fast from the colosseum. As eyes fall on them, they're met with two reactions: northerners raising fists of respect to their chest, as if blindly trusting fate's decision to give them two successors, and as many or more who wear deep scowls and shout the likes of, "Nast richti!" *It's not right.* "Ren nasmi a sigen!" *We need one victor!*

Falcon cares nothing about the title right now. Something bone deep burns for Ophelia.

"Kess." He motions his brother with him toward the long, rectangular stone well that squats ahead in the square. It'll bypass some of the crowds, help them spot Reya.

Scaling the short wall, Falcon balances along the lip of stone, keeping his chin down. Past where a Bender of Flame's doing fire tricks for the crowd, he leaps to the ground and catches sight of Reya again. Just beyond her, though, is a slew of silver armor. In the middle, closer now, is Rune in that royal cape that feels like a kick to the ribs.

Soldiers congregating around the prince and his aide hold weapons they've clearly been allowed to keep. Men who bleed gray for the monarchy and probably want to see Falcon dead, before he can turn the elders against the crown.

He spins for Kessan to figure out a better path through, but his brother's fallen behind. Bodies swim between them. When Falcon finally reaches him, Kessan's staring straight ahead at the royal entourage.

"They haven't seen us yet, Kess. Come on."

Kessan winces as though a great force weighs on him. He doesn't move.

"Kess. You alright?"

Kessan shakes his head slowly, then reaches for the chain he wears on his neck, holding his sharp, blue scale in his palm as his eyes shutter. When they flash open, he yanks the scale free of its chain and crushes his hand around it.

Blood drips from Kessan's fist as the scale cracks.

"What the hell are you doing!"

Kessan doesn't look at him. "I cannot take another step. The oath will not let me betray my alliance."

"Then I'll fucking carry you!"

Falcon reaches out, but Kessan throws a hand out to keep Falcon back. "I will only try to kill you. But there is one way. A...loophole." Kessan's eyes darken deep as caverns. "I am sorry, bruden."

Letting the crushed scale fall, Kessan grabs Falcon in a hard hug to whisper in his good ear, "Take your goddess to the Virstone." Then, before Falcon can reply, Kessan shoves him hard, sending him staggering through the crowds.

As he catches his balance, confounded at the shove and Kessan's plea, the air quivers, wind gusts, and out of nowhere a roar like a mortal-world train bleats from the direction of the *seshen* camps.

An ironspade drecora sweeps down from the sky without warning. Rakúa flies so low over the road she almost skims heads. The unexpected arrival of the North's fiercest is met with screams, and the people duck as one. As she barrels toward Falcon, someone knocks him to the ground.

"Smugger!" Trix shouts as they collide. Ashë's at her side, and they're both out of breath. "We've been looking everywhere for you!"

Falcon can't deal with that right now. Rakúa is coming full tilt like she has a target, her jaws opening wide to brandish deadly, spear-sharp teeth. He's not one to freeze, but he's paralyzed with confusion. Then suspicion.

Spinning in his crouch, he sees Kessan's the only one still on his feet—in Rakúa's path.

A deep pit of fear opens in Falcon at the sight of his brother's head bowed, his expression calm as a summer lake, his arms lifting wide at his sides as if to welcome his beast.

"No!"

But while drecora respect and heed a *volorost*, they have their own wills. Foremost, they do what protects the North. Rakúa doesn't veer. There's no dragonfire, but her jaws snatch Kessan off his feet with a snap and gutting crunch of bones.

A cry that could shake the moons down screams up Falcon's throat as he vaults to his feet, seized by shock and the feeling Rakúa just clawed his heart out. Her wicked tail lashes in her wake as she pulls up, mounting the sky in a loop around the village.

"Rakúa!" His scream is a blade. *No, no, no. Fucking no!*

In that paralyzing moment, the image of what's just happened imprints on Falcon's soul. He'll relive it till the day he dies.

"Falcon!" A hand seizes his arm.

He reefs it away and rears, ready to hit something. But it's Trix. There are northerners around them rising to their feet, too, disbelief rolling through the village. And then...some cheers—*cheers*—as they must realize Falcon is the last heir standing and they have their successor.

Trix is saying something, but everything is noise and nothing's all right as a searing picture of Kessan's calm face brands itself in Falcon's mind.

His eyes catch a brown, thick fabric, falling from the sky. A sickening shred of leather. As it lands at his boot, a burst of energy slams through him, causing him to stagger into Trix. He can feel the moment the Great Sight finds him, when the gateways and cliffs and doors reappear at the edge of his mind, reuniting two halves of the *volorost* power.

Kessan is dead.

Rare tears prick his eyes at the irrevocable, stinging, hollowing truth. A minute ago, brothers made amends. A minute ago, he had hope.

Sei braven.

Falcon told him to be brave and this—*this* is what Kessan does. He finds a loophole in his blood oath to defy the crown.

In a mirror of his grief, Rakúa pierces the night with a shriek so loud half the village ducks again. Her grave voice floods Falcon's head: *"The title cannot be shared, wild one. An honorable death was Kessan's final request."*

Falcon grabs his head between his hands. *"Request? You fucking ate him!"* Kessan, the favored. Kessan, who would've succeeded Ryke if Falcon hadn't come back to Kúzlo.

A rumble of Rakúa's sorrow. *"This has been the way for centuries. Death by one's drecora is a noble end. He is no longer of the earth, but everywhere. In death, he will have his glory."*

"Fuck that!" The truth is no balm to the gut-wrenching pain of knowing Kessan did the only thing he could think of to help. Sacrificing himself, severing the alliance with the Gray King, freeing Rakúa to return to her first welded.

Falcon can feel eyes on him. "Was that what I think it was?" Trix's voice is steel, no trace of empathy. It's probably what he needs, but he hates it anyway. When he looks bitterly at her, she says, "It was. Rakúa chose you. You did it, smugger. You won."

"Won?" His fury sharpens on her, ready with a lashing bite, ready to shout that he just figured out he does have a soul and what the hell good is that when everything that matters keeps slipping through his fingers? But behind Trix and Ashë, there's a flash of someone familiar.

With her hair flying behind her, Reya breaks toward them. "Falcon!" Her blue eyes are wet, incredulous. Her mouth, frozen open as if he's to blame.

Falcon's eyes shutter in regret as he grits out, "Rakúa said it's what he wanted. A noble fucking death and a way out of his blood oath with the crown."

Reya's composure cracks right there, then she launches into his arms. He hugs her back, his heart in a knot. She was never googly-eyed for Kessan or seemed to lust after him, not like Falcon craves Ophelia. But between them, there was a love that went back a long time, and the sacred bond of *Amati*. He had been her chosen.

"Kessan..." Reya's whisper is charged with regret, her fingers digging into Falcon's back.

And Falcon can see the four of them—him, Kaitriona, Kessan, and Reya—stealing through the Valley of Iron when they were *nakommen*, a warrior's song on their lips as they snuck sweetbread off the baking racks in the *yurten* that Malea, Yuli's wife, kept. They would scramble up the ladder on the side of Reya's stone cottage to eat their goods and watch the patrols fly until twilight, imagining how one day they'd be masters of the sky. It was all Falcon wanted then—to make a difference from the air.

"I'm going to weld a fury-skull," Kait declared. "I'll be the fastest *seshen* who ever rode."

"I want a flame-horn," Reya said. "All the fiercest legends rode them. What about you, Kessan?"

He looked at the stars. "I want to command our fates," he dreamed. "I want to be remembered..."

"Kess will be remembered, Rey," Falcon whispers in her ear now. "He'll be remembered."

"*Wild one!*" At the intrusion in his head, Falcon's teeth gnash, but Rakúa bellows urgently, "*The wing has found the goddess. She is gravely injured.*"

His heart stops as he pulls away from Reya. "*Where?*" Quiet. "*Where!*"

"*Yuli has taken her to the cabin in the Dragonwood. I will come for you.*"

"Fuck!" he explodes.

"What now?" Reya pulls away from him with alarm.

Getting a grip on his panic, he says, "We'll grieve Kess later, properly, but Ophelia's in the valley. Rakúa says she's hurt." As fear spears him, Falcon looks to Trix, who's gone still. He can see her mind awhirl the same as his at what this might mean.

If Ophelia's come back, something went off the rails or she got the Dark Shadow Dagger. Or both. The things that would set in motion, according to Cleo's prophecy...

He doesn't think of that now.

"No more summons with the legion," Falcon tells Trix and Ashë. "No more feigning whose side we're on."

The women nod, but with a glance in the direction of royal soldiers and Rune across the road, Trix urges, "We need to do something about them. Royal Army can't catch a whiff that she's in Kúzlo. Not if she's vulnerable."

It's Ashë—the wraith, the quiet observer of their rebel crew—who answers, signing, "I don't think we need to worry about that." She motions to signal overhead.

In the sky, Falcon counts a wing of seven drecora, led by Rakúa, coming in for a landing in the village square.

"Get off the road!" Falcon barks to the northerners nearest him, but the warning's unnecessary this time. They recognize the particular flight pattern.

Carts are wheeled under eaves, children are grabbed by the scruff of their furs, and citizens disappear into inns or shops or back toward the colosseum tunnels, leaving few on the road but visitors from other territories, and the Royal Army with the false confidence their guns give them.

"Reya"—Falcon's voice catches as he turns to her—"I'm so fucking sorry about Kessan, but I need you. The tribal council..."

She nods solemnly. "They will not all accept you easily, but they will expect you to address the people."

"And I will, but I need time." To Trix and Ashë. "Go with Reya as my proxies. Tell the council the truth, Trix. Tell them what's coming. It'll go easier with support of the elders."

Trix goes to stand at Reya's side, threading her fingers through hers. "And Rune?" Trix asks.

Wind rushes up and the ground shakes as the drecora land with shrieks and growls, fanning along the road to surround the Royal Army. Rakúa edges ten feet from Falcon, her attention bladed on Rune

Ethera, who's in conversation with his aide and flanked by soldiers raising guns.

Falcon can feel the drecora's intake of icy breath as she prepares to lay fire.

"Stop!" he shouts, instinct belting the rigid command, hoping she will listen.

Rakúa's chest expands with an irritated growl.

"Rune Ethera's as much a prisoner as Kessan was," he tells her. He won't lose another man who's become a brother to him. He'll figure out how to get Rune out of the Gray King's hold, but he can't if his drecora makes him dragon food.

Rakúa spits a shriek so loud it causes half of Rune's men to drop their guns and raise their hands in surrender. As those soldiers start to kneel, Falcon catches sight of Xakai and Sunder, Serinna and Argan, then Aris and Ronan, all running from the tunnels. The heirs are late to the party and wearing confusion on their faces at the sight of their drecora gathered. They must've been stuck in the hold till now.

Flying on instinct, Falcon channels to the seven drecora. *"I need you to call your flyers. Tell them the guests of the crown are no longer guests; they forced our brother's death. Keep them alive for now, but let's get them off the street."*

The drecora don't deliberate long.

As his half-siblings make for their mounts—some looking shocked, some reluctant—they nod at Falcon, the one who now holds the revered title of high lord.

Weapons in hand, the other heirs circle Rune and his entourage while drecora fix hungry, menacing stares. As Xakai calls for royal soldiers to drop their guns, drecora hiss to emphasize the point and Falcon's gaze meets Rune's.

The prince exchanges a word with his aide, then addresses his soldiers: "Lower your weapons." Reluctantly, the kingsguards do, and Xakai and the heirs move in.

Falcon can't stand it a second longer. He has to get to the Dragonwood.

To Trix, Reya, and Ashë, he says, "The patrol will take the prince and his friends to more rigid accommodations and we'll deal with them later. Go now. Find Thorin and talk to the council." Striding to Rakúa, he catches sight of the missing scale in the shape of a diamond on her tail, the one he removed fifteen years ago that night with Kessan. The one Kessan saved and Falcon now wears on his neck.

Echoes of that moment in the nesting ground haunt him as he mounts.

You're sure if I bring the scale back, they'll honor me?

They'll be bowing at your feet.

It's Falcon the Kúzloans bow to now. The heir who was never meant to be. He seats himself behind Rakúa's neck and fastens a grip on her rider's plume. *"Take me to her."*

As Rakúa turns her massive form, preparing to launch to the sky, he glimpses Rune once more, staring up at him with that boring, emerald gaze, raven curls combed back in a tidy coiffure, as his hands are bound.

Falcon has to remind himself that's not Rune, but a captive he'll have to free. *Soon,* he swears. First, Ophelia.

CHAPTER 63
LIFE & DEATH

In the cabin, Ophelia is cloaked in blood, her face pale and smooth as tide-swept rocks in a frigid sea.

Her skin is cold. The kind of cold that conjures gravestones in a moss-laced wood that hasn't seen the light in a century.

Yuli has laid her on a bed of pelts, and Falcon hovers near her face, listening to the shallow drag of breaths eking from her beautiful lips as the *seshen* hulks in the door. He's saying something about two others who were with her, that he found wounds in her back and staunched them as best he could, but that he's going to fetch the healers.

Falcon doesn't get his gratitude out before Yuli leaves the room.

There's so much blood all over her. All over him as he lays a hand on her stomach and listens hard to assure himself she's breathing.

A glow of particles fills the window near the bed, but when he pulls back, it's something in her cloak that catches his eye. Some long weapon, hidden in fabric.

Undoing the cloth, Falcon straightens like a bolt at the sight of the onyx dagger. The Darkwielder's relic. He stares at it a full second, realizing that he was right—her return is the start of what's to come—but he won't worry about that now. *Ophelia first.*

She'll need the dagger safe. Using the fabric, he grasps the hilt without touching the blade and feeds the relic into his skin sheath. A rolling shudder sweeps through him when it's swallowed—he hasn't forgotten what it feels like to have darkness near—but it's not the same as the marking he bore on his neck once. This Shadow is sealed in the relic. Still, a weight settles, heavy, in the ink it leaves behind on his chest.

He's tucking his shirt back in place when he notices the only other object Ophelia's got with her, snug in the sheath of her leather boot, right where he's always told her to keep her weapon of choice.

He trails a finger over the *A* in its hilt, hoping somehow she might hear him as he confesses, "The night I saw you hold this dragonblade, something clicked into place inside me. I almost lost my shit." A breath shudders out of him. "It was like I'd been hearing just an echo of a song since I was a kid, and when you stroked a finger over its edge, I burned in my chest—burned for *you*—and suddenly every note of the melody was clear." He runs a thumb across the grooves carved in the hilt. "When I gave you this, I had no idea what was coming, and I didn't care. I only knew, whatever the future held, there was no one else meant for my *Amati* blade but you."

Ophelia gasps a breath, drawing Falcon back. Her eyes are squeezed shut, and he tracks for the pain she must be reacting to. Wounds on her back, Yuli said.

Just beneath her, Falcon sees the blood where it seeped in a perilous pool before Yuli staunched it. With care, he eases her shoulder up enough to steal a look under the cloth, finding a bullet wound that makes him swallow. A wound that bears an amber-green sheen, which means the gunpowder was laced with *migth*.

"What the hell happened?" he whispers. This is why she's not healing. The bullet's still inside her. Her breath stutters, and Falcon grips the side of the bed. "Ophelia?"

She doesn't answer, but her inhales wane, ebbing in a fitful pattern.

Falcon scrubs a hand down his face, feeling the walls close in. Feeling like he can't wait for healers. The *migth* is killing her. It's not normal ammo—it's meant to combust. Gods, moving her was a risk! Yuli must've felt there wasn't a choice.

In a growling whisper, he says, "Don't you fucking die."

He's not a praying man, but he worships her. And on this night that the deities are supposed to be listening, for the first time since he was twelve, since his mother died, Falcon Thames bargains, *Let her live. You can have me, if that's your goddamn design, but not her.*

He swears right then, if Ophelia lives he'll accept the death that waits for him in war. He'll accept the fate—the part of the vision—he's been keeping to himself.

The death Trix's sister predicted.

"Are you sure you want to know what Cleo saw?" Trix asked him on the edge of Jagst before their mission into Kúzlo. When he dead-eyed her, she nodded. "In an ambush, it's you or her. Only one of you can live."

His heart bled for a future that would never be his, but then it steeled. Men like him weren't meant for happy endings. After leaving Kúzlo as a boy, he had never let himself even dream of it—not until Ophelia walked into those woods at the Constelli and over the next four years made him respect her, made him look at her, made his soul hope...

Made him love her.

"It's not a choice," he told Trix. He'd die a thousand deaths for her. "She lives."

She lives! Falcon shouts at the gods. *Tell me what to do!* His hand curls beneath the crown of her head, and he brings his forehead to hers.

A reply comes like a bell. *"Volorost..."*

Falcon stiffens at the all-commanding voice. It's not drecora.

He cuts a look at the moons as that voice overcomes him. *"Born in fire. Bathed in blood. Search within you to create what was."*

Falcon's mind races. "Create what was...?"

"Animater," the voice—of the gods?—resounds. *"Search within."*

He can't think of anything in his sheath that would remove a bullet. Not even a primordial relic. Anything that would make it like she'd never been shot—

Bolting upright, he yanks up his tunic. The fire seems to flare in the hearth, encouraging him, as he shucks off his shirt, finding the small pool of ink where he buried the object below his hip. Ink that holds the sliver of the *vis stagisi* horn he broke off before gifting the rest of the animal's pelt and rack to the Gatekeeper.

In this single sliver, he has a power that's been said to remake things broken, withered, dying. A power he always knew he'd never use on himself. Falcon removes it from his sheath, then kisses Ophelia's forehead before gently pulling her toward him, onto her side so he can see her back more clearly.

She doesn't cry out, doesn't respond, not even as he removes Yuli's staunching cloth and blood seeps anew.

There are two bullet wounds, each laced with *migth*.

Without hesitation, Falcon grits his teeth and follows what the old stories say, dragging the sharp tip of the horn across her skin to open one of the wounds up farther. He's met with that shimmer in her blood that tells him she's strong. A goddess, a queen, a survivor, his partner—his soul.

She's fucking everything.

He rests the sliver inside the gaping wound, waiting for it to sink and dissolve. Waiting for her to come back to him. When her wounds glow, when the bullets spit onto the bed, he swears the moons flicker and their frost fades and the dust outside the window sighs in relief. Beyond the cabin, there's a long, baying howl.

"Live," he whispers.

In the fire's glow, Ophelia rouses under his blood-covered hands, her eyelids fluttering. "Falcon?"

He lays his head against hers, heat radiating in his chest, though he can feel the shadow of death on his shoulder. "Live," he echoes. "You're going to live."

AFTER

KIER

O n the dark king's arrival, the sea is a mirror of his rage.

Kier greets the fury of black waters that crash against the seafarers' dinghy with a loathing look as he's led out of the boat into ice-cold, shallow tides. Into his exile at the edge of the worlds, as ordered by the Council of Guilds.

Frigid claws swipe at his legs. *I bring death,* the sea howls from its depths.

I am made of death, he answers. As a crisp wind whips the smell of brine and leaves and rotted mushrooms, Kier bores a look at the four mammoth seafarers—pirates—who prod him toward shore. *And when I get free of these spellshackles, my enemies will be reminded of it.*

Waves slam his calves in reply. *There's no leaving the Isle of Nix, least of all with your wits.*

You don't know me or my mind.

The sea laughs, spitting dark foam at his heels as he wades ashore. Awaiting him is the rising Tower of Lost Souls and a jungle that ensnares the isle.

Exile.

"You played your part well," his mother told him days ago, as he lingered in the paralysis of poison. "Finding Ophelia Dannan, bringing her to Ghastly, teaching her. But how complicated it became. If only she had truly loved you." Saira stroked his hair. "I might have told you I intended to test her—to see if she would go through with the poison. But you needed to be tested, too. Could the goddess draw you to reason? Or were your ghosts too strong to be slayed?"

With pity in her eyes, Saira produced a pair of spelled manacles, shackling Kier at the wrists, then neck. He quaked with malice as Saira tipped an antidote to his mouth and said, "It seems your ghosts *are* strong, and our new queen cares only for the destruction of our relics. But your exile may fix both, starting with denying the goddess access to you—someone she will need in order to destroy the instruments."

Bitterness rose up his throat as the antidote slipped down, his limbs soon tingling and his thoughts sparking fully to life again.

She is mine, Kier tried to growl. *She is mine! And you poisoned her against me,* he wanted to scream. *I will end you for it!*

As guards came for him and Saira seemed to register his fury, she leaned in to whisper, "As one who called a prison tower home for thirty years, I warn you not to let old ghosts be your demise. Please, my son, use the next century of your sentence to become something better than your father was."

Seabirds caw above the shore, the noise shackling him again to the present.

Kier bites back his wrath and the utter sting of betrayal as he faces the Isle of Nix, an isolated land to which he has banished plenty of men before. Men who deserved a horrid fate.

A seafarer shoves him forward, stirring shadows that leap in him for release. To his ire, they meet the spellshackles at his wrists with a hiss, banishing the darkness back into him.

A laugh on the wind, as if the isle is goading him, stoking his embers the way Jas always did, like his mother—like all those who never saw past his darkness.

Delphine did once. And for a glimmer, Ophelia.

Ophelia. Her name is crushing in his skull, eliciting a haunting memory of a tear slipping down her face as she leaned over him with his birthright—his dagger—in her possession. Yet it wasn't the dagger he struggled against the poison for. It was that tear. He wanted to reach for it, to taste her pain that felt the same as his, to pull her to him and feel her warmth and confess he regretted it all.

If he'd told her the truth of his heart—that he feared losing her the way he lost Delphine—rather than rush to force the bond, perhaps things would have gone differently. Perhaps he would be different.

The sea scrapes her icy nails across the tops of his feet. *And what but a monster will you become on my island?* she asks as he's forced to shore by the seafarers, up and into the Tower of Lost Souls where prisoners' screams claw his head. Led up, and up, past irons bars where silhouettes thin as bones grasp their heads and howl, where he hears a familiar, tortured cry. "Darkwielder!"

Irony chaining his gaze to a figure behind bars, he looks with loathing on Vesh Derringer, who is right where Kier sent him.

"Move along, *king*." A seafarer nudges him and Kier's fists clench where they're bound.

With Derringer's useless cries at his back, a small light flickers through a window high above, and he thinks of the plea Ophelia left him with. A plea for redemption.

Yet the sea's taunting question echoes in his mind: What but a monster would he become here?

Death, he vows to the ghosts that haunt him. *I will become the death of you all.*

To be continued in book three of the
Whispers of Dust & Darkness series...coming soon!

ACKNOWLEDGEMENTS

I have a lump in my throat as I write. This story grew beyond my wildest imaginings this year—a year that was wrought with loss in my family—and the book is so special to me for how hard fought every word was.

An immense thank you to my writing team. Beth Stedman, you gave me the confidence to write bravely and the courage to continue the series into a third installment. *Every Thread of Light* would be a pile of bones if it weren't for your vision. J Mercer, you're ever the calm voice of reason. From the first to the final read, you got the story and were its biggest champion. You're the reason readers are able to forest their way through my wild prose. And Rhiannon Rollness, thank you for your kind heart, your early input, and your cheerleading to help the story find its way.

To Sarah Hansen, for the brilliant cover. And to @lesyablackbird, @koijix, @ladyhedi, and @lictoria_art for bringing the characters to life with your exquisite artwork.

Thank you to my amazing beta team for early reads and screaming in my DMs: Aubrey Sanders, Jaden Hoy, Bethany White, Kelsey Kennedy, and Brandi Clappsy.

My everlasting gratitude also to my loud and proud street team, including: @sydneysreadingrealm, @fireheart_13_, @thatbookishteach, @pagesbyadelyn, @fichtandco, @jadadadondada, @mamalightsbooks, @bookashhh, @need.new.reads, @writer.m.a.brown, @authormorgankielisch, @_bookishescape, @tairen_soul, @you.do.not.yield_beth, @readingwithkathleen, @sleeping.book.junkie, @_allisomreads, @literary_dystopia, @lxstinneverland, @covenofbooksandbrews, @bookish.apothecary, @knot.sew.bookish, @mary_garrn_nyc, @cinnabunbooks, @bookdragonbrunette, @hullbooknook, @tay.talks.books, @themedschoolbookfairy, @tupelos.library, @reannareadsbooks, @elis.endless.tbr, @bookedinwisco, @readwithharp, @dani.readss, @pagesandpjs, @cat_but_leo_con_libr, @bookishvibesclub, @serafina.reader, @hanji.targaryen, @magsreadz, @raelovesreading, @stevieslittlelibrary, @danireadsbooks3, @hollyjorgensen1, and @trinhelium.

Thank you to all the incredible authors I have met since this journey began, for your support, collaboration and rooting each other on, including Samantha Amstutz, Mary Dublin, Anne Kendsley, and EL Canney.

To you, holding this book, for continuing the journey with Ophelia and her morally grey cast.

To every family member, friend, and reader who has cheered me on, asked how they could support the series, and gave me the courage to keep writing. I love you guys.

And, most importantly and never least, to Andrew and Fox, who are my entire world beyond Magus. The very, very best parts of real life exist because of you. Thank you for letting me disappear into these fantasy realms to indulge this dream.

TRIGGER WARNINGS

Every Thread of Light contains elements of: emotional trauma and anxiety, mental and physical torture, (magical) racism, oppressive language, gunfire, physical abuse of minors (implied), substance abuse, blood/bleeding and wounds, death of a child (flashback memory), fighting for sport, dubious consent, sex work, gaslighting, physical and emotional manipulation, loss of body autonomy, imprisonment, consensual open-door intimacy and sexual experiences, loss of a parent, loss of a sibling, death of animals, and war violence.

About the Author

Sarah Zimm discovered at age six she could climb a high maple carrying a blank notebook. She's been writing ever since. Sarah lives in the Midwest with her husband, son, and shadow-chasing mutt. The Whispers of Dust & Darkness is her debut dark fantasy romance series. You can find her online at @authorsarahzimm or authorsarahzimm.com.